PENNY DORA
AND THE WISHING BOX

PENNY DORA
AND THE WISHING BOX

MICHAEL STOCK
WRITER

SINA GRACE
ARTIST

TAMRA BONVILLAIN
COLORIST

HOPE LARSON
LETTERER

COVER BY
SINA GRACE
& TAMRA BONVILLAIN

CREATED BY:
NICO LUDWIG-STOCK (AGE 8 AT THE TIME)
& HER PAPA, MICHAEL STOCK

LOGO DESIGNED BY TIM DANIEL

IMAGE COMICS, INC.
Robert Kirkman - chief operating officer
Erik Larsen - chief financial officer
Todd McFarlane - president
Marc Silvestri - chief executive officer
Jim Valentino - vice-president

Corey Murphy - Director of Sales
Jeremy Sullivan - Director of Digital Sales
Kat Salazar - Director of PR & Marketing
Emily Miller - Director of Operations
Branwyn Bigglestone - Senior Accounts Manager
Sarah Mello - Accounts Manager

Drew Gill - Art Director
Jonathan Chan - Production Manager
Meredith Wallace - Print Manager
Randy Okamura - Marketing Production Designer
David Brothers - Content Manager
Addison Duke - Production Artist

Vincent Kukua - Production Artist
Sasha Head - Production Artist
Tricia Ramos - Production Artist
Emilio Bautista - Sales Assistant
Jessica Ambriz - Administrative Assistant
www.imagecomics.com

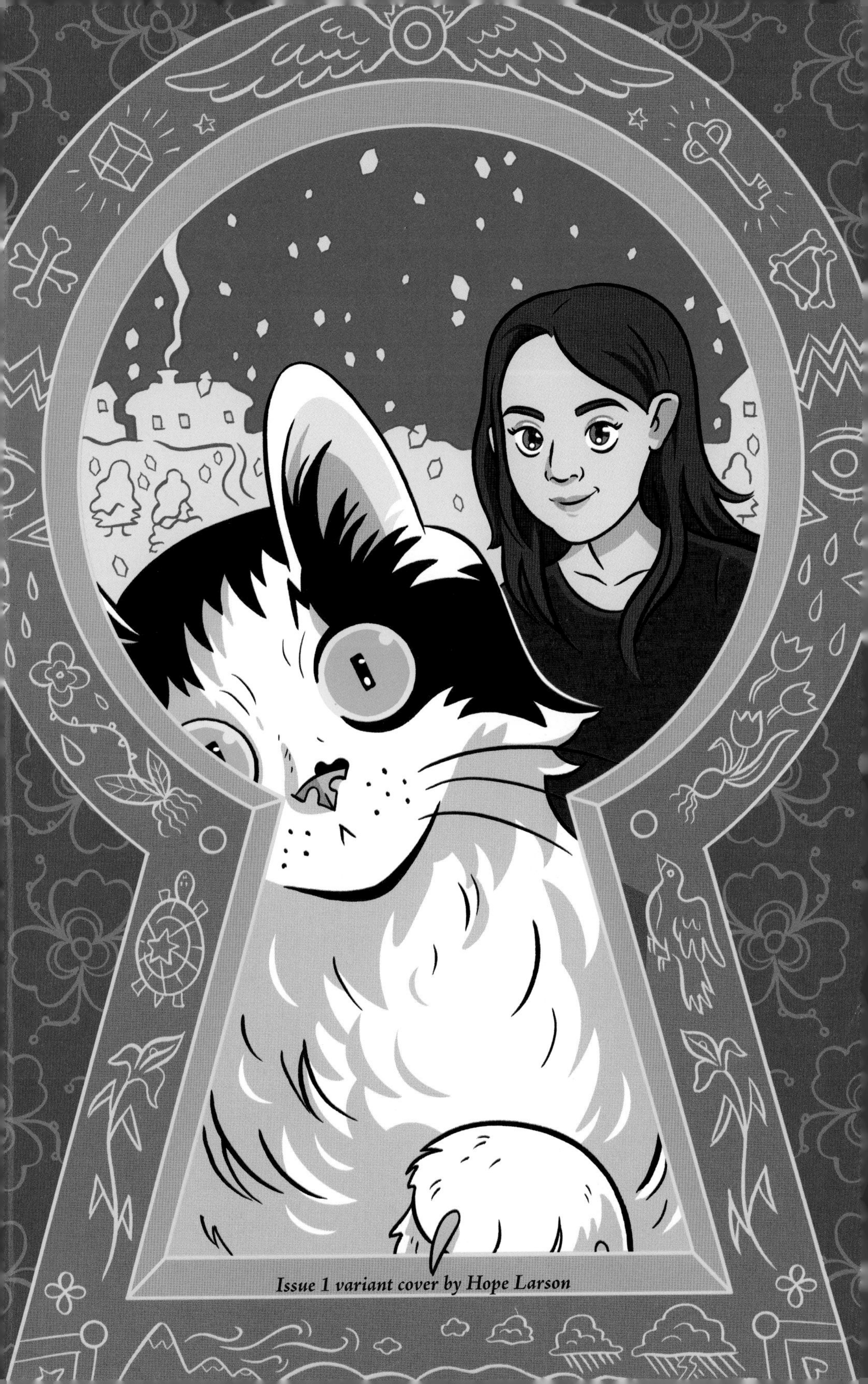

Issue 1 variant cover by Hope Larson

Chapter One

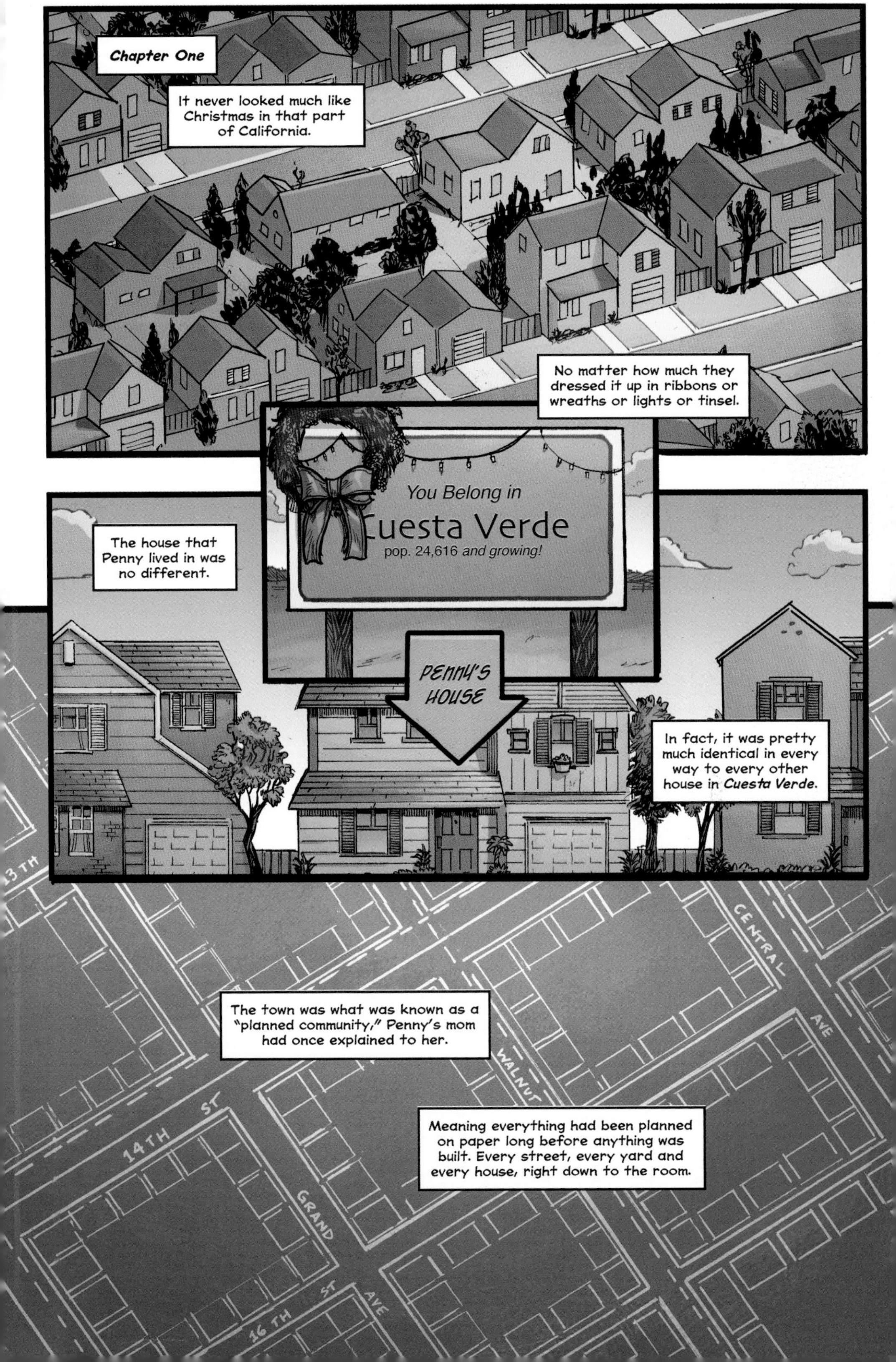
Chapter One
It never looked much like Christmas in that part of California.
No matter how much they dressed it up in ribbons or wreaths or lights or tinsel.
You Belong in
Cuesta Verde
pop. 24,616 and growing!
The house that Penny lived in was no different.
PENNY'S HOUSE
In fact, it was pretty much identical in every way to every other house in Cuesta Verde.
The town was what was known as a "planned community," Penny's mom had once explained to her.
CENTRAL AVE
WALNUT
14TH ST
GRAND
16TH ST
AVE
Meaning everything had been planned on paper long before anything was built. Every street, every yard and every house, right down to the room.

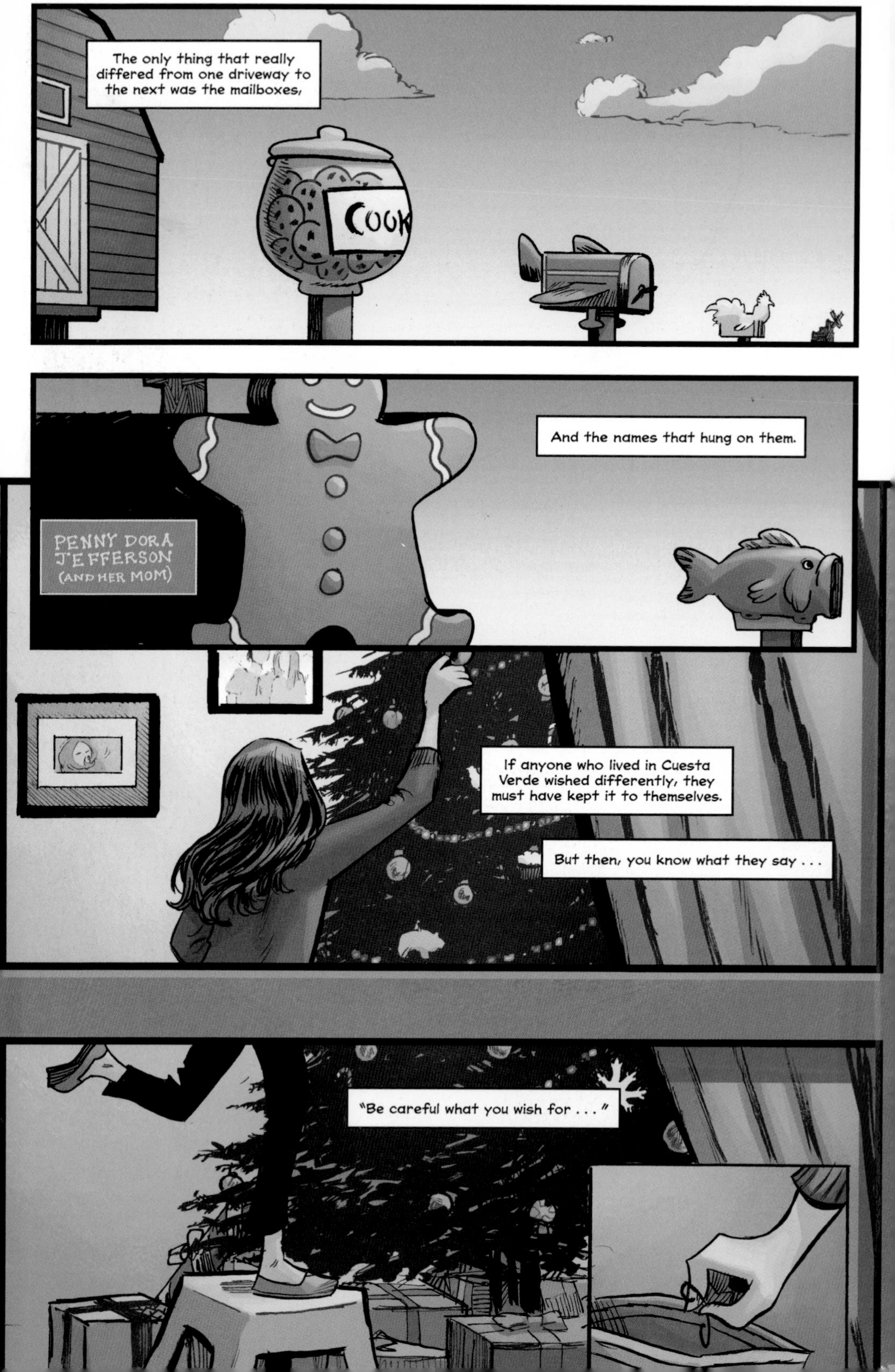
The only thing that really differed from one driveway to the next was the mailboxes,
COOK
And the names that hung on them.
PENNY DORA JEFFERSON (AND HER MOM)
If anyone who lived in Cuesta Verde wished differently, they must have kept it to themselves.
But then, you know what they say . . .
"Be careful what you wish for . . ."

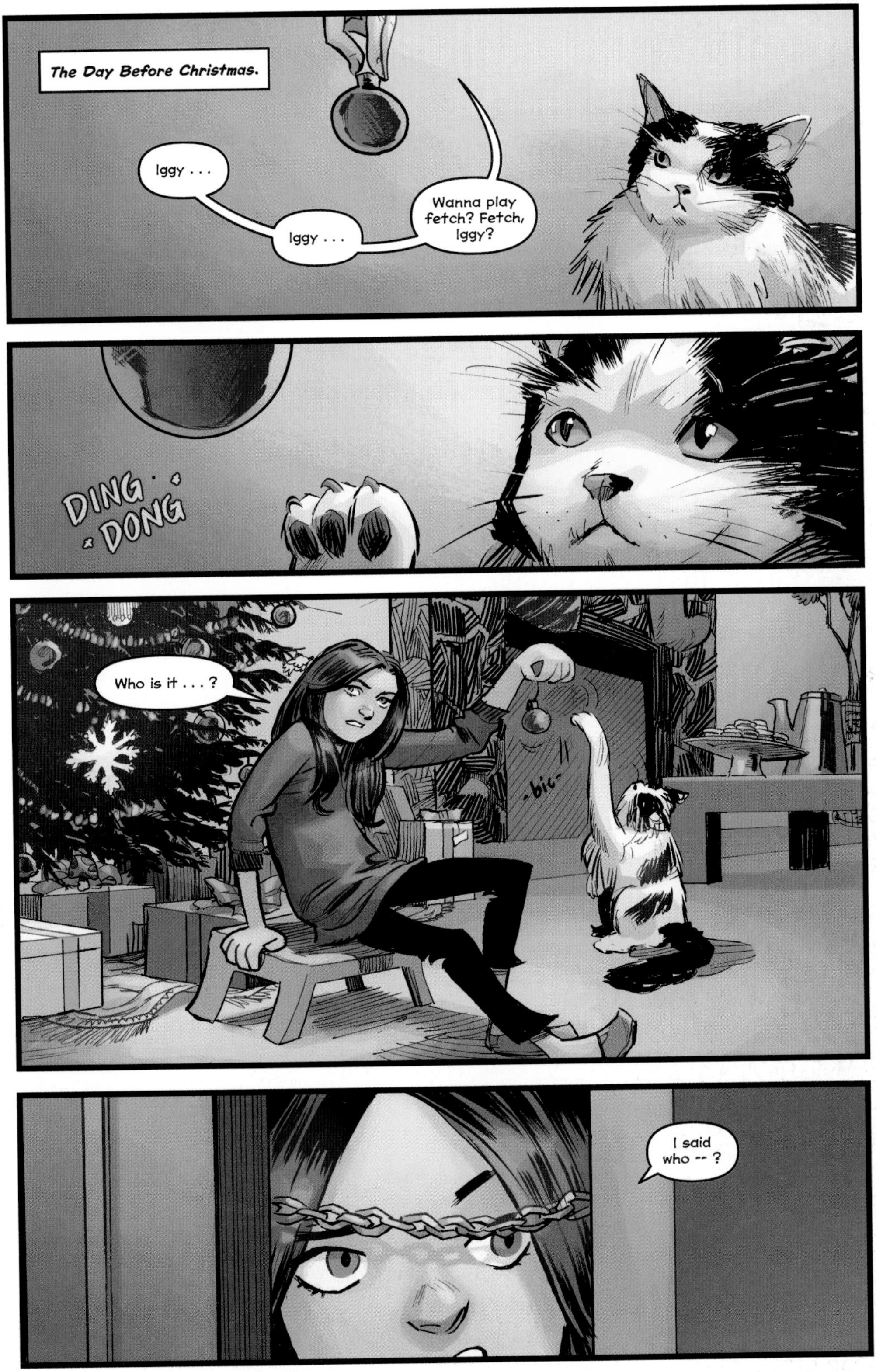
The Day Before Christmas.
Iggy . . .
Iggy . . .
Wanna play fetch? Fetch, Iggy?
DING · DONG
Who is it . . . ?
-bic-
I said who -- ?

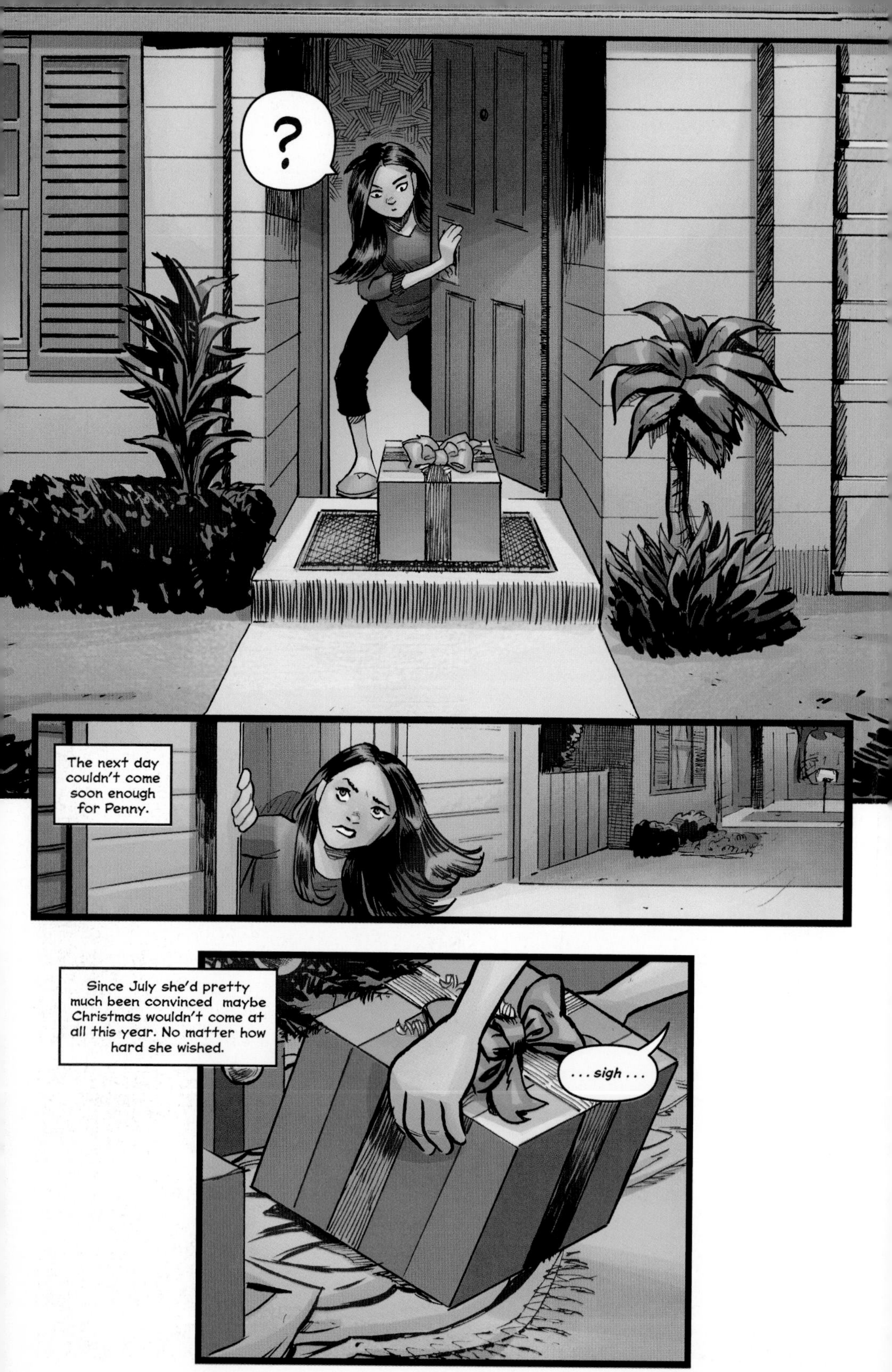
?
The next day couldn't come soon enough for Penny.
Since July she'd pretty much been convinced maybe Christmas wouldn't come at all this year. No matter how hard she wished.
. . . sigh . . .

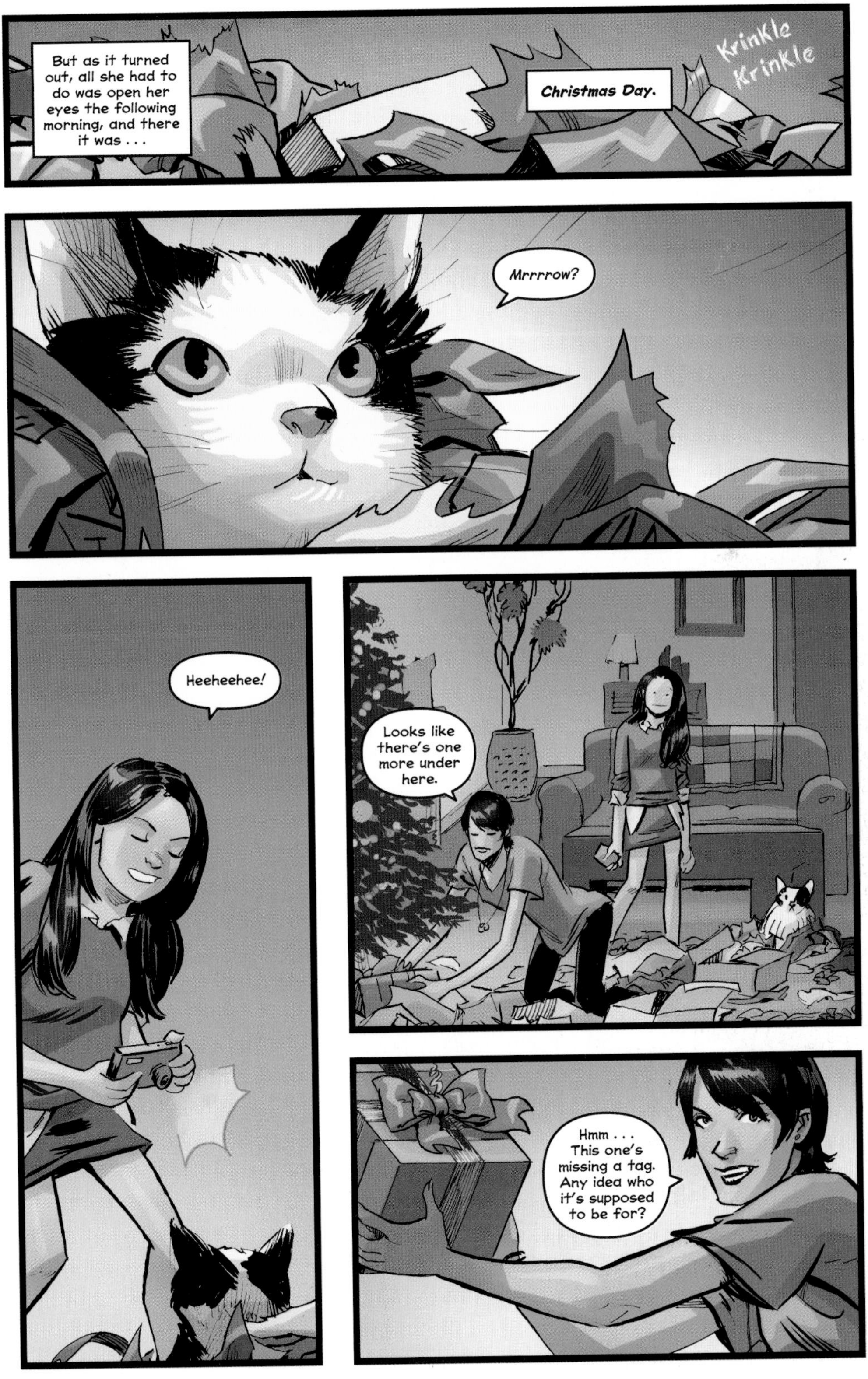

But as it turned out, all she had to do was open her eyes the following morning, and there it was . . .
Christmas Day.
Krinkle Krinkle
Mrrrrow?
Heeheehee!
Looks like there's one more under here.
Hmm . . . This one's missing a tag. Any idea who it's supposed to be for?

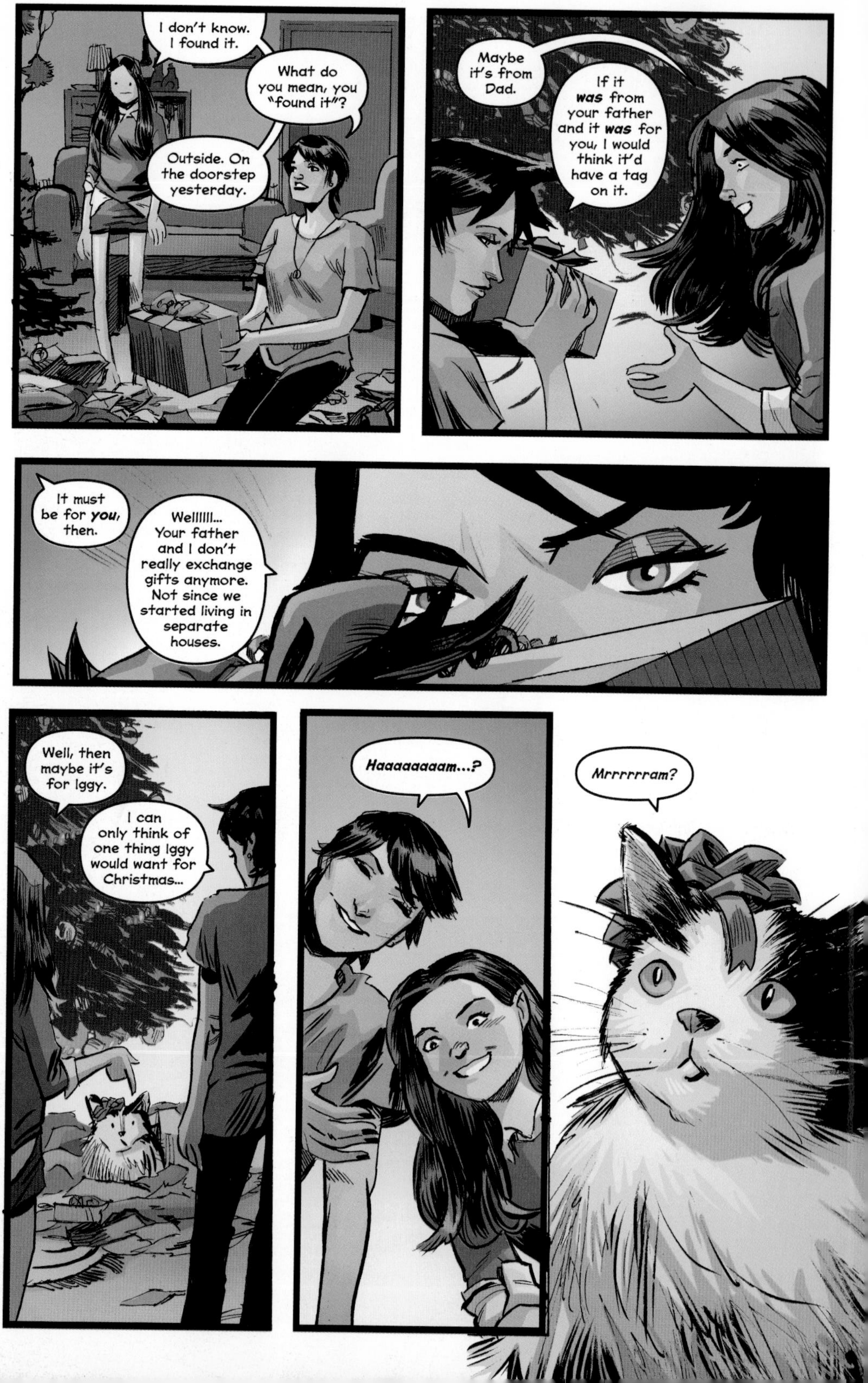
I don't know. I found it.
What do you mean, you "found it"?
Outside. On the doorstep yesterday.
Maybe it's from Dad.
If it *was* from your father and it *was* for you, I would think it'd have a tag on it.
It must be for *you*, then.
Wellllll... Your father and I don't really exchange gifts anymore. Not since we started living in separate houses.
Well, then maybe it's for Iggy.
I can only think of one thing Iggy would want for Christmas...
Haaaaaaaam...?
Mrrrrrram?

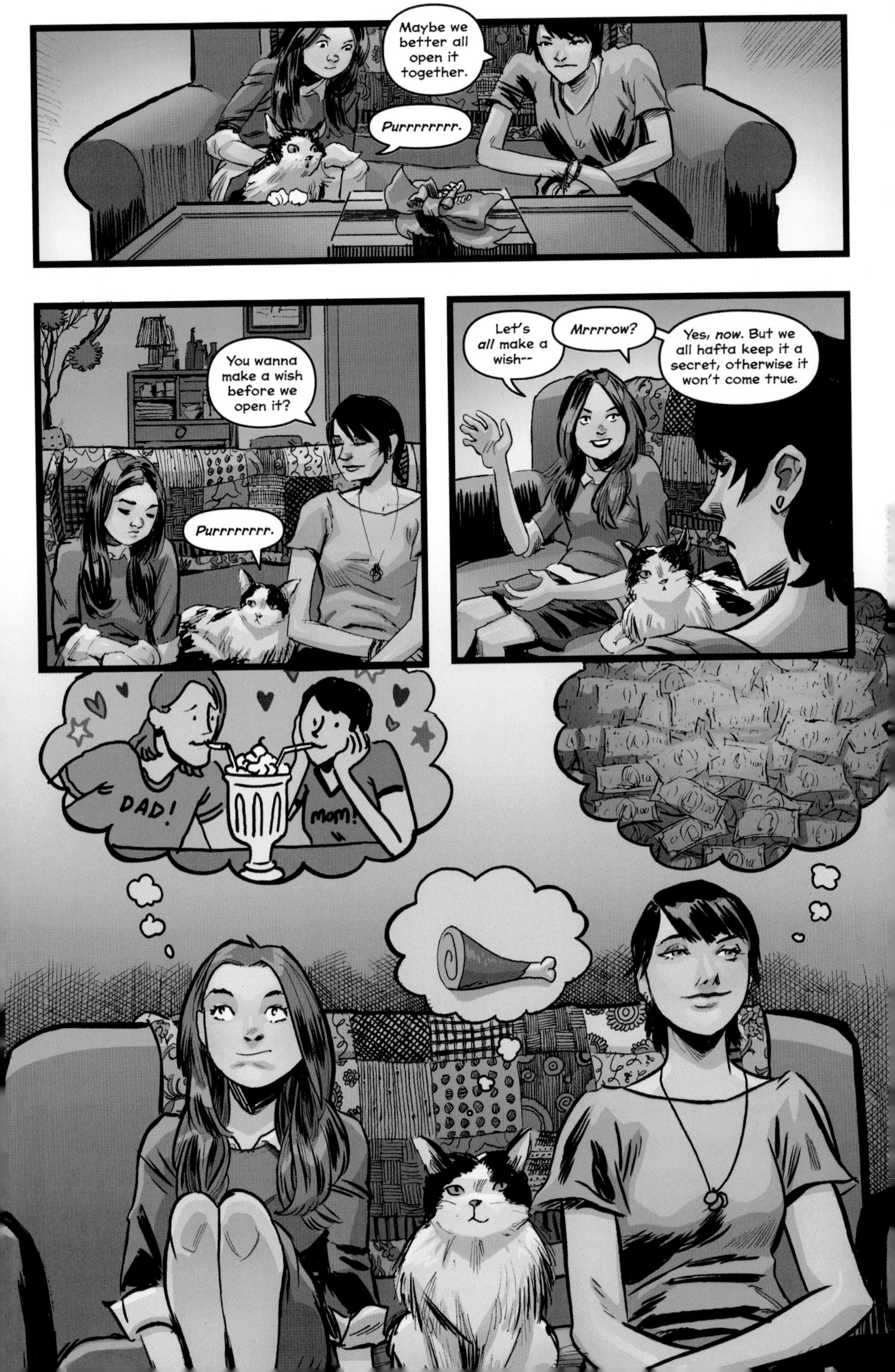
Maybe we better all open it together.
Purrrrrrrr.
You wanna make a wish before we open it?
Purrrrrrrr.
Let's *all* make a wish--
Mrrrrow?
Yes, *now*. But we all hafta keep it a secret, otherwise it won't come true.
DAD!
MOM!

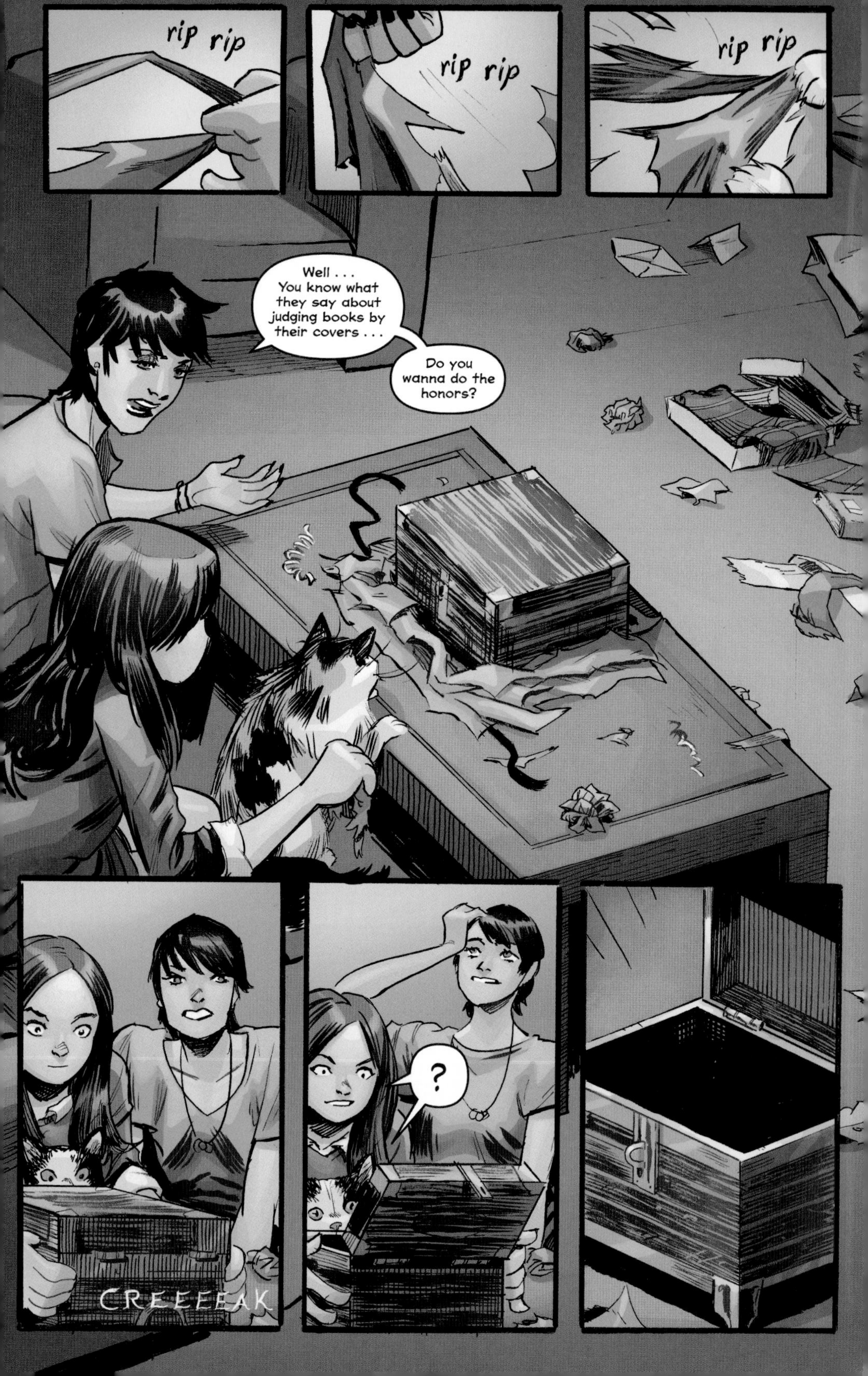
rip rip
rip rip
rip rip
Well . . . You know what they say about judging books by their covers . . .
Do you wanna do the honors?
CREEEEAK
?

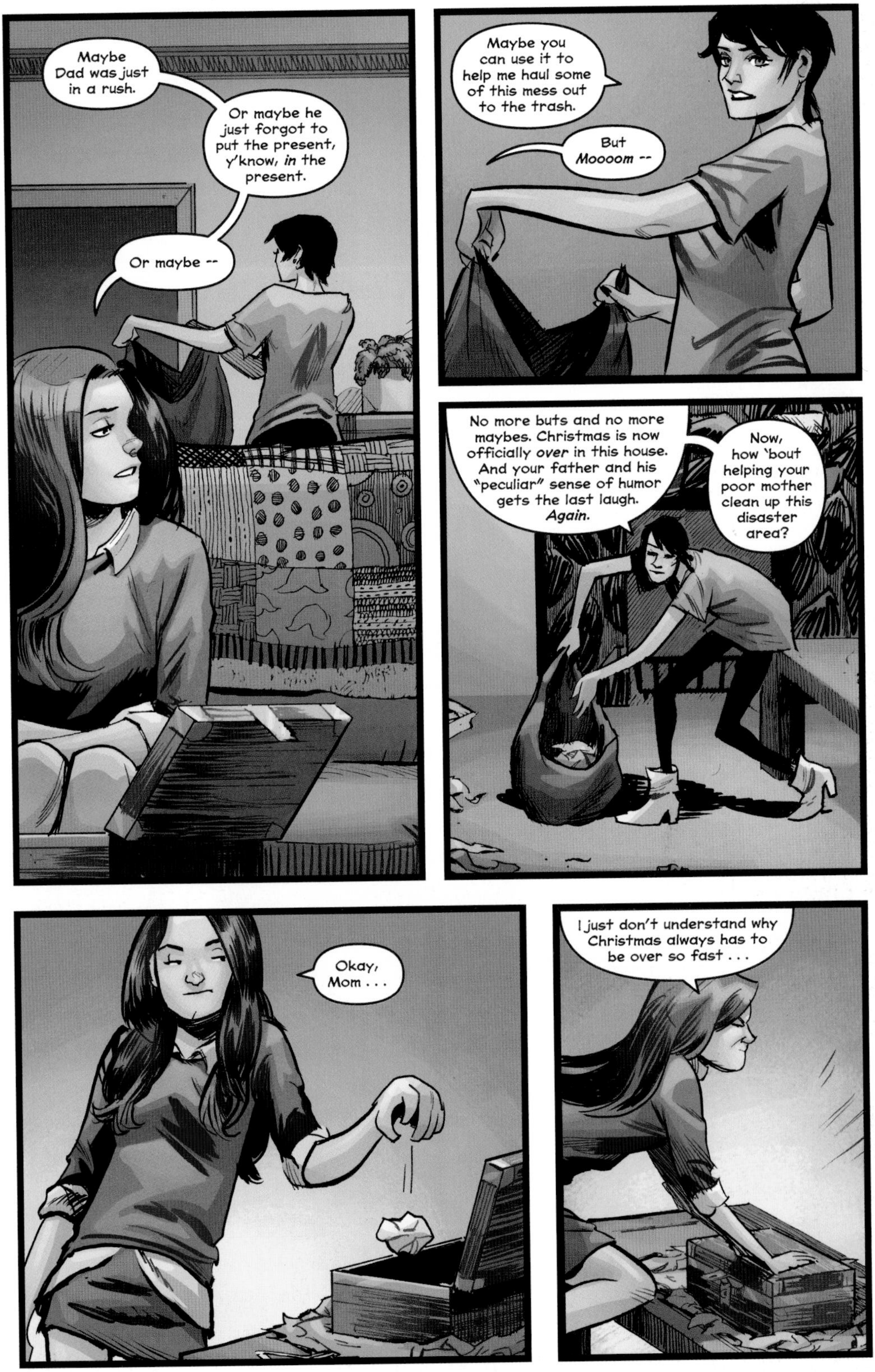
Maybe Dad was just in a rush.
Or maybe he just forgot to put the present, y'know, *in* the present.
Or maybe --
Maybe you can use it to help me haul some of this mess out to the trash.
But *Moooom* --
No more buts and no more maybes. Christmas is now officially *over* in this house. And your father and his "peculiar" sense of humor gets the last laugh. ***Again.***
Now, how 'bout helping your poor mother clean up this disaster area?
Okay, Mom . . .
I just don't understand why Christmas always has to be over so fast . . .

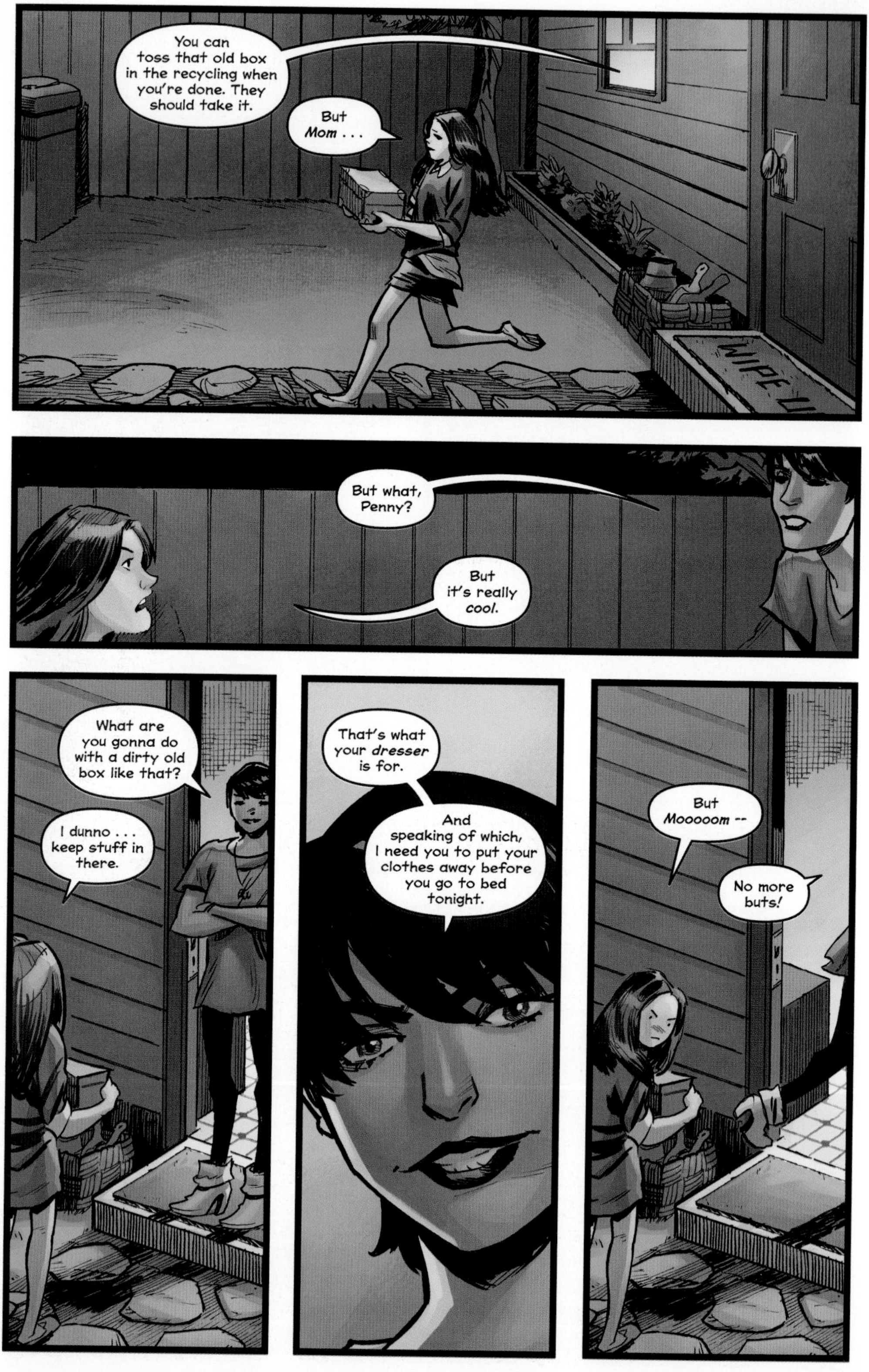
You can toss that old box in the recycling when you're done. They should take it.
But *Mom* . . .
WIPE
But what, Penny?
But it's really *cool*.
What are you gonna do with a dirty old box like that?
I dunno . . . keep stuff in there.
That's what your *dresser* is for.
And speaking of which, I need you to put your clothes away before you go to bed tonight.
But *Mooooom* --
No more buts!

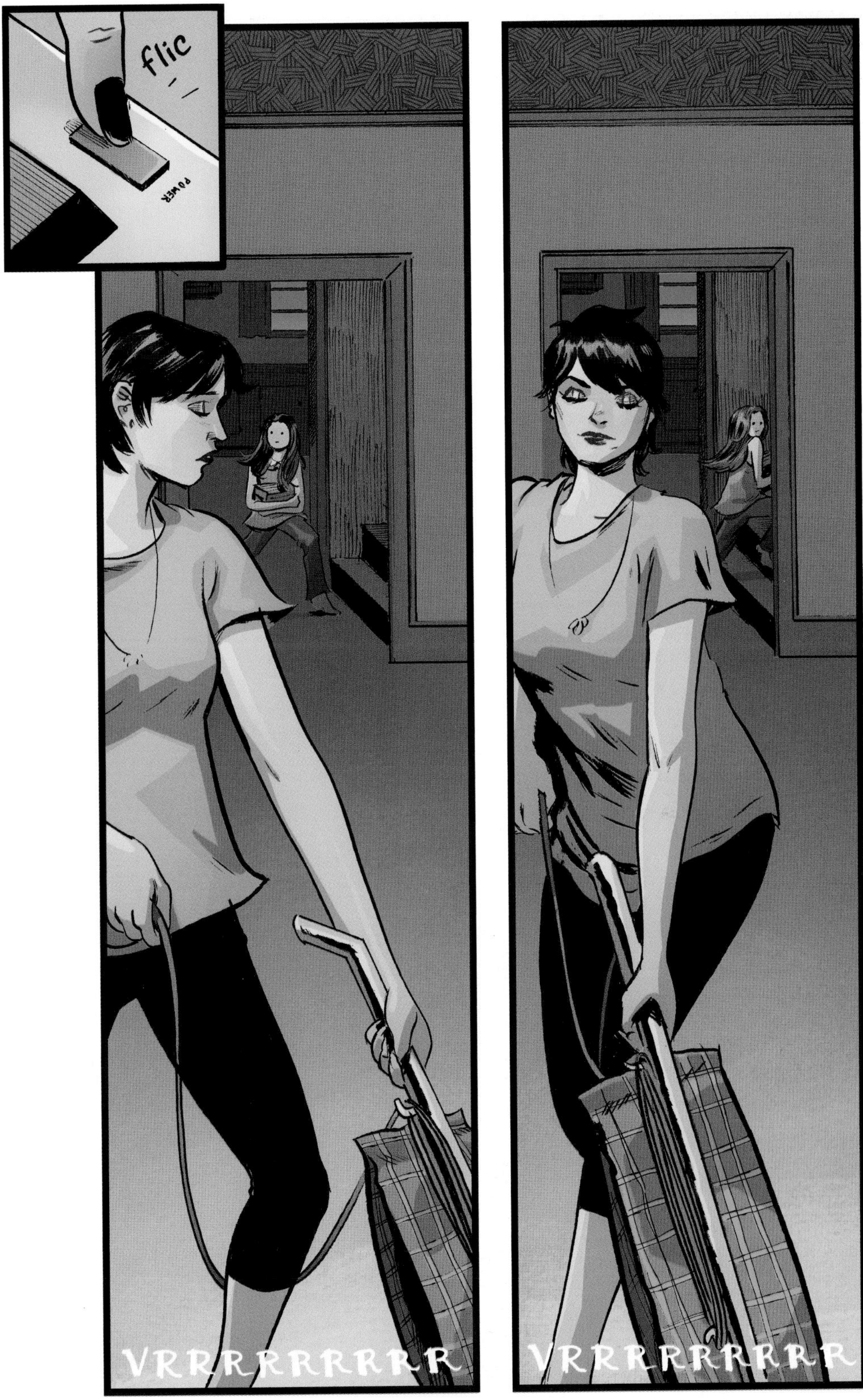
flic
POWER
VRRRRRRRRR
VRRRRRRRRR

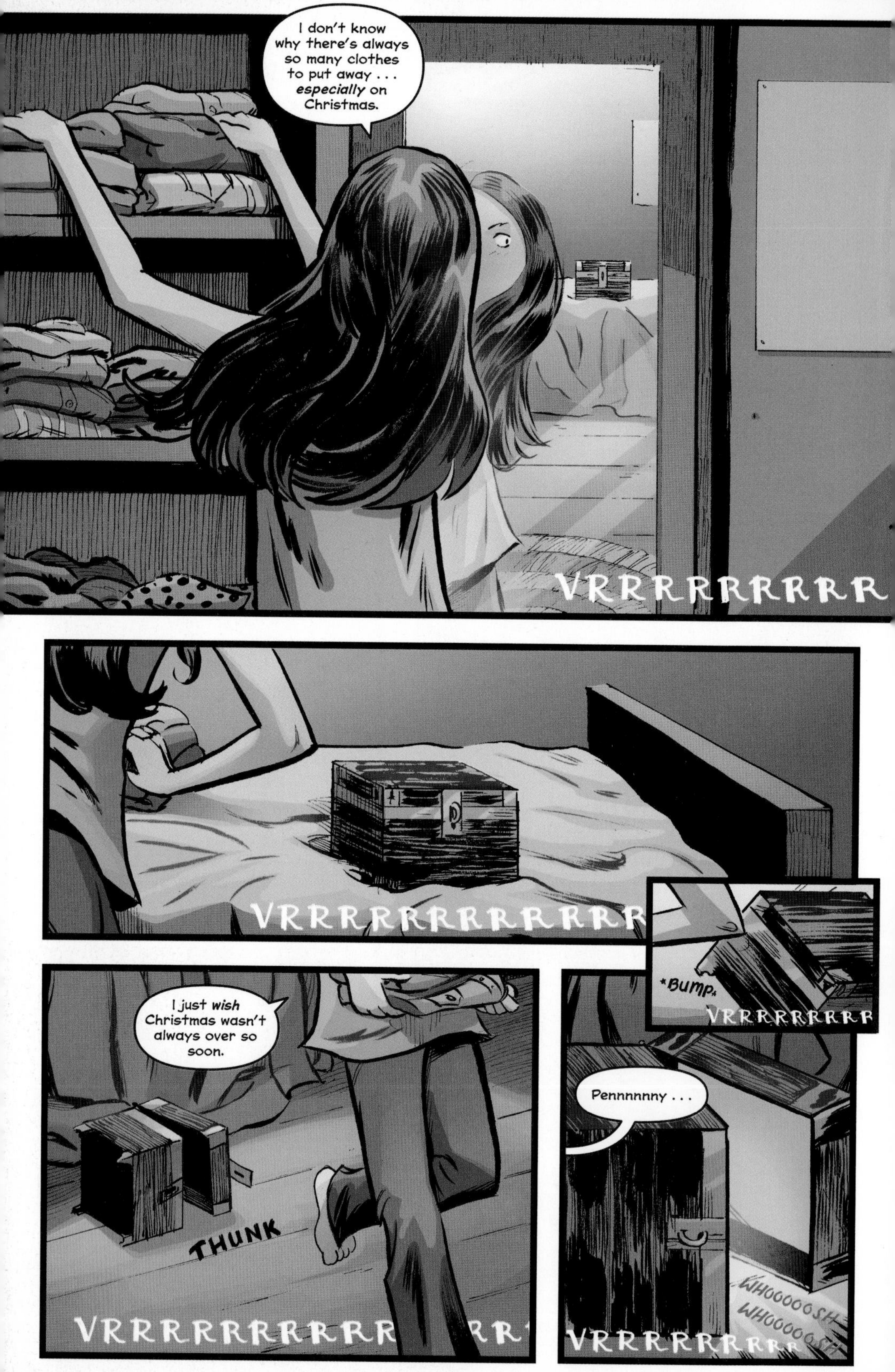
I don't know why there's always so many clothes to put away . . . *especially* on Christmas.
VRRRRRRRRR
VRRRRRRRRRRRR
BUMP
VRRRRRRRRR
I just *wish* Christmas wasn't always over so soon.
THUNK
VRRRRRRRRRRRR
Pennnnnny . . .
WHOOOOOSH
WHOOOOOSH
VRRRRRRRRRR

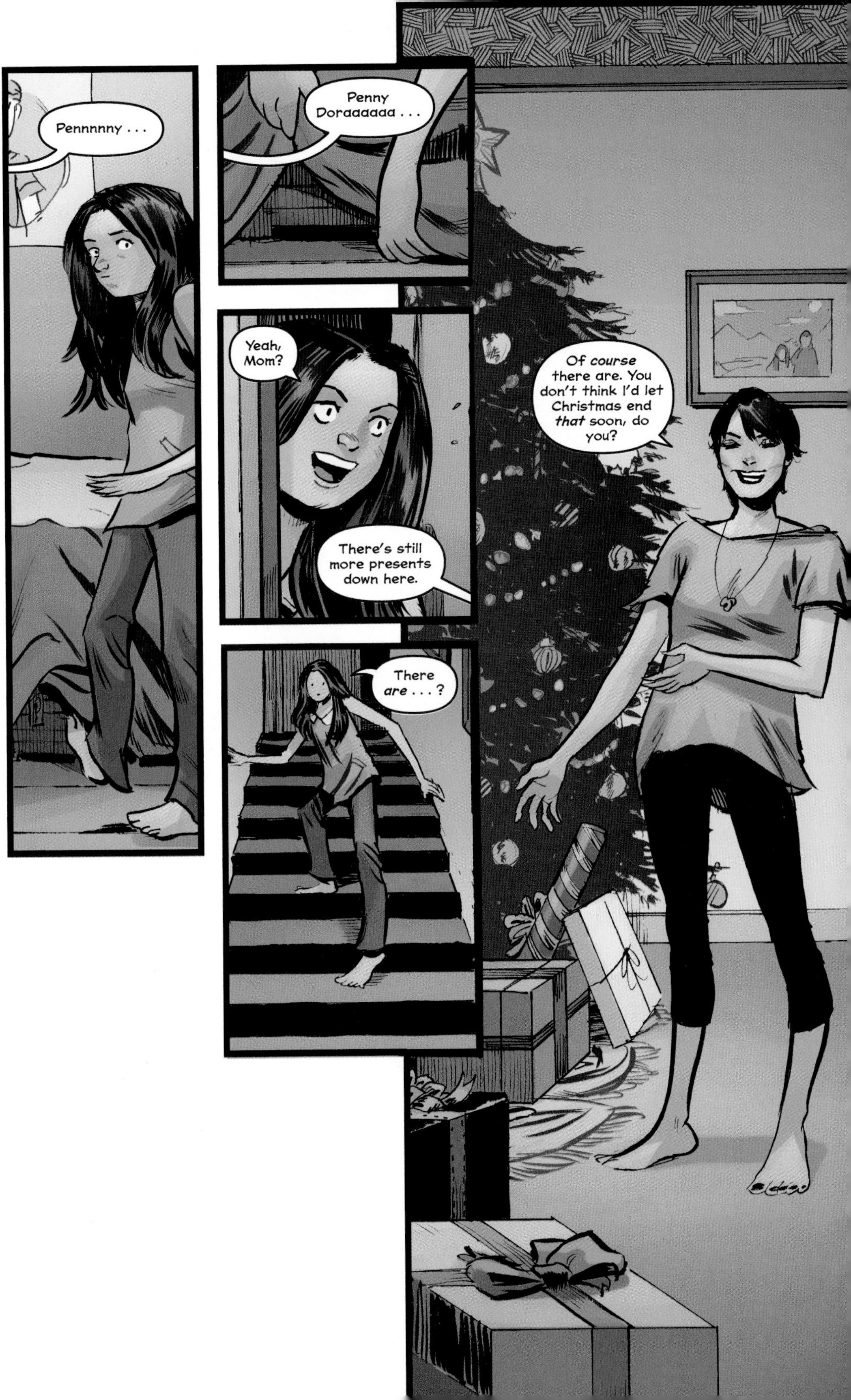
Pennnnny . . .
Penny Doraaaaaa . . .
Yeah, Mom?
There's still more presents down here.
There are . . . ?
Of course there are. You don't think I'd let Christmas end that soon, do you?

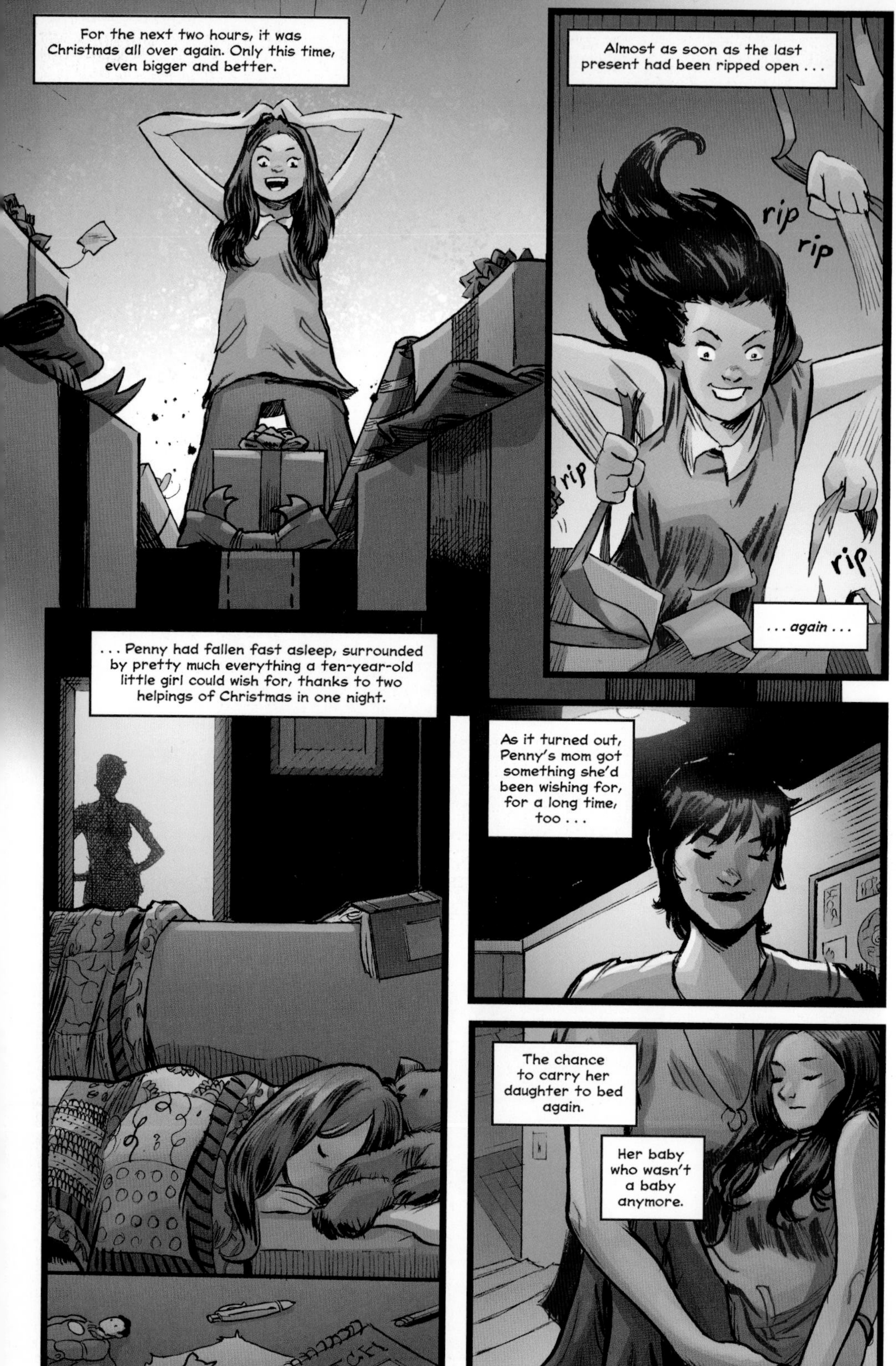
For the next two hours, it was Christmas all over again. Only this time, even bigger and better.
Almost as soon as the last present had been ripped open . . .
rip
rip
rip
rip
. . . again . . .
. . . Penny had fallen fast asleep, surrounded by pretty much everything a ten-year-old little girl could wish for, thanks to two helpings of Christmas in one night.
As it turned out, Penny's mom got something she'd been wishing for, for a long time, too . . .
The chance to carry her daughter to bed again.
Her baby who wasn't a baby anymore.

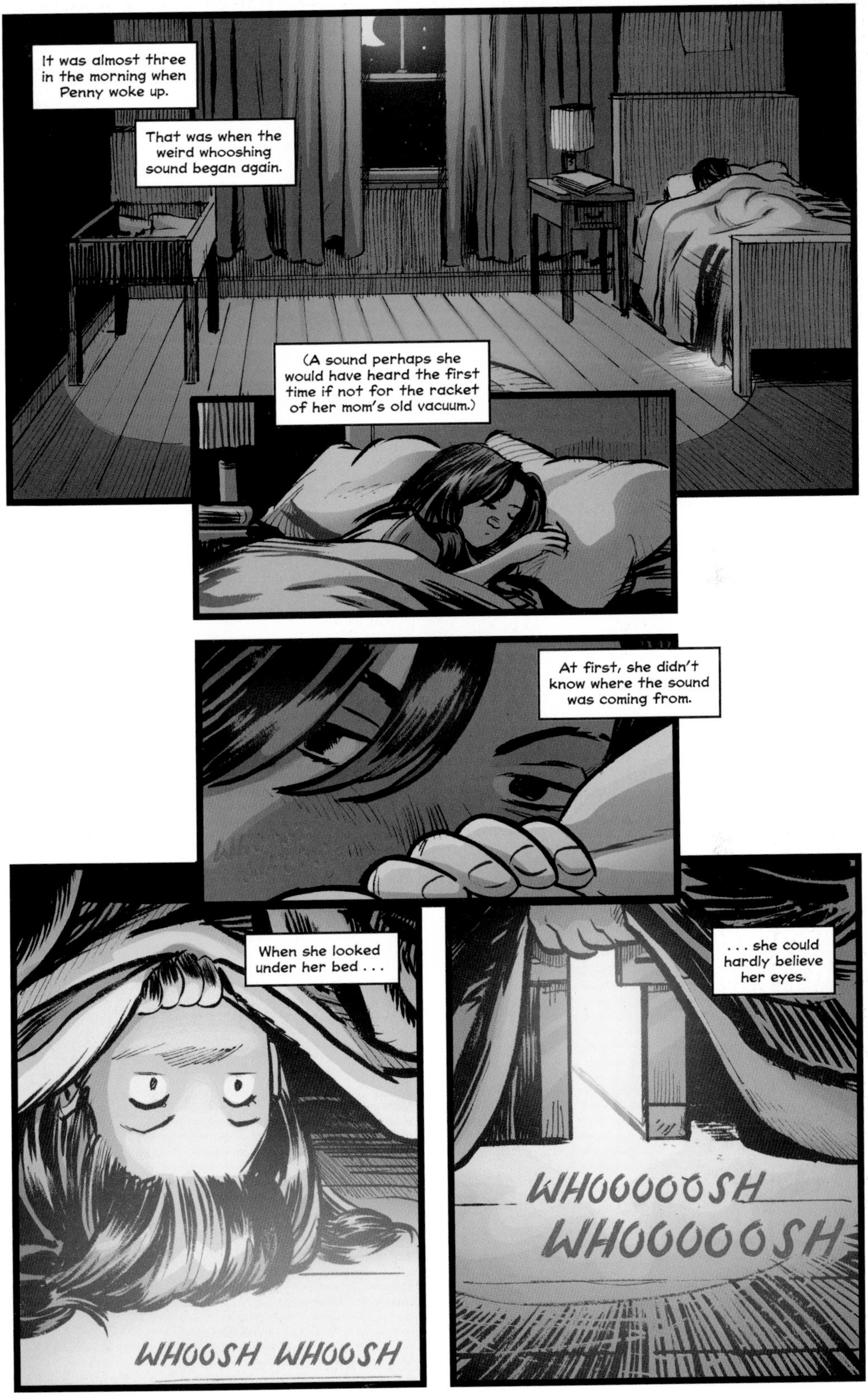

It was almost three in the morning when Penny woke up.
That was when the weird whooshing sound began again.
(A sound perhaps she would have heard the first time if not for the racket of her mom's old vacuum.)
At first, she didn't know where the sound was coming from.
When she looked under her bed . . .
WHOOSH WHOOSH
. . . she could hardly believe her eyes.
WHOOOOOOSH
WHOOOOOOSH

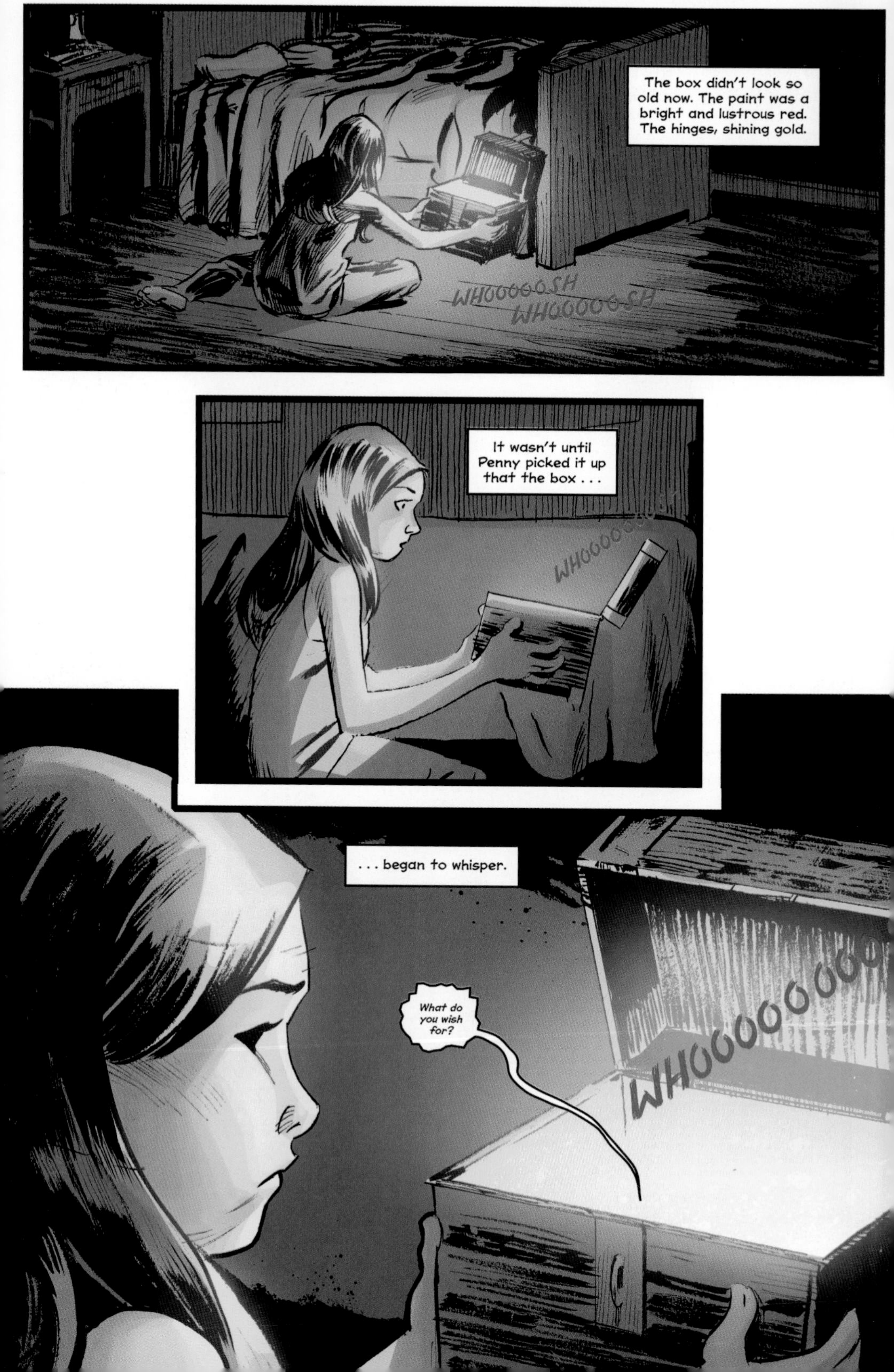
The box didn't look so old now. The paint was a bright and lustrous red. The hinges, shining gold.
WHOOOOOOSH
WHOOOOOOSH
It wasn't until Penny picked it up that the box . . .
. . . began to whisper.
What do you wish for?
WHOOOOOOOO

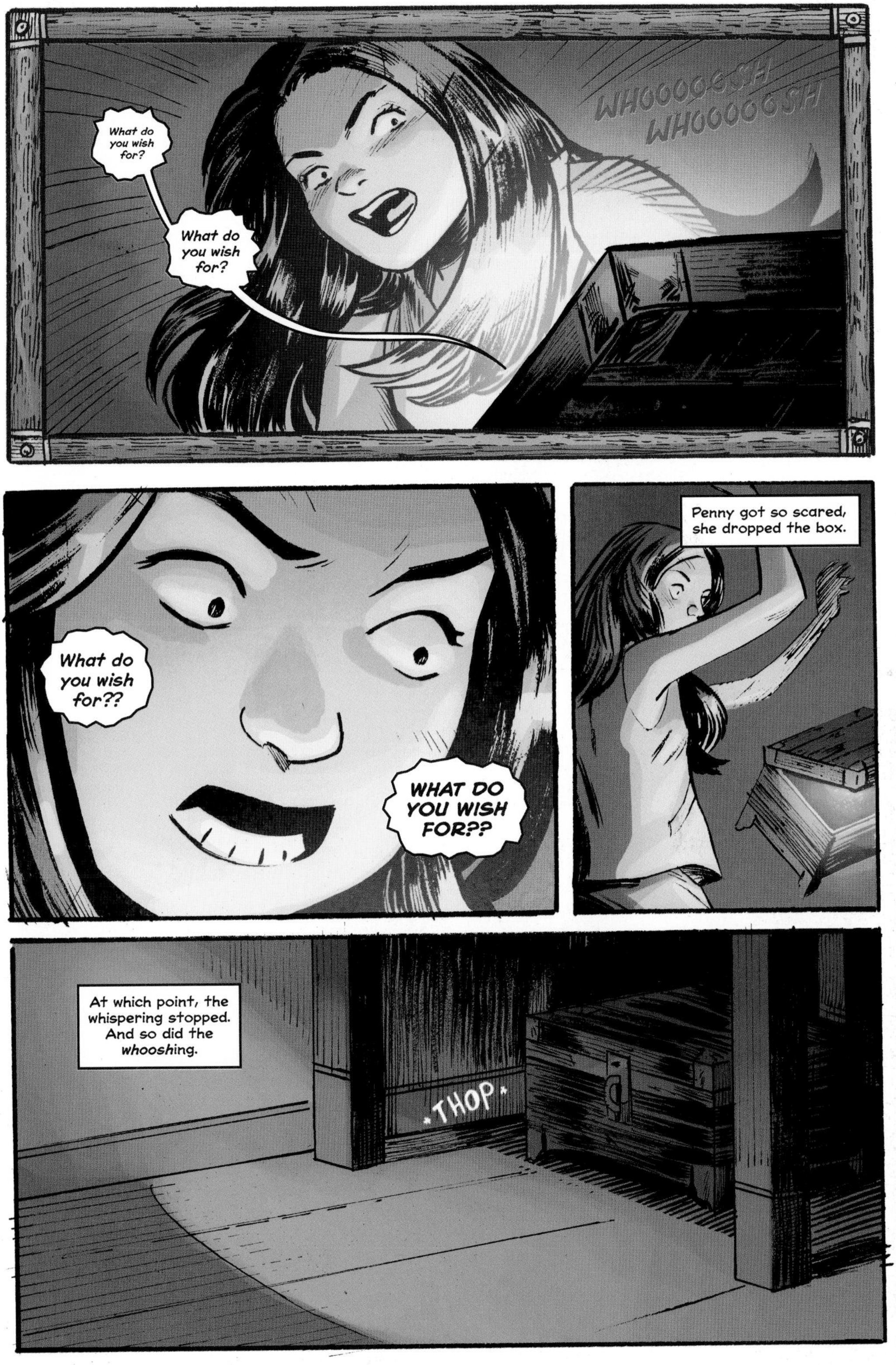
What do you wish for?
What do you wish for?
WHOOOOOSH WHOOOOOSH
What do you wish for??
WHAT DO YOU WISH FOR??
Penny got so scared, she dropped the box.
At which point, the whispering stopped. And so did the *whooshing*.
THOP

Penny tip-toed across the room and dug around in the back of her closet.

She settled on a weapon.

Then she poked at the box with it -- just once -- and very softly.

tic

When nothing happened . . .

. . . she pushed the box out of the shadows and into the bright patch of moonlight on the floor in front of her window.

SLIIIIDE

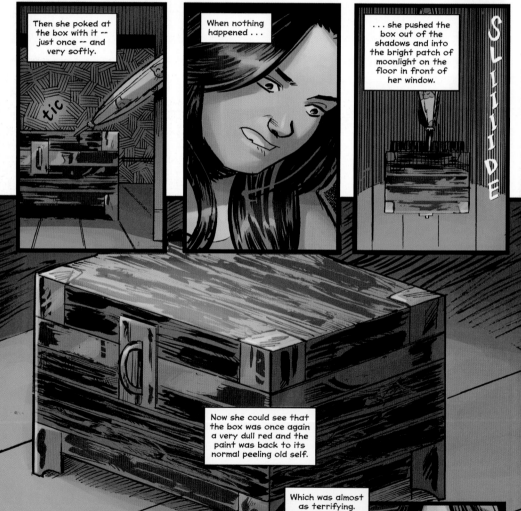

Now she could see that the box was once again a very dull red and the paint was back to its normal peeling old self.

Which was almost as terrifying.

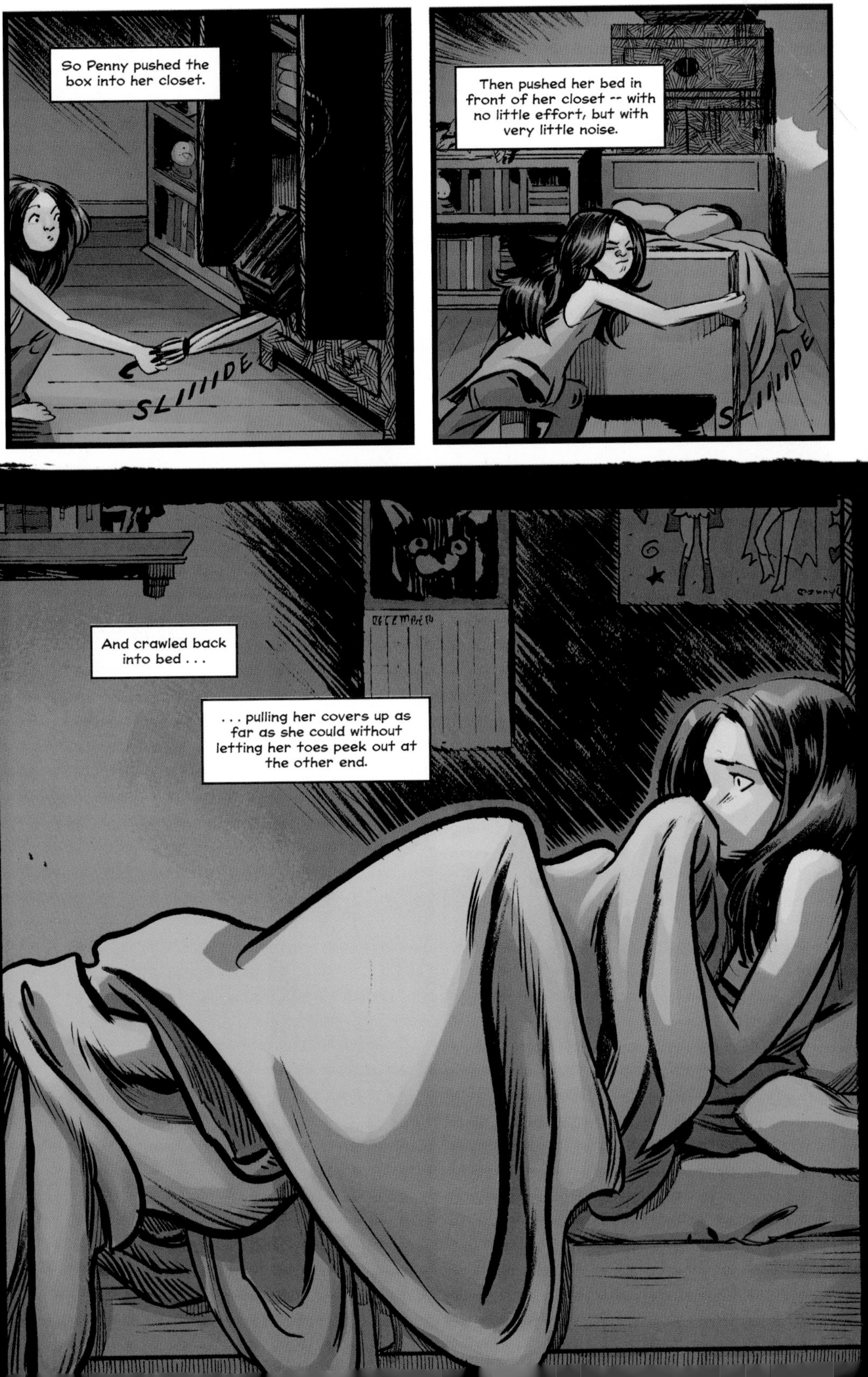
So Penny pushed the box into her closet.
SLIIIIDE
Then pushed her bed in front of her closet -- with no little effort, but with very little noise.
SLIIIIDE
And crawled back into bed . . .
. . . pulling her covers up as far as she could without letting her toes peek out at the other end.

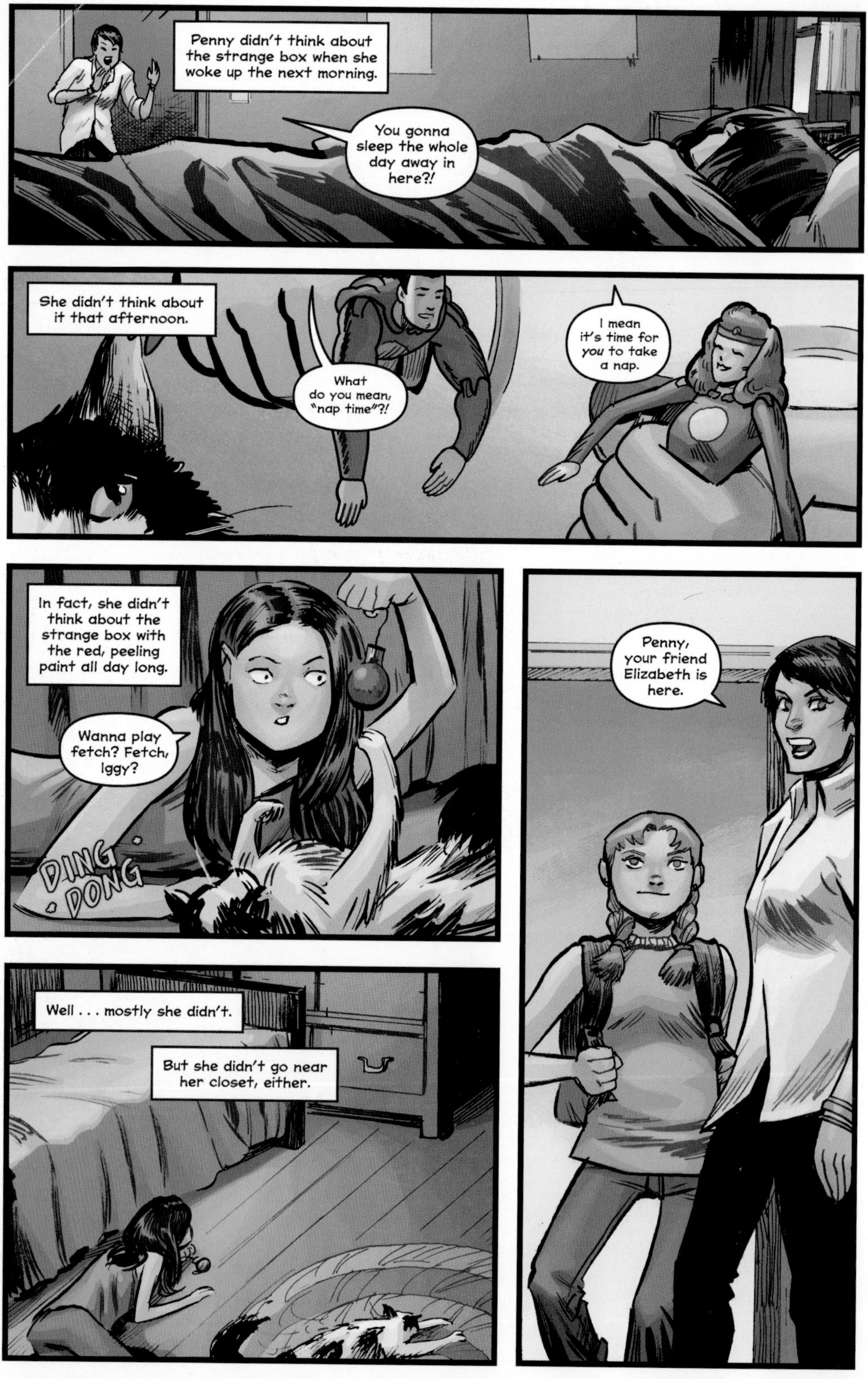
Penny didn't think about the strange box when she woke up the next morning.
You gonna sleep the whole day away in here?!
She didn't think about it that afternoon.
What do you mean, "nap time"?!
I mean it's time for *you* to take a nap.
In fact, she didn't think about the strange box with the red, peeling paint all day long.
Wanna play fetch? Fetch, Iggy?
DING DONG
Penny, your friend Elizabeth is here.
Well . . . mostly she didn't.
But she didn't go near her closet, either.

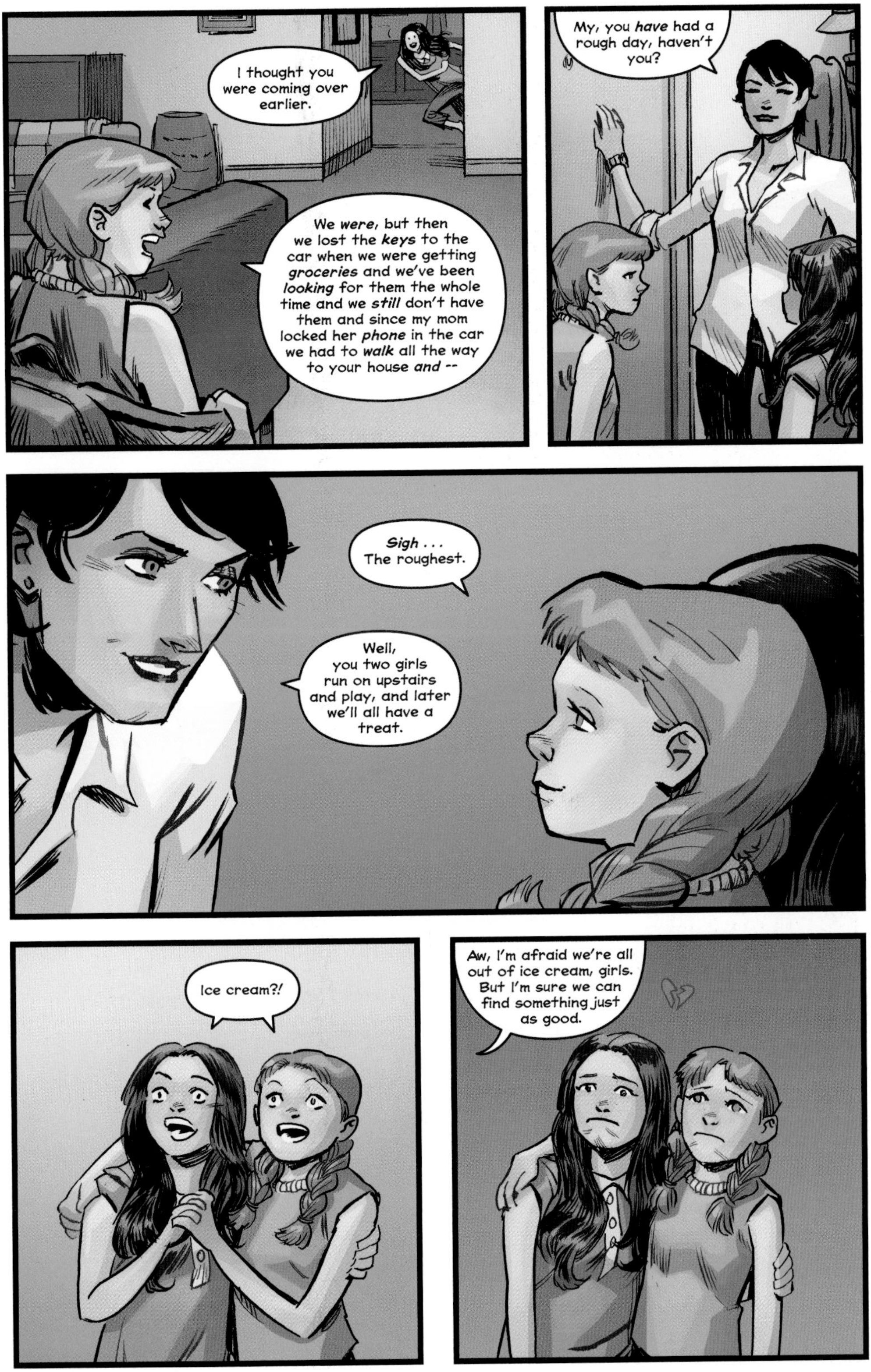
I thought you were coming over earlier.
We *were,* but then we lost the *keys* to the car when we were getting *groceries* and we've been *looking* for them the whole time and we *still* don't have them and since my mom locked her *phone* in the car we had to *walk* all the way to your house *and* --
My, you *have* had a rough day, haven't you?
Sigh . . . The roughest.
Well, you two girls run on upstairs and play, and later we'll all have a treat.
Ice cream?!
Aw, I'm afraid we're all out of ice cream, girls. But I'm sure we can find something just as good.

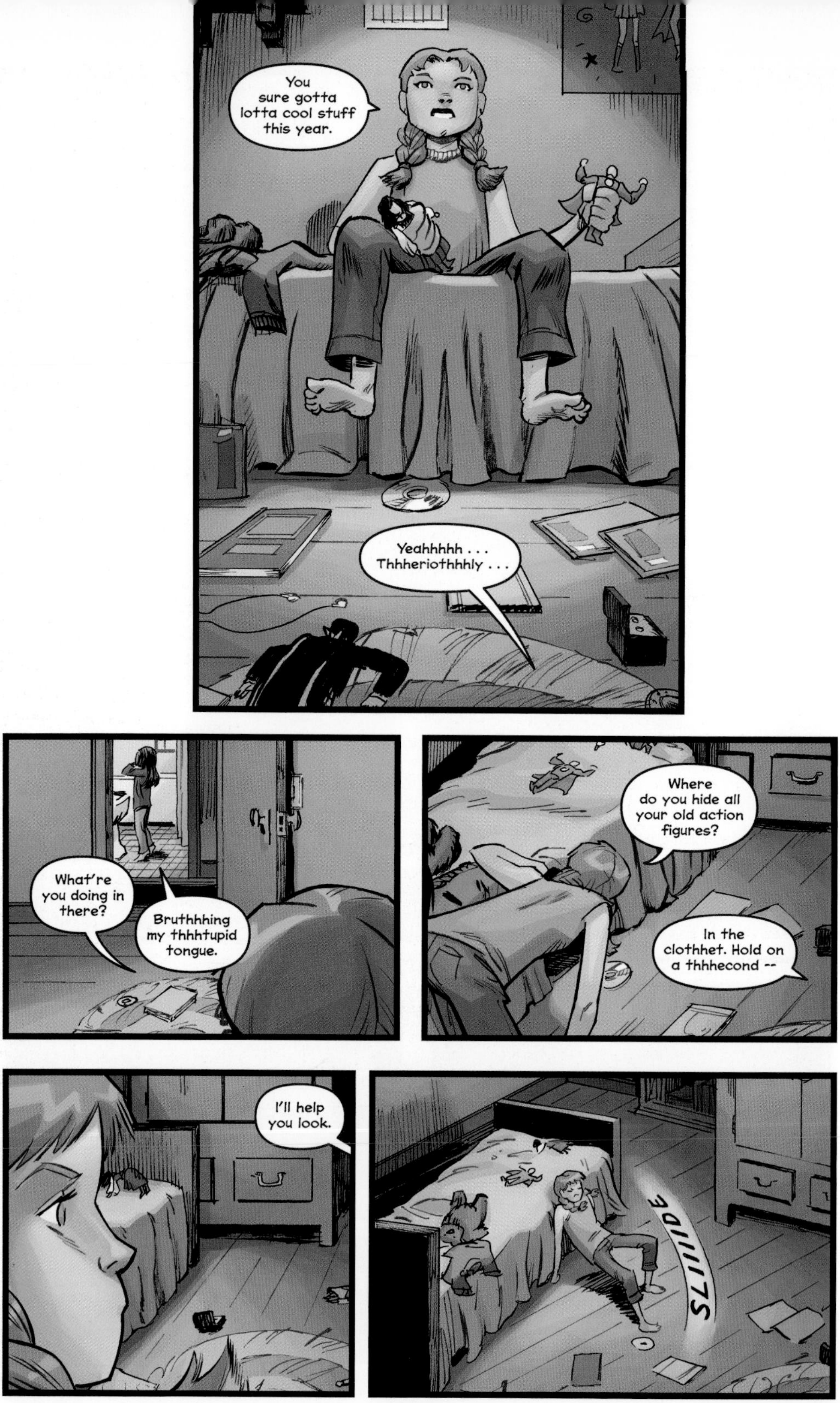
You sure gotta lotta cool stuff this year.
Yeahhhhh . . . Thhheriothhhly . . .
What're you doing in there?
Bruthhhing my thhhtupid tongue.
Where do you hide all your old action figures?
In the clothhet. Hold on a thhhecond --
I'll help you look.
SLIIIIDE

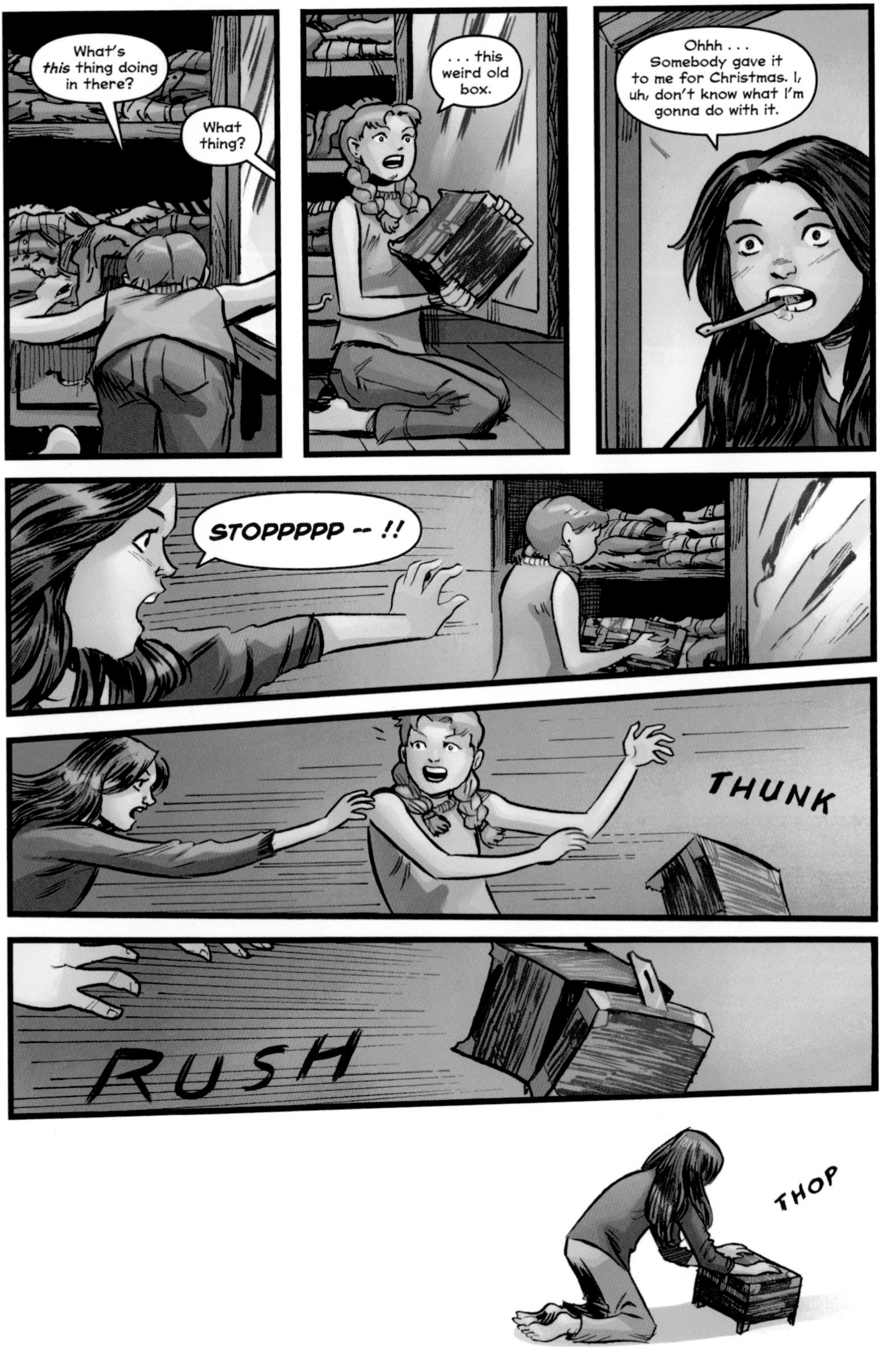

What's *this* thing doing in there?
What thing?
. . . this weird old box.
Ohhh . . . Somebody gave it to me for Christmas. I, uh, don't know what I'm gonna do with it.
STOPPPPP -- !!
THUNK
RUSH
THOP

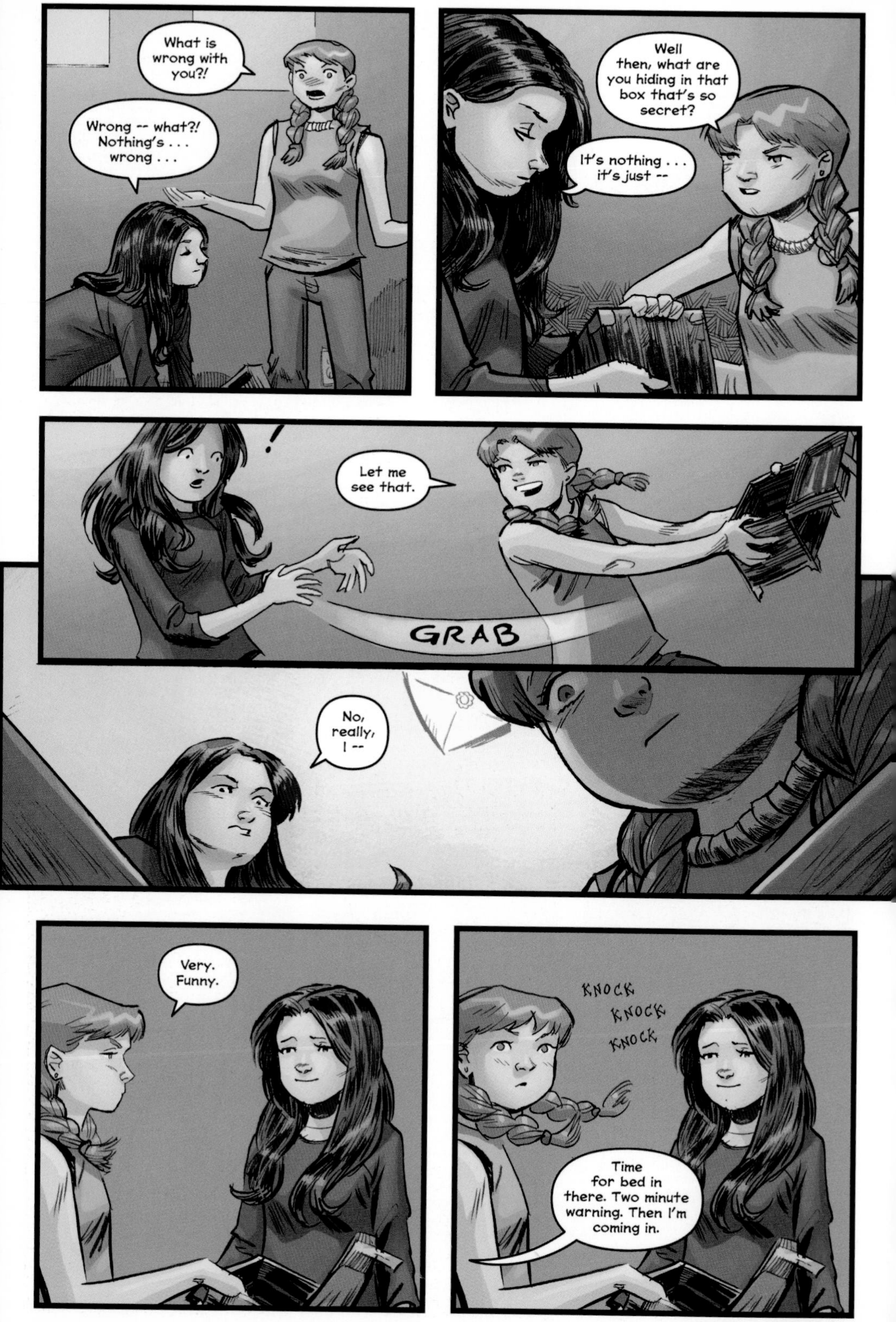
What is wrong with you?!
Wrong -- what?! Nothing's . . . wrong . . .
Well then, what are you hiding in that box that's so secret?
It's nothing . . . it's just --
!
Let me see that.
GRAB
No, really, I --
Very. Funny.
KNOCK KNOCK KNOCK
Time for bed in there. Two minute warning. Then I'm coming in.

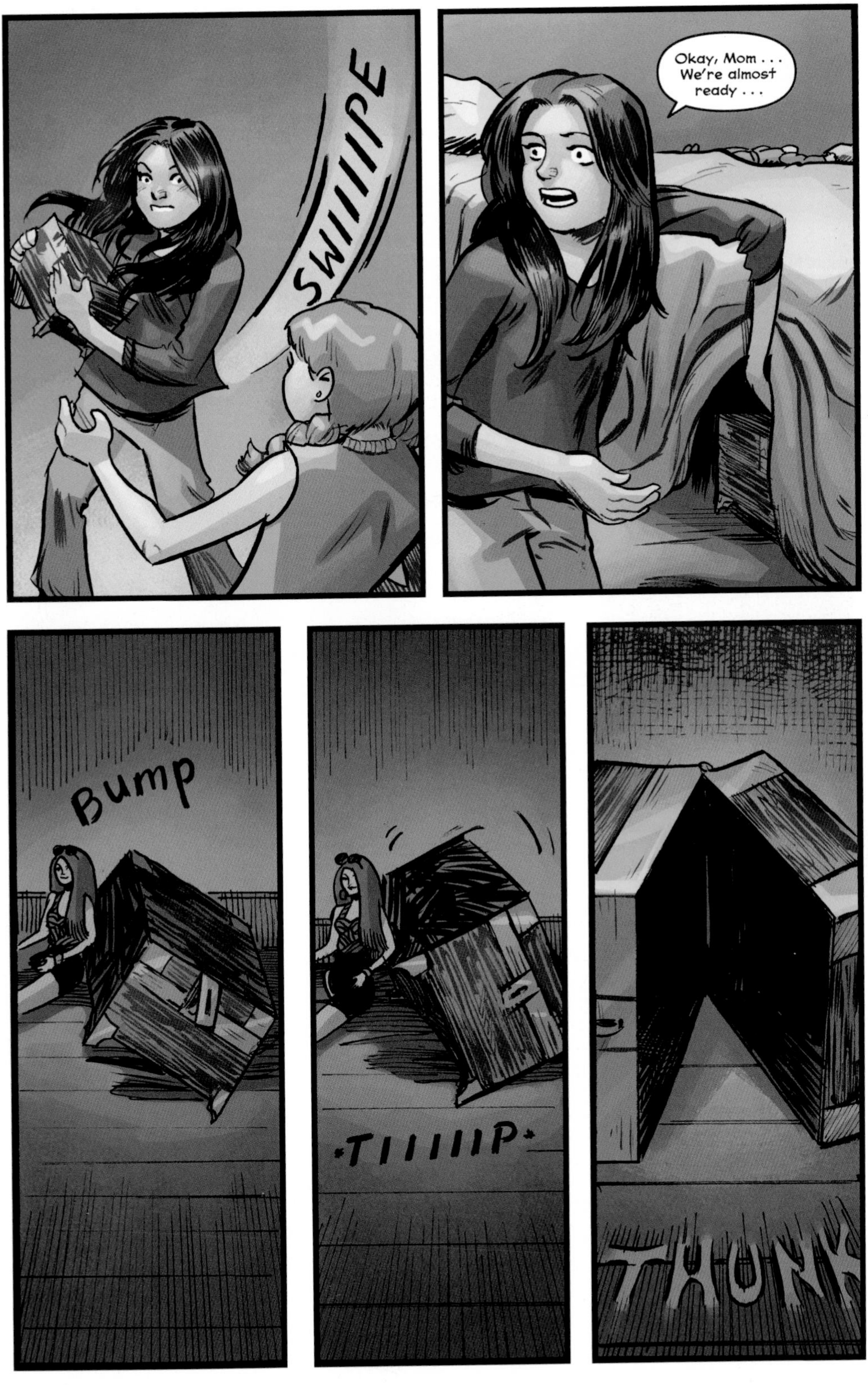
SWIIIPE
Okay, Mom . . . We're almost ready . . .
Bump
TIIIIIP
THUNK

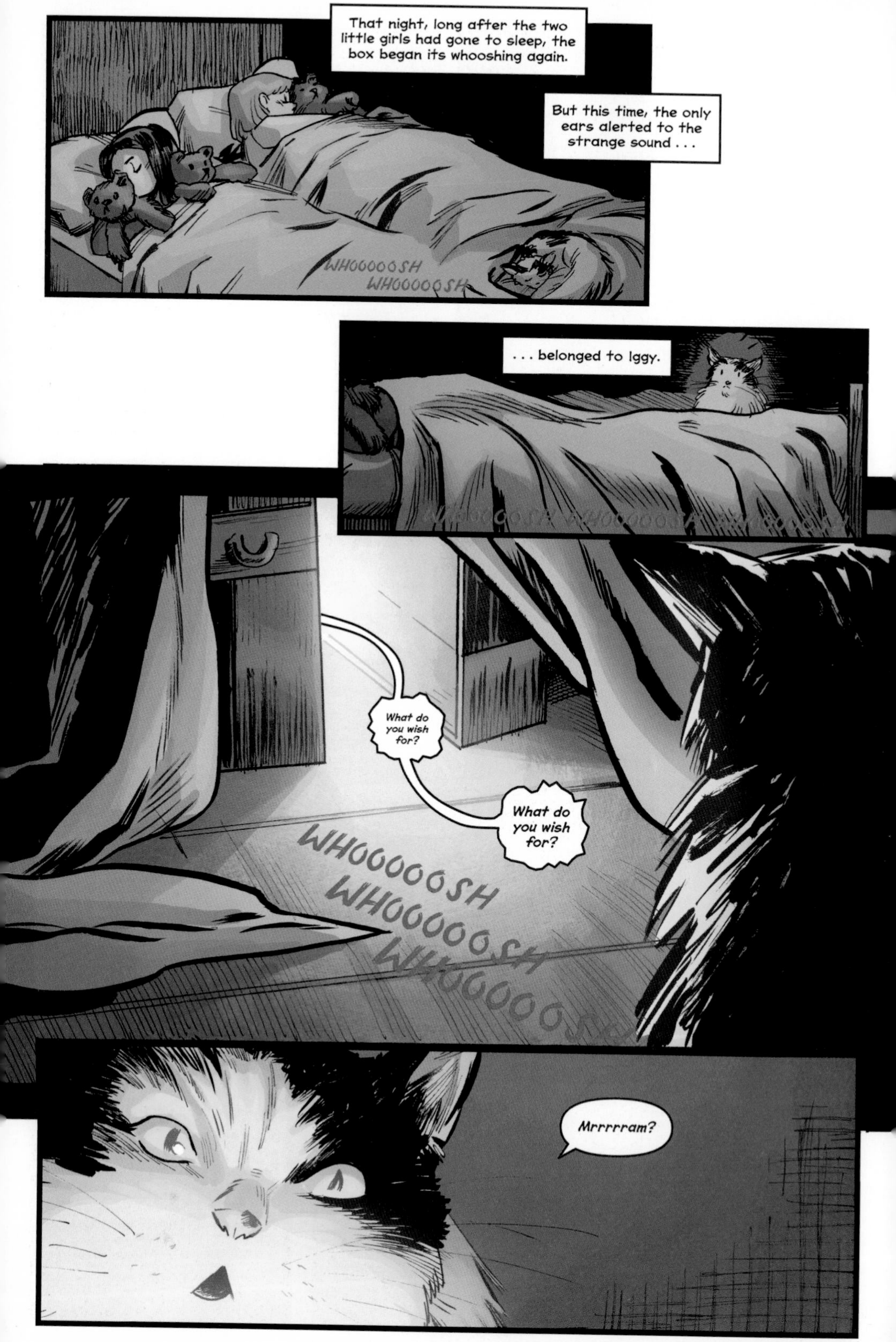
That night, long after the two little girls had gone to sleep, the box began its whooshing again.
But this time, the only ears alerted to the strange sound . . .
WHOOOOOSH
WHOOOOOSH
. . . belonged to Iggy.
What do you wish for?
What do you wish for?
WHOOOOOOSH
WHOOOOOOSH
Mrrrrram?

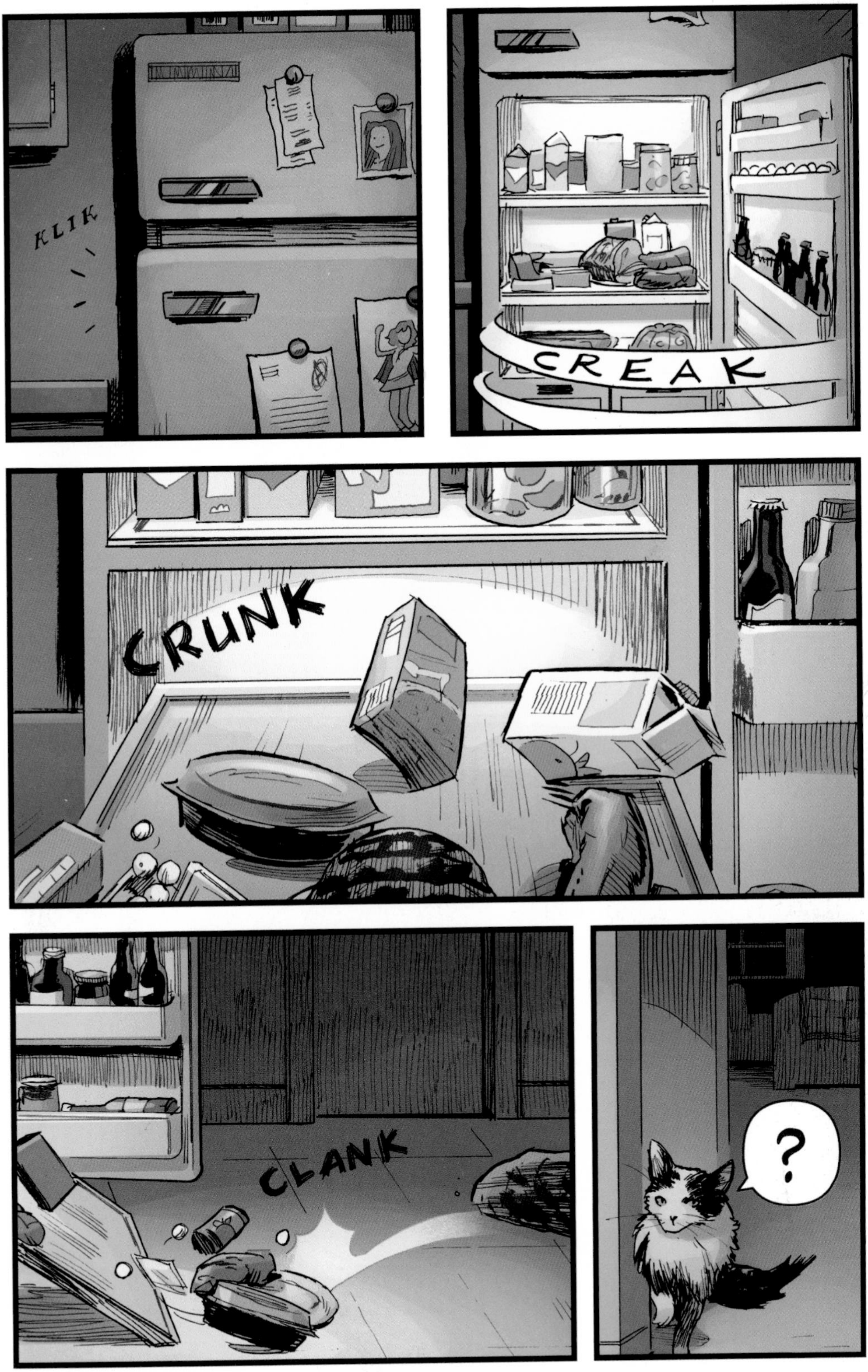
KLIK
CREAK
CRUNK
CLANK
?

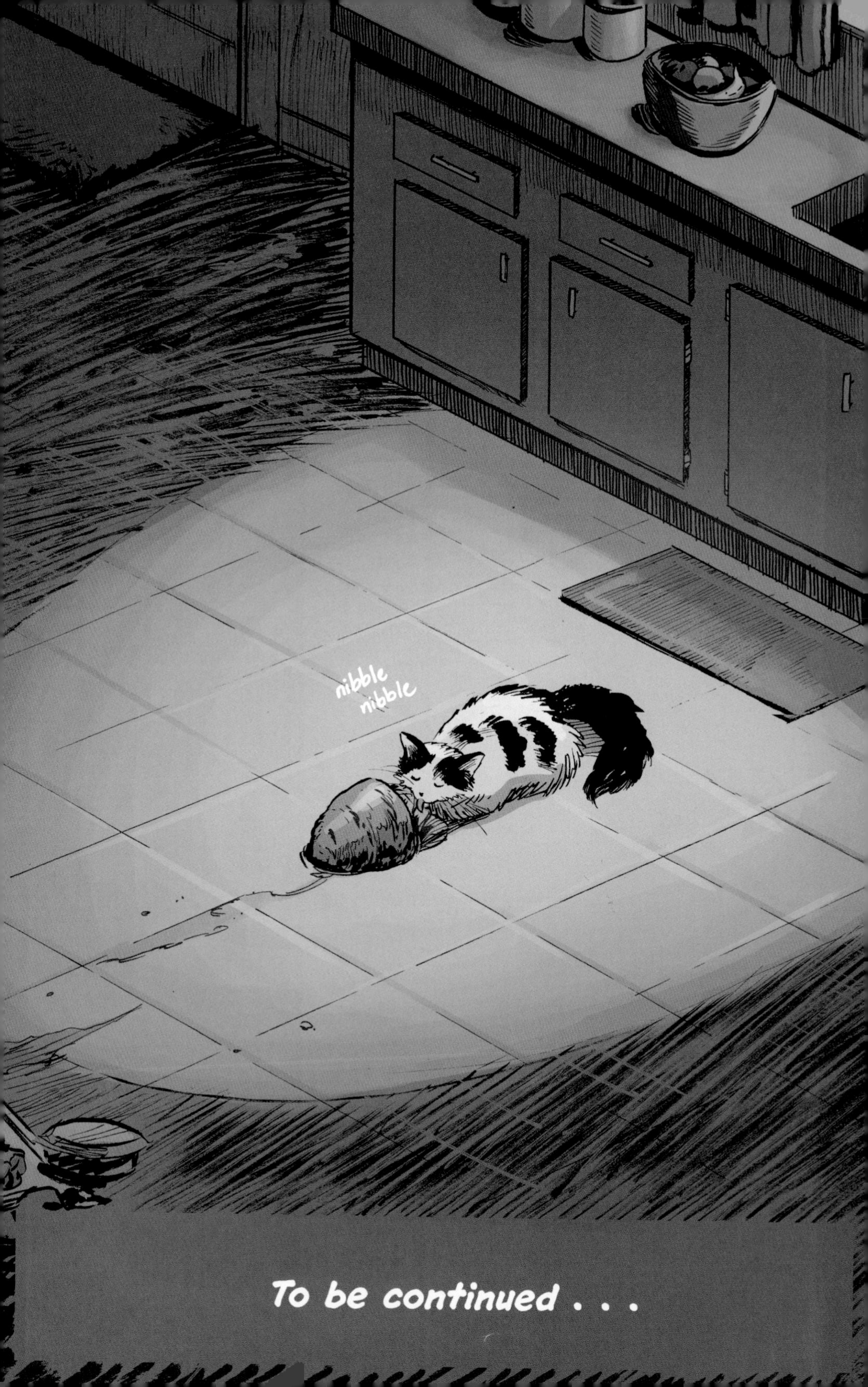
nibble
nibble
To be continued . . .

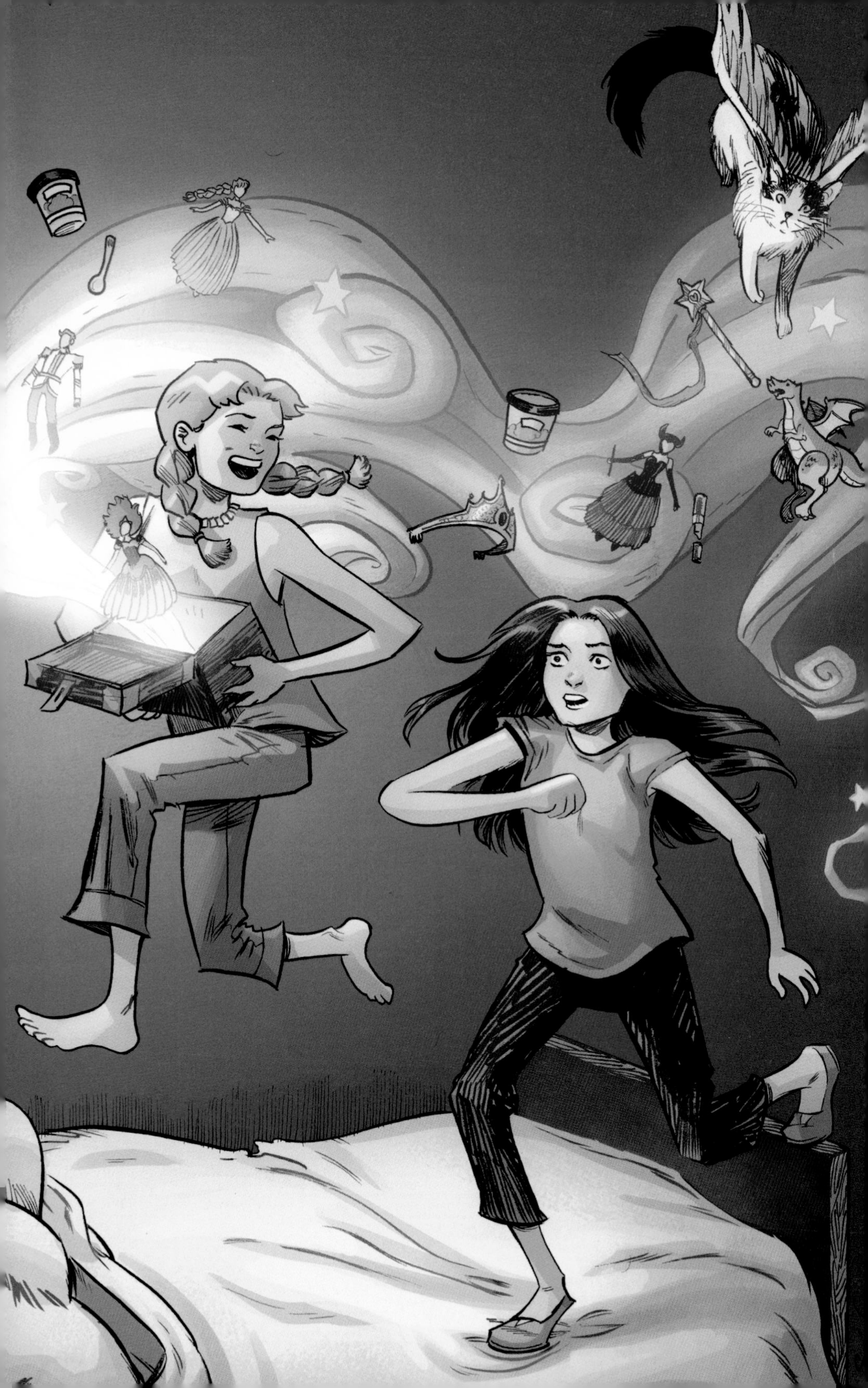

Chapter Two

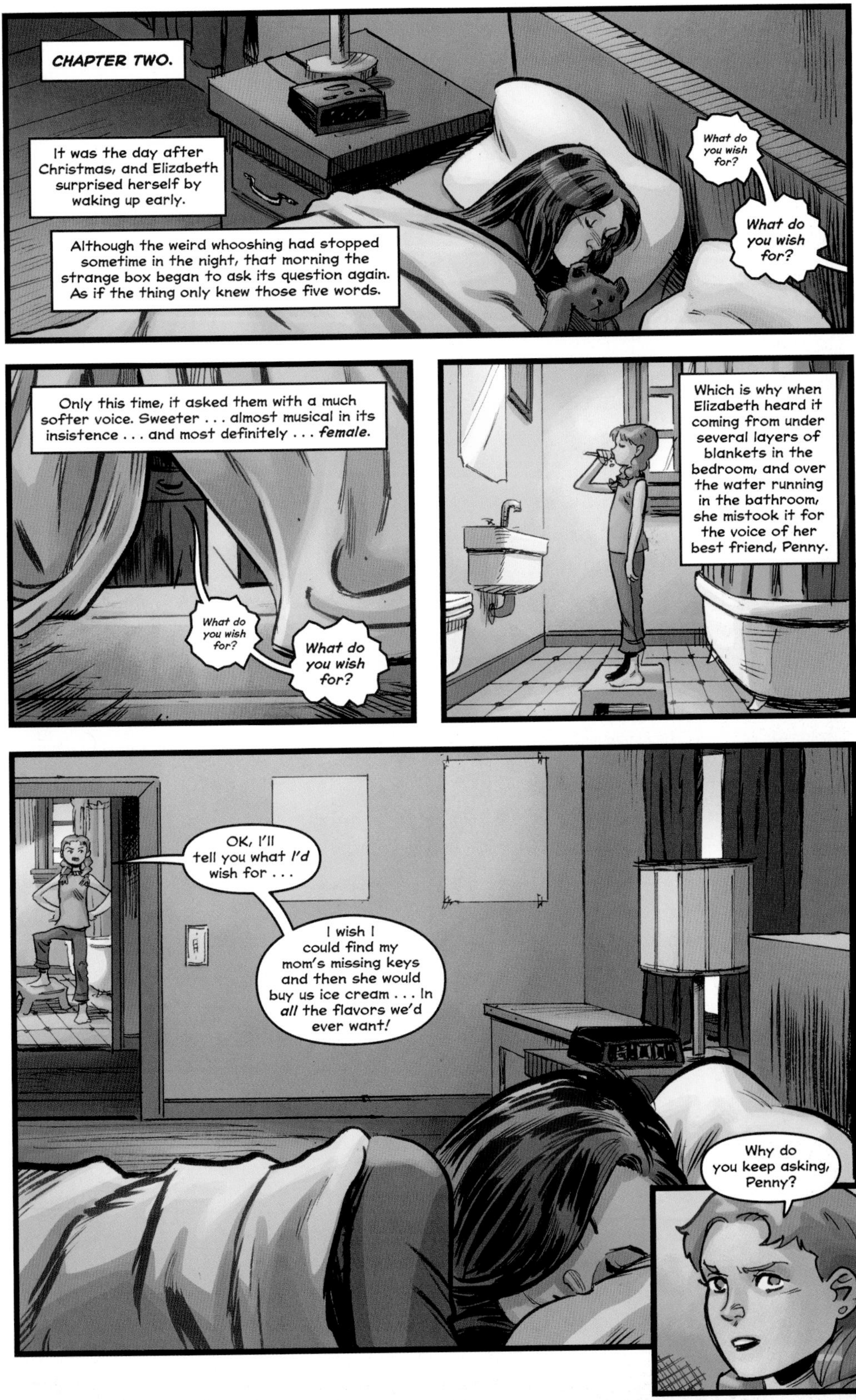
CHAPTER TWO.
It was the day after Christmas, and Elizabeth surprised herself by waking up early.
Although the weird whooshing had stopped sometime in the night, that morning the strange box began to ask its question again. As if the thing only knew those five words.
What do you wish for?
What do you wish for?
Only this time, it asked them with a much softer voice. Sweeter . . . almost musical in its insistence . . . and most definitely . . . *female*.
What do you wish for?
What do you wish for?
Which is why when Elizabeth heard it coming from under several layers of blankets in the bedroom, and over the water running in the bathroom, she mistook it for the voice of her best friend, Penny.
OK, I'll tell you what *I'd* wish for . . .
I wish I could find my mom's missing keys and then she would buy us ice cream . . . In *all* the flavors we'd ever want!
Why do you keep asking, Penny?

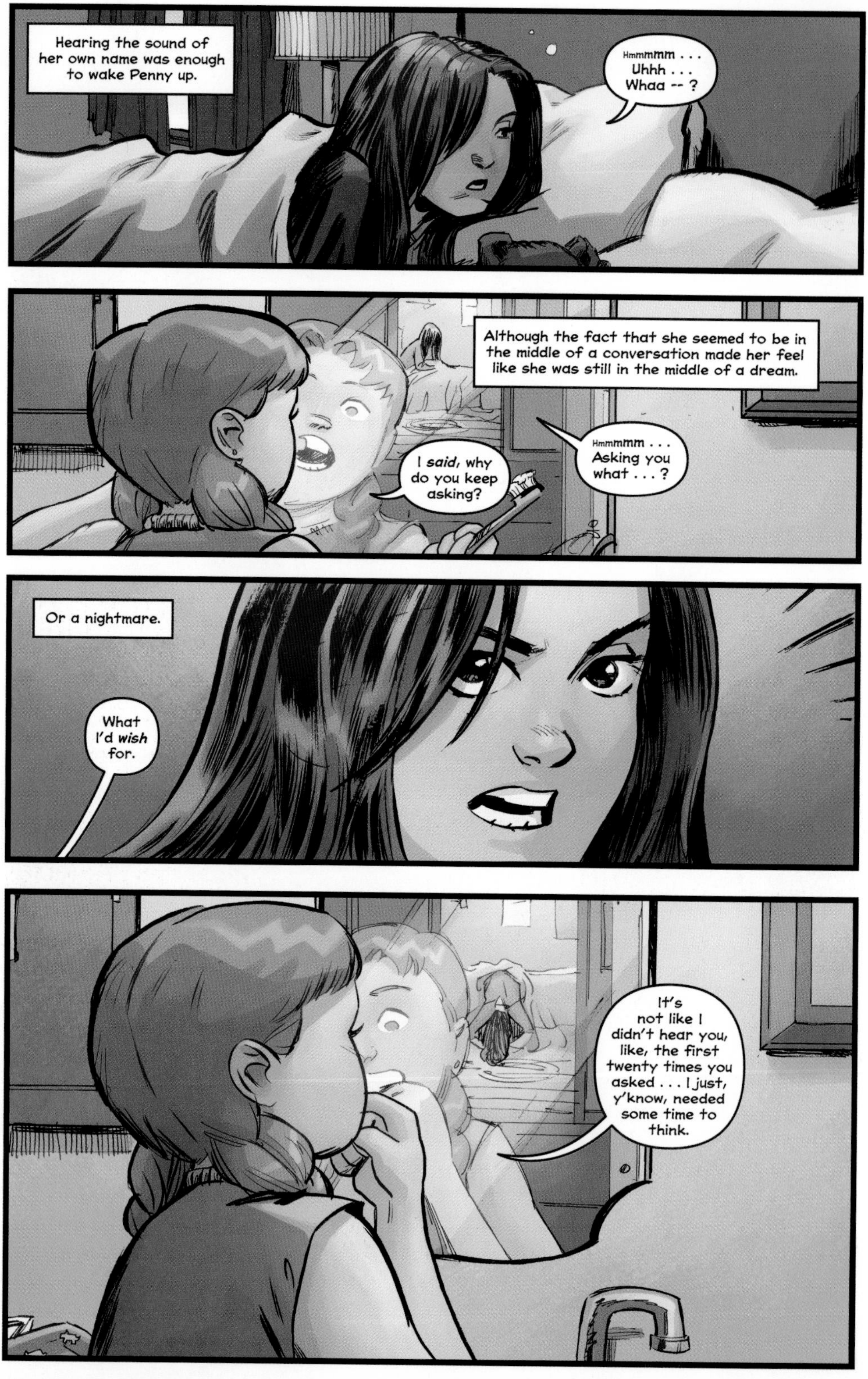
Hearing the sound of her own name was enough to wake Penny up.
Hmmmmm . . . Uhhh . . . Whaa -- ?
Although the fact that she seemed to be in the middle of a conversation made her feel like she was still in the middle of a dream.
I *said*, why do you keep asking?
Hmmmmm . . . Asking you what . . . ?
Or a nightmare.
What I'd *wish* for.
It's not like I didn't hear you, like, the first twenty times you asked . . . I just, y'know, needed some time to think.

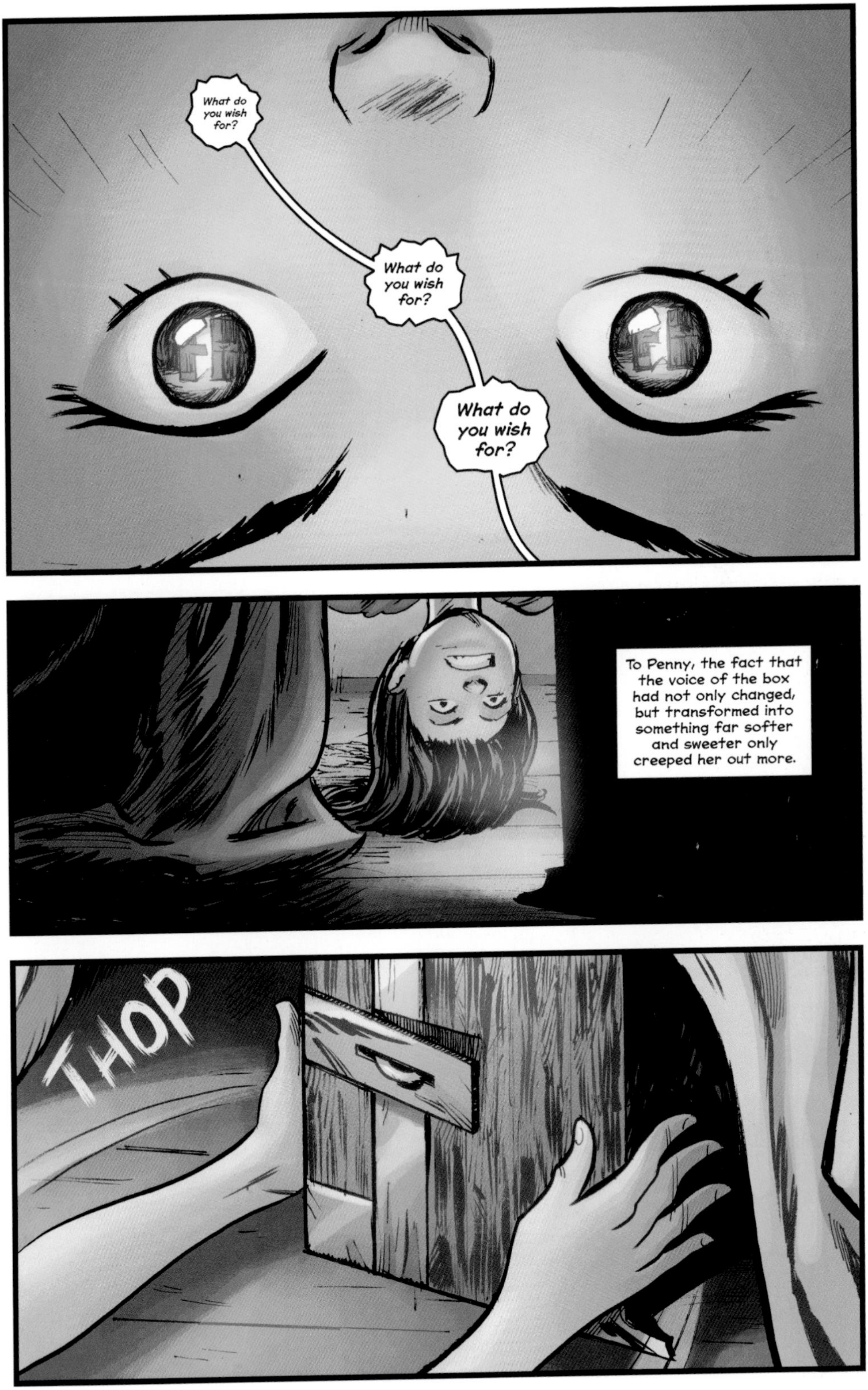
What do you wish for?
What do you wish for?
What do you wish for?
To Penny, the fact that the voice of the box had not only changed, but transformed into something far softer and sweeter only creeped her out more.
THOP

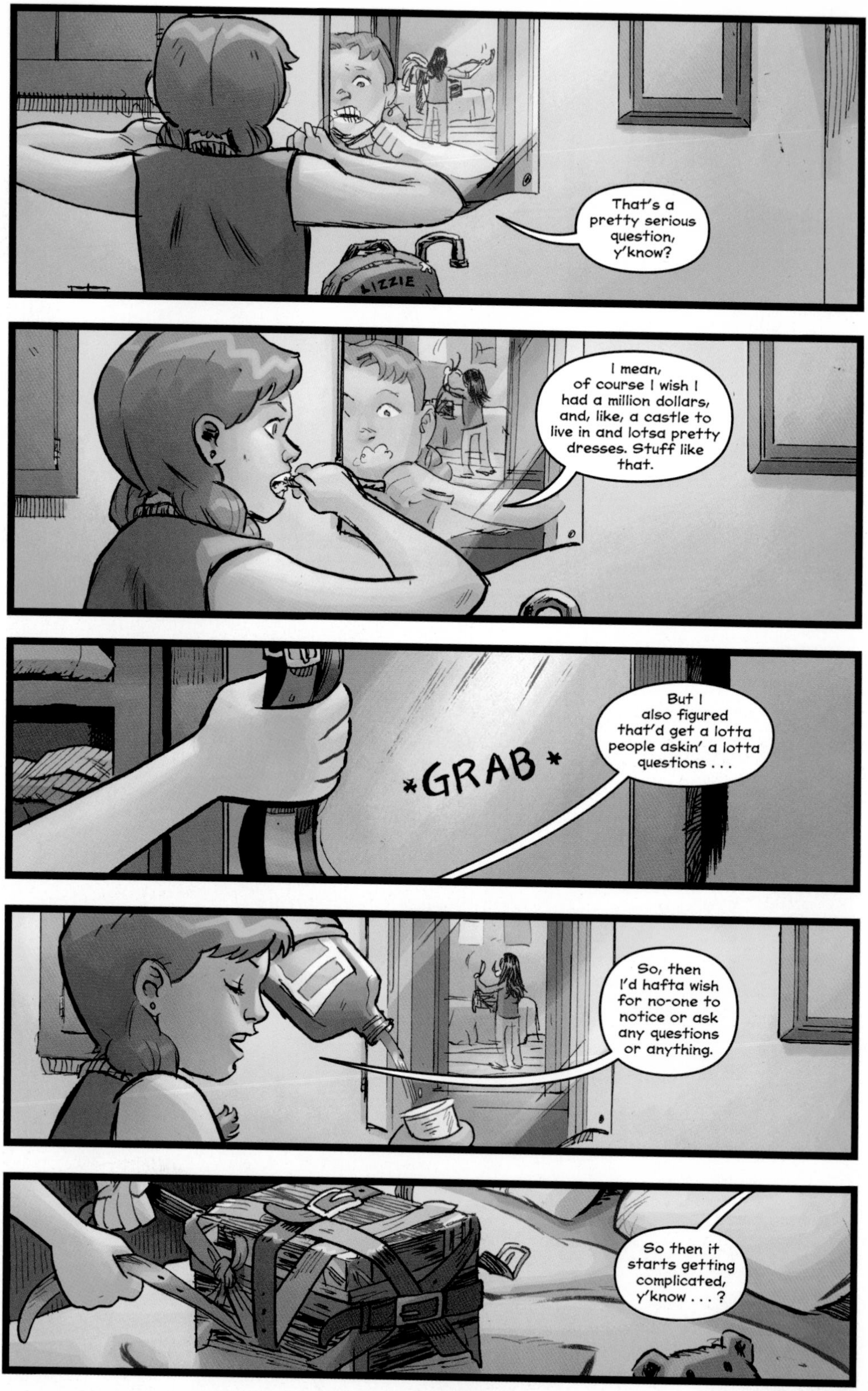
LIZZIE
That's a pretty serious question, y'know?
I mean, of course I wish I had a million dollars, and, like, a castle to live in and lotsa pretty dresses. Stuff like that.
But I also figured that'd get a lotta people askin' a lotta questions . . .
GRAB
So, then I'd hafta wish for no-one to notice or ask any questions or anything.
So then it starts getting complicated, y'know . . . ?

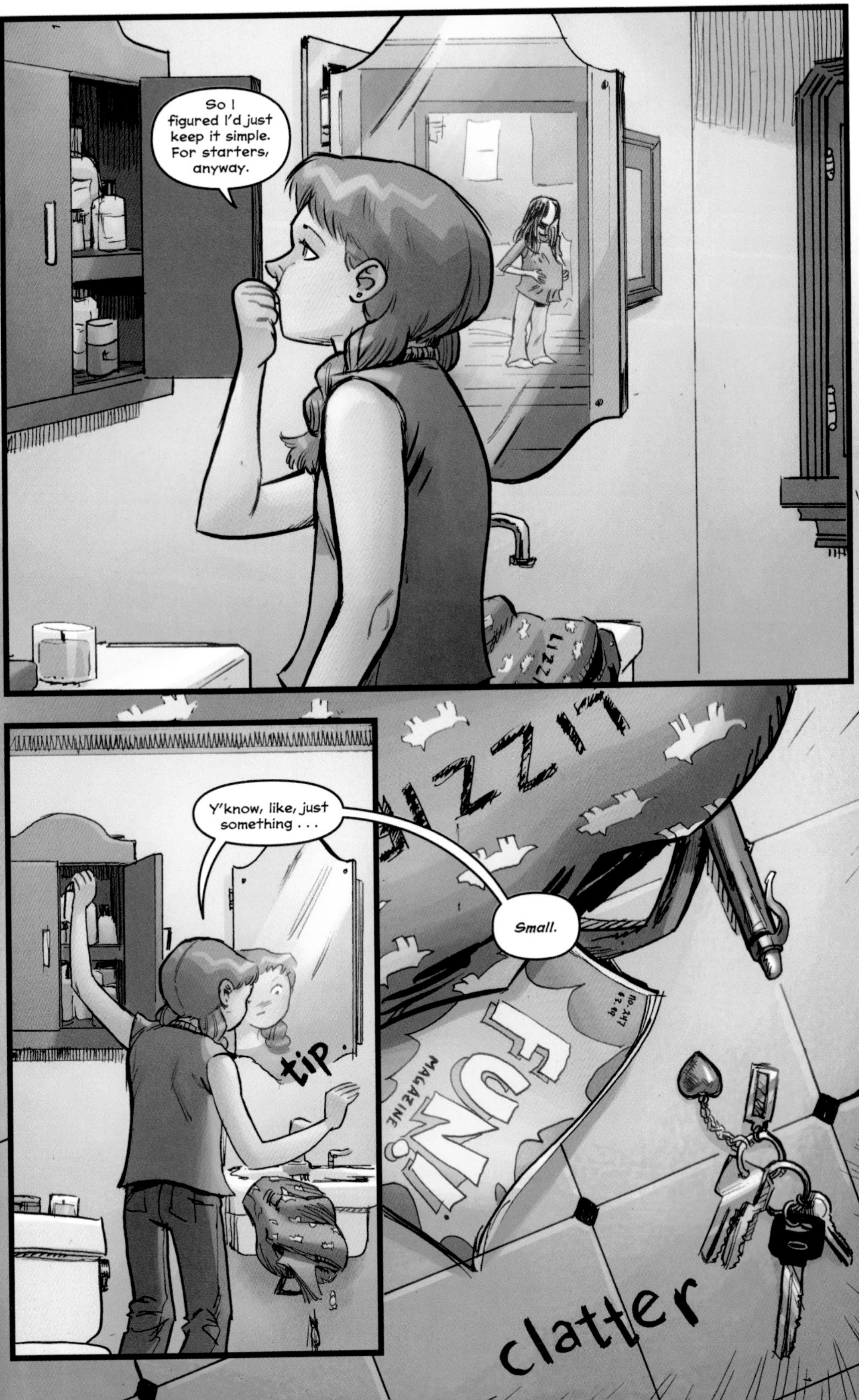

So I figured I'd just keep it simple. For starters, anyway.
LIZZI
Y'know, like, just something . . .
Small.
tip.
LIZZI
FUN! MAGAZINE
clatter

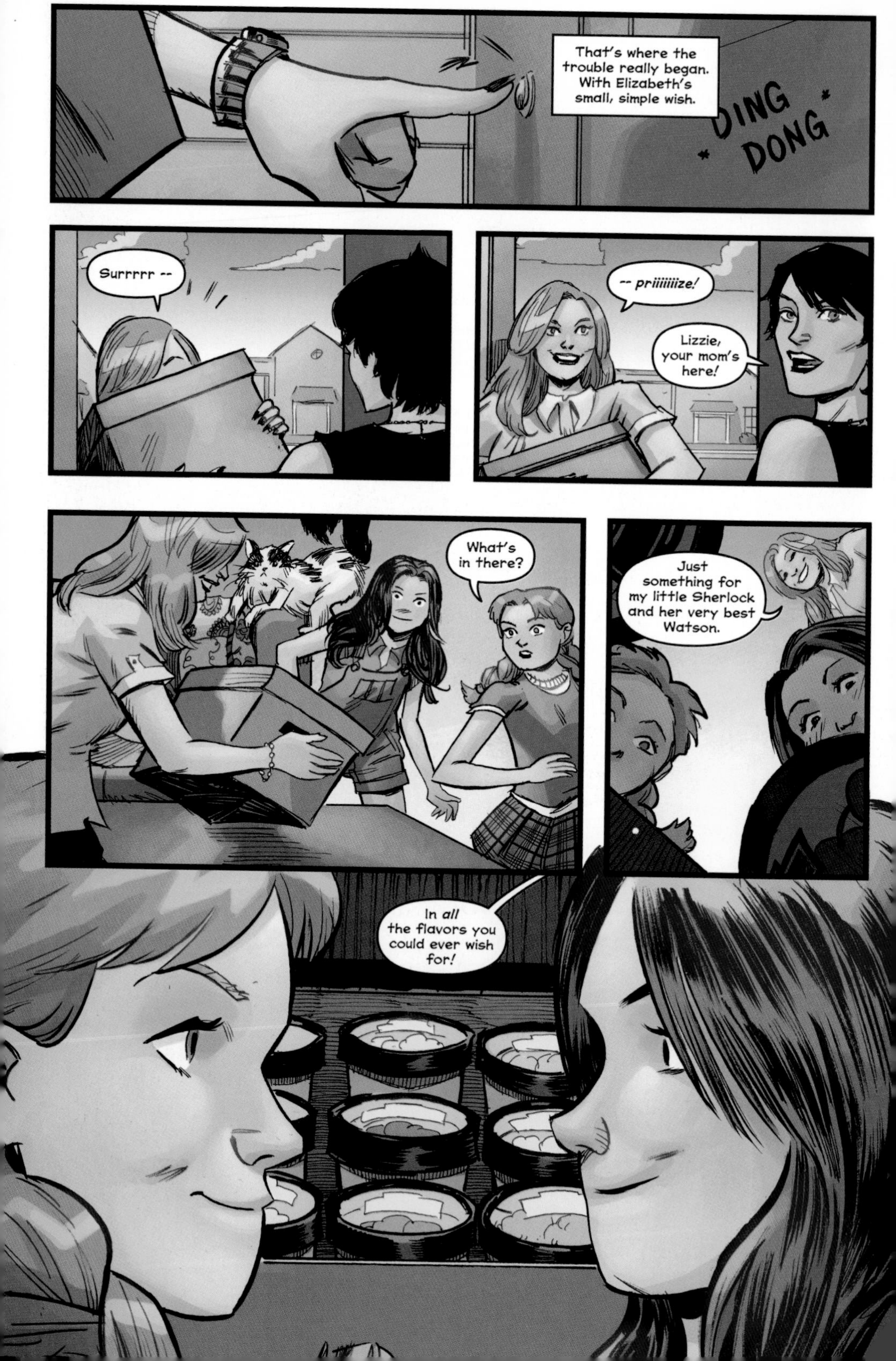
That's where the trouble really began. With Elizabeth's small, simple wish.
DING DONG
Surrrrr --
-- priiiiiiize!
Lizzie, your mom's here!
What's in there?
Just something for my little Sherlock and her very best Watson.
In *all* the flavors you could ever wish for!

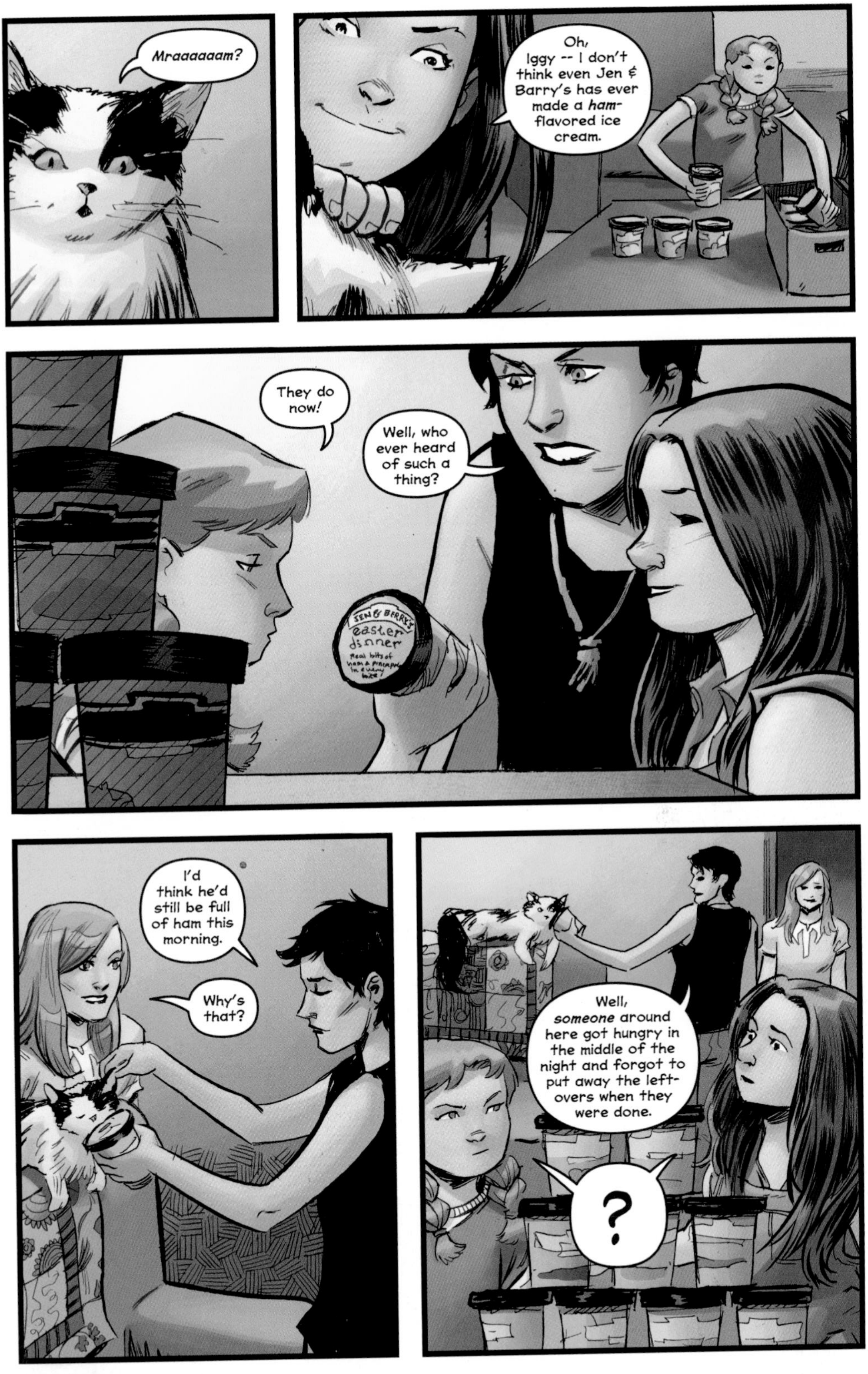
Mraaaaaam?
Oh, Iggy -- I don't think even Jen & Barry's has ever made a *ham*-flavored ice cream.
They do now!
Well, who ever heard of such a thing?
JEN & BARRY'S
easter dinner
I'd think he'd still be full of ham this morning.
Why's that?
Well, *someone* around here got hungry in the middle of the night and forgot to put away the left-overs when they were done.
?

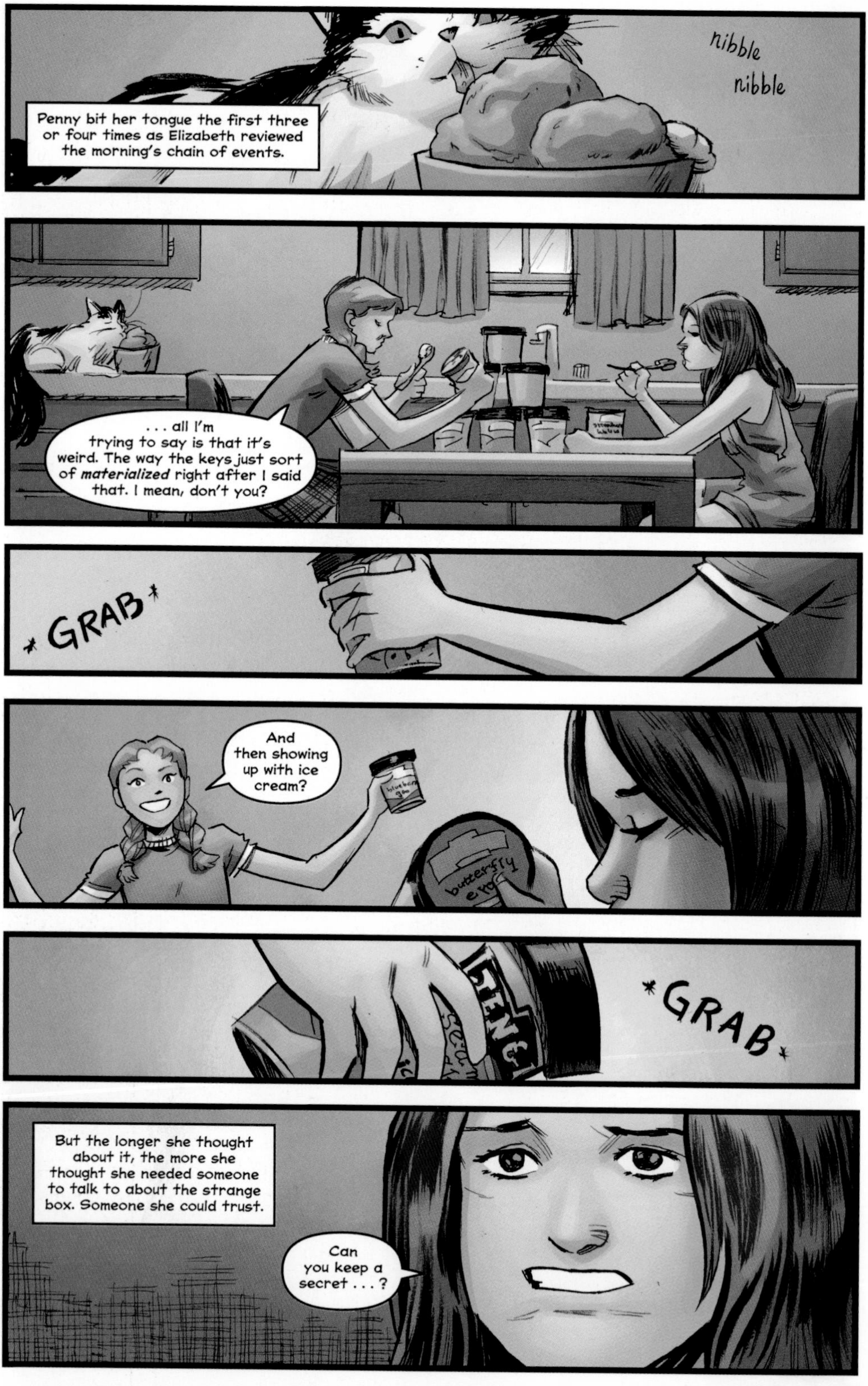
Penny bit her tongue the first three or four times as Elizabeth reviewed the morning's chain of events.
nibble
nibble
. . . all I'm trying to say is that it's weird. The way the keys just sort of *materialized* right after I said that. I mean, don't you?
GRAB
And then showing up with ice cream?
butterfly
GRAB
But the longer she thought about it, the more she thought she needed someone to talk to about the strange box. Someone she could trust.
Can you keep a secret . . . ?

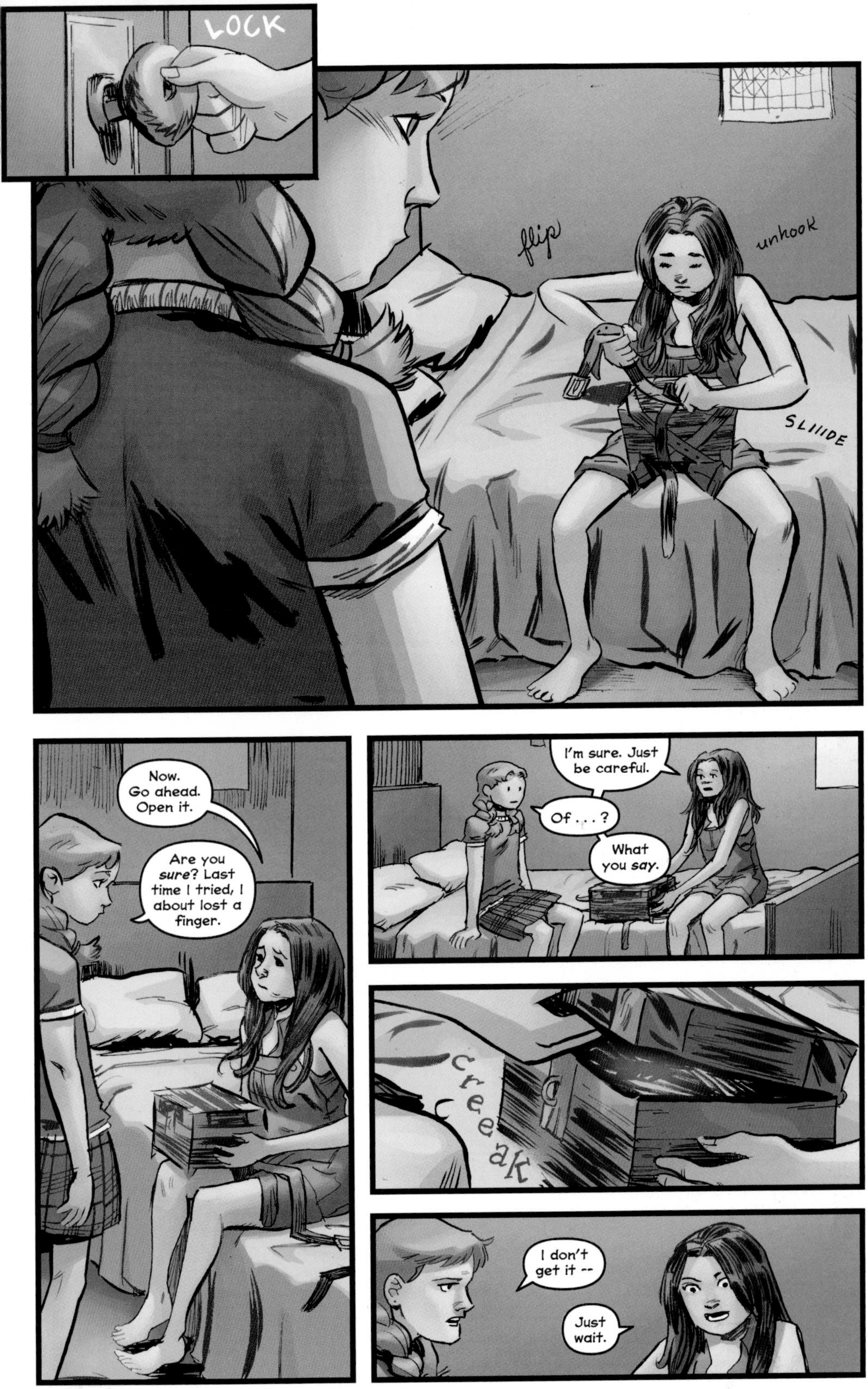
LOCK
flip
unhook
SLIIIDE
Now. Go ahead. Open it.
Are you *sure*? Last time I tried, I about lost a finger.
I'm sure. Just be careful.
Of . . . ?
What you *say*.
creeak
I don't get it --
Just wait.

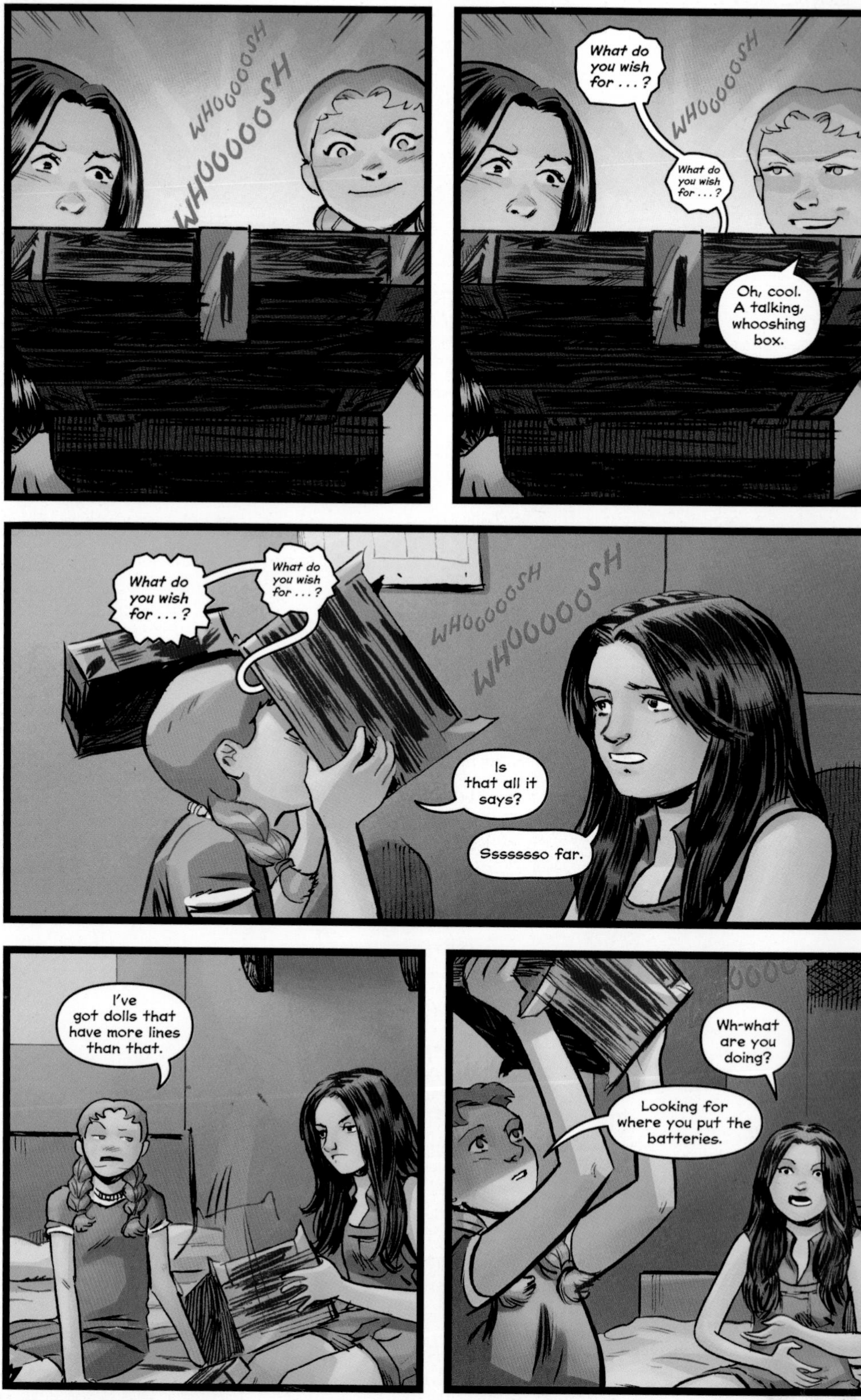
WHOOOOOSH
WHOOOOOSH
What do you wish for . . . ?
WHOOOOOSH
What do you wish for . . . ?
Oh, cool. A talking, whooshing box.
What do you wish for . . . ?
What do you wish for . . . ?
WHOOOOOSH
WHOOOOOOSH
Is that all it says?
Sssssso far.
I've got dolls that have more lines than that.
Wh-what are you doing?
Looking for where you put the batteries.

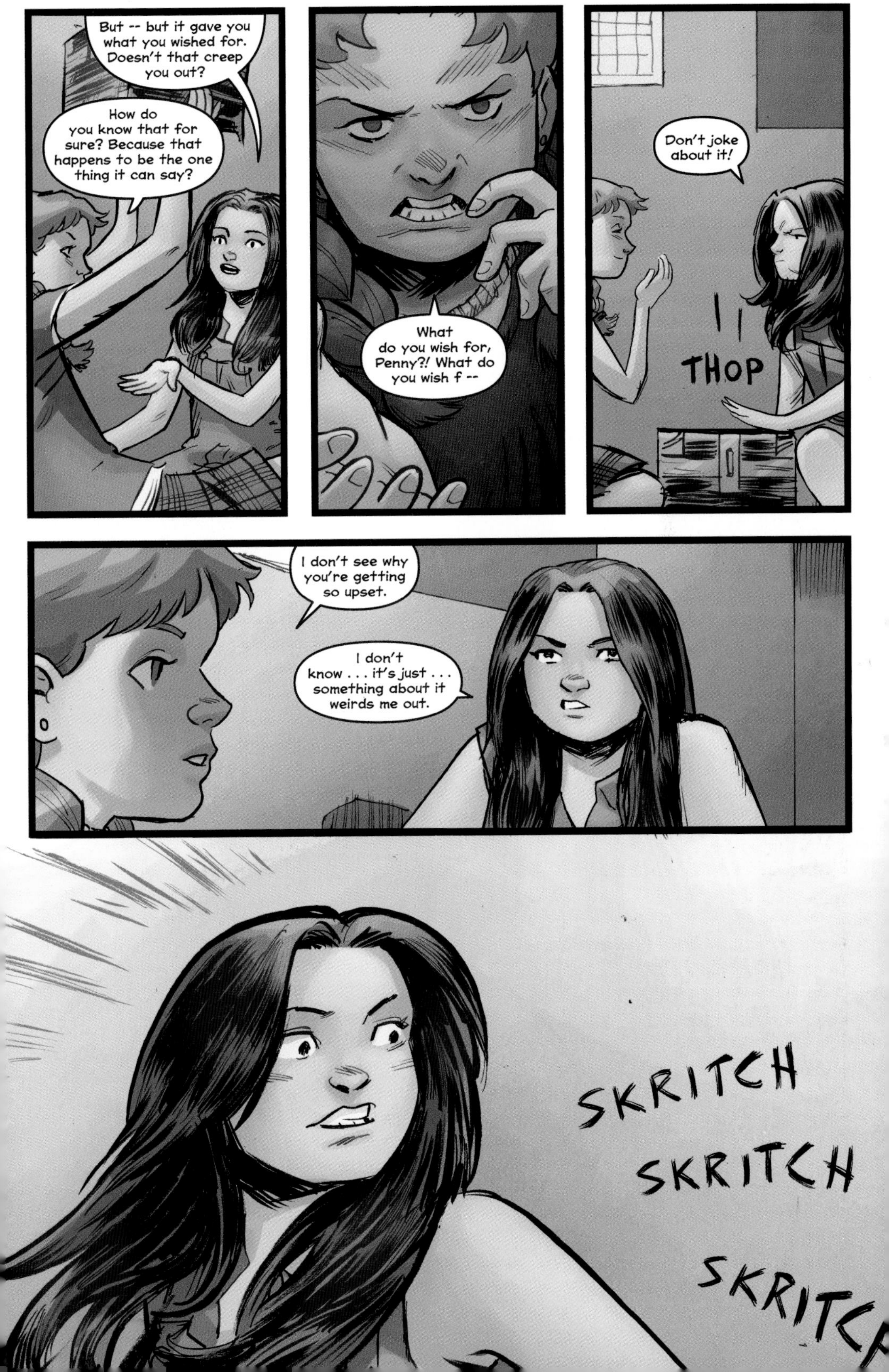

But -- but it gave you what you wished for. Doesn't that creep you out?
How do you know that for sure? Because that happens to be the one thing it can say?
What do you wish for, Penny?! What do you wish f --
Don't joke about it!
THOP
I don't see why you're getting so upset.
I don't know . . . it's just . . . something about it weirds me out.
SKRITCH
SKRITCH
SKRITCH

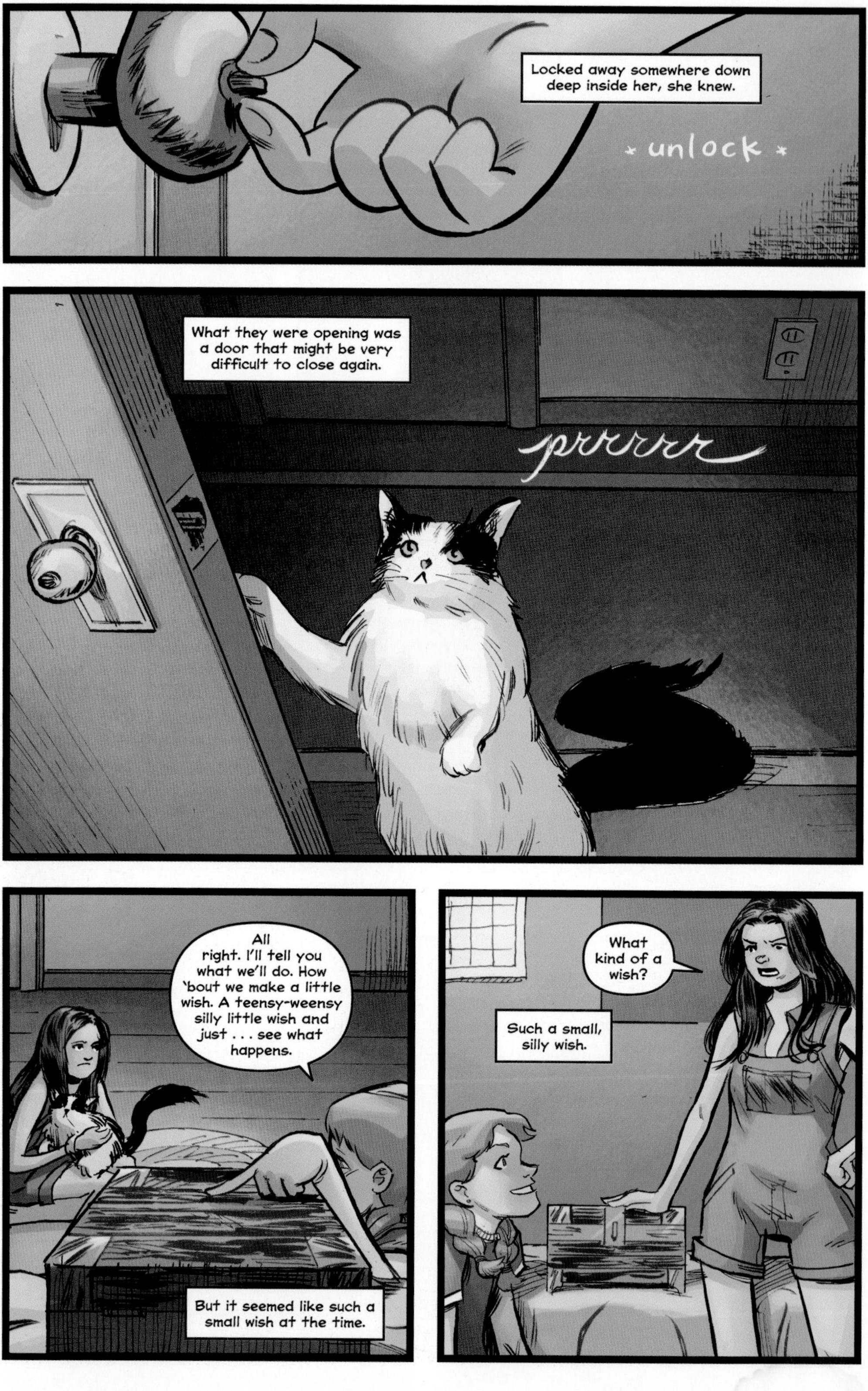
Locked away somewhere down deep inside her, she knew.
unlock
What they were opening was a door that might be very difficult to close again.
prrrrr
All right. I'll tell you what we'll do. How 'bout we make a little wish. A teensy-weensy silly little wish and just . . . see what happens.
But it seemed like such a small wish at the time.
What kind of a wish?
Such a small, silly wish.

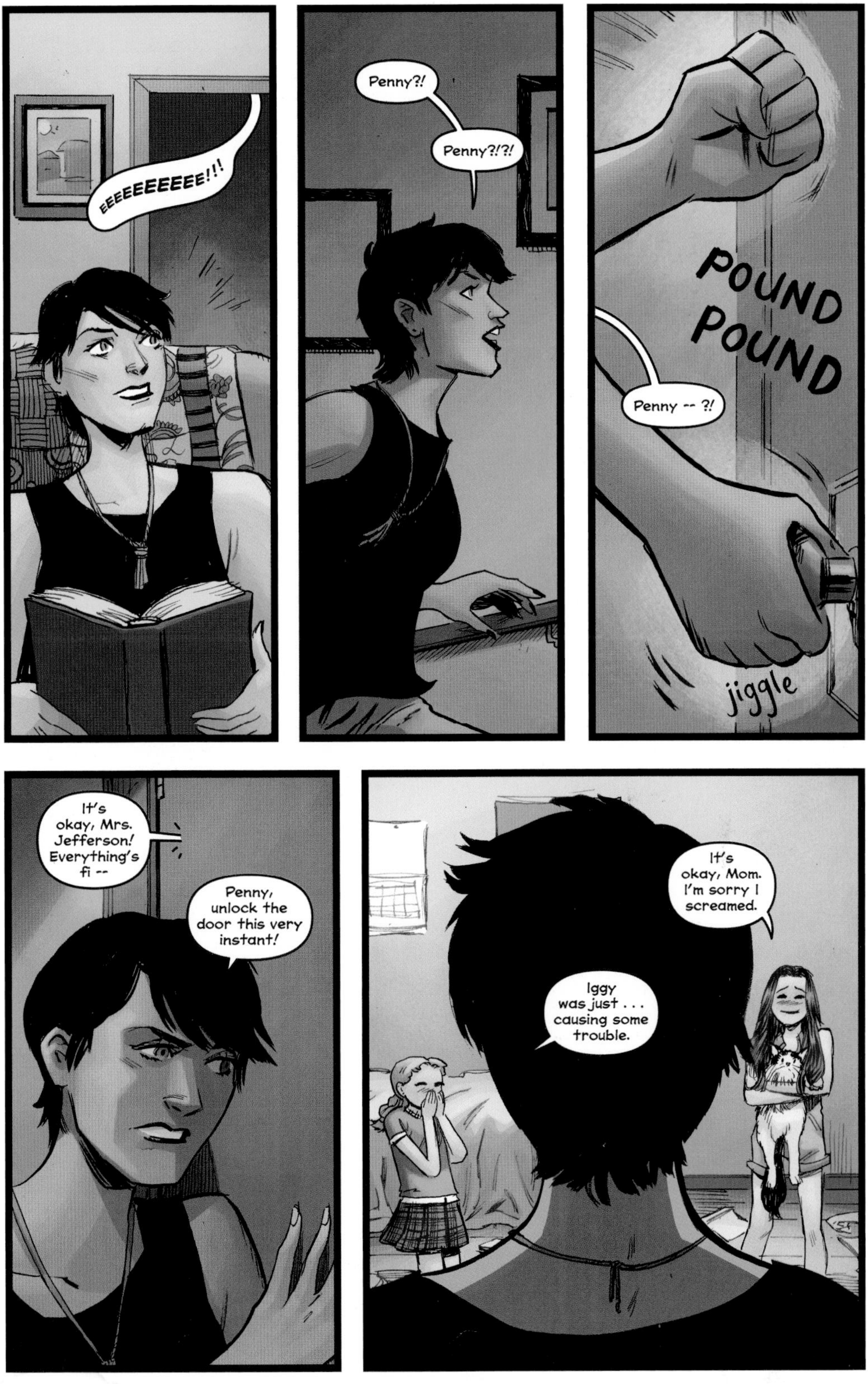
EEEEEEEEEE!!!
Penny?!
Penny?!?!
POUND POUND
Penny -- ?!
jiggle
It's okay, Mrs. Jefferson! Everything's fi --
Penny, unlock the door this very instant!
It's okay, Mom. I'm sorry I screamed.
Iggy was just . . . causing some trouble.

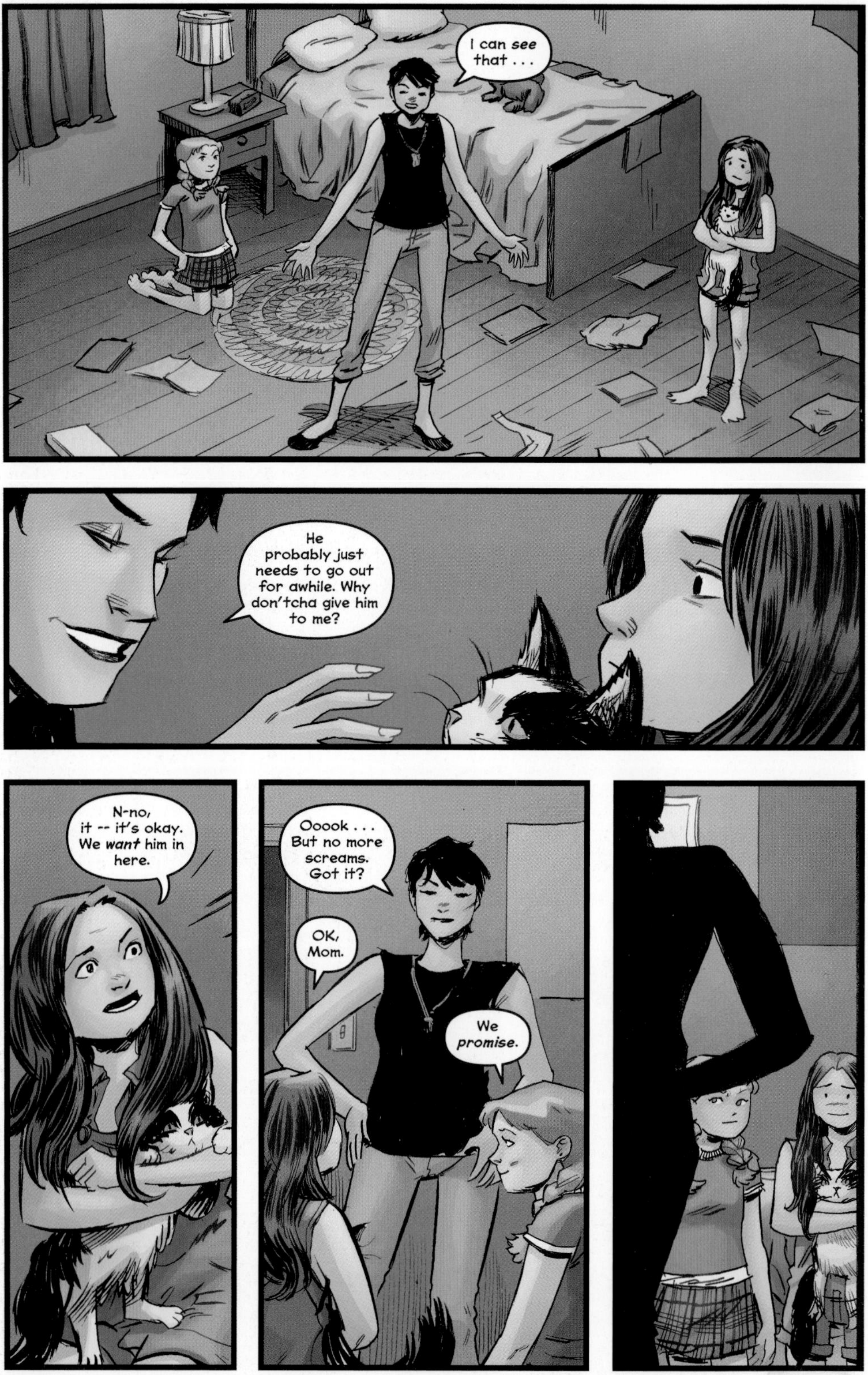
I can *see* that . . .
He probably just needs to go out for awhile. Why don'tcha give him to me?
N-no, it -- it's okay. We *want* him in here.
Ooook . . . But no more screams. Got it?
OK, Mom.
We *promise*.

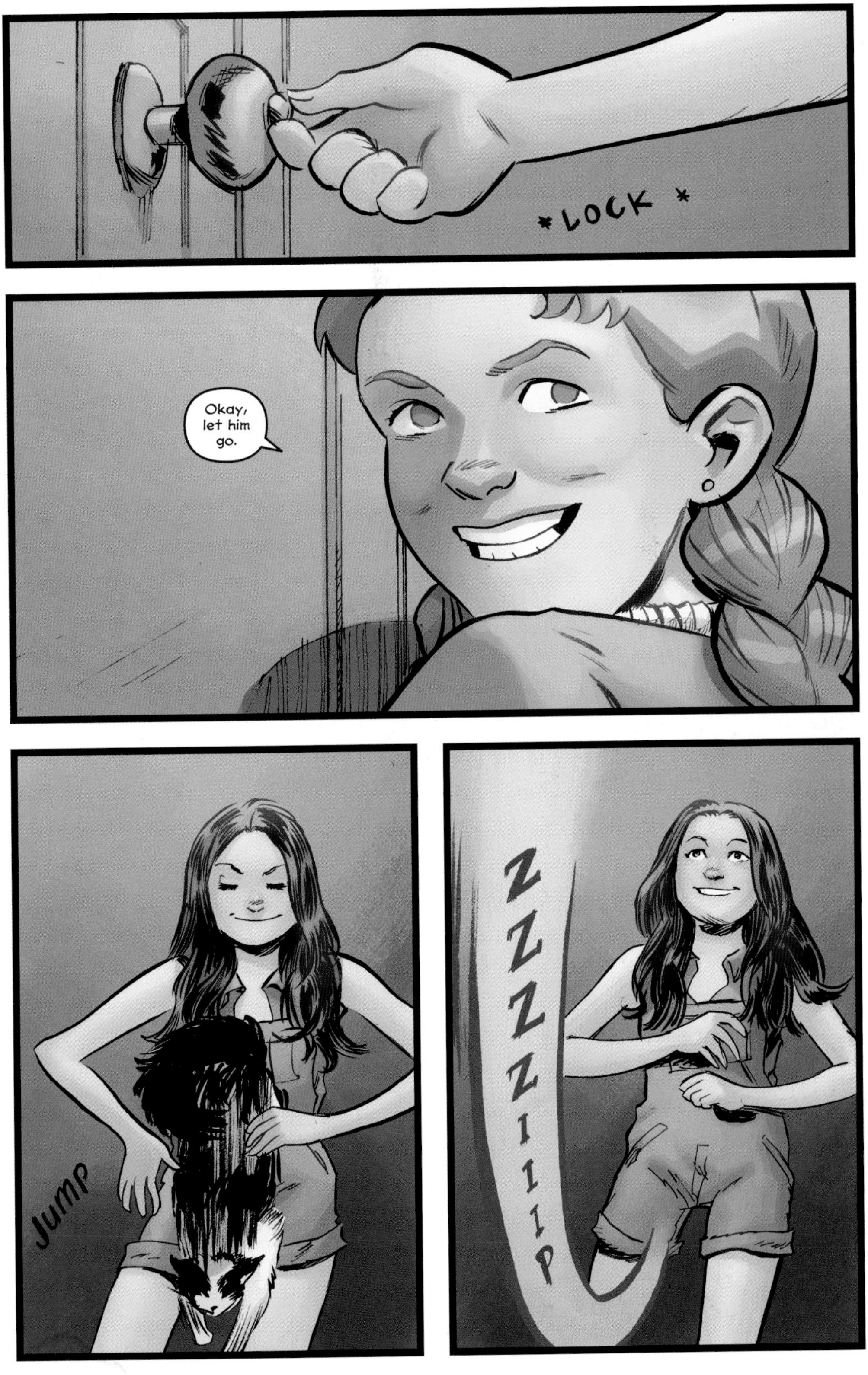
LOCK
Okay, let him go.
JUMP
ZZZZIIIP

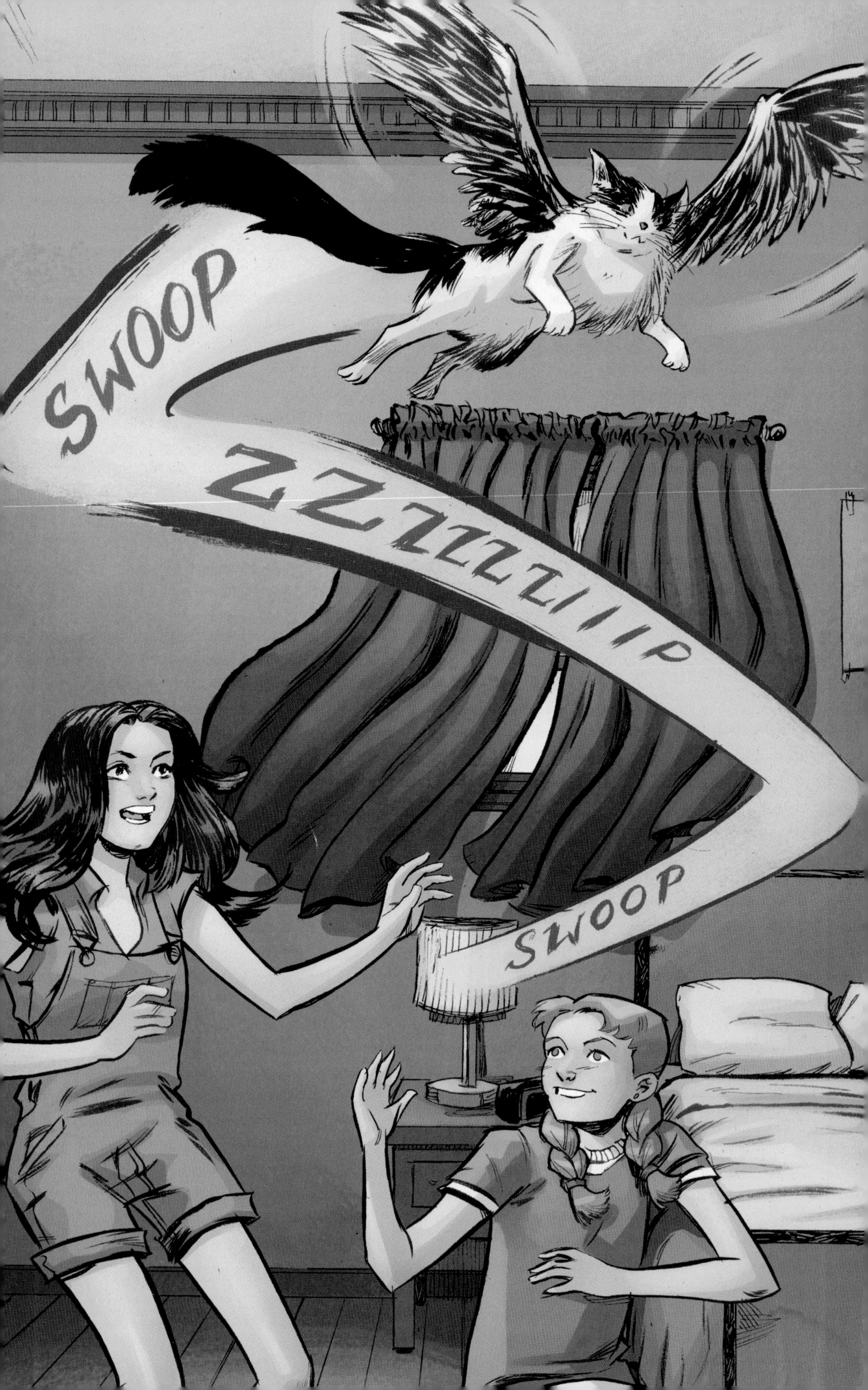
SWOOP
ZZZZZZZIIIIP
SWOOP

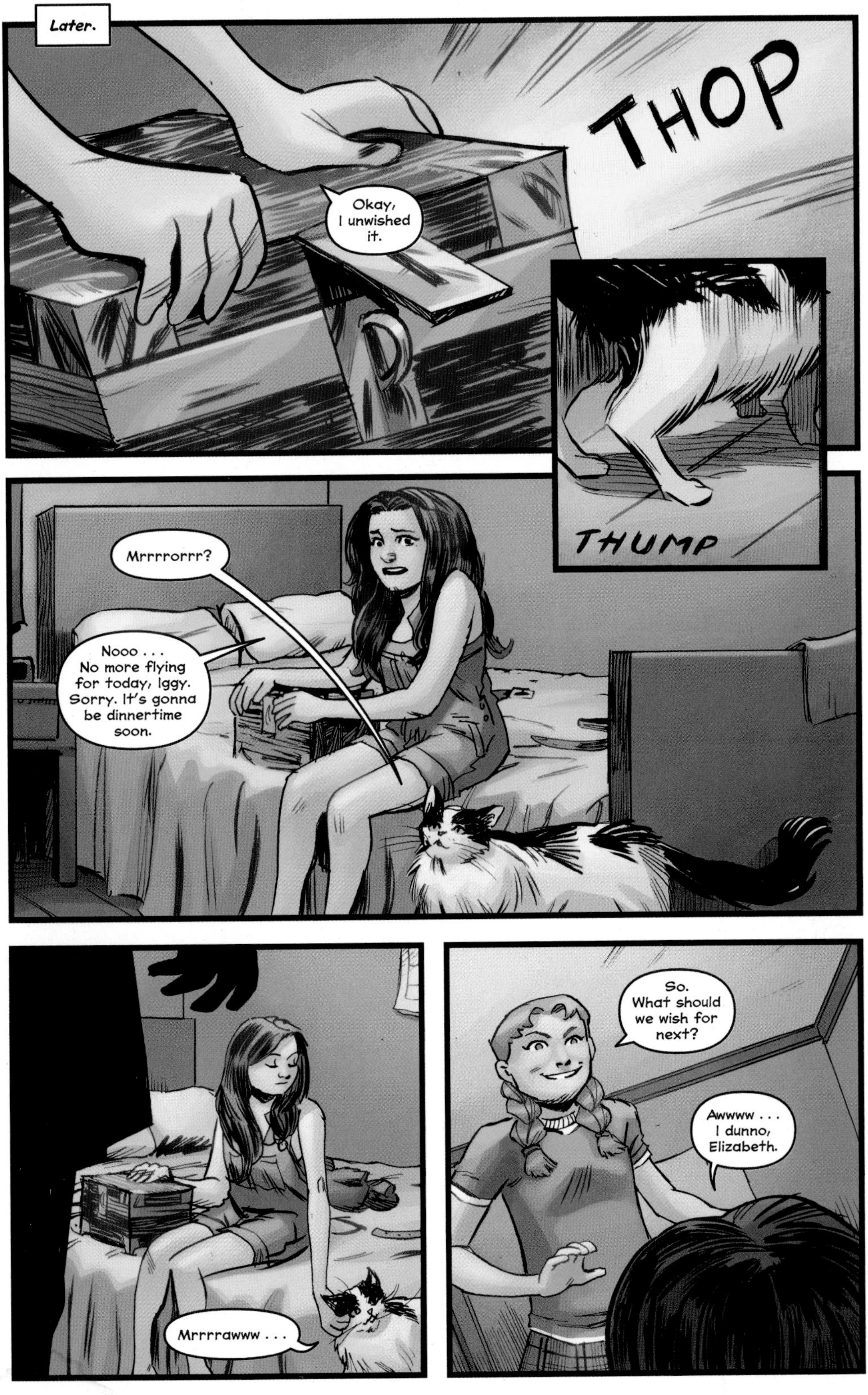
Later.
THOP
Okay, I unwished it.
THUMP
Mrrrrorrr?
Nooo . . . No more flying for today, Iggy. Sorry. It's gonna be dinnertime soon.
Mrrrrawww . . .
So. What should we wish for next?
Awwww . . . I dunno, Elizabeth.

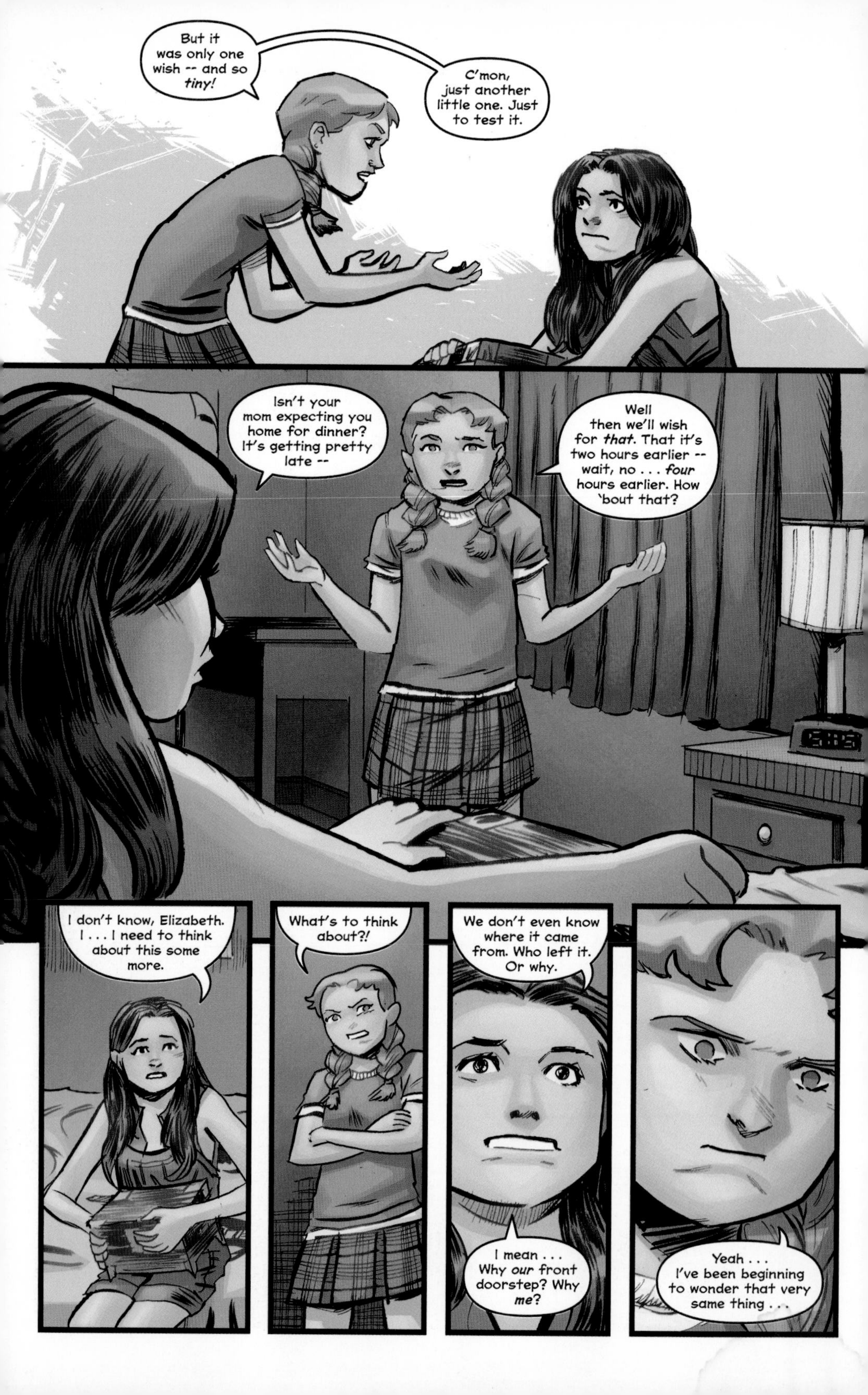
But it was only one wish -- and so *tiny!*
C'mon, just another little one. Just to test it.
Isn't your mom expecting you home for dinner? It's getting pretty late --
Well then we'll wish for *that*. That it's two hours earlier -- wait, no . . . *four* hours earlier. How 'bout that?
I don't know, Elizabeth. I . . . I need to think about this some more.
What's to think about?!
We don't even know where it came from. Who left it. Or why.
I mean . . . Why *our* front doorstep? Why *me*?
Yeah . . . I've been beginning to wonder that very same thing . . .

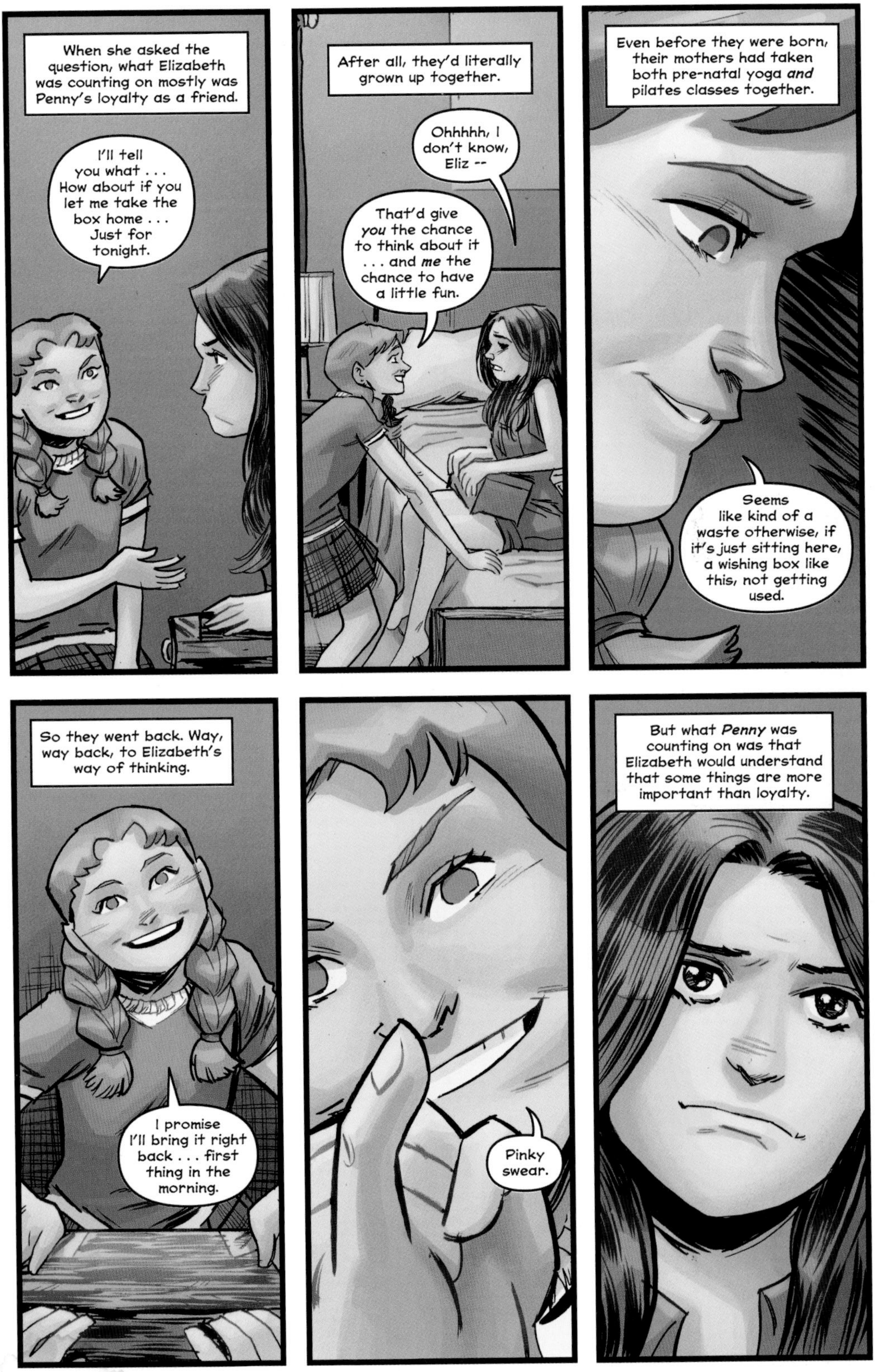
When she asked the question, what Elizabeth was counting on mostly was Penny's loyalty as a friend.
I'll tell you what . . . How about if you let me take the box home . . . Just for tonight.
After all, they'd literally grown up together.
Ohhhhh, I don't know, Eliz --
That'd give *you* the chance to think about it . . . and *me* the chance to have a little fun.
Even before they were born, their mothers had taken both pre-natal yoga *and* pilates classes together.
Seems like kind of a waste otherwise, if it's just sitting here, a wishing box like this, not getting used.
So they went back. Way, way back, to Elizabeth's way of thinking.
I promise I'll bring it right back . . . first thing in the morning.
Pinky swear.
But what *Penny* was counting on was that Elizabeth would understand that some things are more important than loyalty.

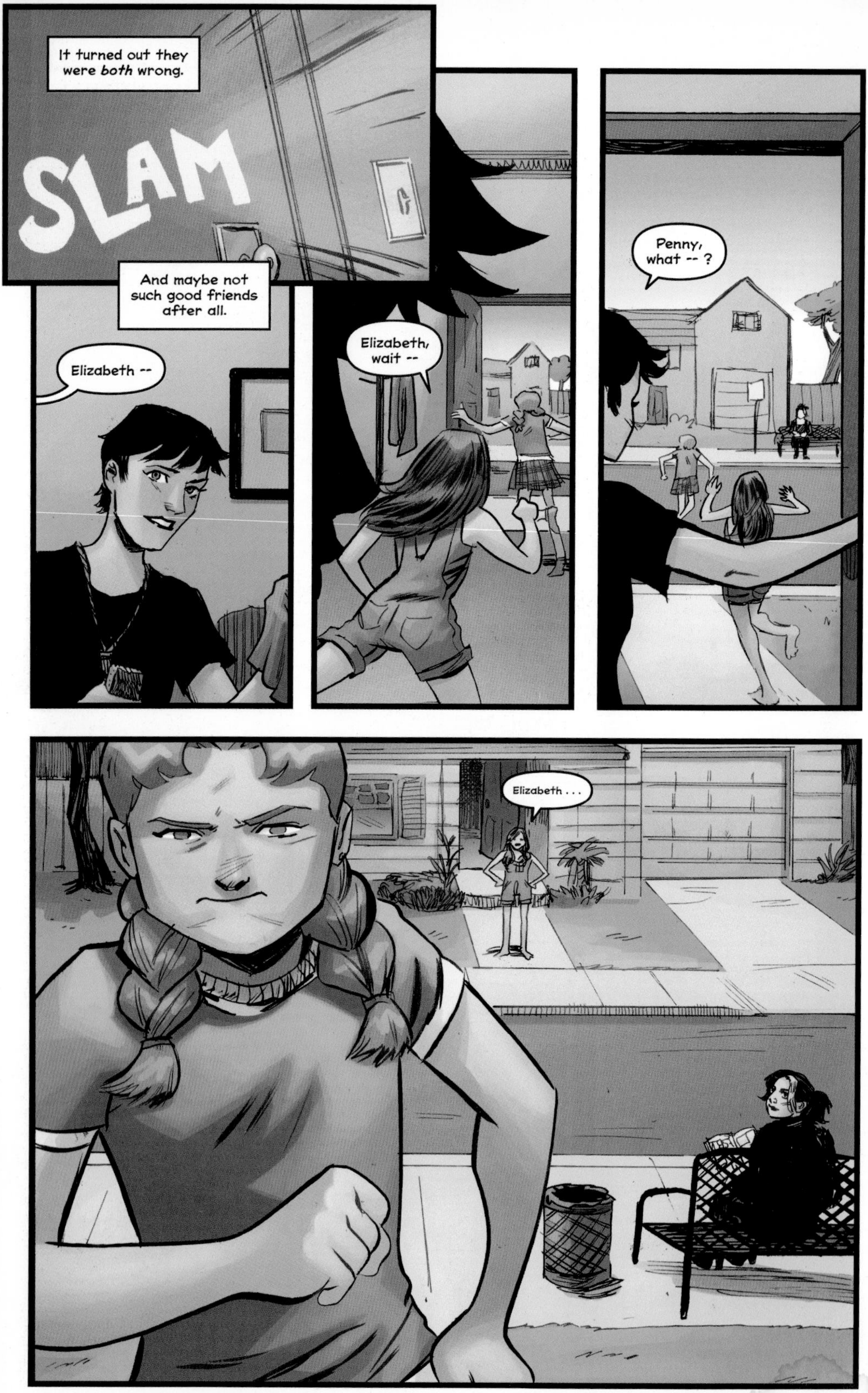
It turned out they were *both* wrong.
SLAM
And maybe not such good friends after all.
Elizabeth --
Elizabeth, wait --
Penny, what -- ?
Elizabeth . . .

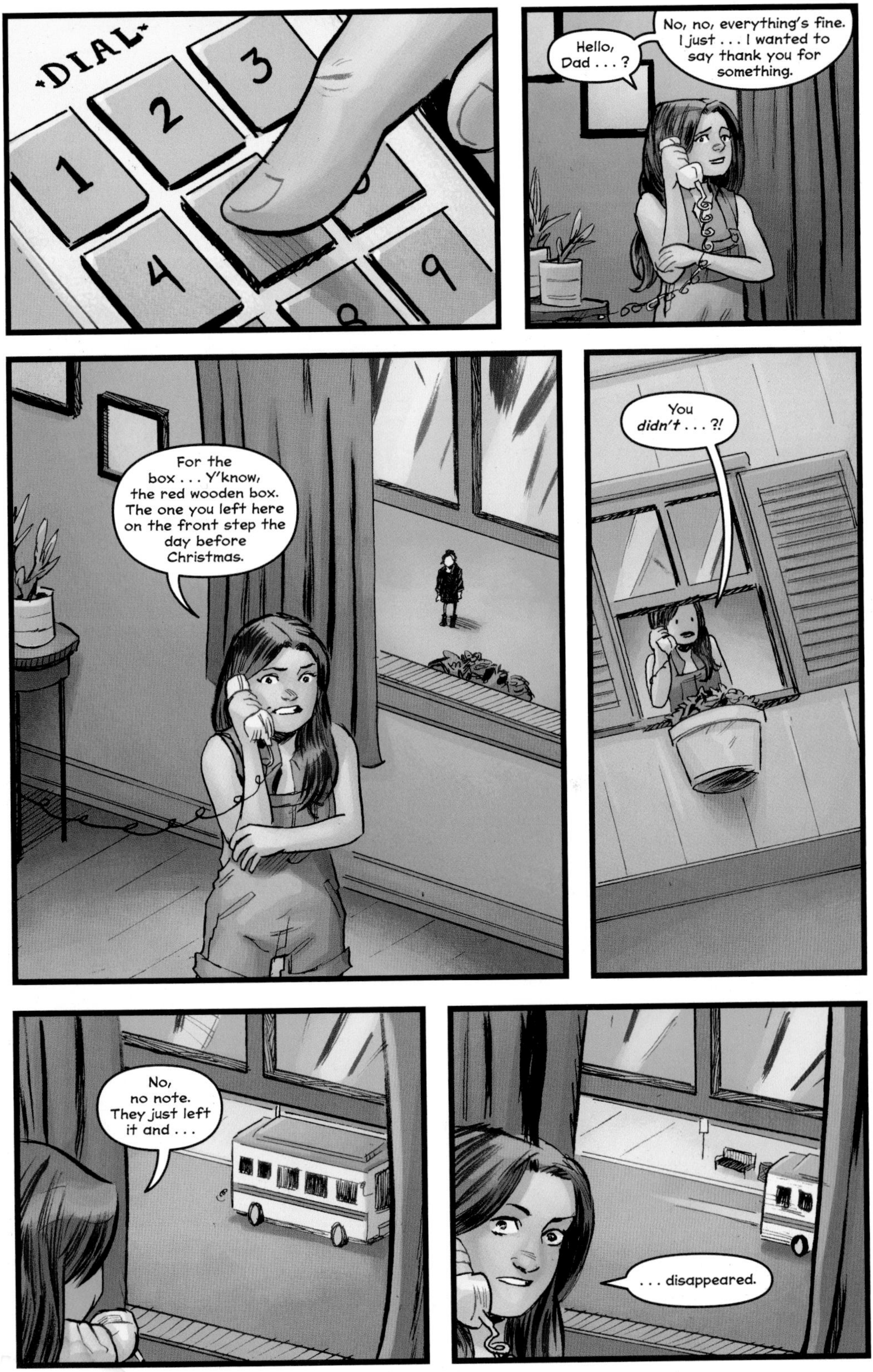
DIAL
Hello, Dad . . . ?
No, no, everything's fine. I just . . . I wanted to say thank you for something.
For the box . . . Y'know, the red wooden box. The one you left here on the front step the day before Christmas.
You *didn't* . . . ?!
No, no note. They just left it and . . .
. . . disappeared.

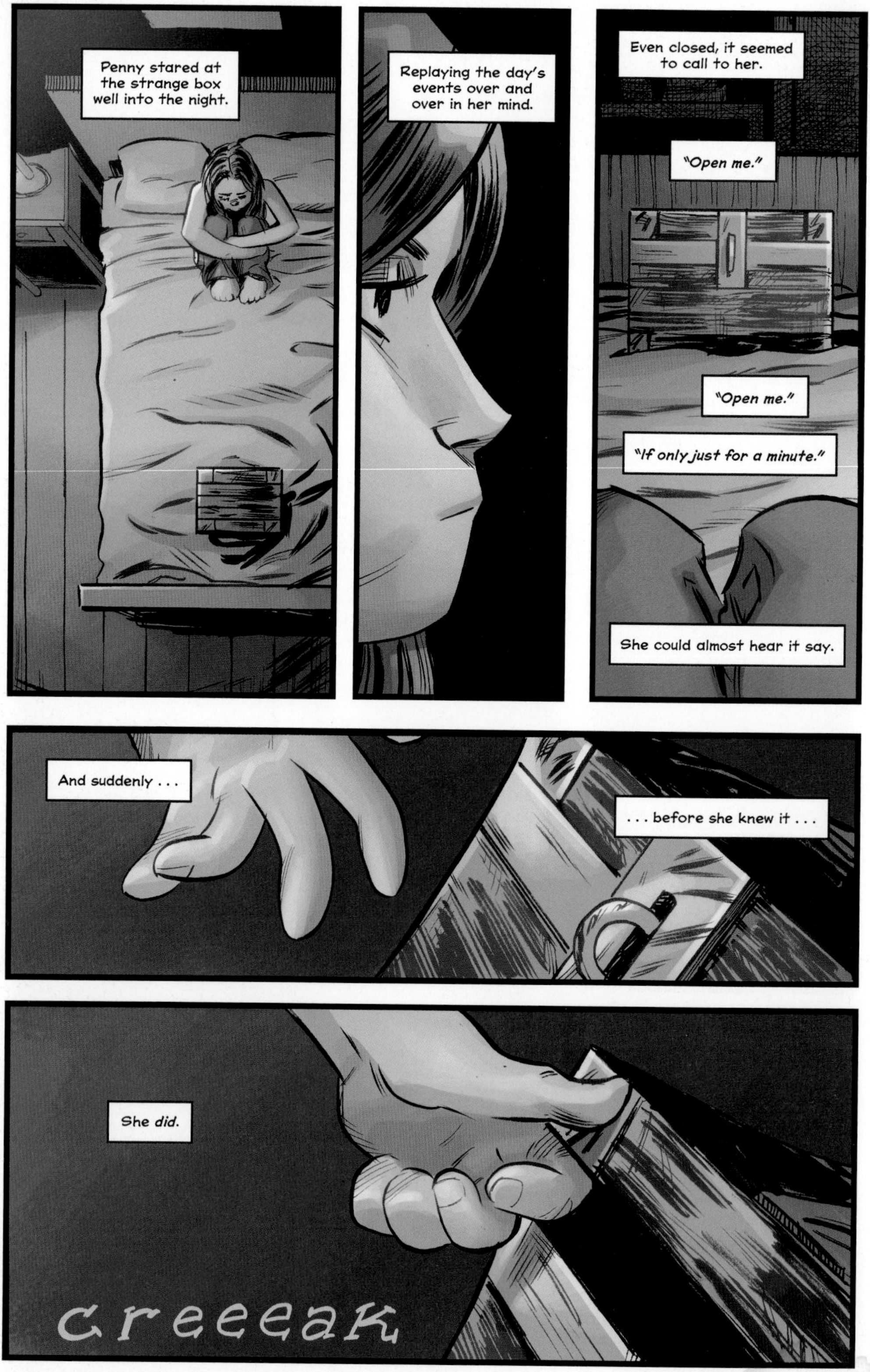
Penny stared at the strange box well into the night.
Replaying the day's events over and over in her mind.
Even closed, it seemed to call to her.
"Open me."
"Open me."
"If only just for a minute."
She could almost hear it say.
And suddenly . . .
. . . before she knew it . . .
She *did*.
creeeak

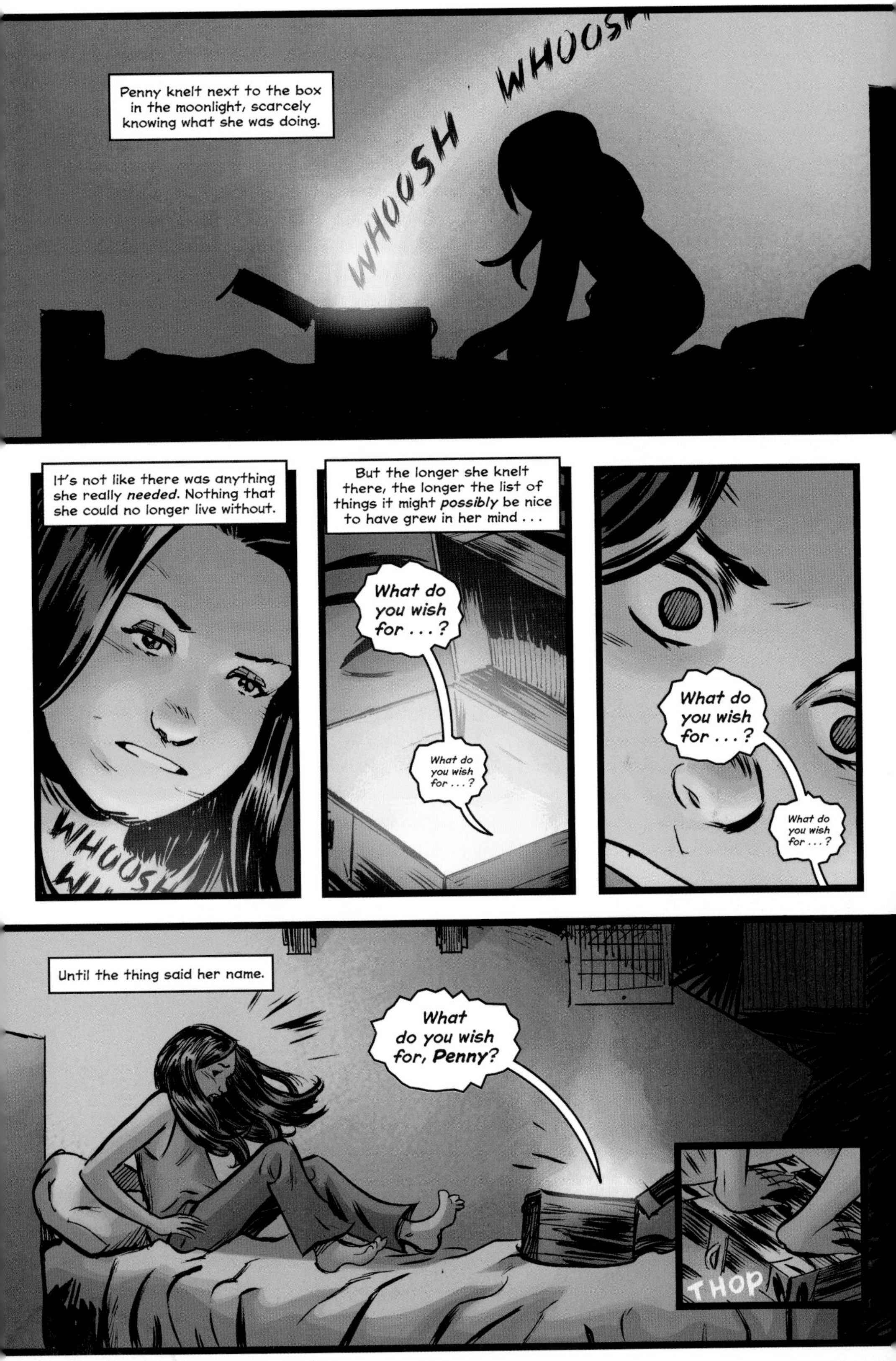

Penny knelt next to the box in the moonlight, scarcely knowing what she was doing.
WHOOSH WHOOSH
It's not like there was anything she really *needed*. Nothing that she could no longer live without.
WHOOSH
But the longer she knelt there, the longer the list of things it might *possibly* be nice to have grew in her mind . . .
What do you wish for . . . ?
What do you wish for . . . ?
What do you wish for . . . ?
What do you wish for . . . ?
Until the thing said her name.
What do you wish for, *Penny*?
THOP

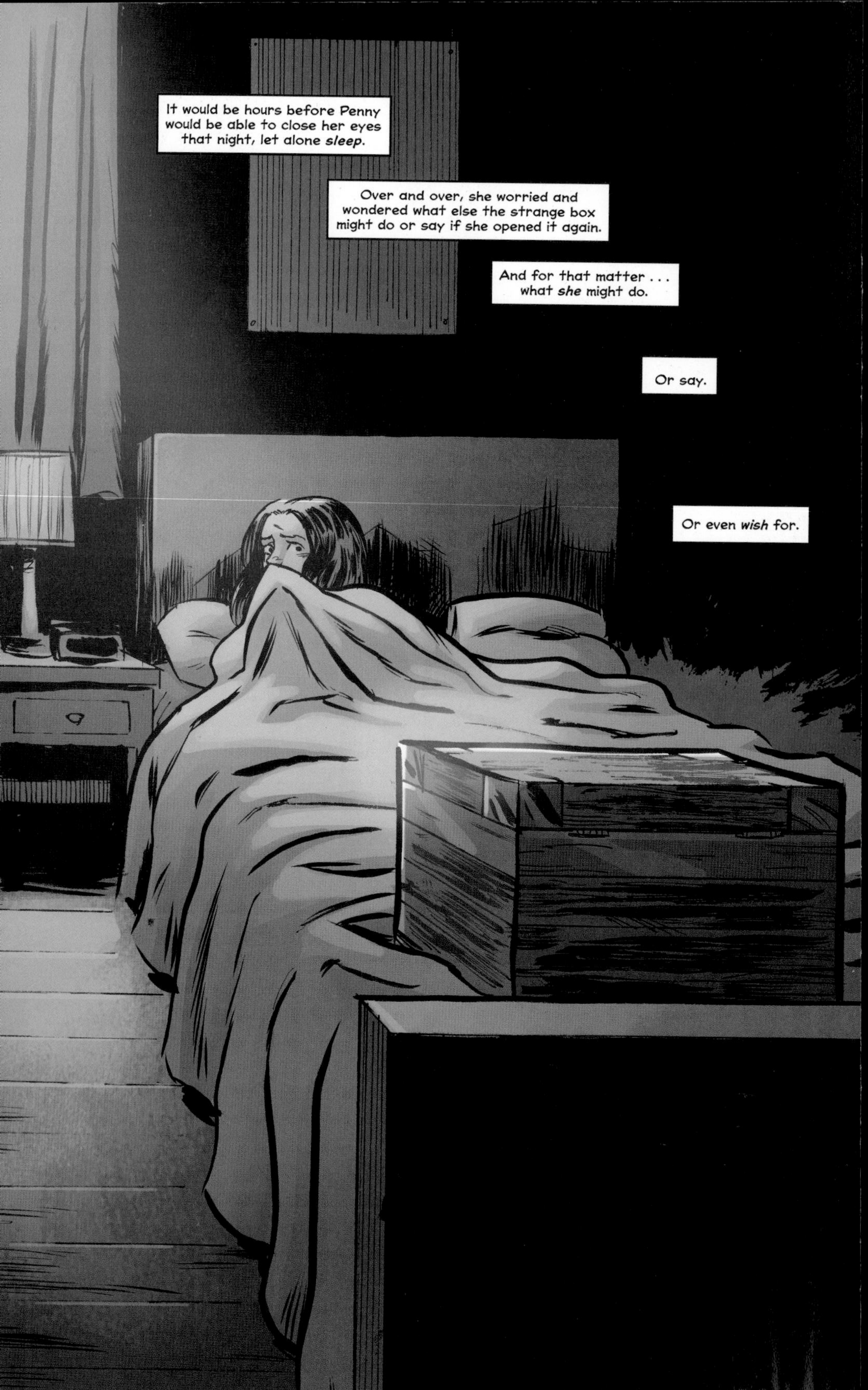
It would be hours before Penny would be able to close her eyes that night, let alone *sleep*.
Over and over, she worried and wondered what else the strange box might do or say if she opened it again.
And for that matter . . . what *she* might do.
Or say.
Or even *wish* for.

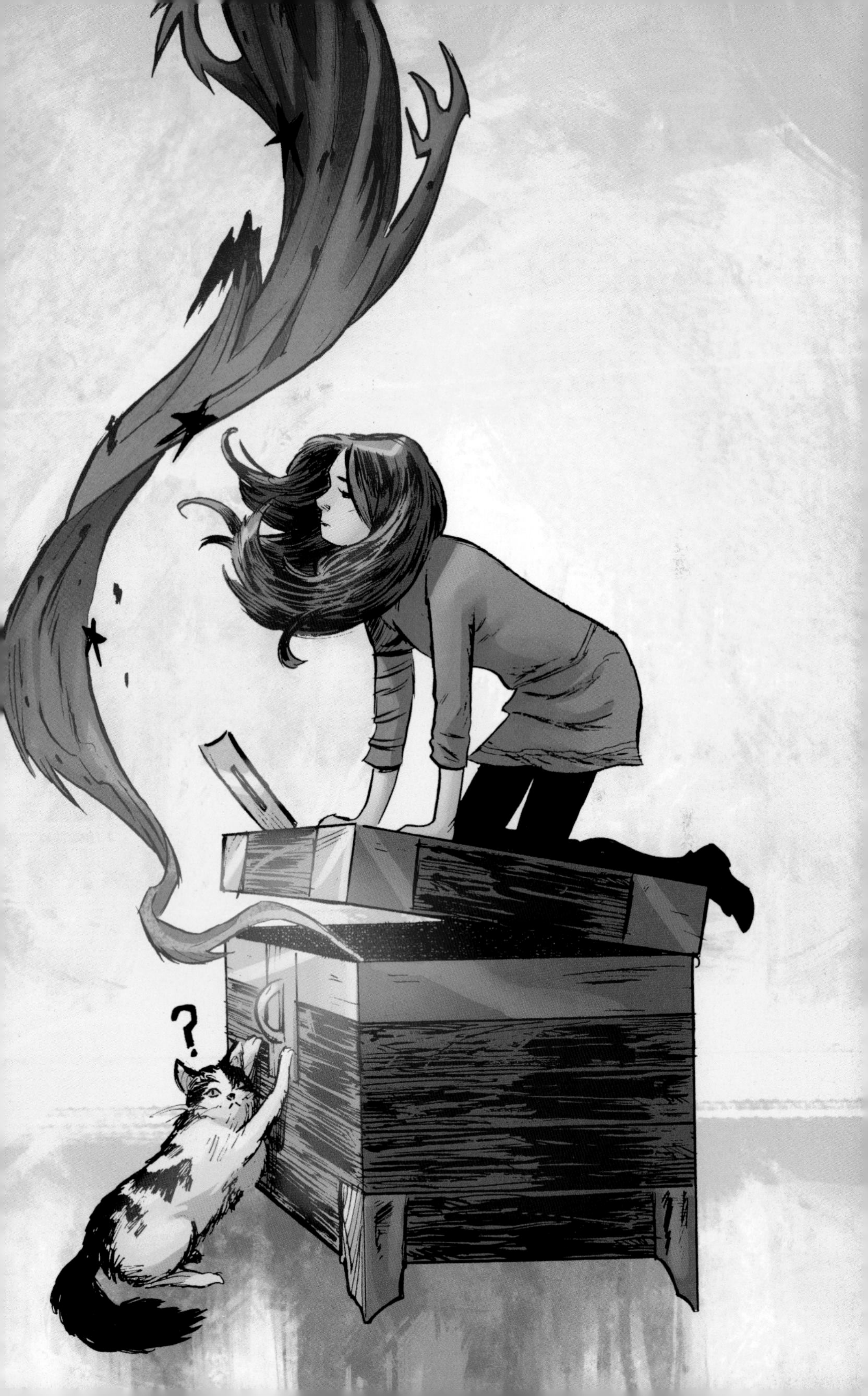
?

Chapter Three

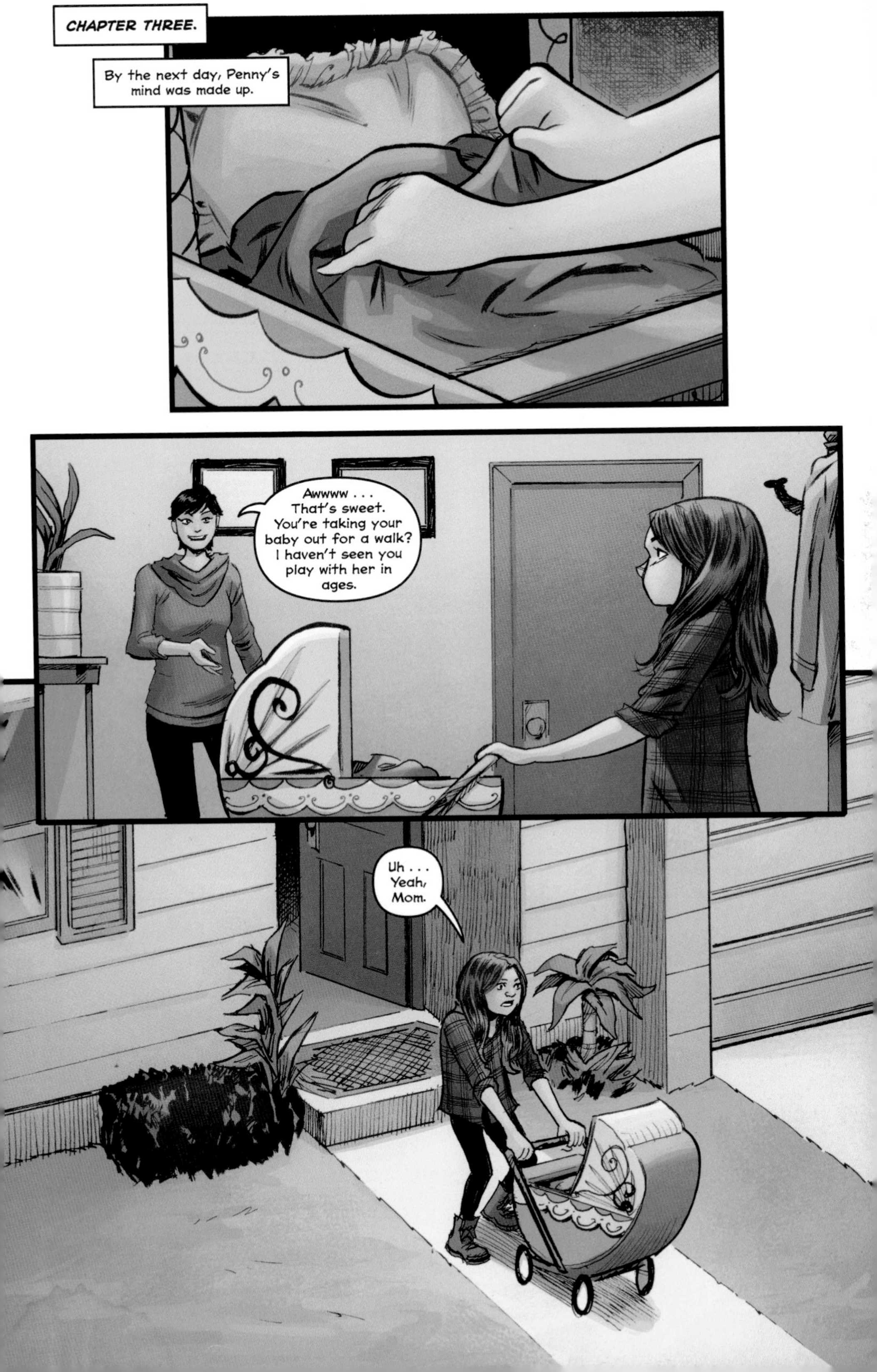
CHAPTER THREE.
By the next day, Penny's mind was made up.
Awwww . . . That's sweet. You're taking your baby out for a walk? I haven't seen you play with her in ages.
Uh . . . Yeah, Mom.

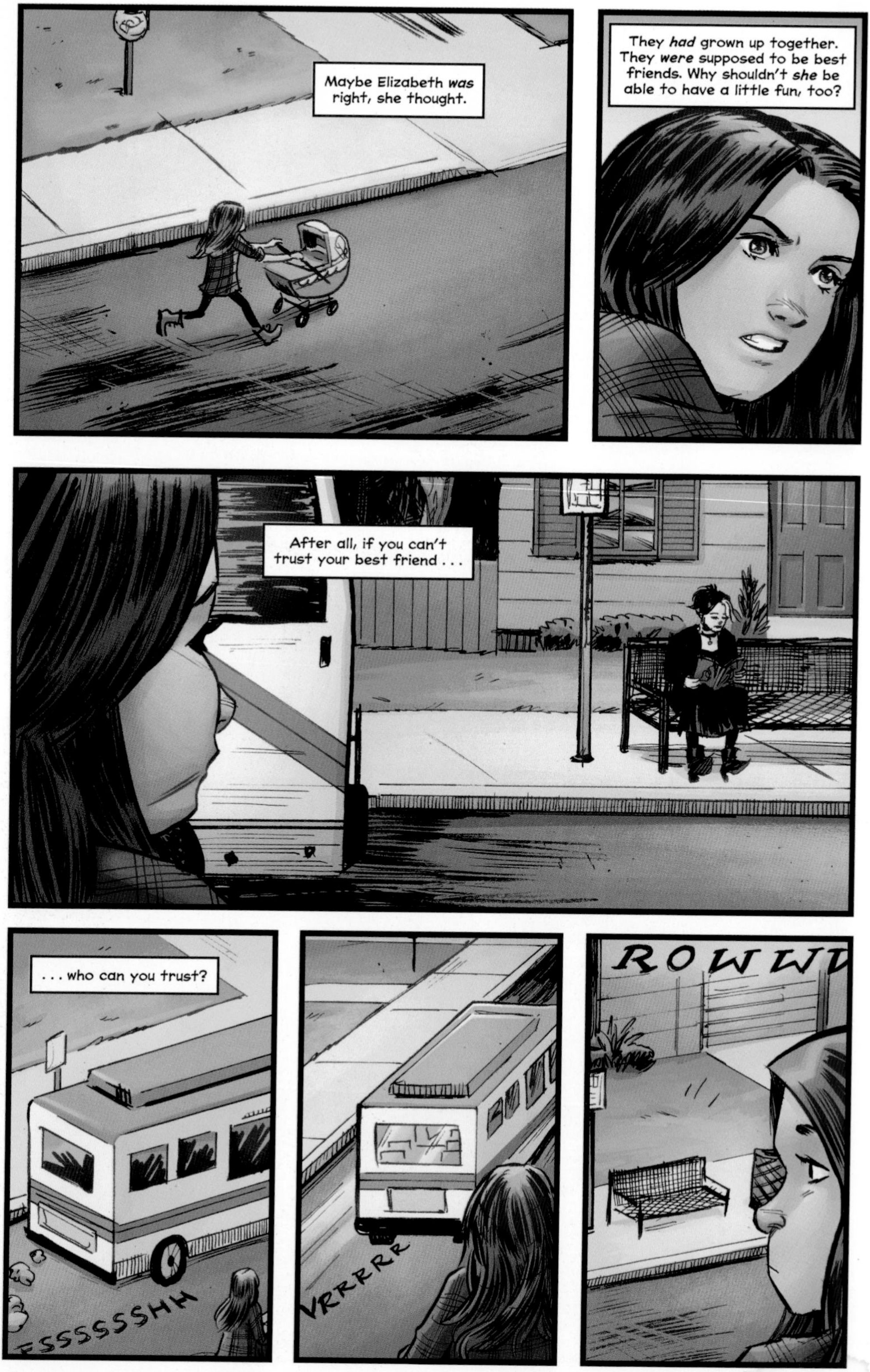
Maybe Elizabeth *was* right, she thought.
They *had* grown up together. They *were* supposed to be best friends. Why shouldn't *she* be able to have a little fun, too?
After all, if you can't trust your best friend . . .
. . . who can you trust?
FSSSSSSHH
VRRRRR
ROWWD

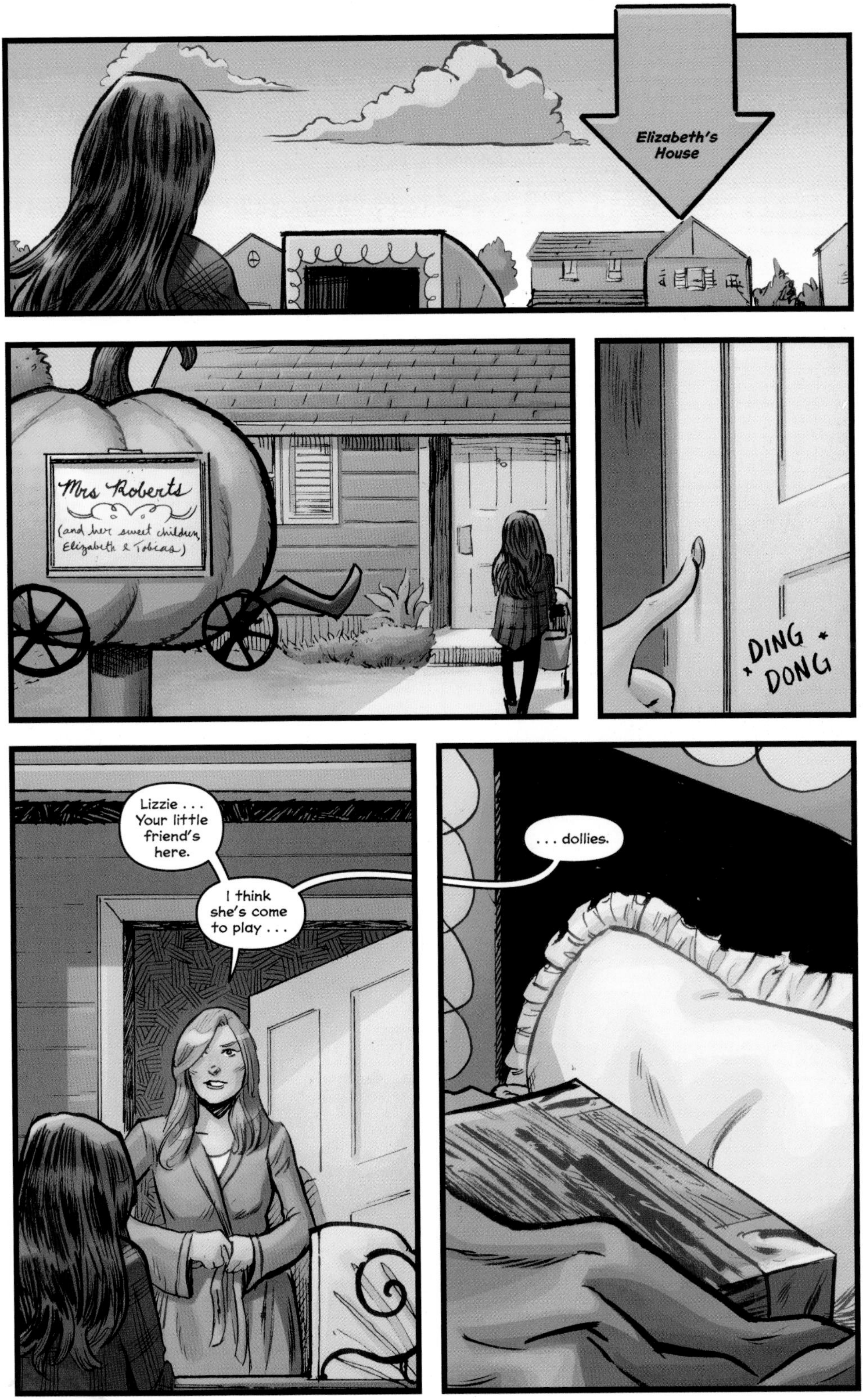
Elizabeth's House
Mrs Roberts
(and her sweet children, Elizabeth & Tobias)
DING DONG
Lizzie . . . Your little friend's here.
I think she's come to play . . .
. . . dollies.

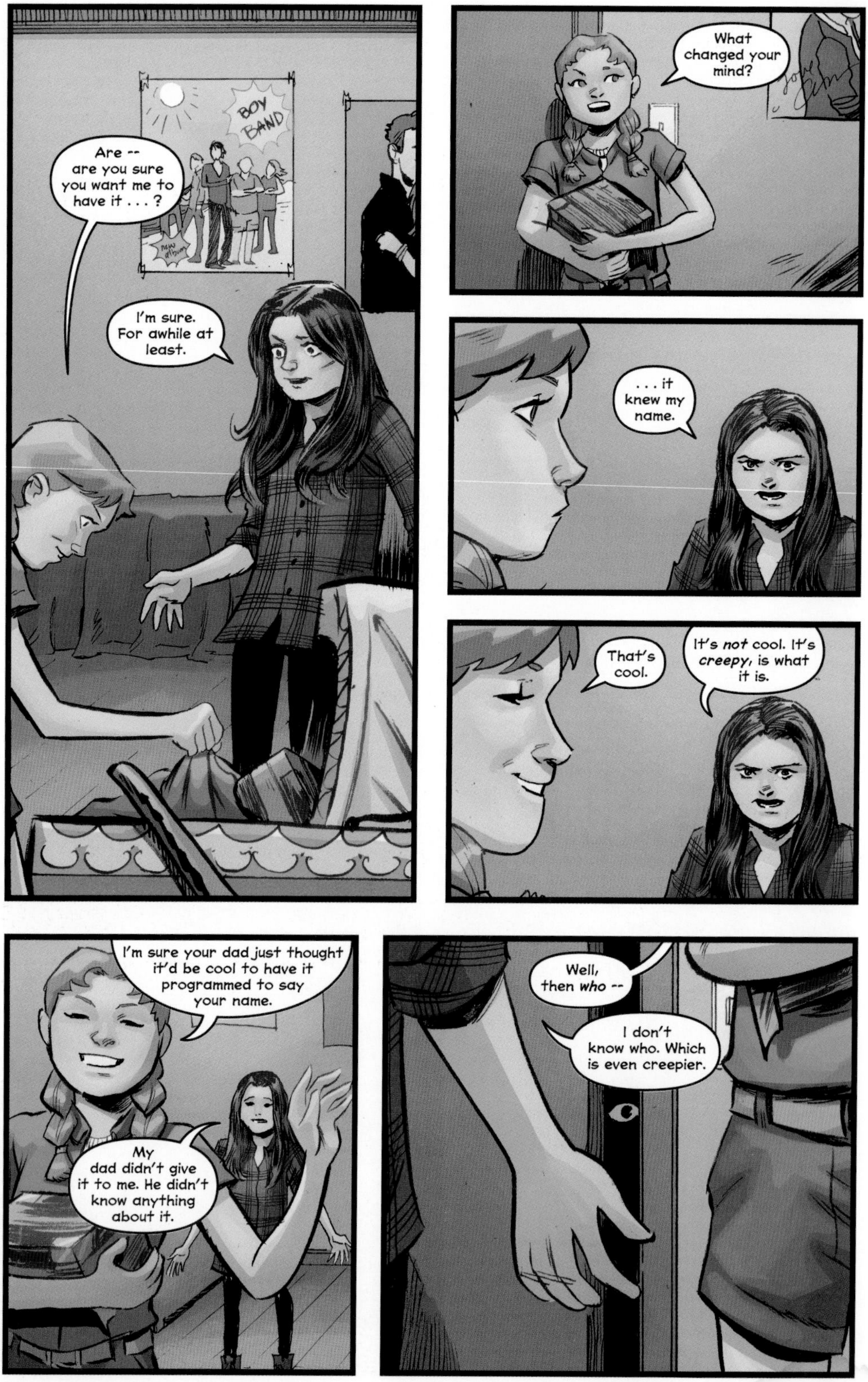
BOY BAND
new album
Are -- are you sure you want me to have it . . . ?
I'm sure. For awhile at least.
What changed your mind?
. . . it knew my name.
That's cool.
It's *not* cool. It's *creepy,* is what it is.
I'm sure your dad just thought it'd be cool to have it programmed to say your name.
My dad didn't give it to me. He didn't know anything about it.
Well, then *who* --
I don't know who. Which is even creepier.

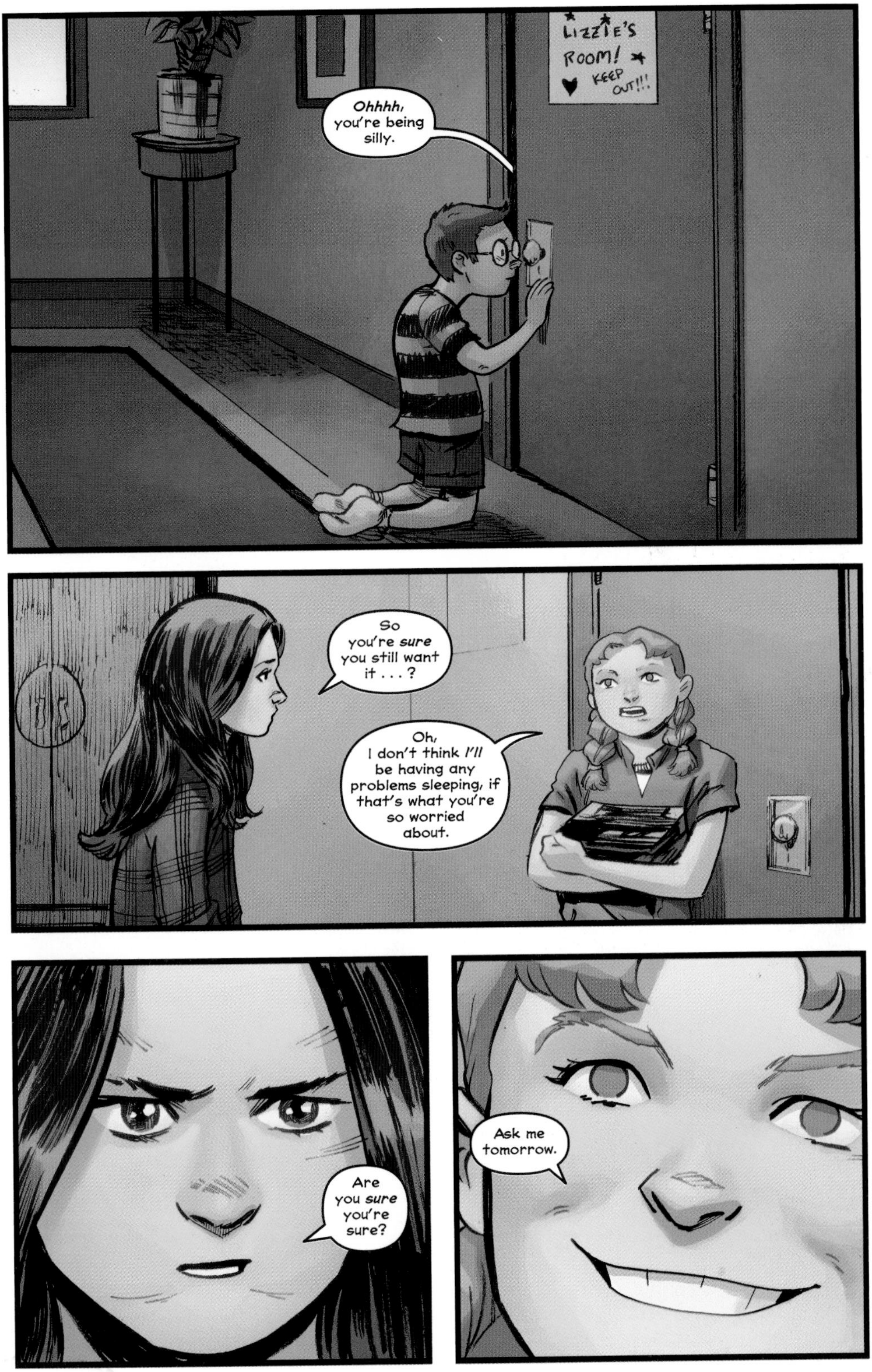
LIZZIE'S ROOM! KEEP OUT!!!
Ohhhh, you're being silly.
So you're *sure* you still want it . . . ?
Oh, I don't think *I'll* be having any problems sleeping, if that's what you're so worried about.
Are you *sure* you're sure?
Ask me tomorrow.

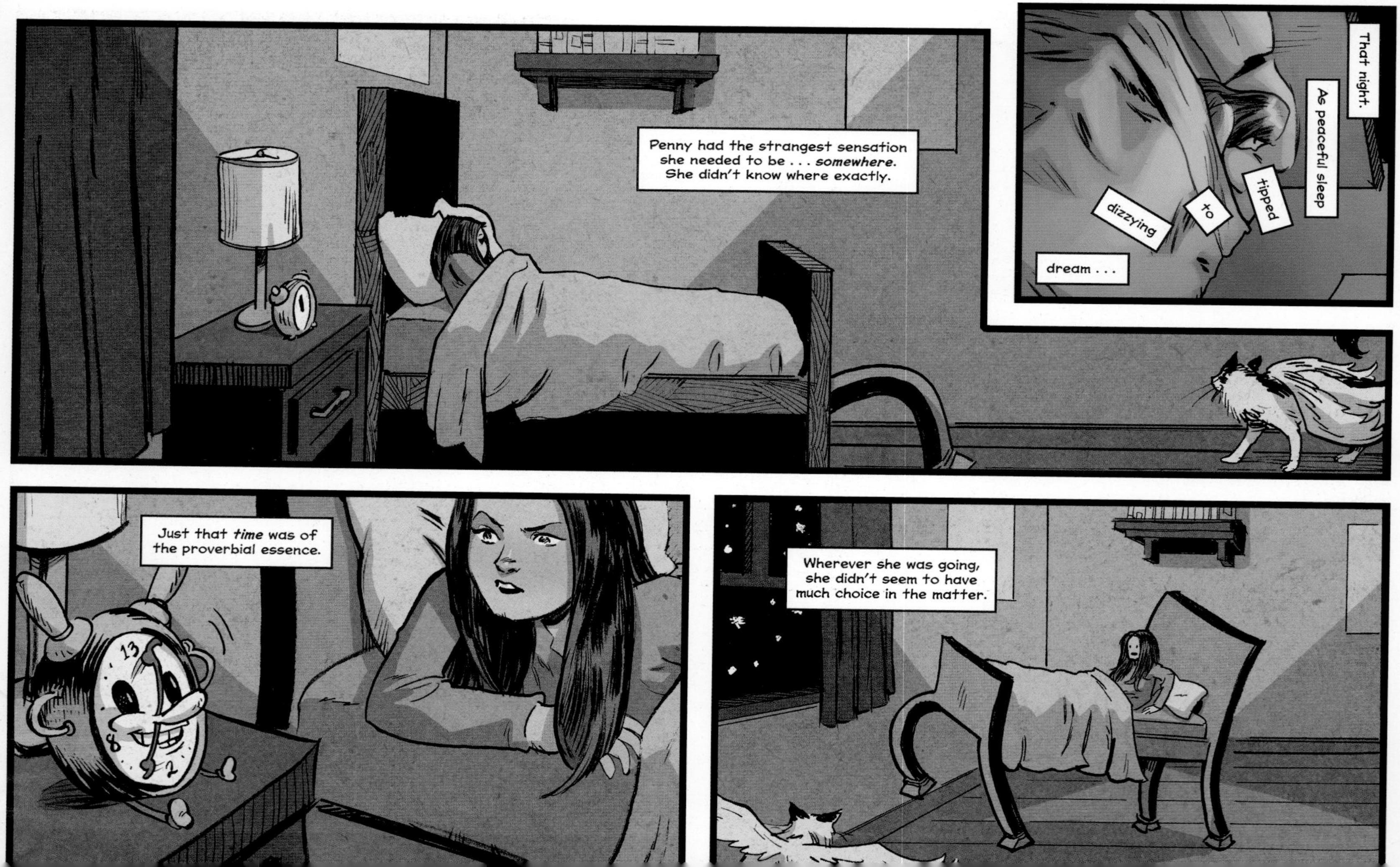
That night.
As peaceful sleep
tipped
to
dizzying
dream . . .
Penny had the strangest sensation she needed to be . . . *somewhere*. She didn't know where exactly.
Just that *time* was of the proverbial essence.
Wherever she was going, she didn't seem to have much choice in the matter.

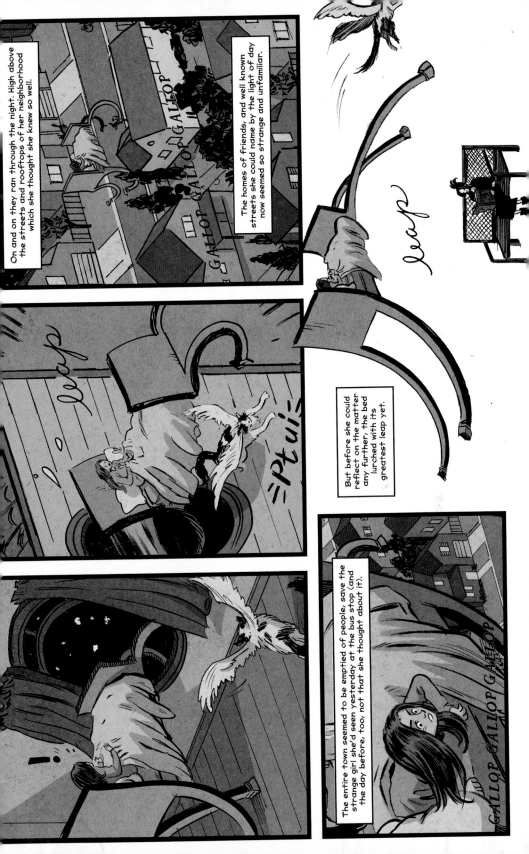

On and on they ran through the night. High above the streets and rooftops of her neighborhood which she thought she knew so well.

The homes of friends, and well known streets she could name by the light of day now seemed so strange and unfamiliar.

leap

=ptui=

But before she could reflect on the matter any further, the bed lurched with its greatest leap yet.

The entire town seemed to be emptied of people, save the strange girl she'd seen yesterday at the bus stop (and the day before, too, not that she thought about it).

GALLOP GALLOP GALLOP
GALLOP GALLOP GALLOP GALLOP

leap

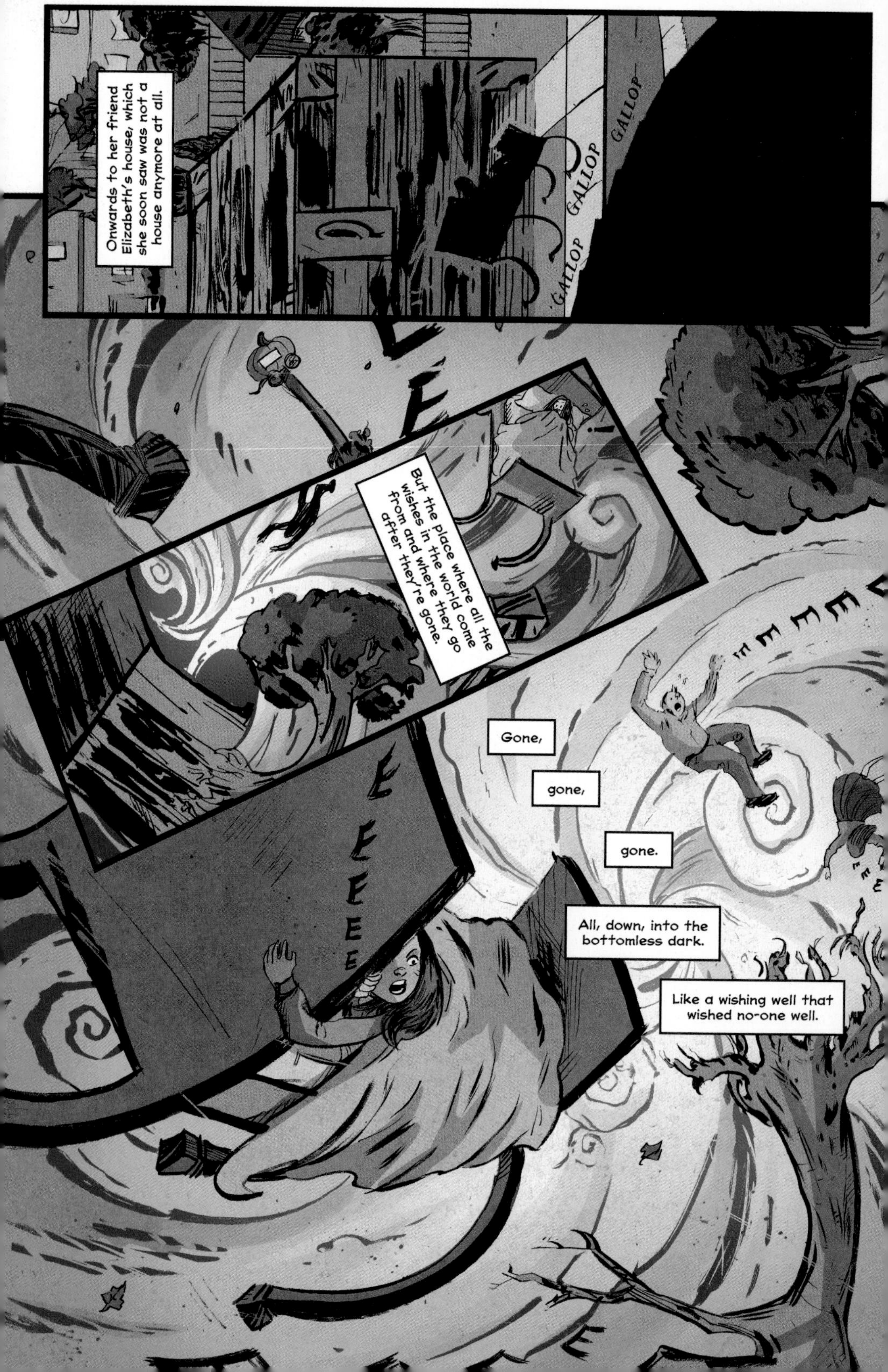
Onwards to her friend Elizabeth's house, which she soon saw was not a house anymore at all.
GALLOP
GALLOP
GALLOP
GALLOP
But the place where all the wishes in the world come from and where they go after they're gone.
Gone,
gone,
gone.
All, down, into the bottomless dark.
Like a wishing well that wished no-one well.

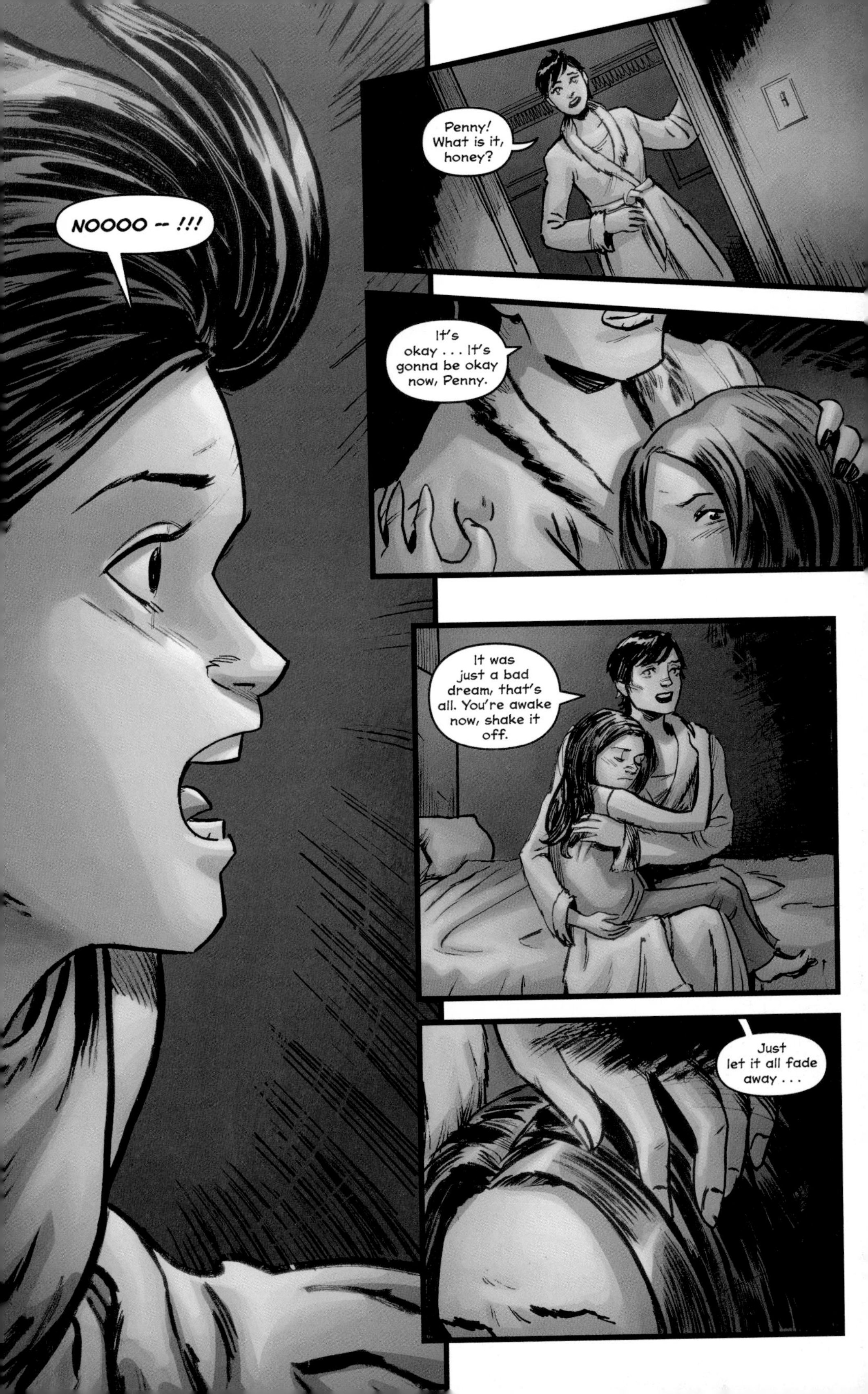
NOOOO -- !!!
Penny! What is it, honey?
It's okay . . . It's gonna be okay now, Penny.
It was just a bad dream, that's all. You're awake now, shake it off.
Just let it all fade away . . .

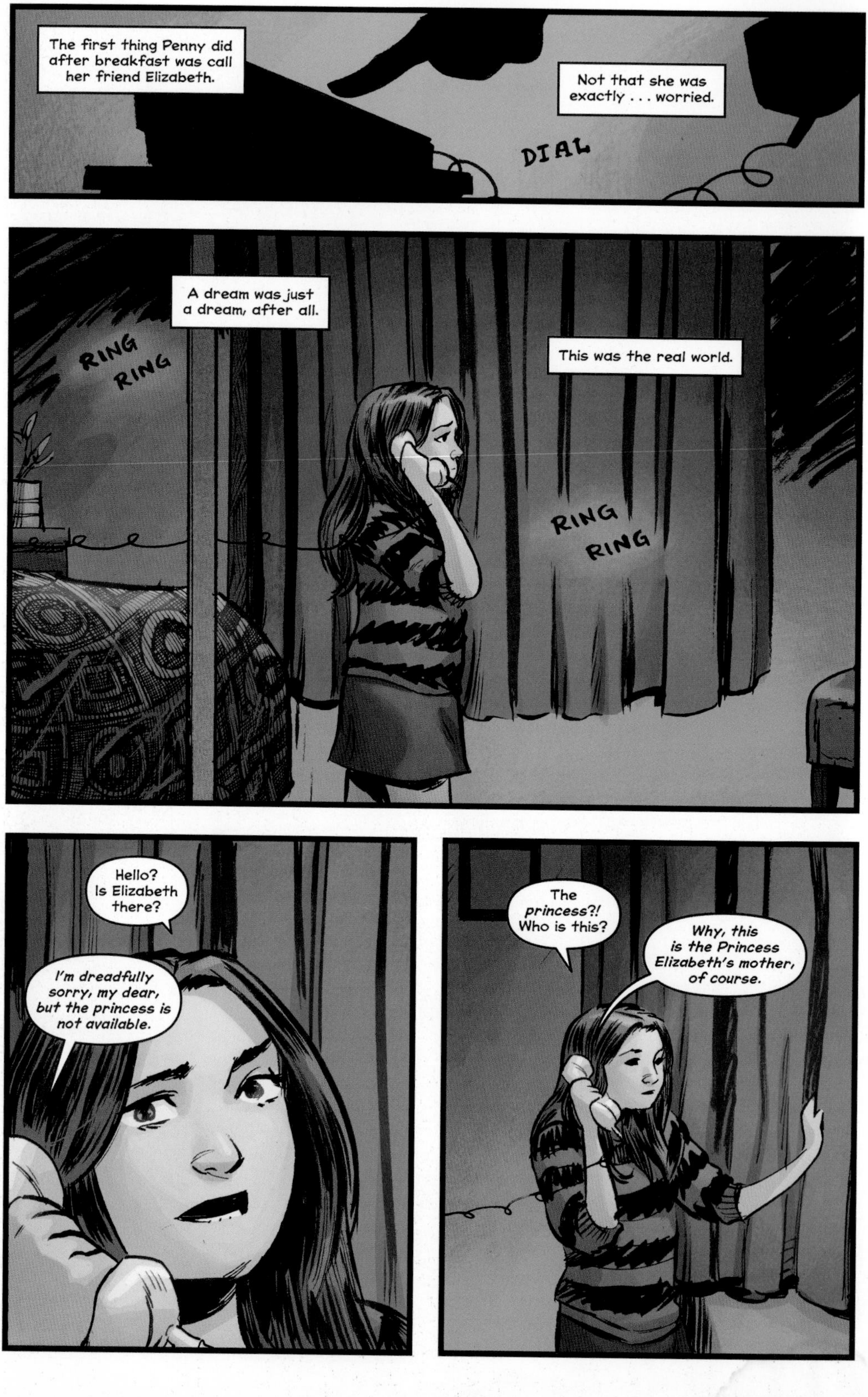
The first thing Penny did after breakfast was call her friend Elizabeth.
Not that she was exactly . . . worried.
DIAL
A dream was just a dream, after all.
RING RING
This was the real world.
RING RING
Hello? Is Elizabeth there?
I'm dreadfully sorry, my dear, but the princess is not available.
The princess?! Who is this?
Why, this is the Princess Elizabeth's mother, of course.

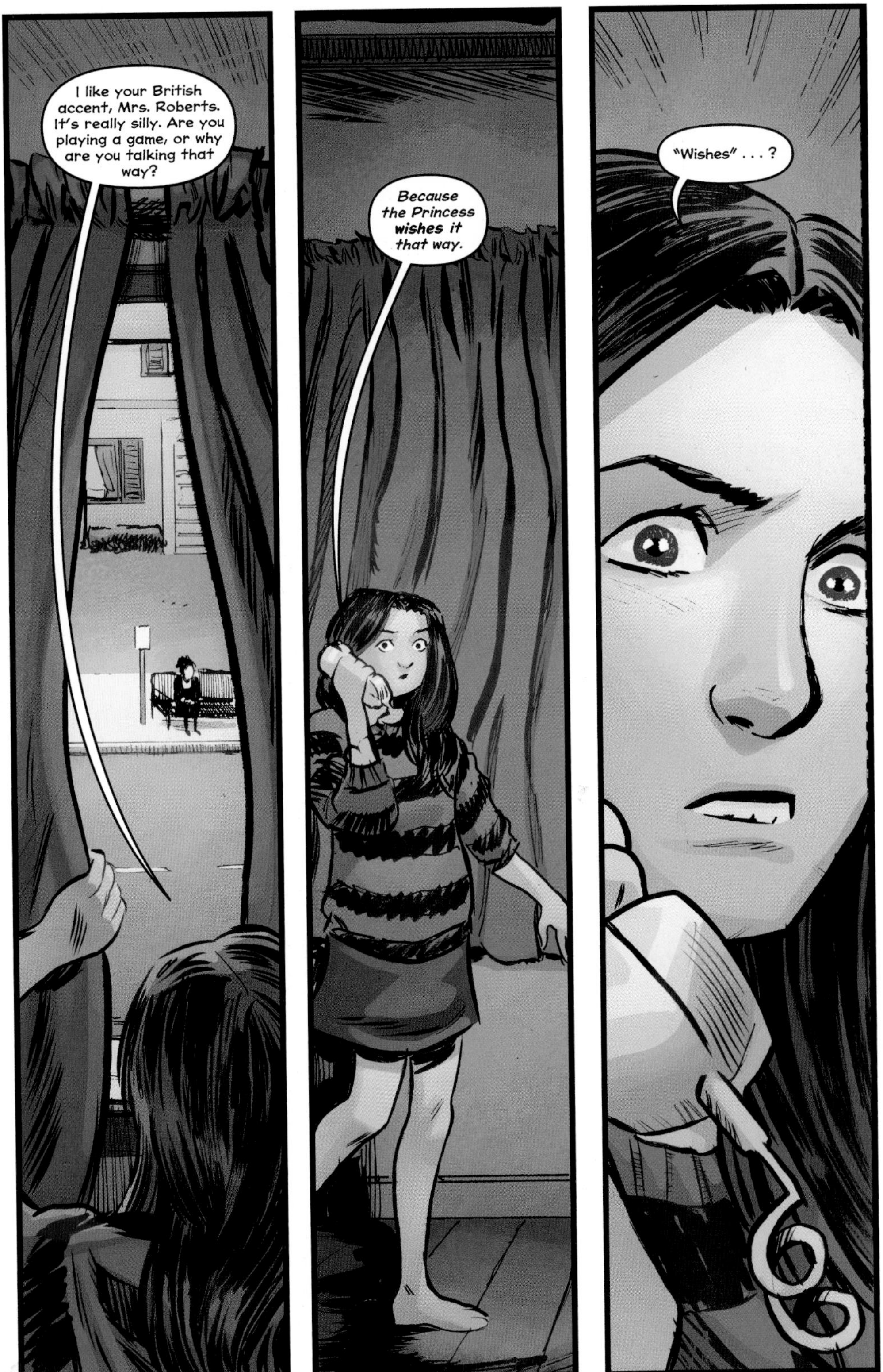
I like your British accent, Mrs. Roberts. It's really silly. Are you playing a game, or why are you talking that way?
*Because the Princess **wishes** it that way.*
"Wishes" . . . ?

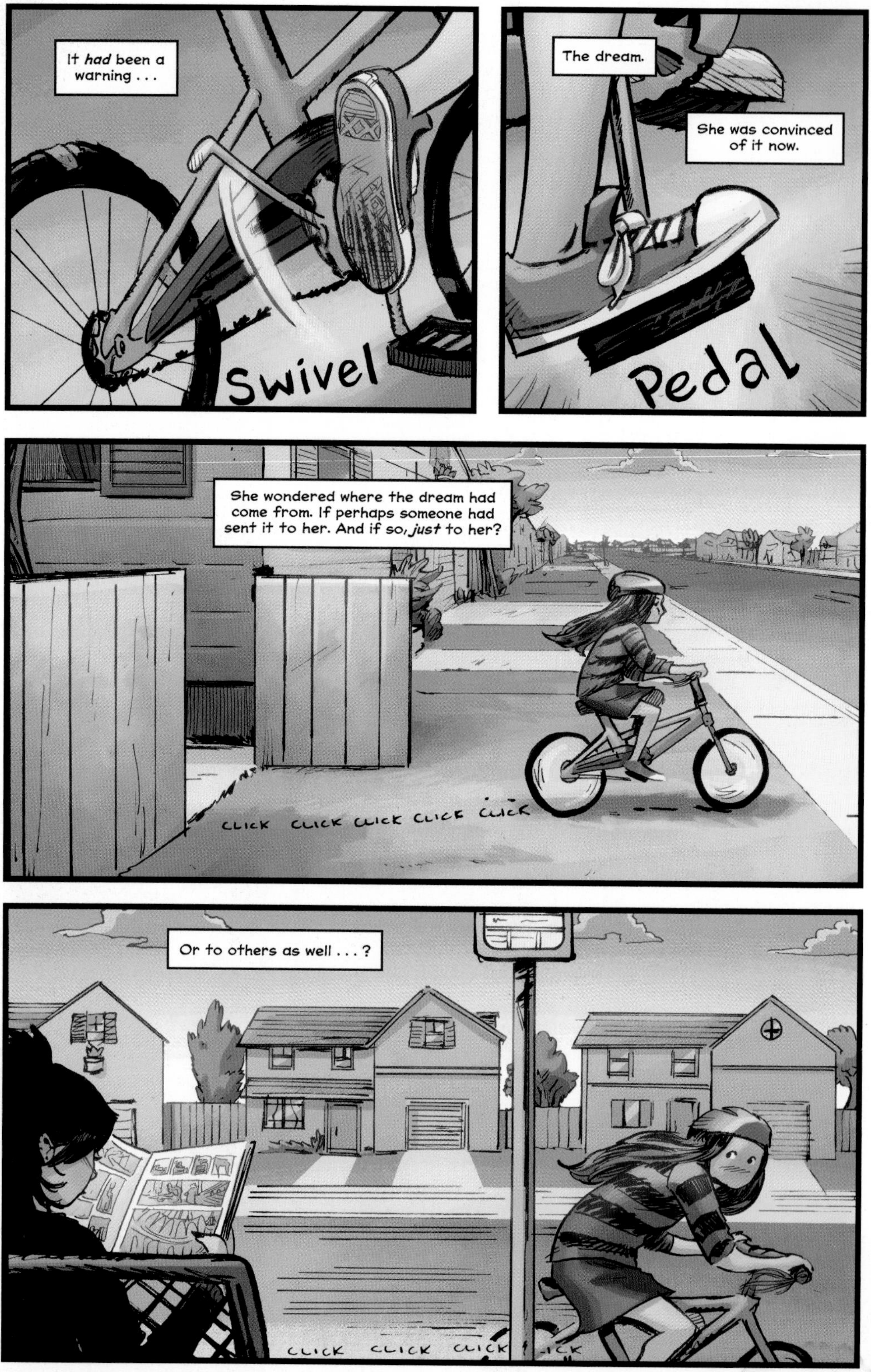
It *had* been a warning . . .
Swivel
The dream.
She was convinced of it now.
Pedal
She wondered where the dream had come from. If perhaps someone had sent it to her. And if so, *just* to her?
CLICK CLICK CLICK CLICK CLICK
Or to others as well . . . ?
CLICK CLICK CLICK

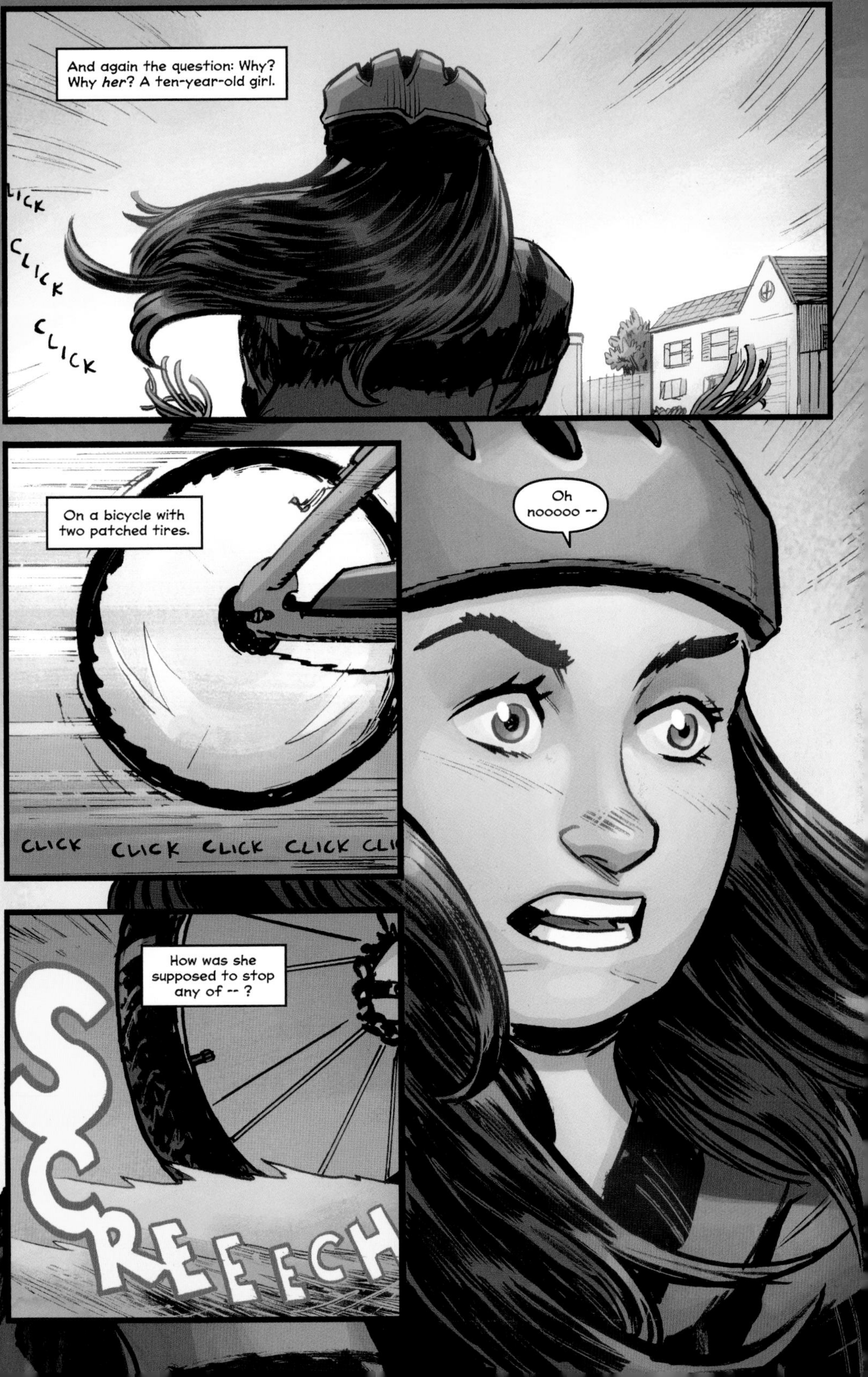
And again the question: Why? Why *her*? A ten-year-old girl.
LICK
CLICK
CLICK
On a bicycle with two patched tires.
CLICK CLICK CLICK CLICK CLI
Oh nooooo --
How was she supposed to stop any of -- ?
SCREEECH

Princess Elizabeth
(and Her Royal Family)
CLICK CLICK CLICK CLICK CLI
ding dong

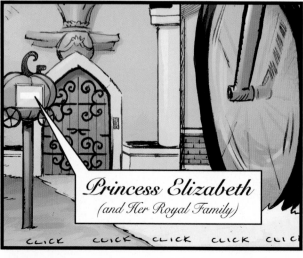

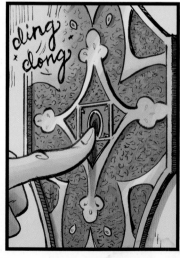

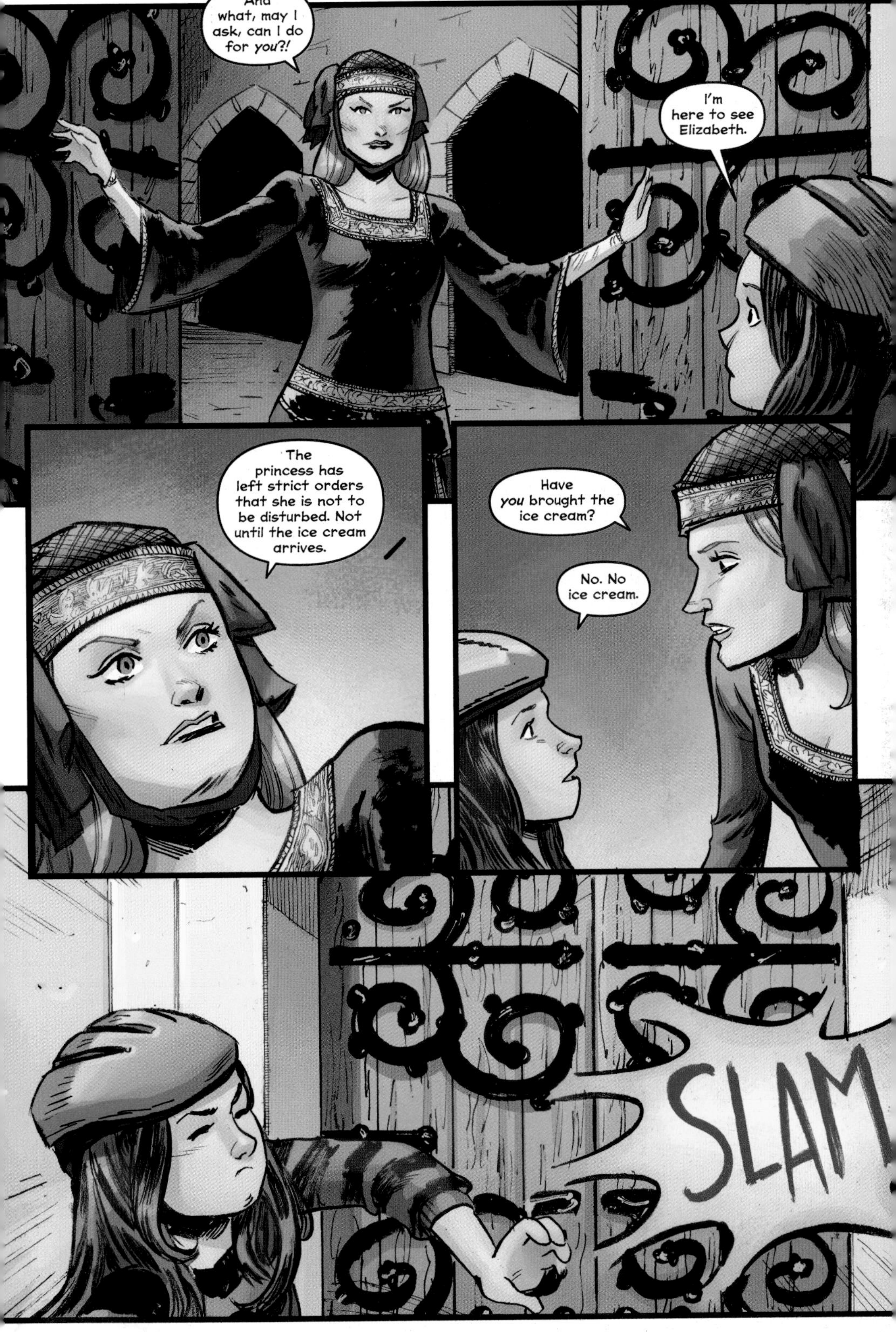
And what, may I ask, can I do for *you*?!
I'm here to see Elizabeth.
The princess has left strict orders that she is not to be disturbed. Not until the ice cream arrives.
Have *you* brought the ice cream?
No. No ice cream.
SLAM

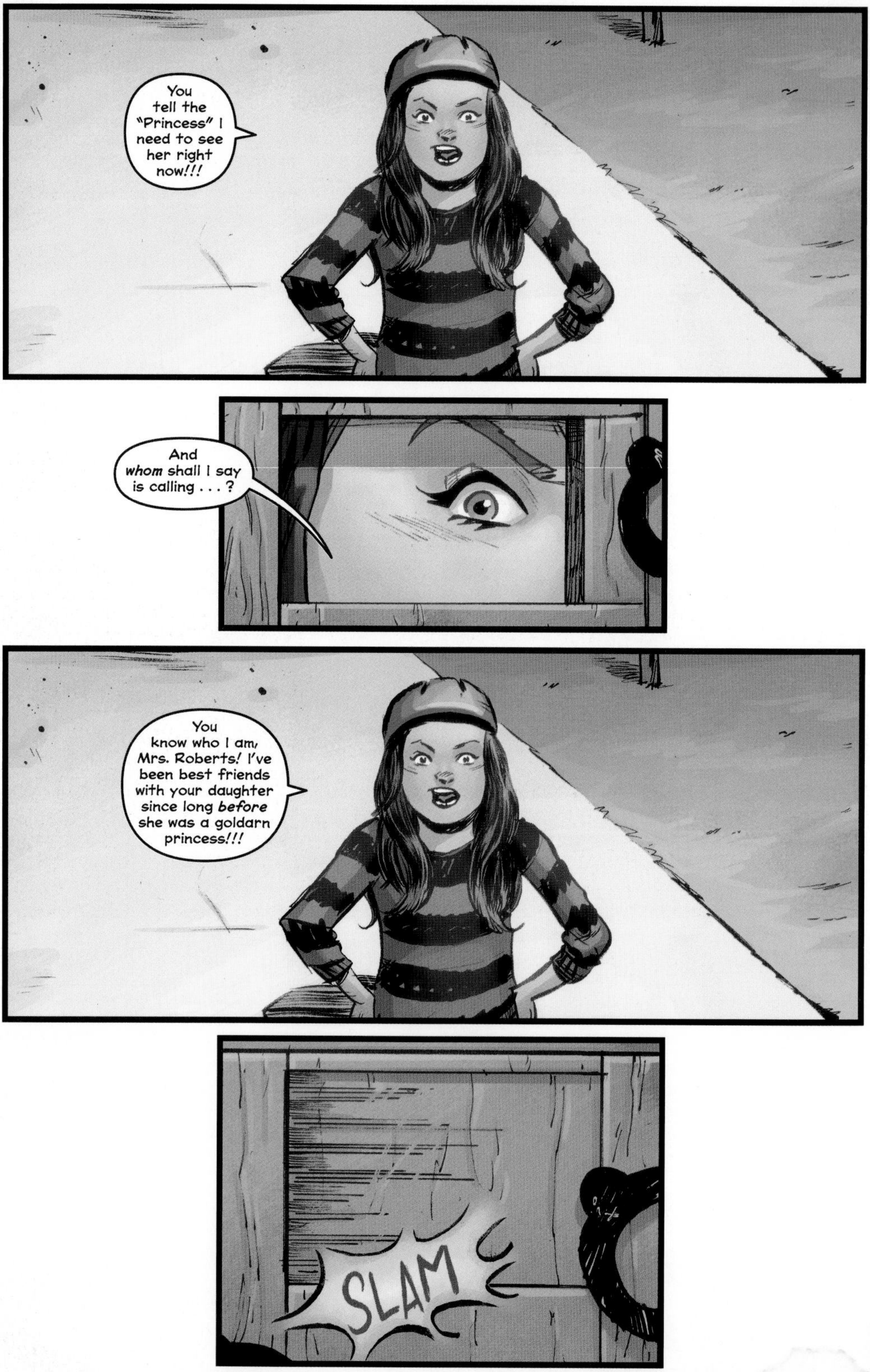
You tell the "Princess" I need to see her right now!!!
And *whom* shall I say is calling . . . ?
You know who I am, Mrs. Roberts! I've been best friends with your daughter since long *before* she was a goldarn princess!!!
SLAM

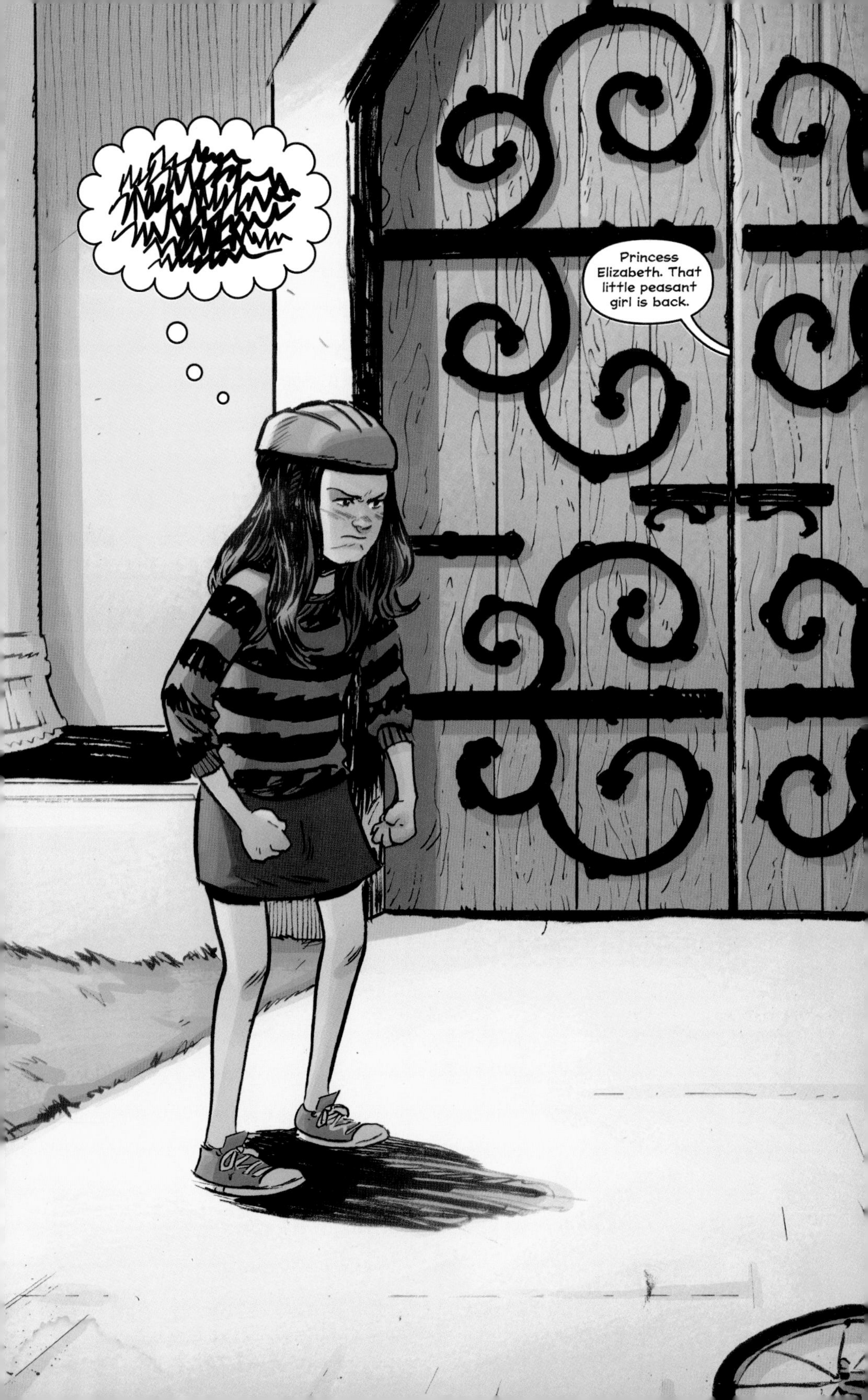
Princess Elizabeth. That little peasant girl is back.

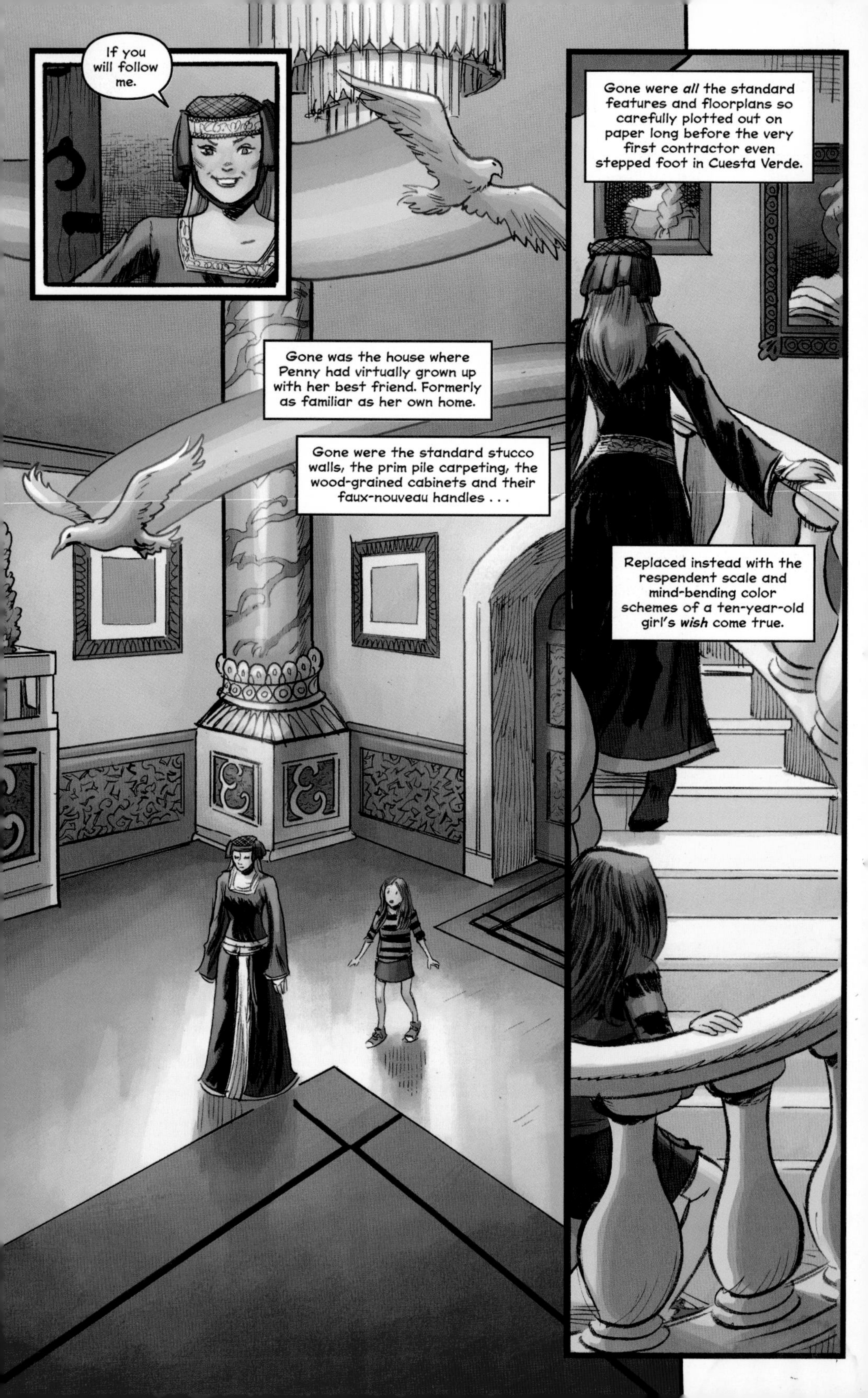
If you will follow me.
Gone was the house where Penny had virtually grown up with her best friend. Formerly as familiar as her own home.
Gone were the standard stucco walls, the prim pile carpeting, the wood-grained cabinets and their faux-nouveau handles . . .
Gone were *all* the standard features and floorplans so carefully plotted out on paper long before the very first contractor even stepped foot in Cuesta Verde.
Replaced instead with the respendent scale and mind-bending color schemes of a ten-year-old girl's *wish* come true.

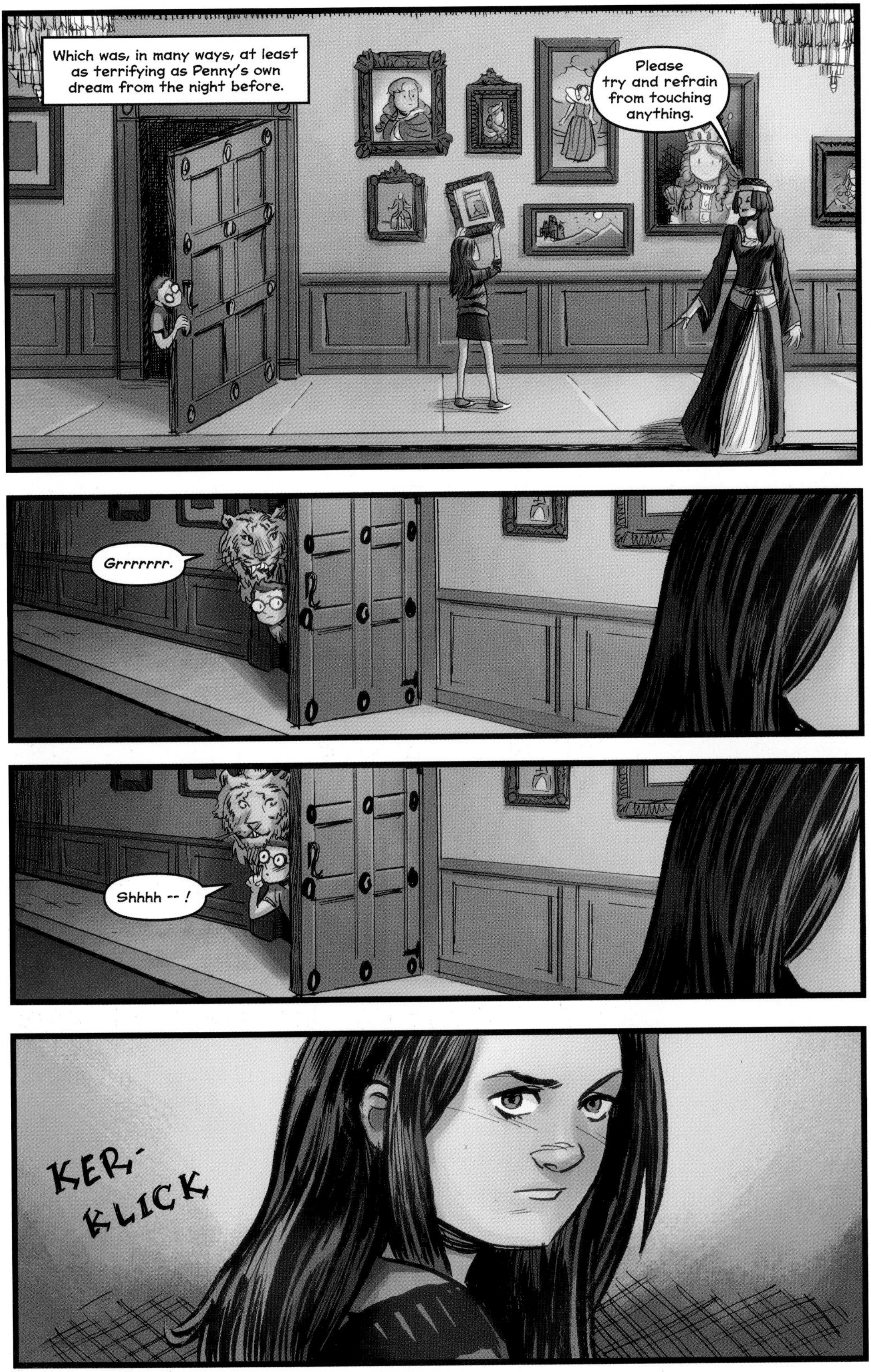

Which was, in many ways, at least as terrifying as Penny's own dream from the night before.
Please try and refrain from touching anything.
Grrrrrrr.
Shhhh -- !
KER-KLICK

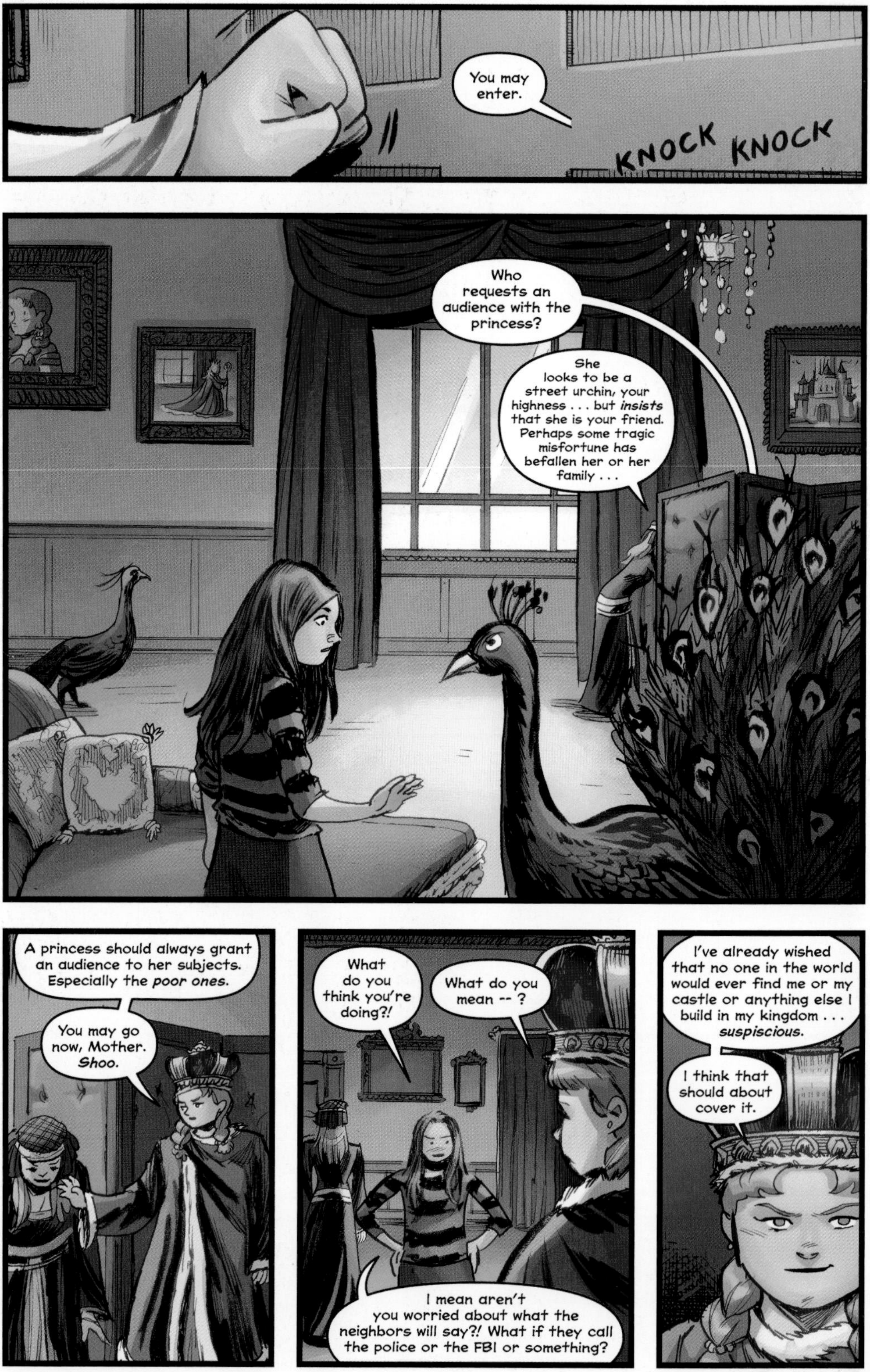
You may enter.
KNOCK KNOCK
Who requests an audience with the princess?
She looks to be a street urchin, your highness . . . but *insists* that she is your friend. Perhaps some tragic misfortune has befallen her or her family . . .
A princess should always grant an audience to her subjects. Especially the *poor ones*.
You may go now, Mother. *Shoo.*
What do you think you're doing?!
What do you mean -- ?
I mean aren't you worried about what the neighbors will say?! What if they call the police or the FBI or something?
I've already wished that no one in the world would ever find me or my castle or anything else I build in my kingdom . . . *suspiscious*.
I think that should about cover it.

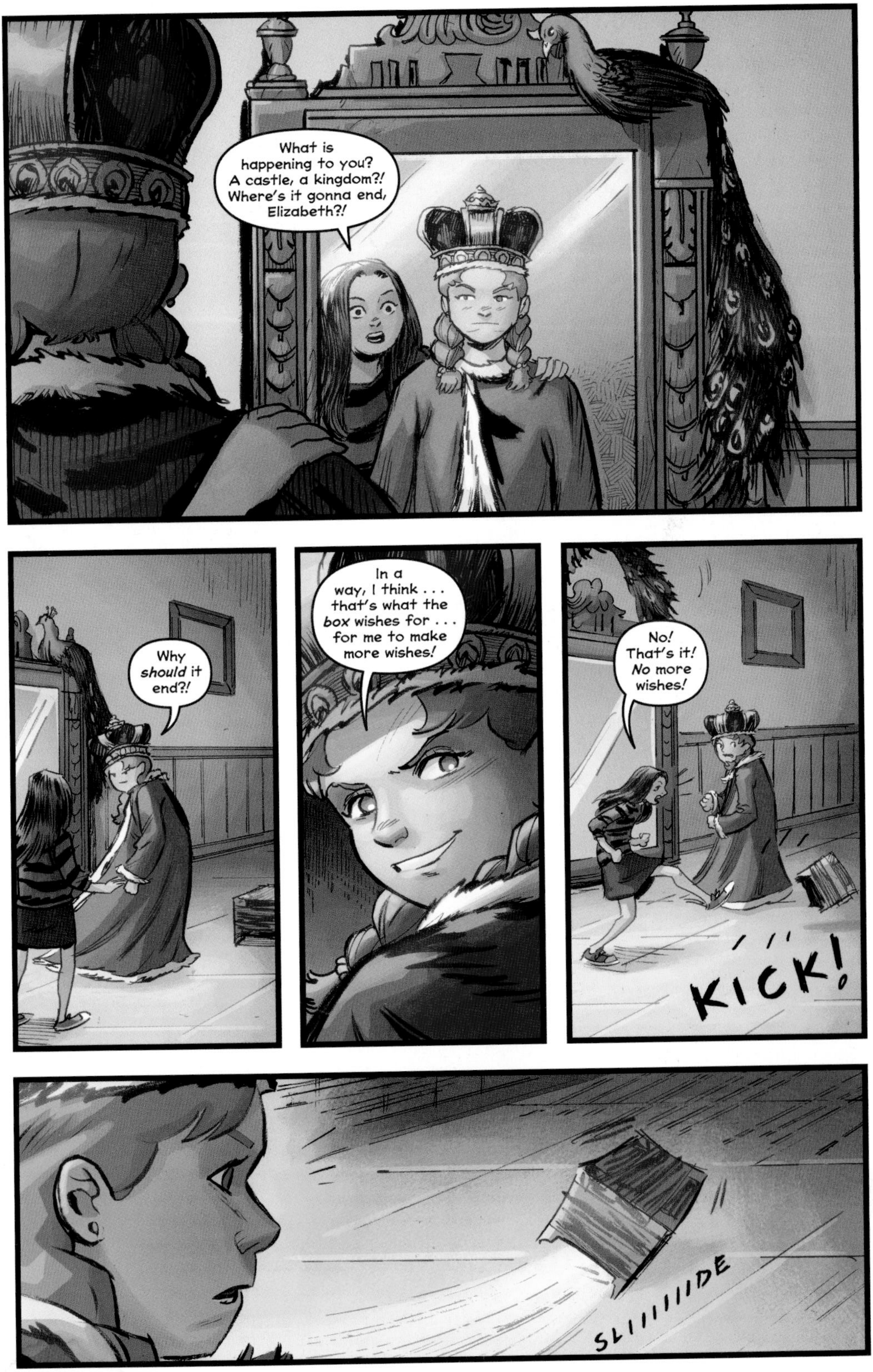
What is happening to you? A castle, a kingdom?! Where's it gonna end, Elizabeth?!
Why *should* it end?!
In a way, I think . . . that's what the *box* wishes for . . . for me to make more wishes!
No! That's it! *No* more wishes!
KICK!
SLIIIIIIDE

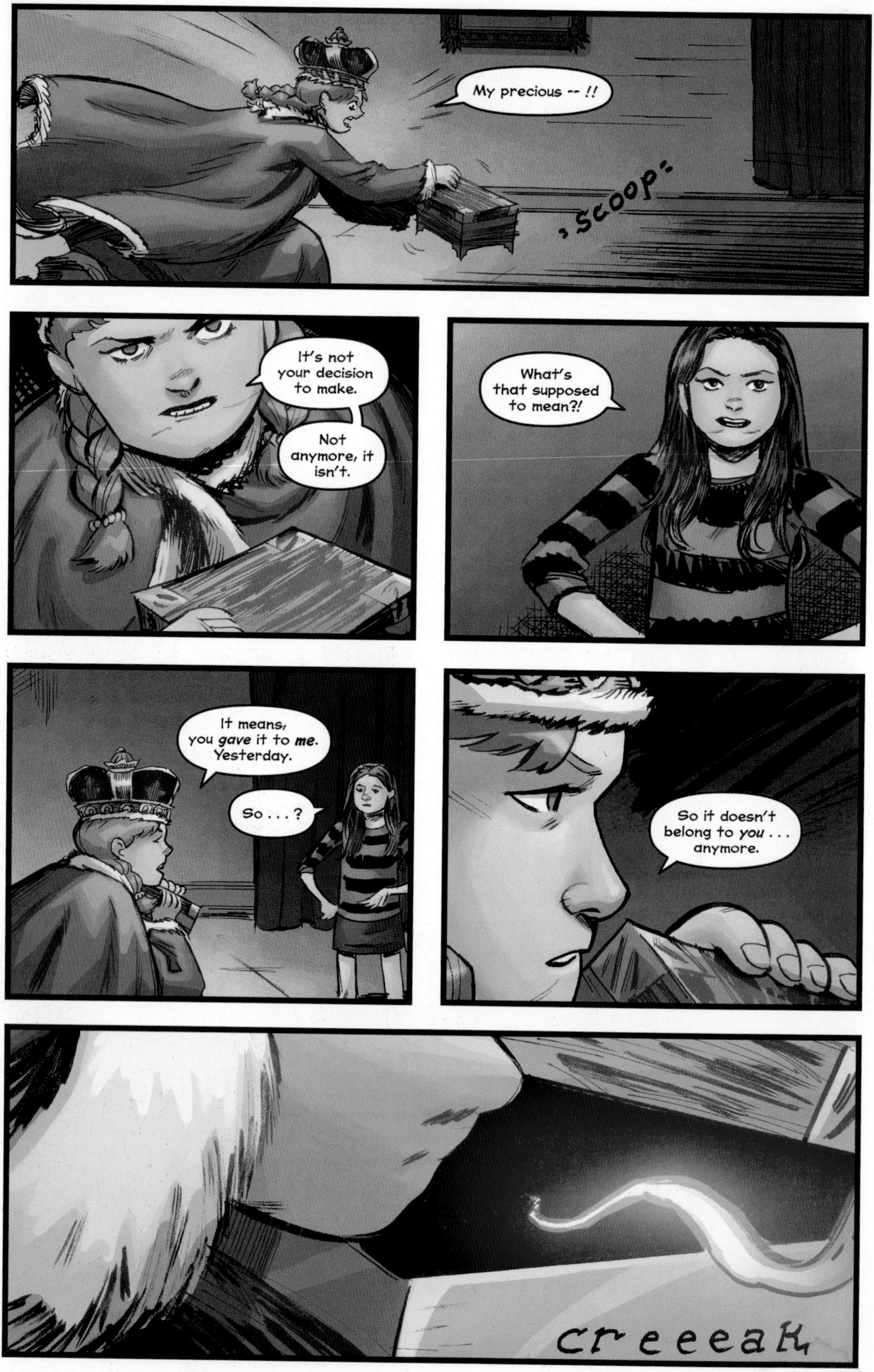
My precious -- !!
SCOOP
It's not your decision to make.
Not anymore, it isn't.
What's that supposed to mean?!
It means, you *gave* it to *me*. Yesterday.
So . . . ?
So it doesn't belong to *you* . . . anymore.
creeeak

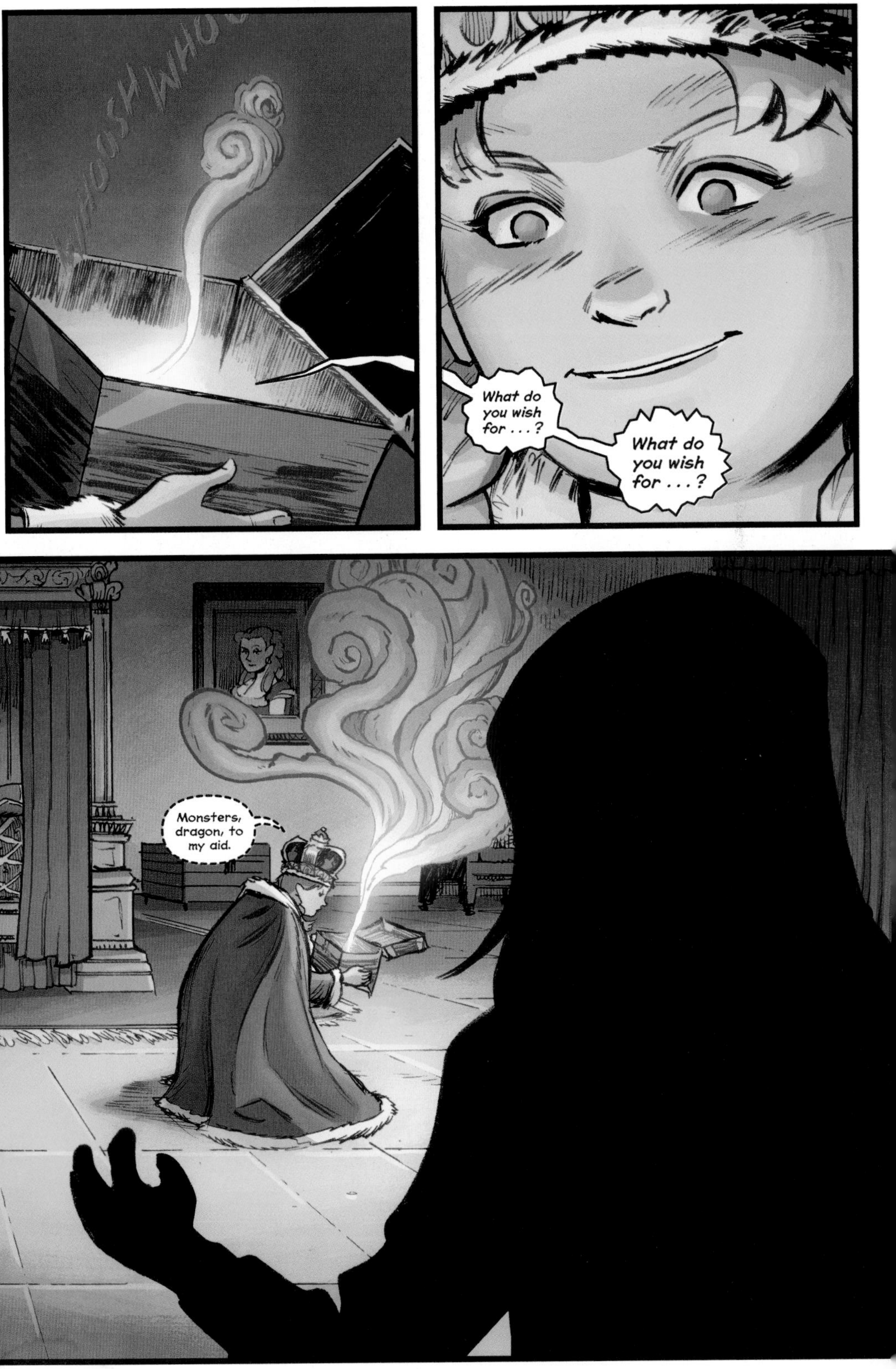
WHOOSHWHOO
What do you wish for . . . ?
What do you wish for . . . ?
Monsters, dragon, to my aid.

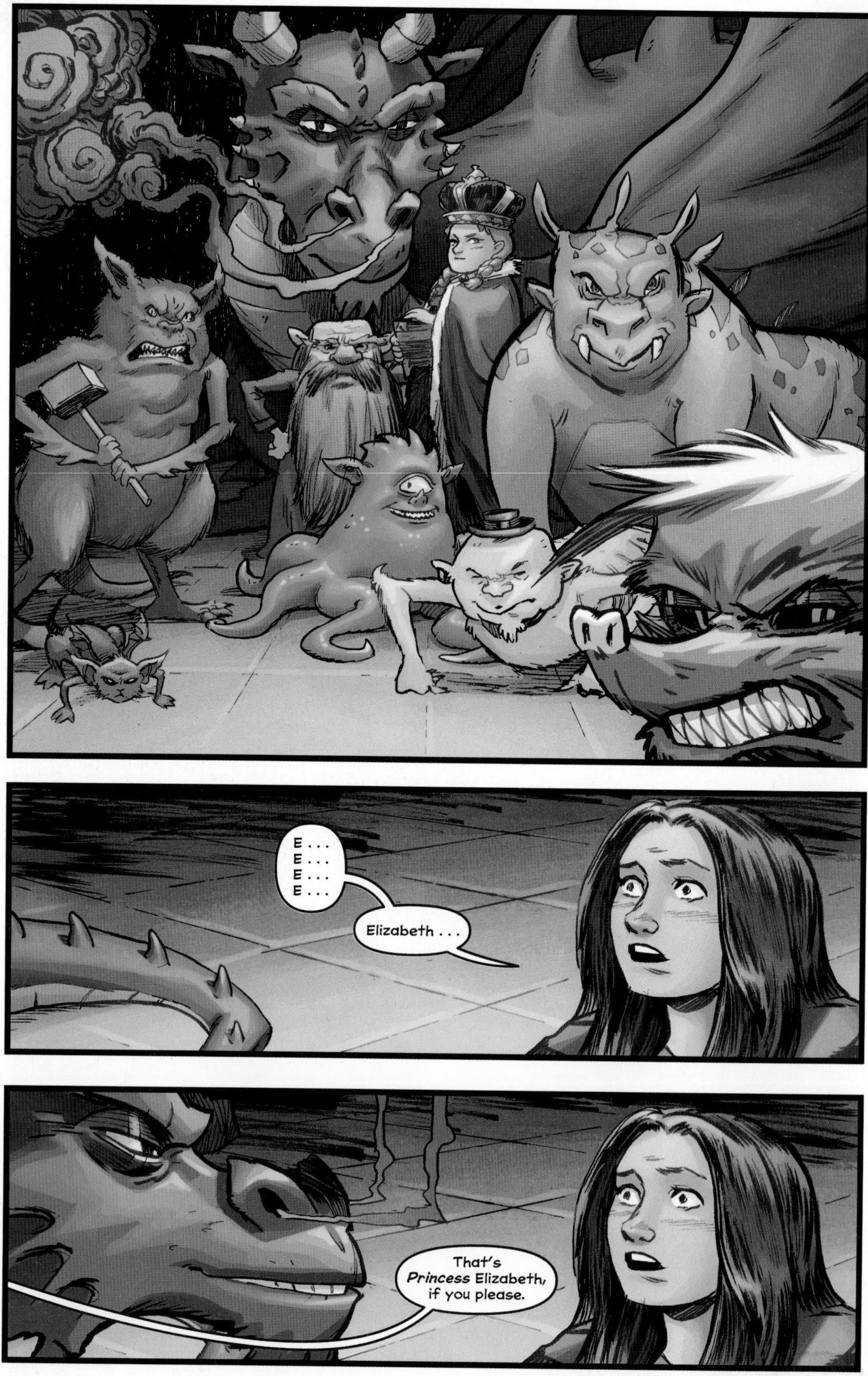
E . . .
E . . .
E . . .
E . . .
Elizabeth . . .
That's *Princess* Elizabeth, if you please.

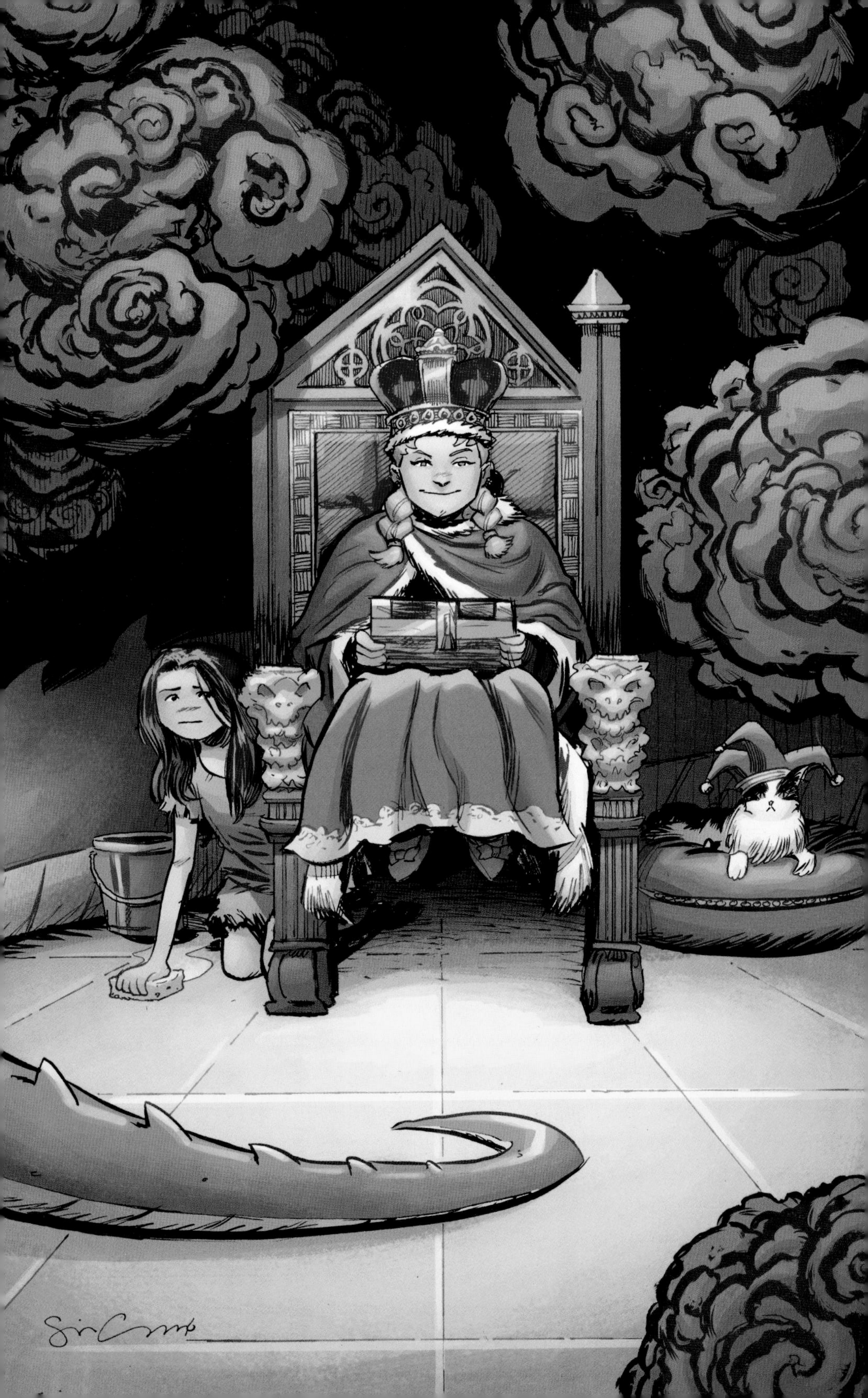

Chapter Four

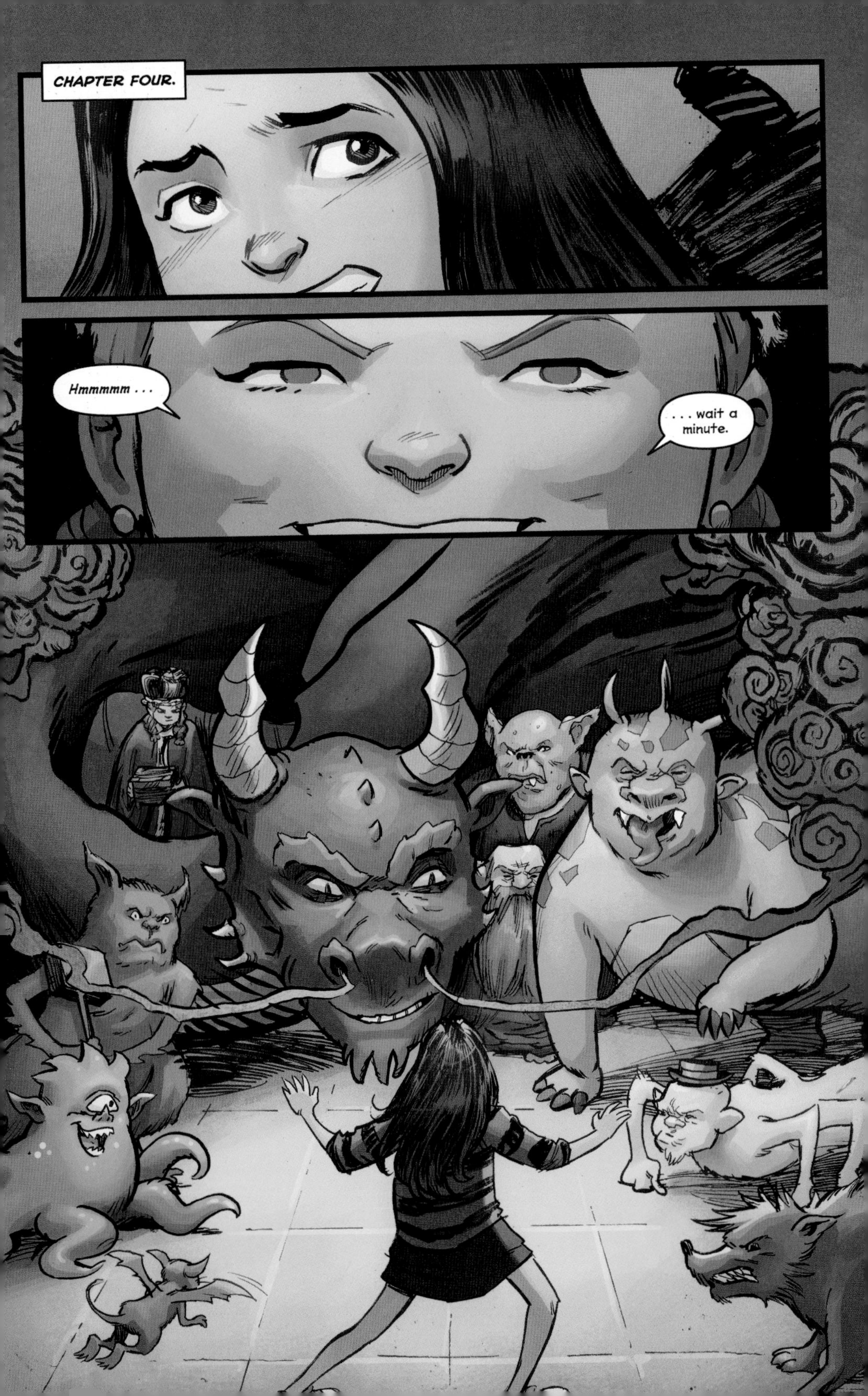
CHAPTER FOUR.
Hmmmmm . . .
. . . wait a minute.

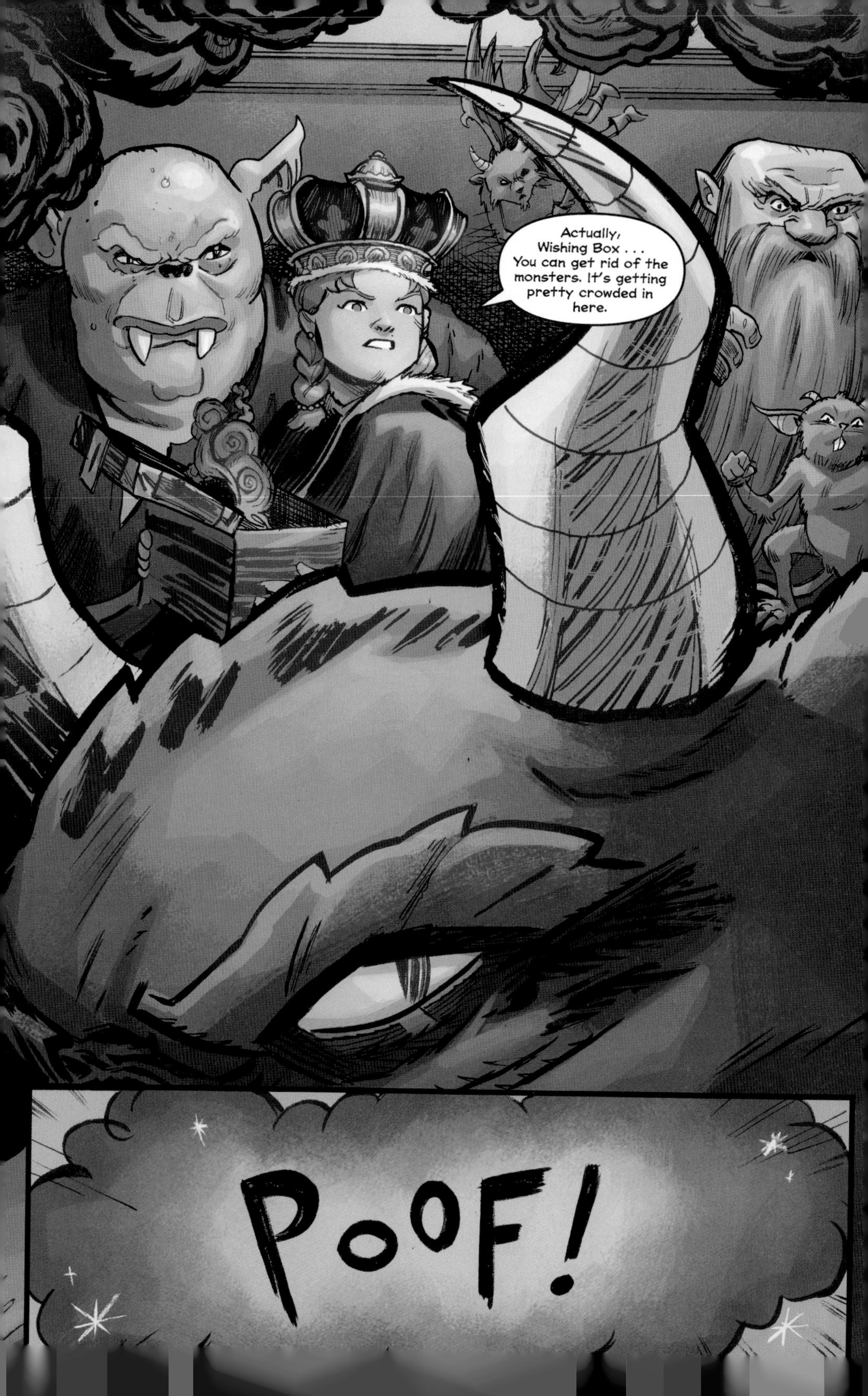
Actually, Wishing Box . . . You can get rid of the monsters. It's getting pretty crowded in here.
POOF!

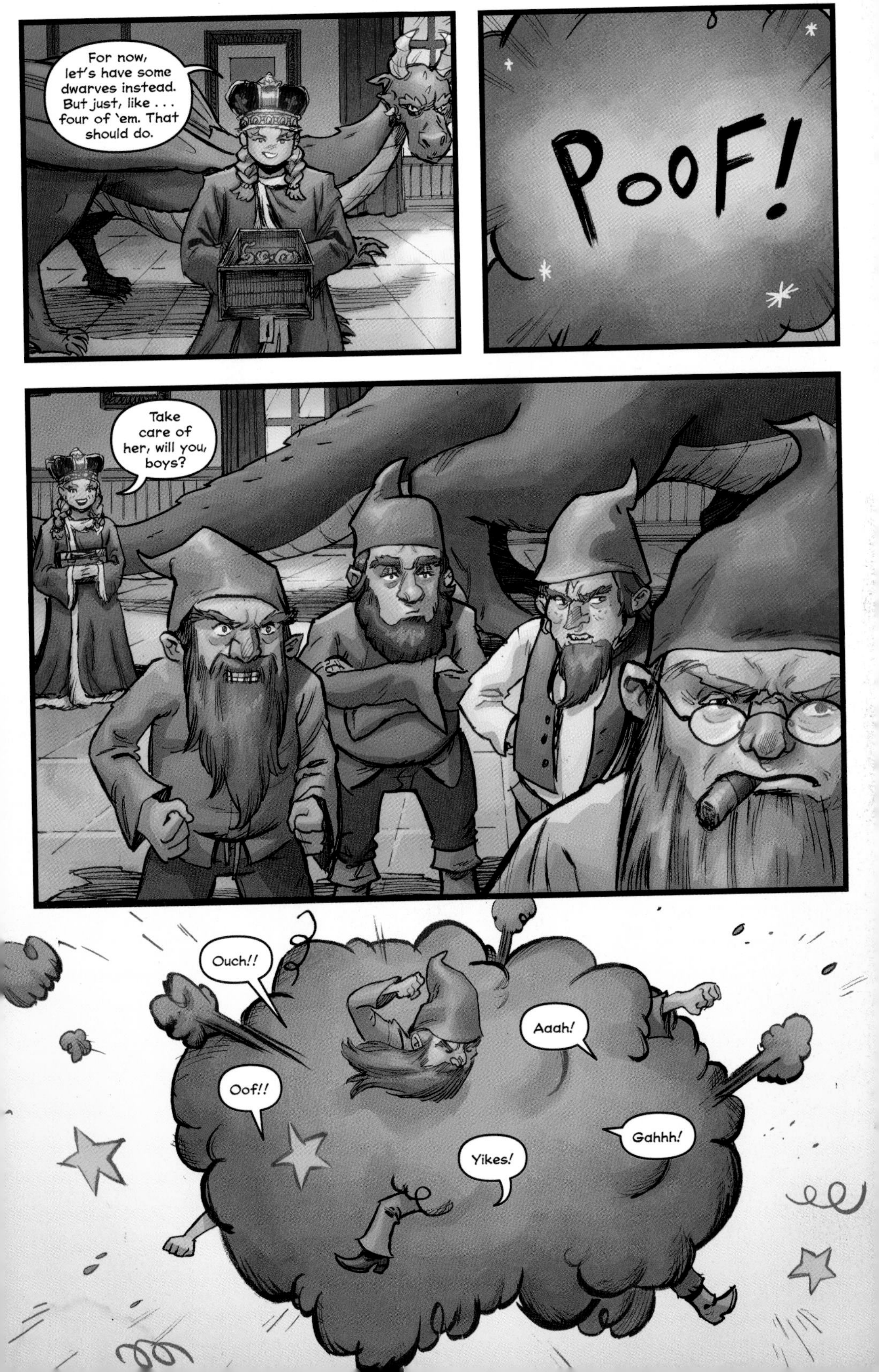
For now, let's have some dwarves instead. But just, like . . . four of 'em. That should do.
POOF!
Take care of her, will you, boys?
Ouch!!
Aaah!
Oof!!
Yikes!
Gahhh!

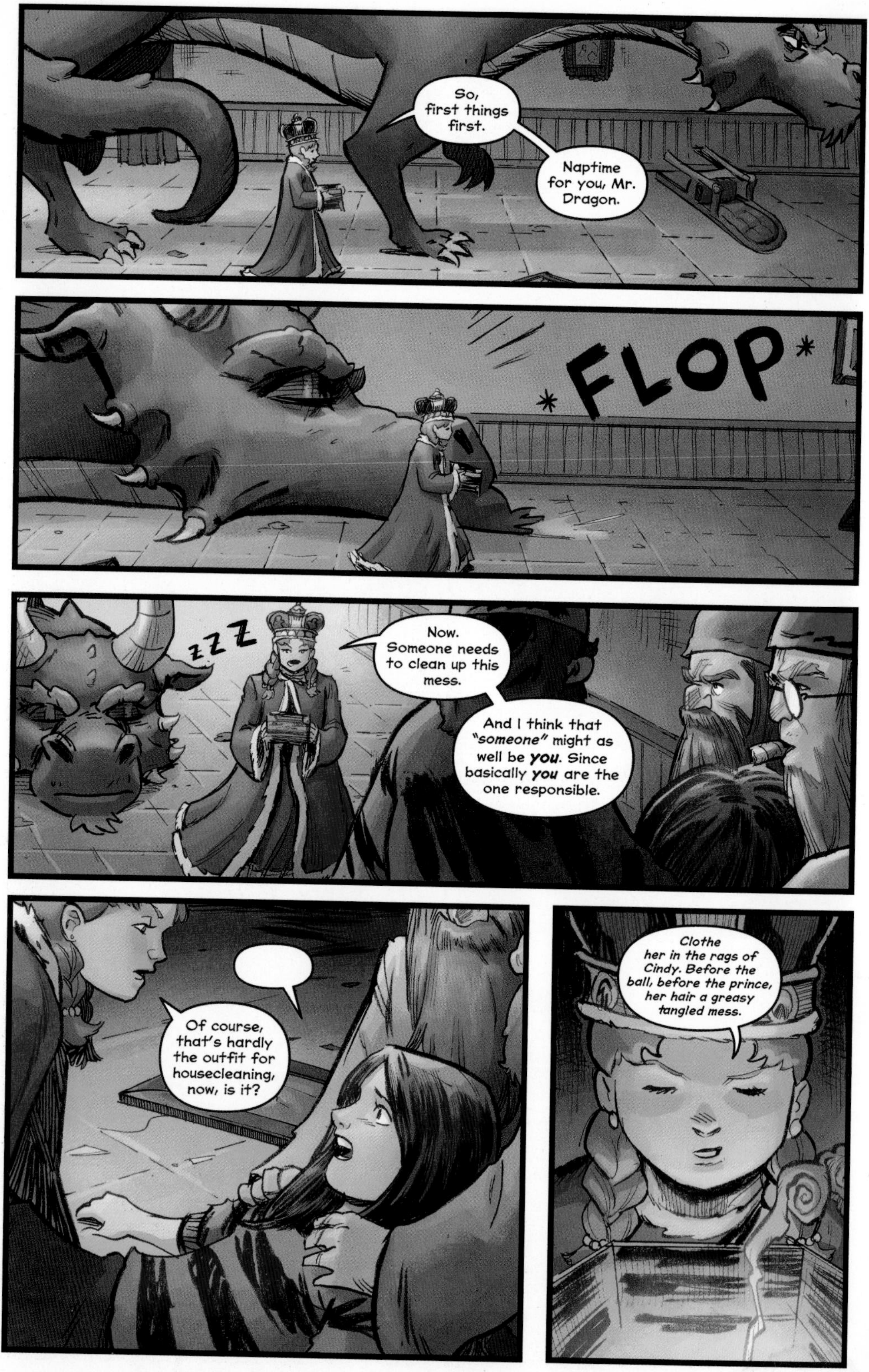
So, first things first.
Naptime for you, Mr. Dragon.
FLOP
ZZZ
Now. Someone needs to clean up this mess.
And I think that "*someone*" might as well be ***you***. Since basically ***you*** are the one responsible.
Of course, that's hardly the outfit for housecleaning, now, is it?
Clothe her in the rags of Cindy. Before the ball, before the prince, her hair a greasy tangled mess.

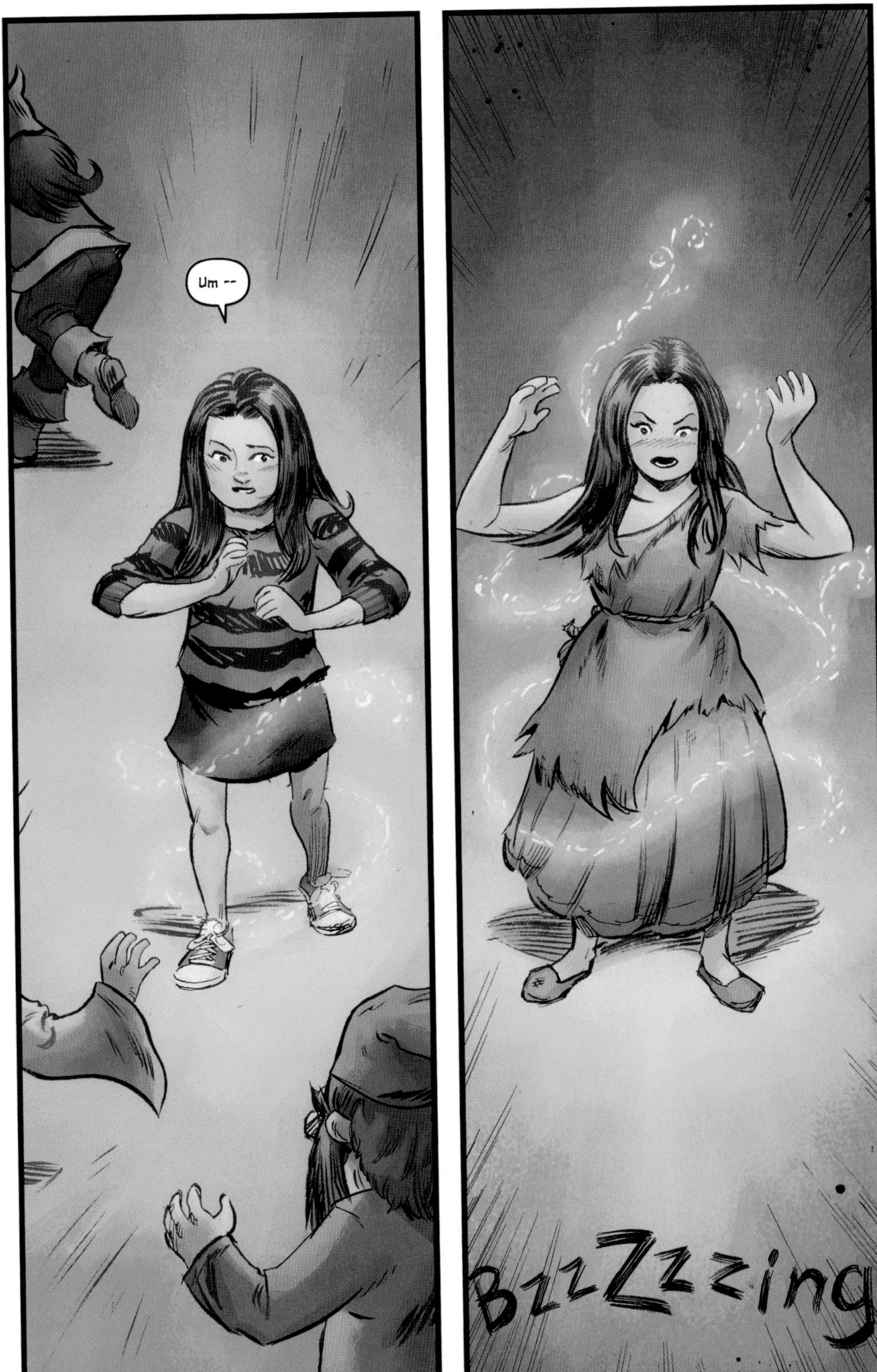
Um --
BzzZzzing

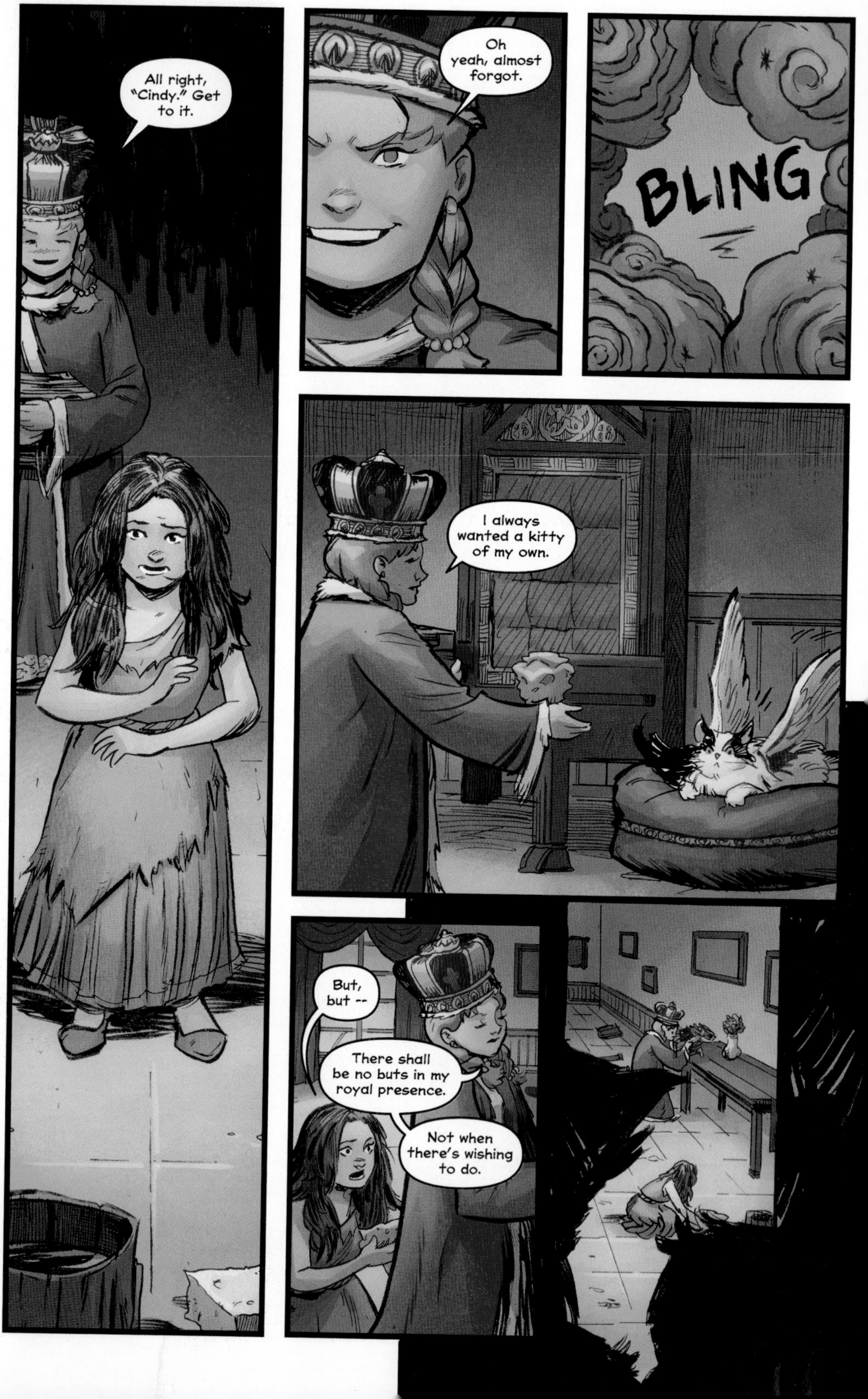
All right, "Cindy." Get to it.
Oh yeah, almost forgot.
BLING
I always wanted a kitty of my own.
But, but --
There shall be no buts in my royal presence.
Not when there's wishing to do.

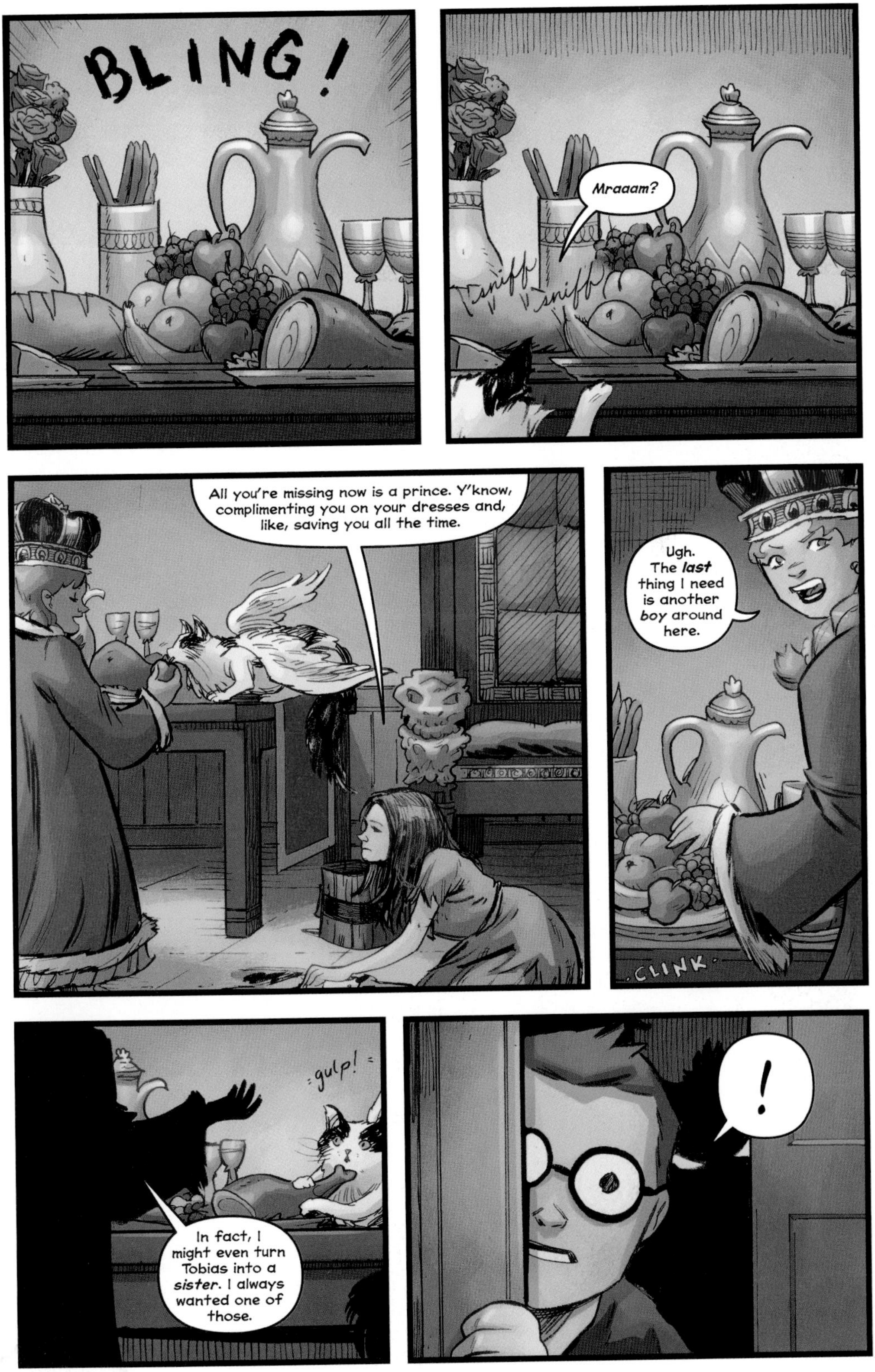
BLING!
Mraaam?
sniff sniff
All you're missing now is a prince. Y'know, complimenting you on your dresses and, like, saving you all the time.
Ugh. The *last* thing I need is another *boy* around here.
CLINK
gulp!
In fact, I might even turn Tobias into a *sister*. I always wanted one of those.
!

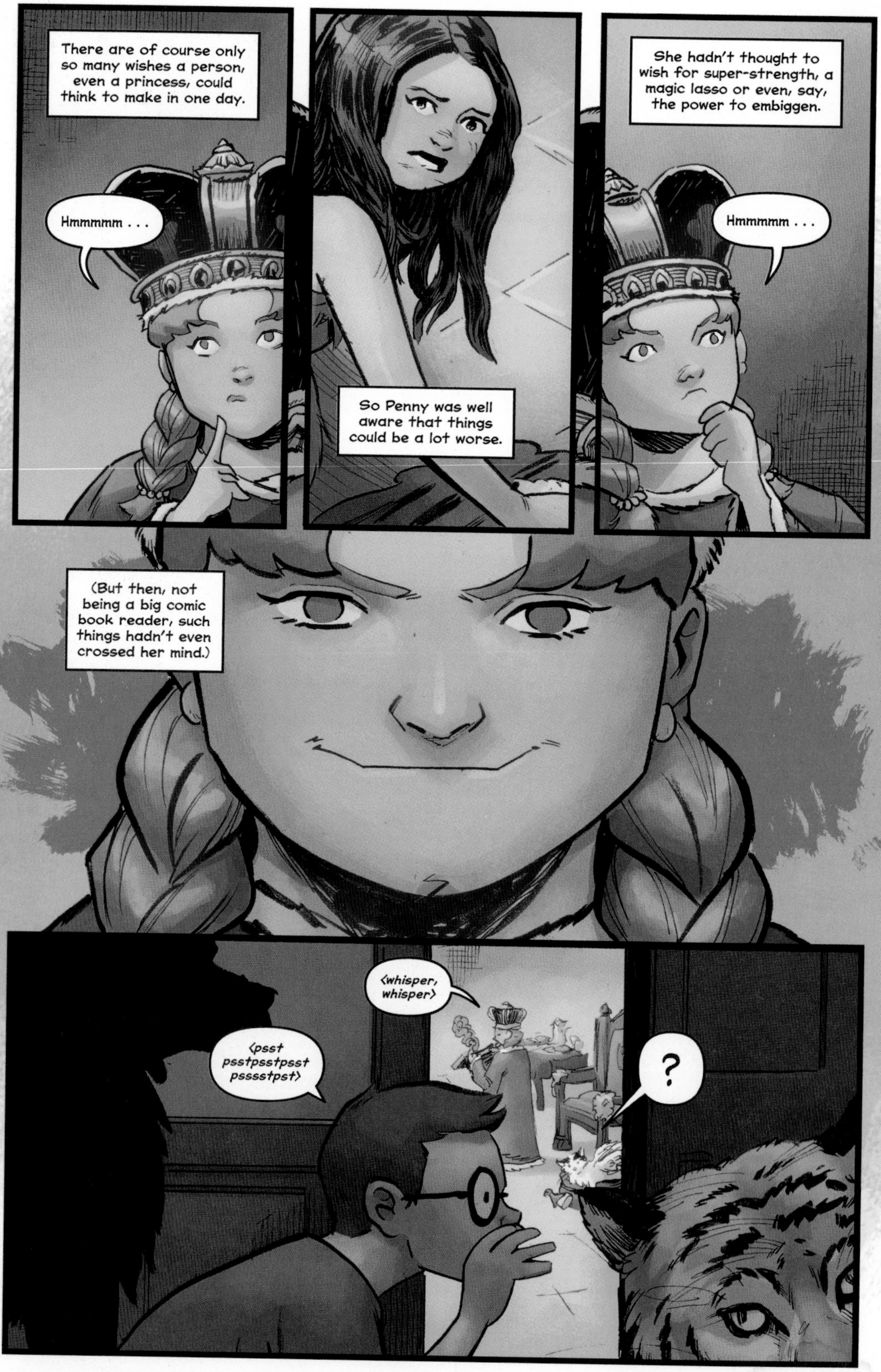
There are of course only so many wishes a person, even a princess, could think to make in one day.
Hmmmmm . . .
So Penny was well aware that things could be a lot worse.
She hadn't thought to wish for super-strength, a magic lasso or even, say, the power to embiggen.
Hmmmmm . . .
(But then, not being a big comic book reader, such things hadn't even crossed her mind.)
<whisper, whisper>
<psst psstpsstpsst psssstpst>
?

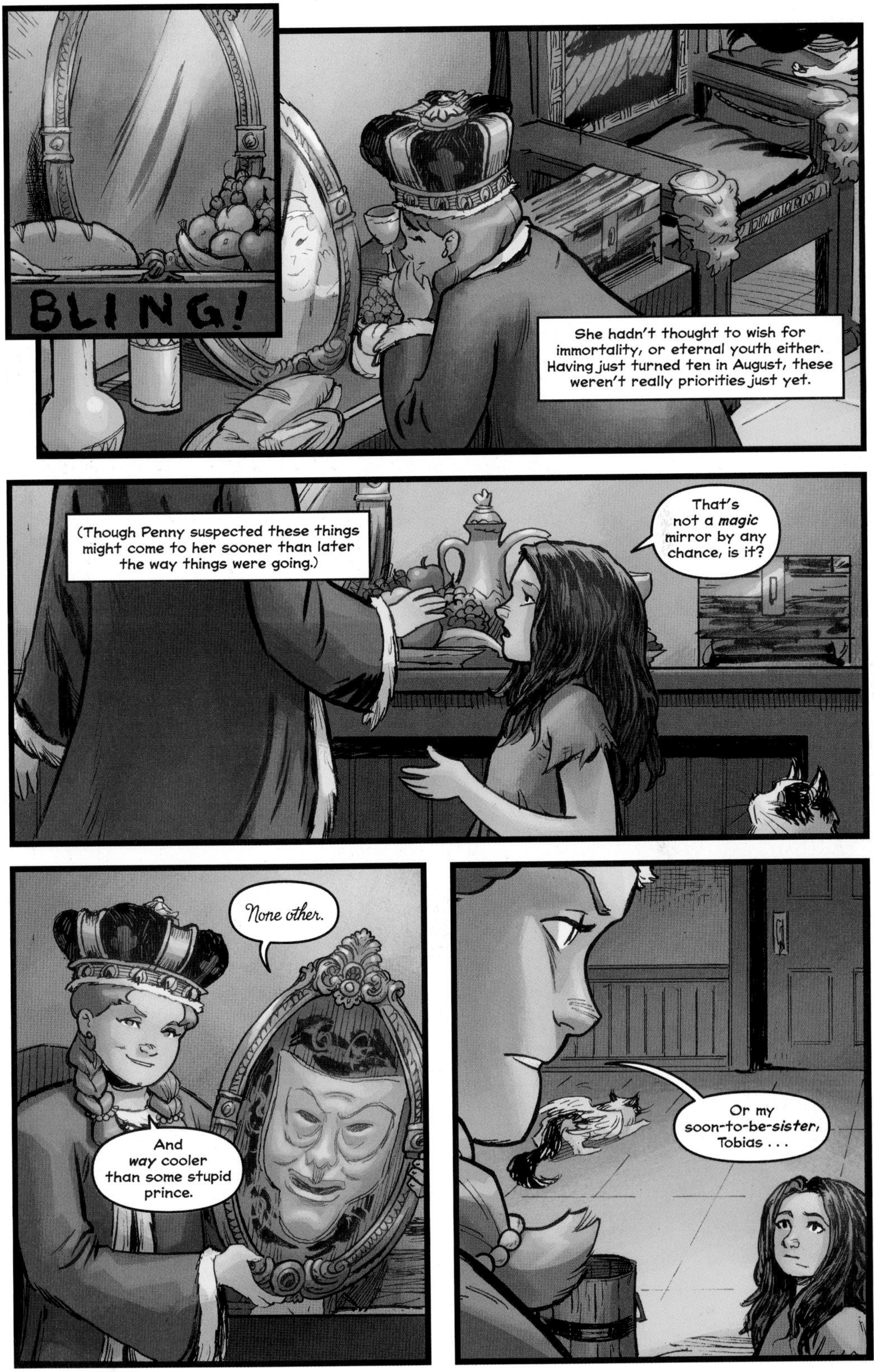
BLING!
She hadn't thought to wish for immortality, or eternal youth either. Having just turned ten in August, these weren't really priorities just yet.
(Though Penny suspected these things might come to her sooner than later the way things were going.)
That's not a *magic* mirror by any chance, is it?
None other.
And *way* cooler than some stupid prince.
Or my soon-to-be-*sister*, Tobias . . .

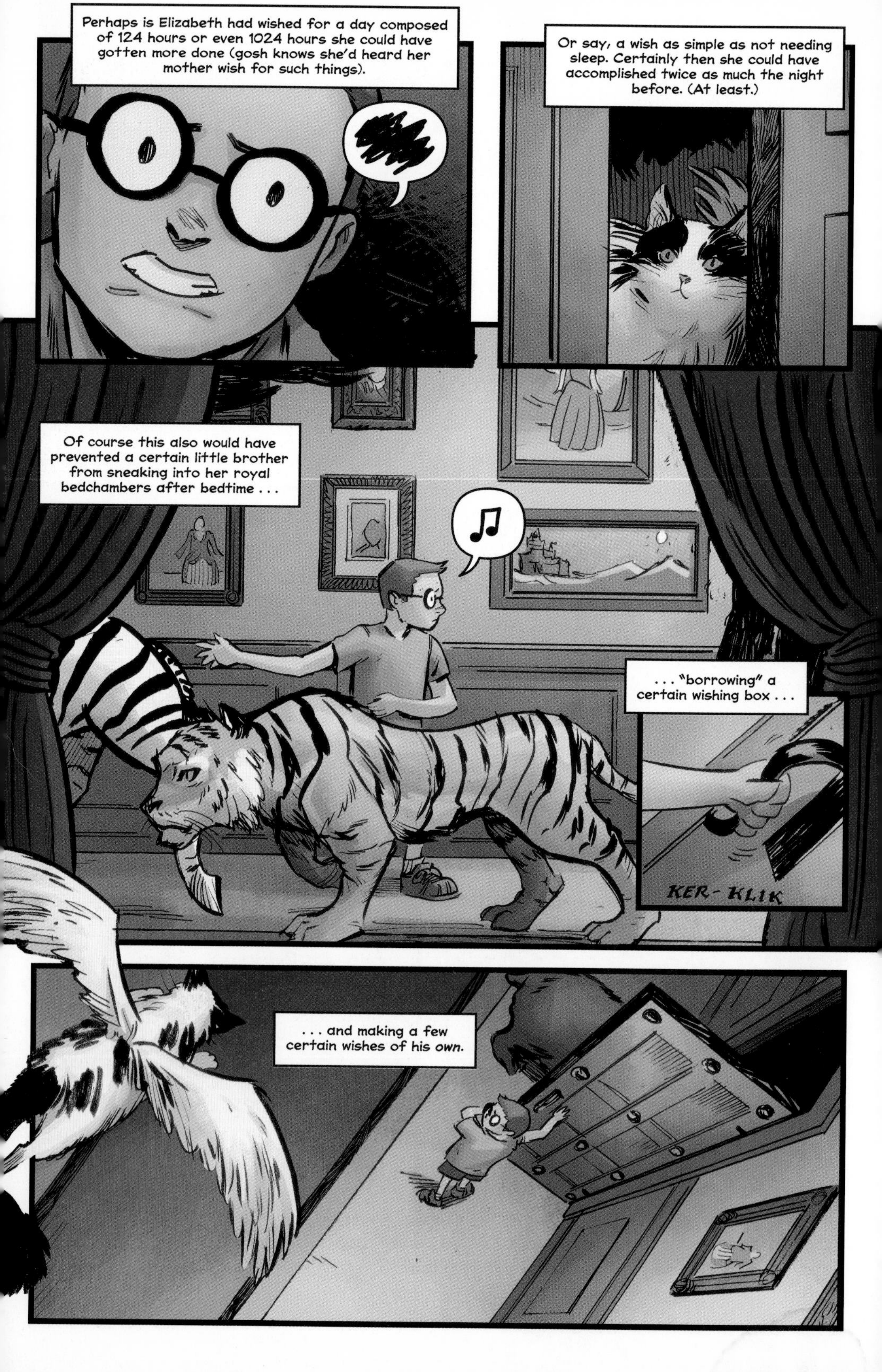
Perhaps is Elizabeth had wished for a day composed of 124 hours or even 1024 hours she could have gotten more done (gosh knows she'd heard her mother wish for such things).
Or say, a wish as simple as not needing sleep. Certainly then she could have accomplished twice as much the night before. (At least.)
Of course this also would have prevented a certain little brother from sneaking into her royal bedchambers after bedtime . . .
. . . "borrowing" a certain wishing box . . .
KER-KLIK
. . . and making a few certain wishes of his *own*.

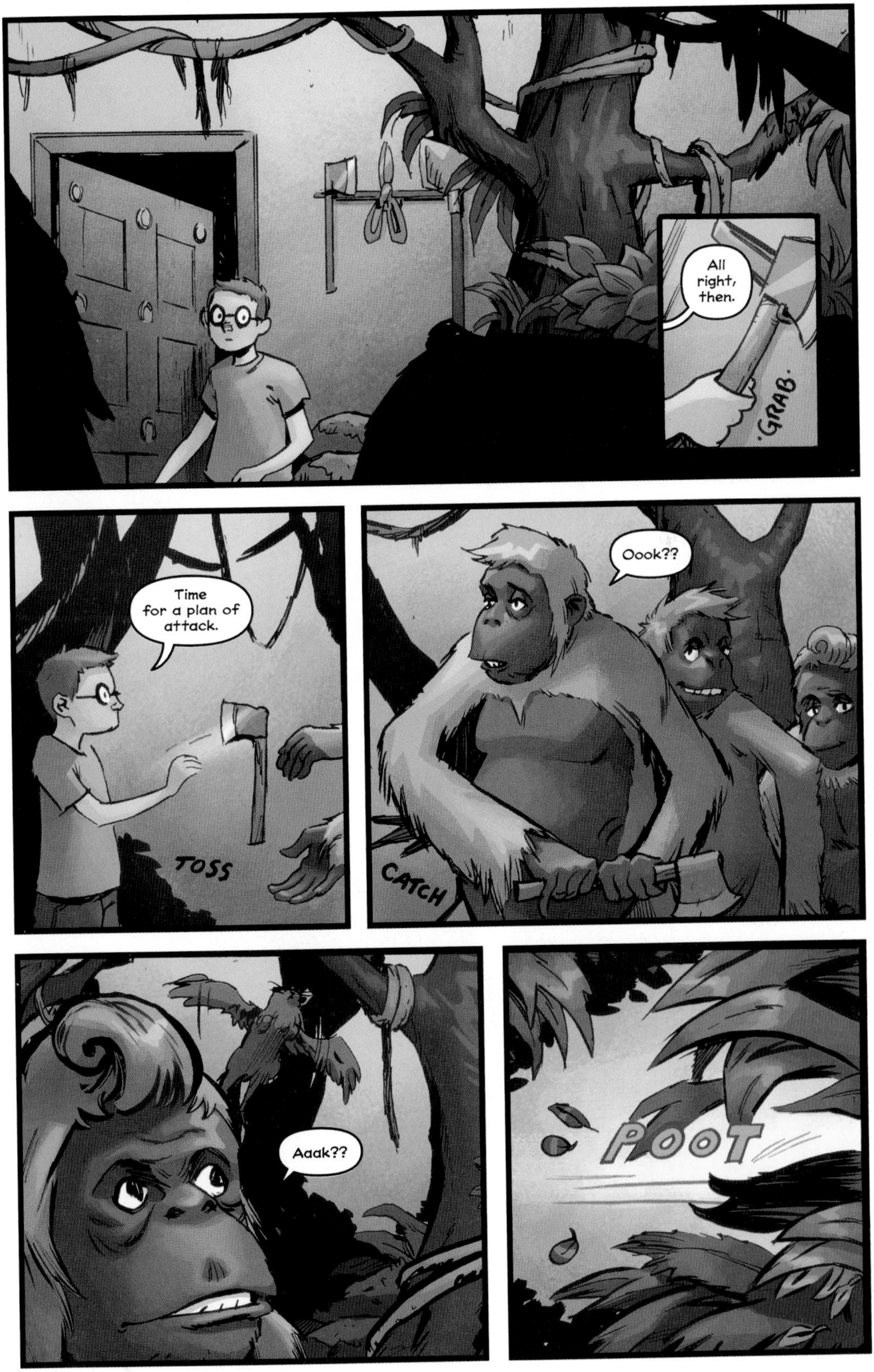
All right, then.
GRAB
Time for a plan of attack.
TOSS
Oook??
CATCH
Aaak??
POOT

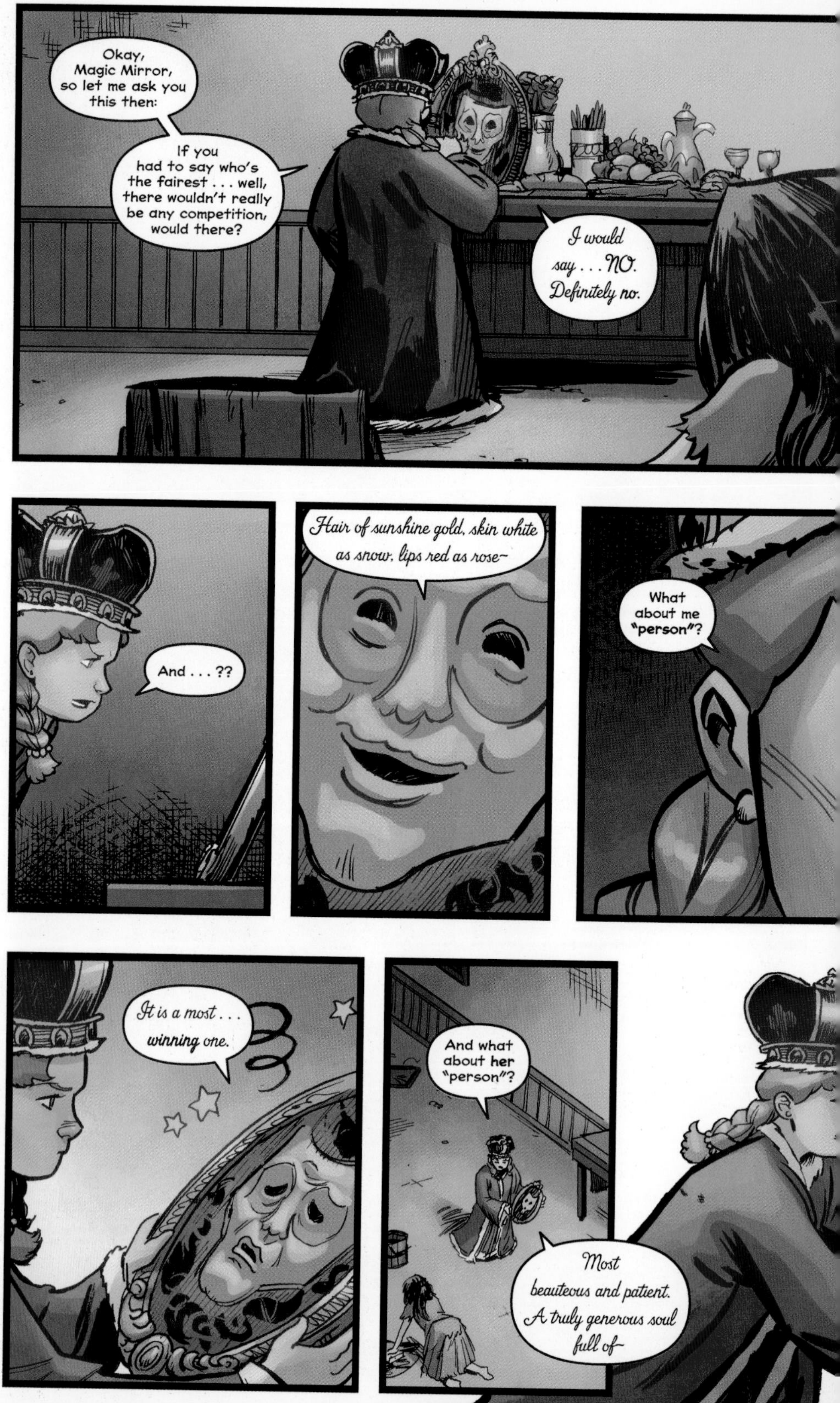
Okay, Magic Mirror, so let me ask you this then:
If you had to say who's the fairest . . . well, there wouldn't really be any competition, would there?
I would say . . . NO. Definitely no.
And . . . ??
Hair of sunshine gold, skin white as snow, lips red as rose~
What about me "person"?
It is a most . . . winning one.
And what about her "person"?
Most beauteous and patient. A truly generous soul full of~

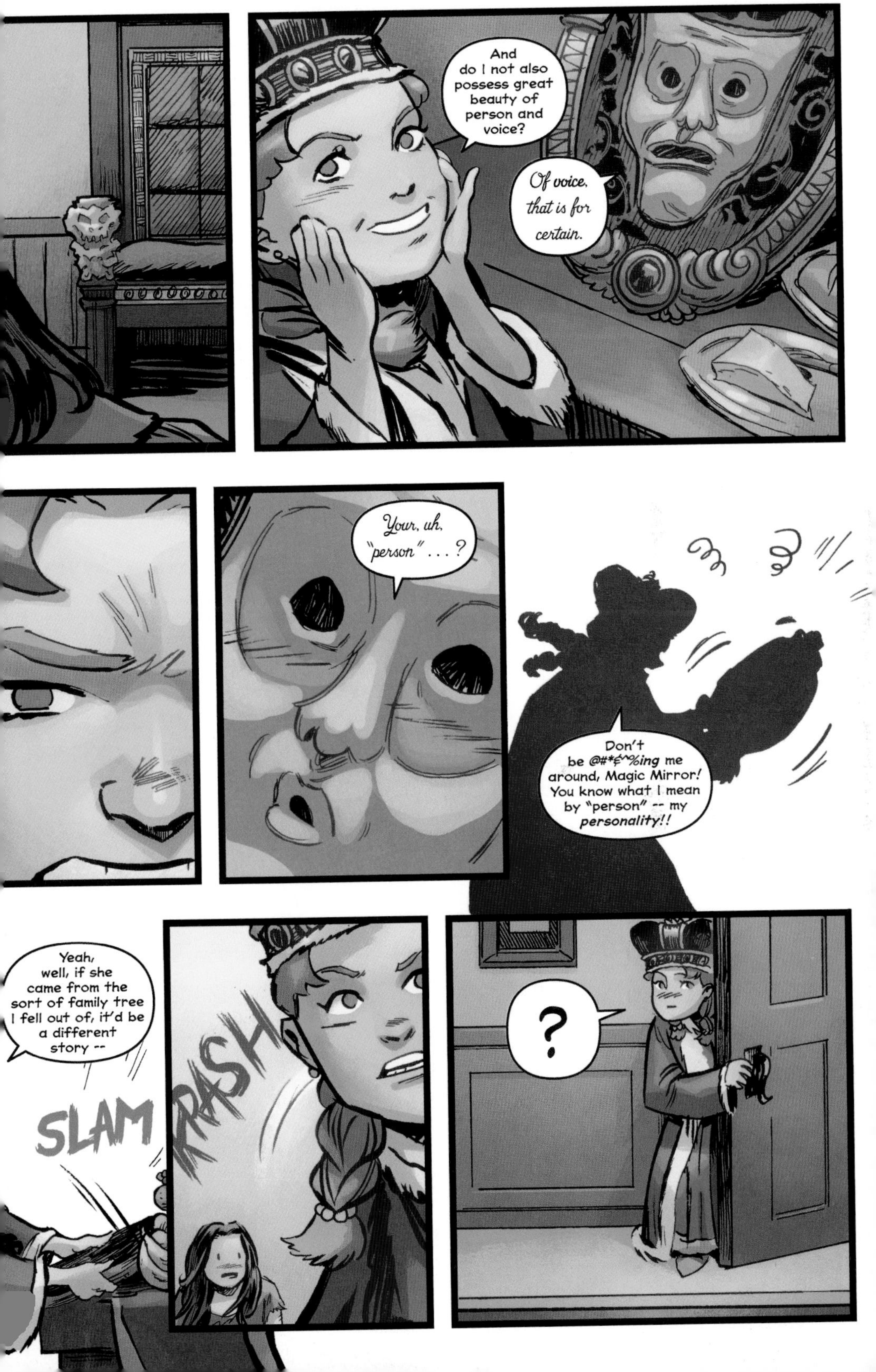
And do I not also possess great beauty of person and voice?
Of voice, that is for certain.
Your, uh, "person" . . . ?
Don't be @#*€^%ing me around, Magic Mirror! You know what I mean by "person" -- my *personality!!*
Yeah, well, if she came from the sort of family tree I fell out of, it'd be a different story --
SLAM
CRASH
?

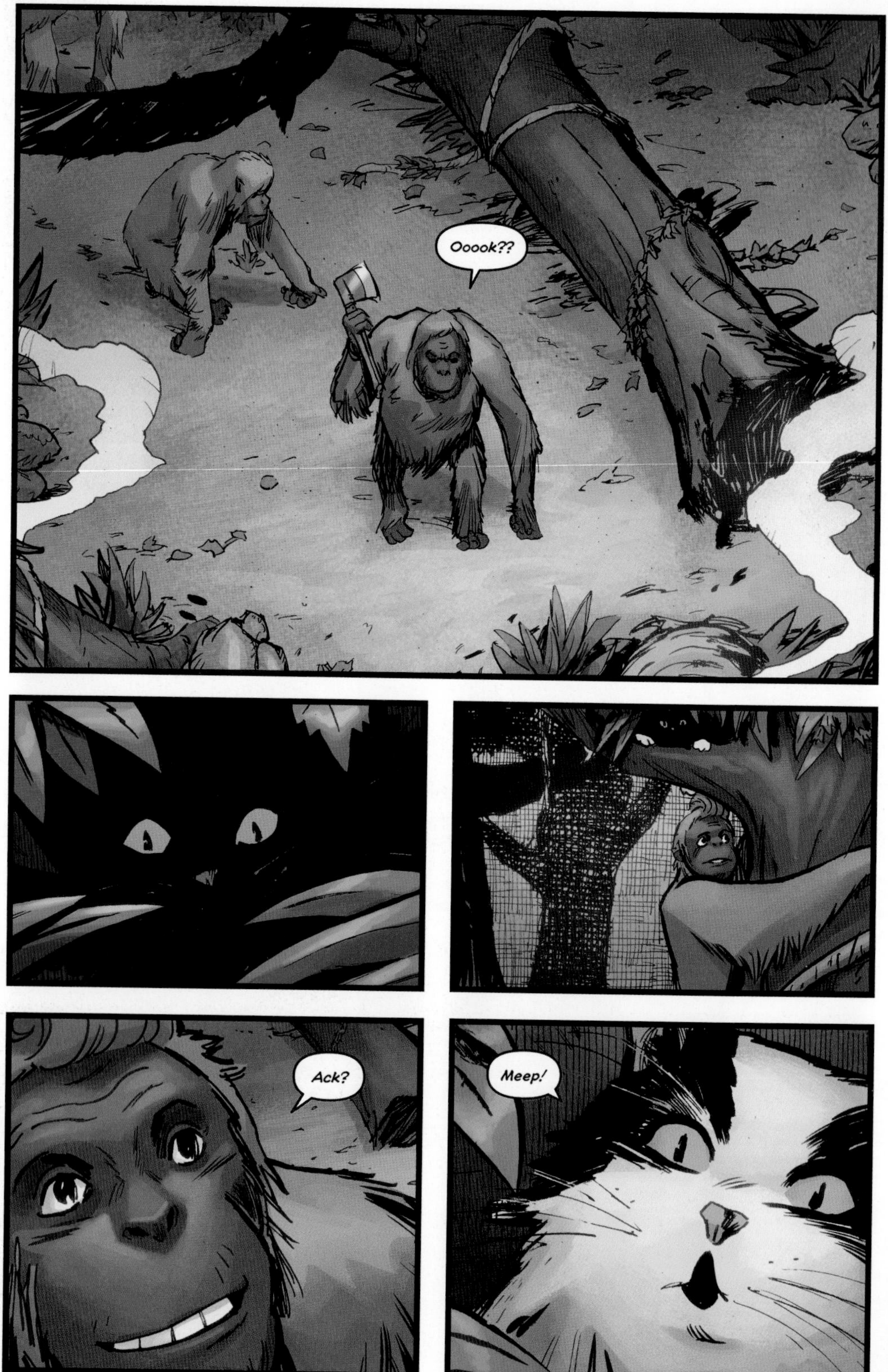
Ooook??
Ack?
Meep!

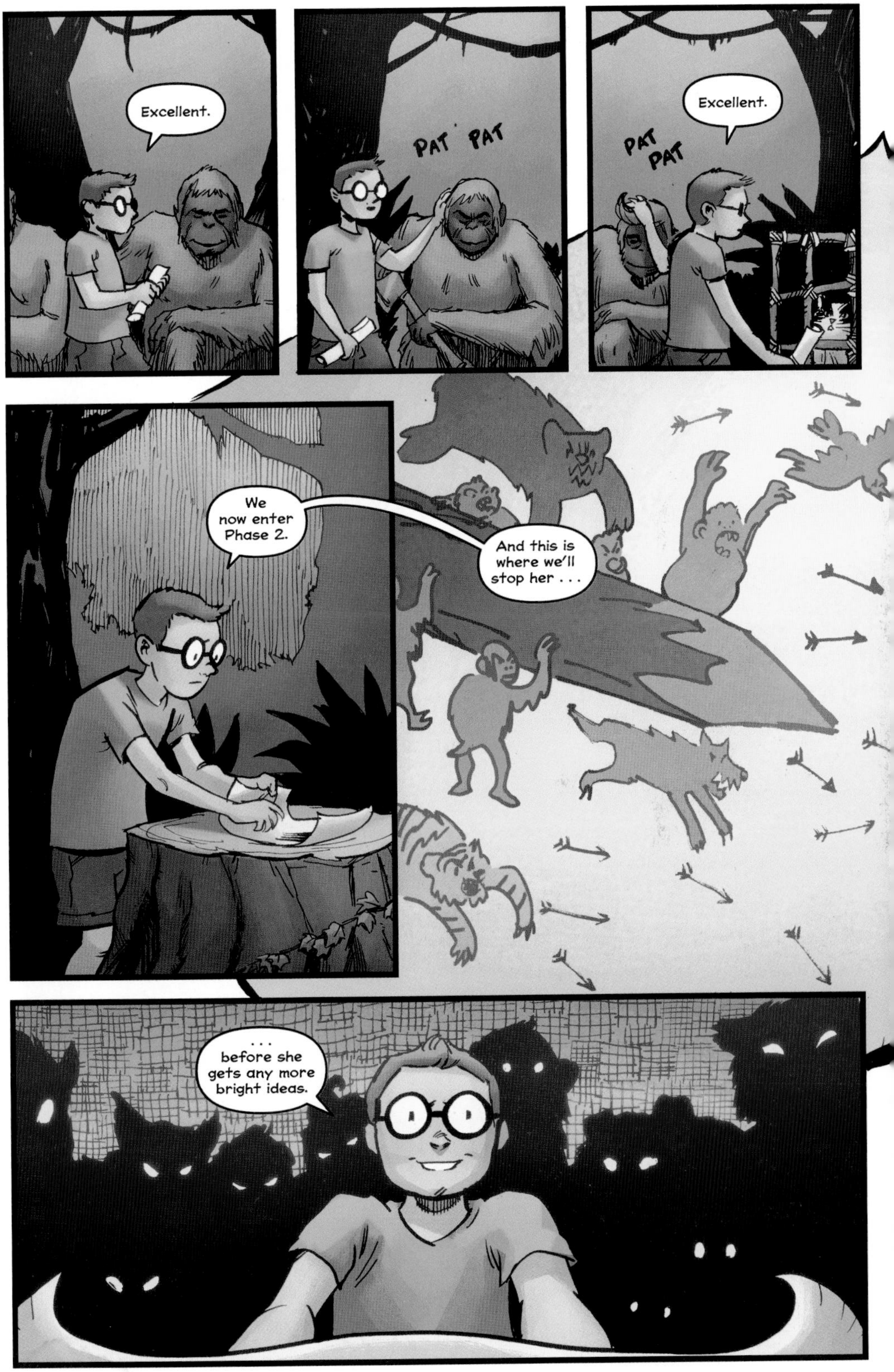
Excellent.
PAT PAT
PAT PAT
Excellent.
We now enter Phase 2.
And this is where we'll stop her . . .
. . . before she gets any more bright ideas.

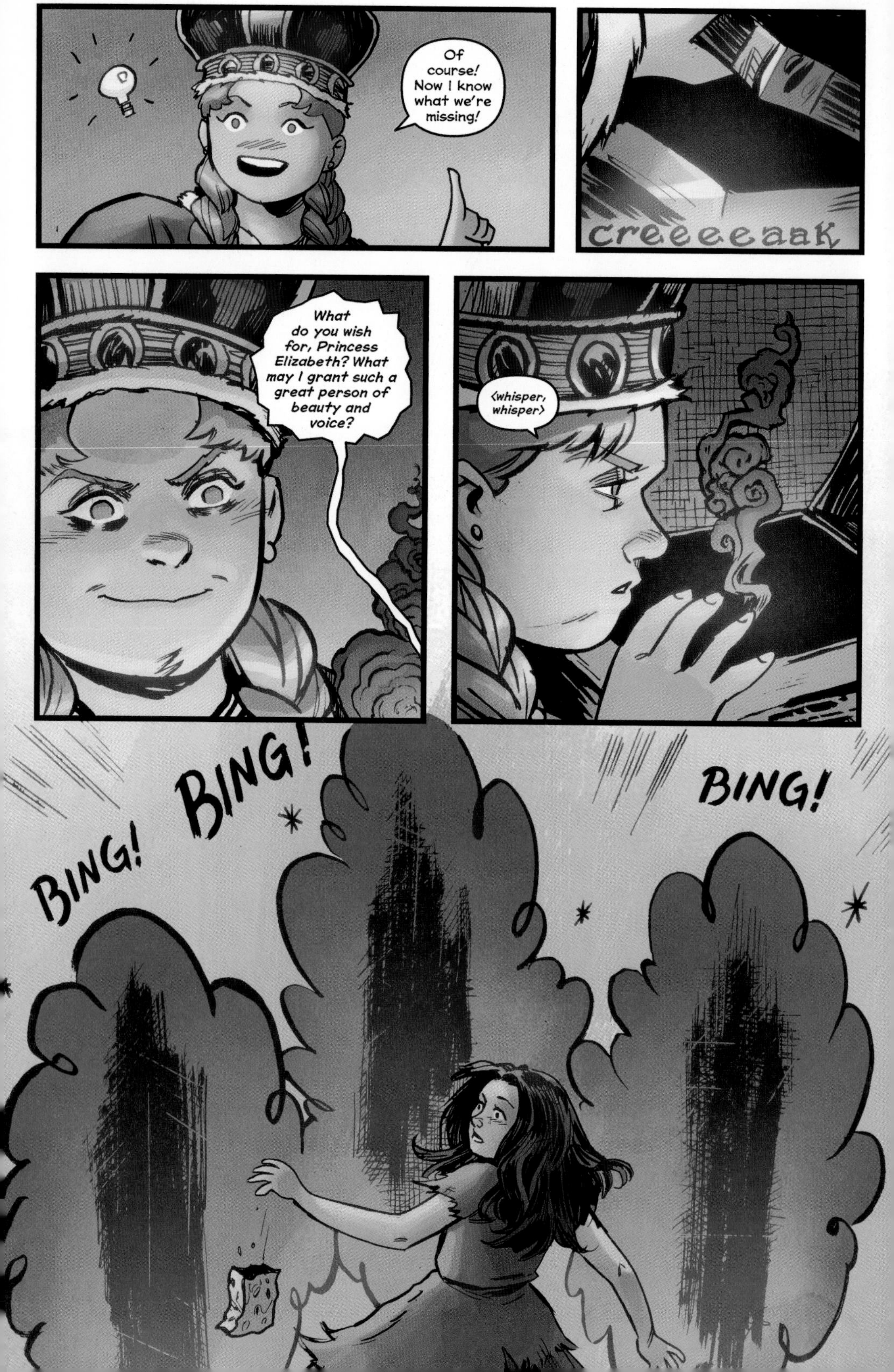

Of course! Now I know what we're missing!
creeeeaak
What do you wish for, Princess Elizabeth? What may I grant such a great person of beauty and voice?
<whisper, whisper>
BING!
BING!
BING!

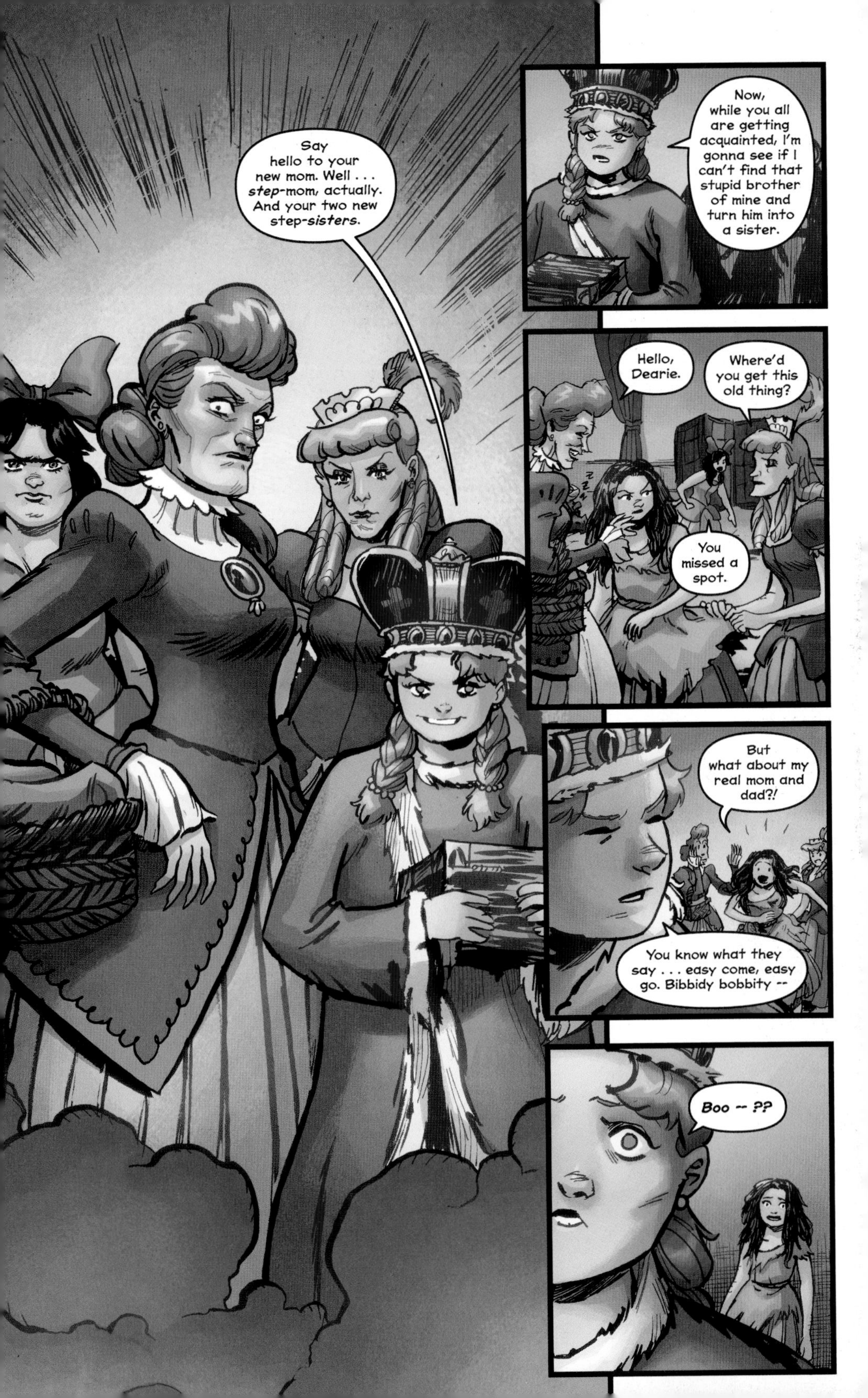
Say hello to your new mom. Well . . . *step*-mom, actually. And your two new step-*sisters*.
Now, while you all are getting acquainted, I'm gonna see if I can't find that stupid brother of mine and turn him into a sister.
Hello, Dearie.
Where'd you get this old thing?
You missed a spot.
But what about my real mom and dad?!
You know what they say . . . easy come, easy go. Bibbidy bobbity --
Boo -- ??

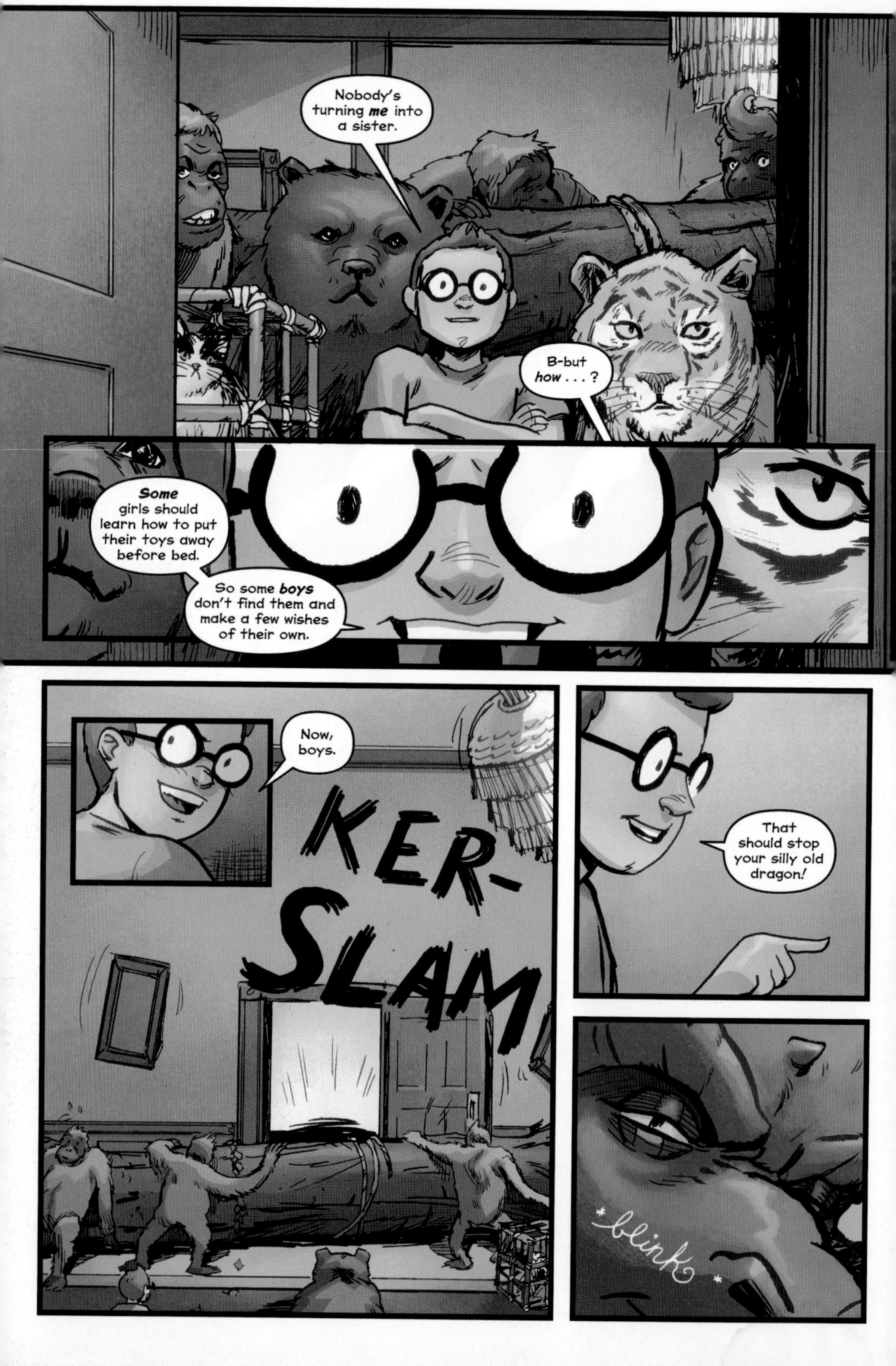
Nobody's turning *me* into a sister.
B-but *how . . .*?
Some girls should learn how to put their toys away before bed.
So some ***boys*** don't find them and make a few wishes of their own.
Now, boys.
KER-SLAM
That should stop your silly old dragon!
blink

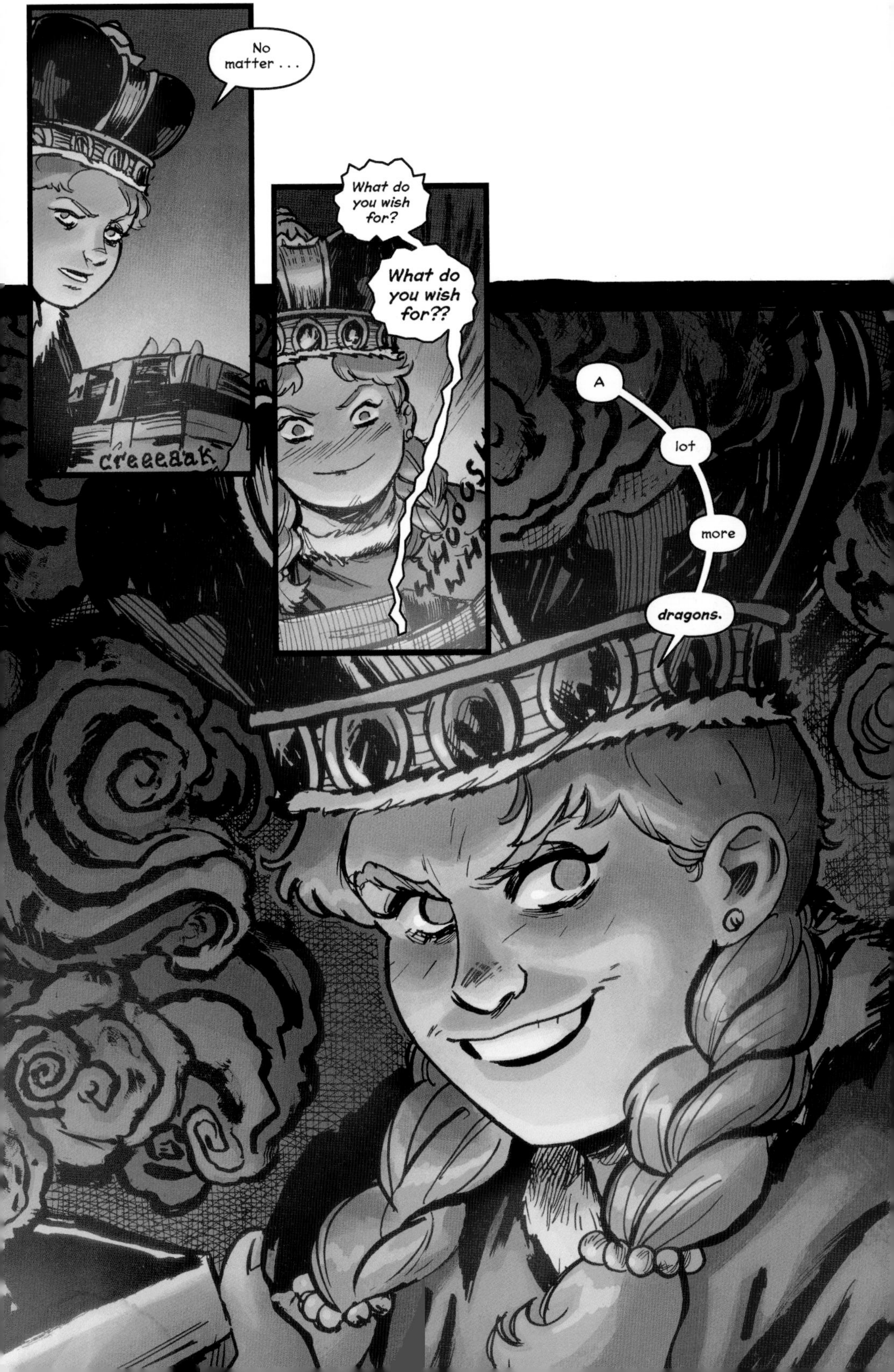
No matter . . .
creeeaak
What do you wish for?
What do you wish for??
A lot more dragons.

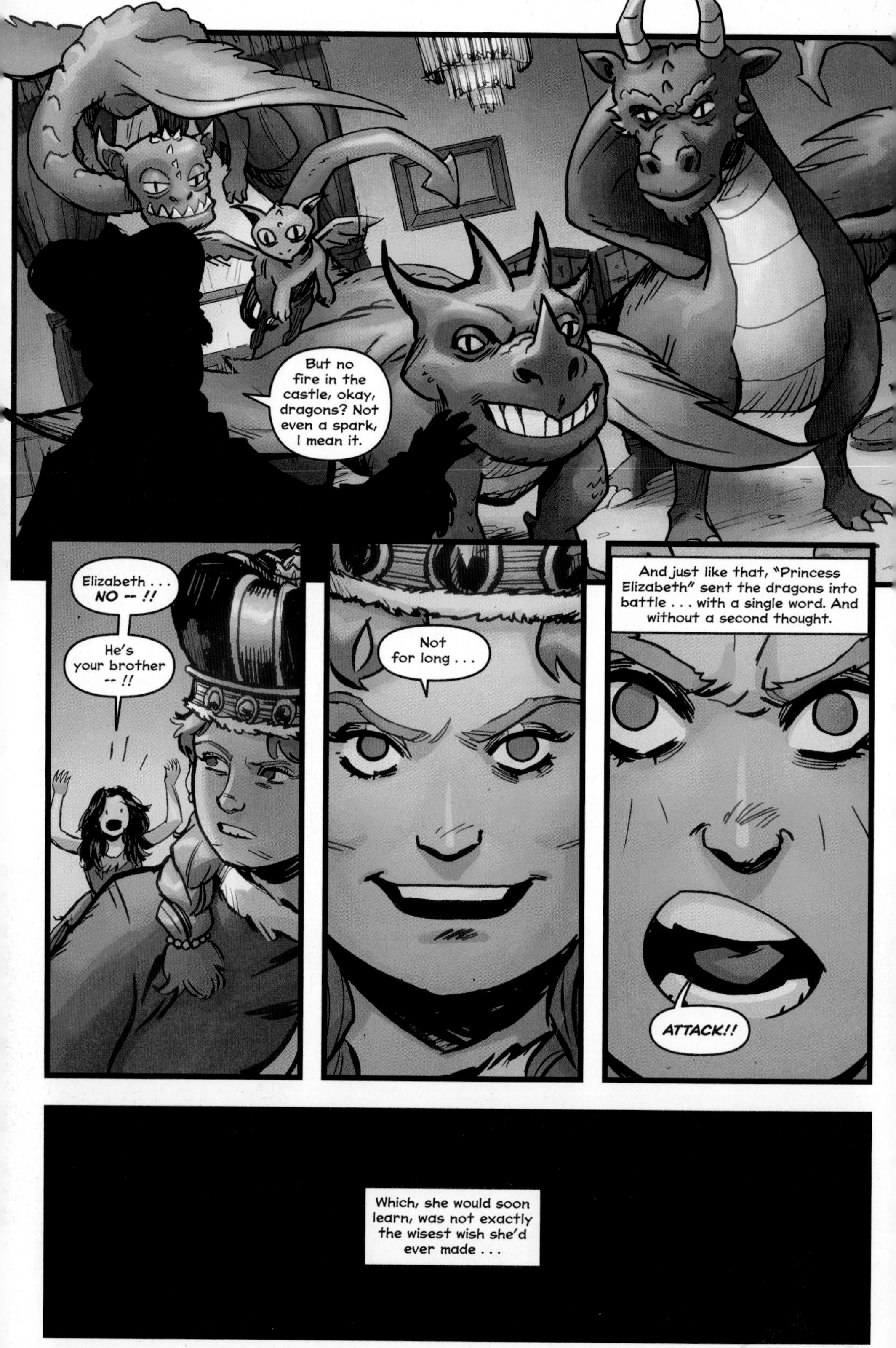
But no fire in the castle, okay, dragons? Not even a spark, I mean it.
Elizabeth . . . ***NO -- !!***
He's your brother -- !!
Not for long . . .
And just like that, "Princess Elizabeth" sent the dragons into battle . . . with a single word. And without a second thought.
ATTACK!!
Which, she would soon learn, was not exactly the wisest wish she'd ever made . . .

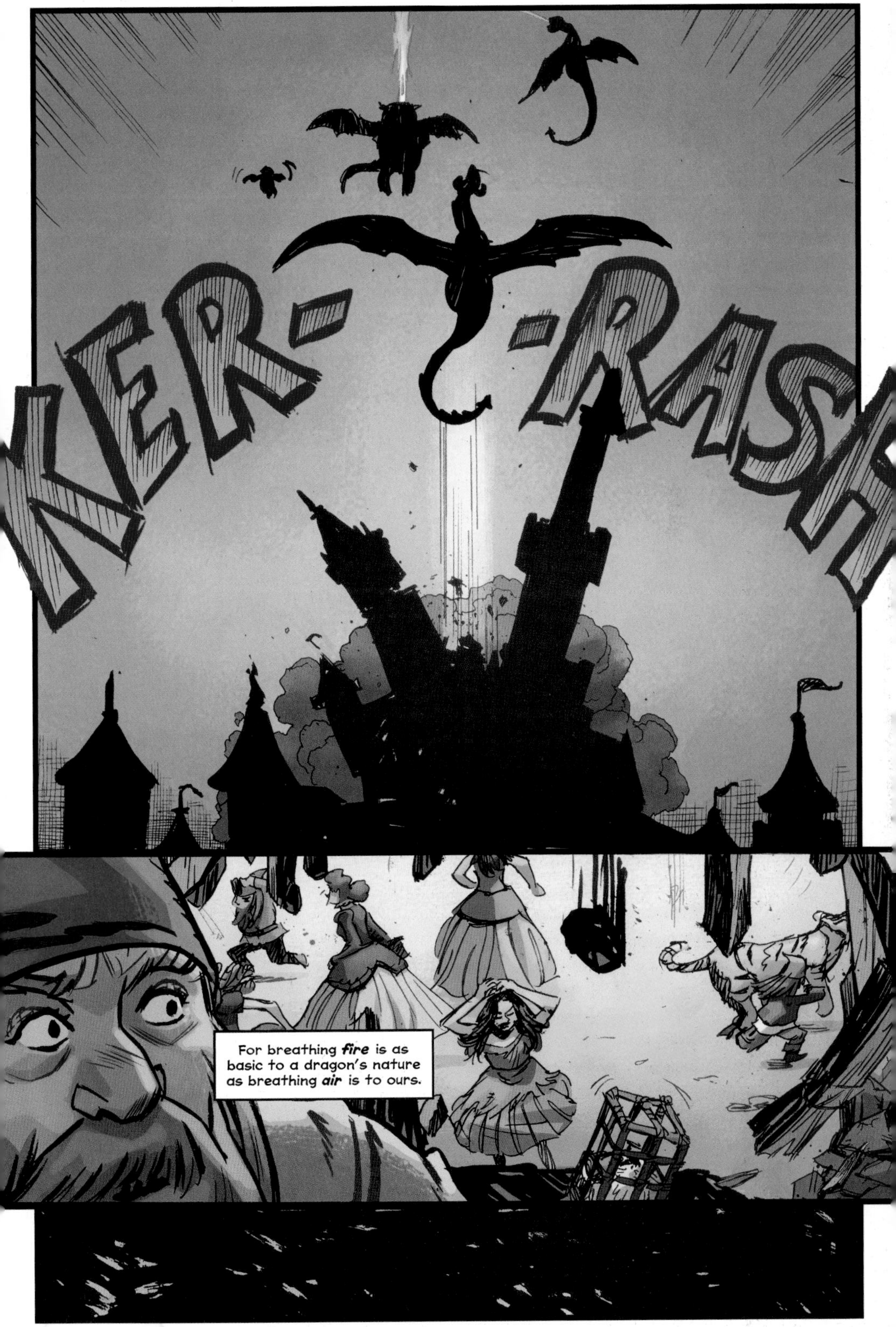
KER-
-RASH
For breathing *fire* is as basic to a dragon's nature as breathing *air* is to ours.

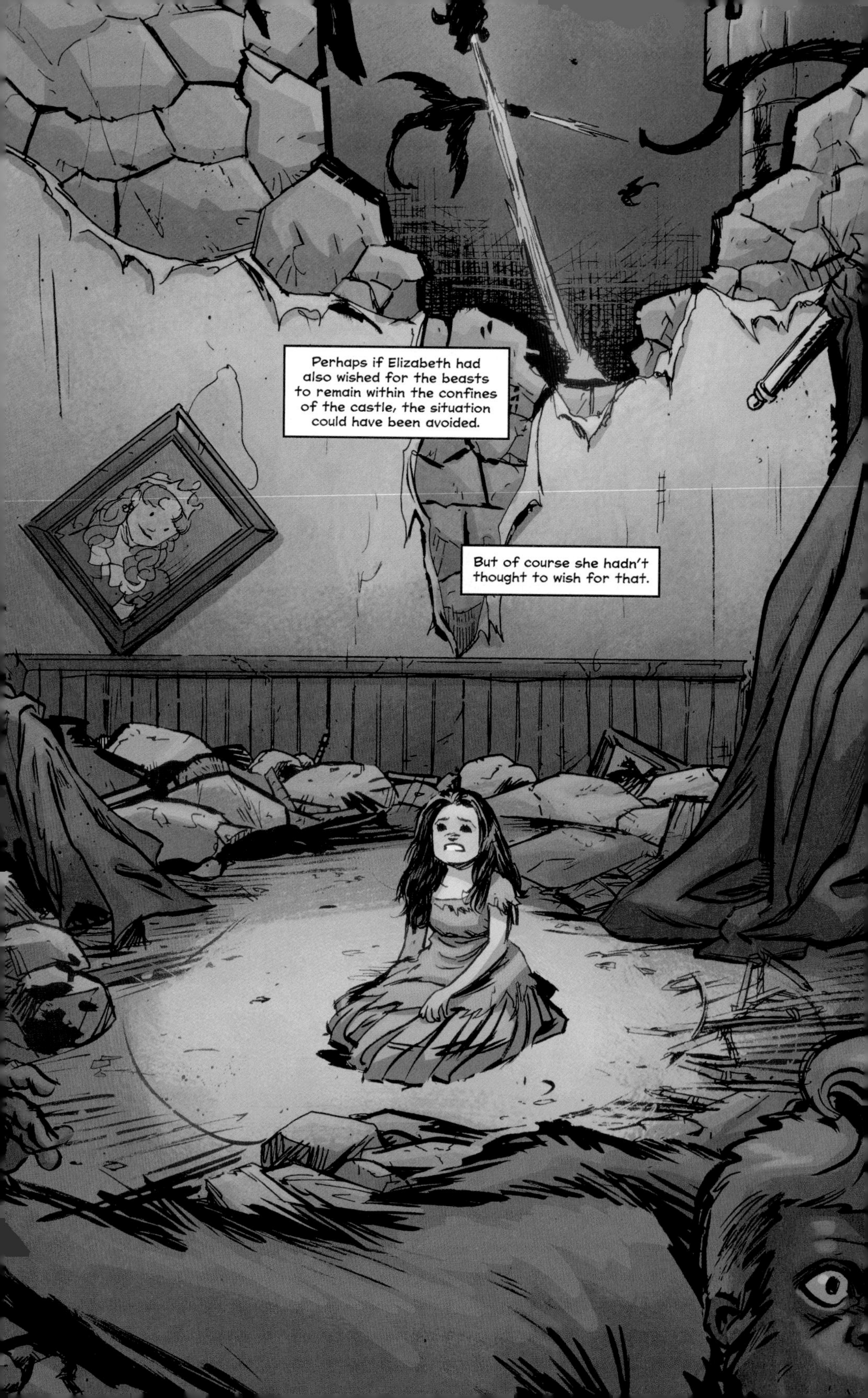
Perhaps if Elizabeth had also wished for the beasts to remain within the confines of the castle, the situation could have been avoided.
But of course she hadn't thought to wish for that.

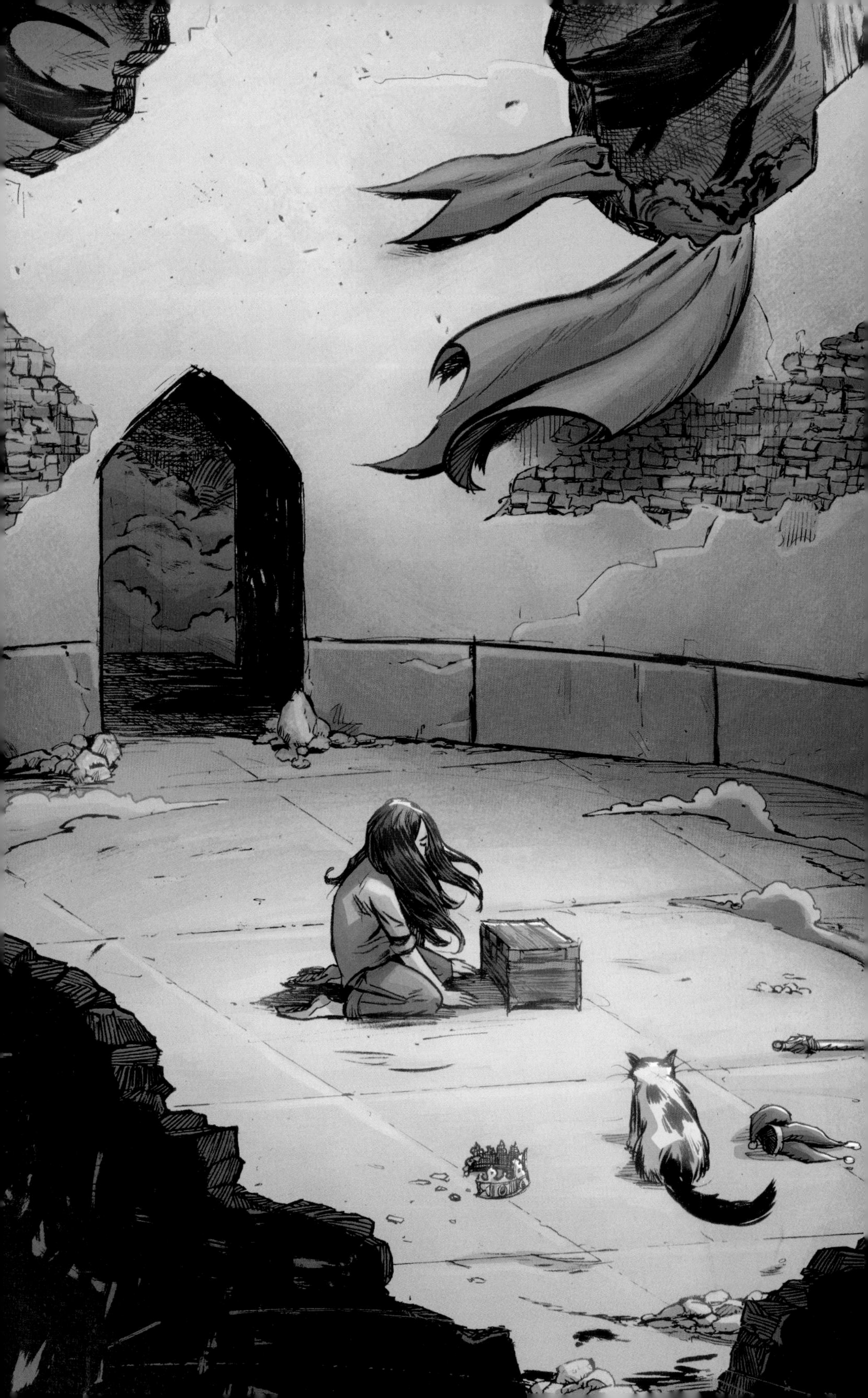

Chapter Five

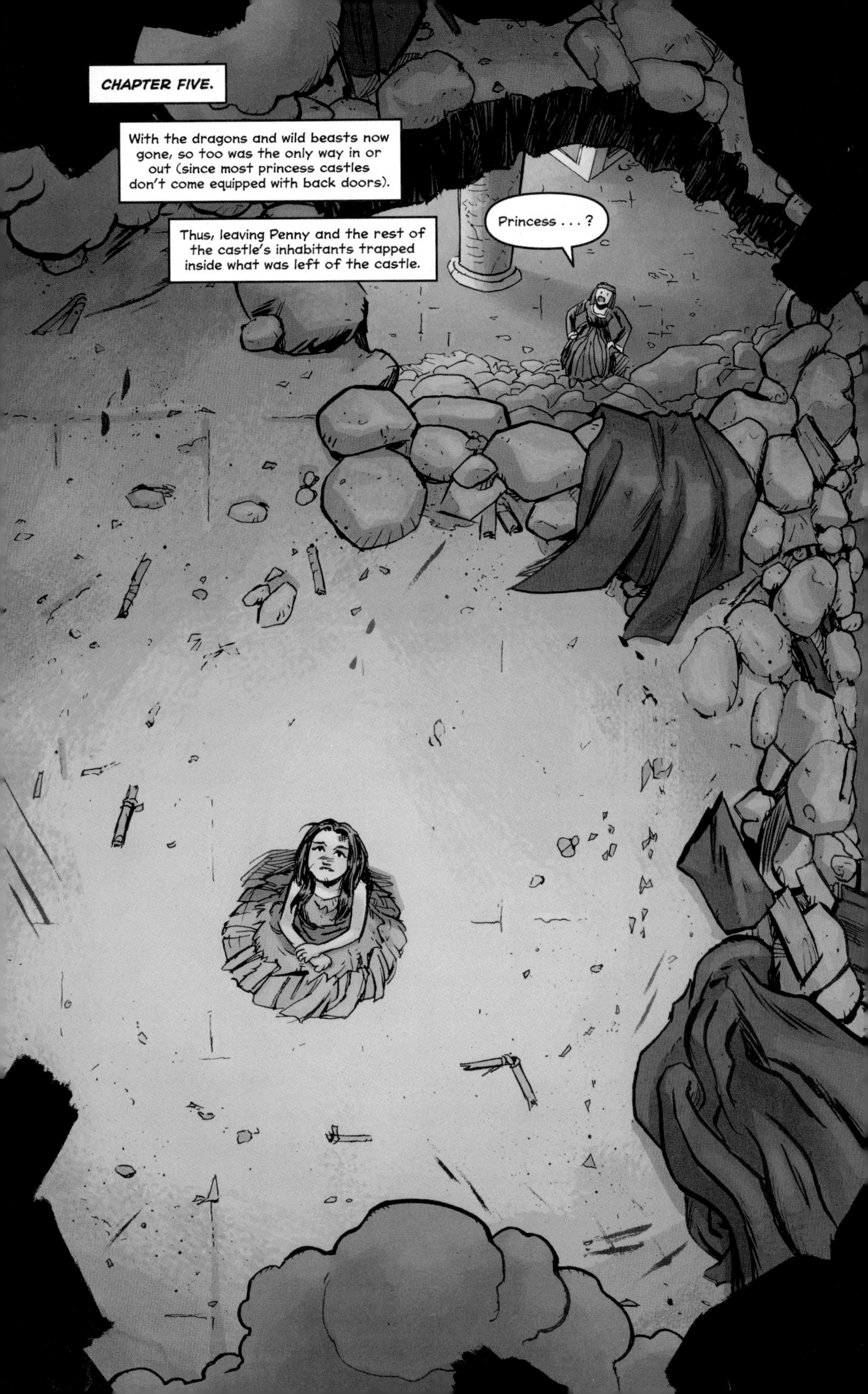
CHAPTER FIVE.
With the dragons and wild beasts now gone, so too was the only way in or out (since most princess castles don't come equipped with back doors).
Thus, leaving Penny and the rest of the castle's inhabitants trapped inside what was left of the castle.
Princess . . . ?

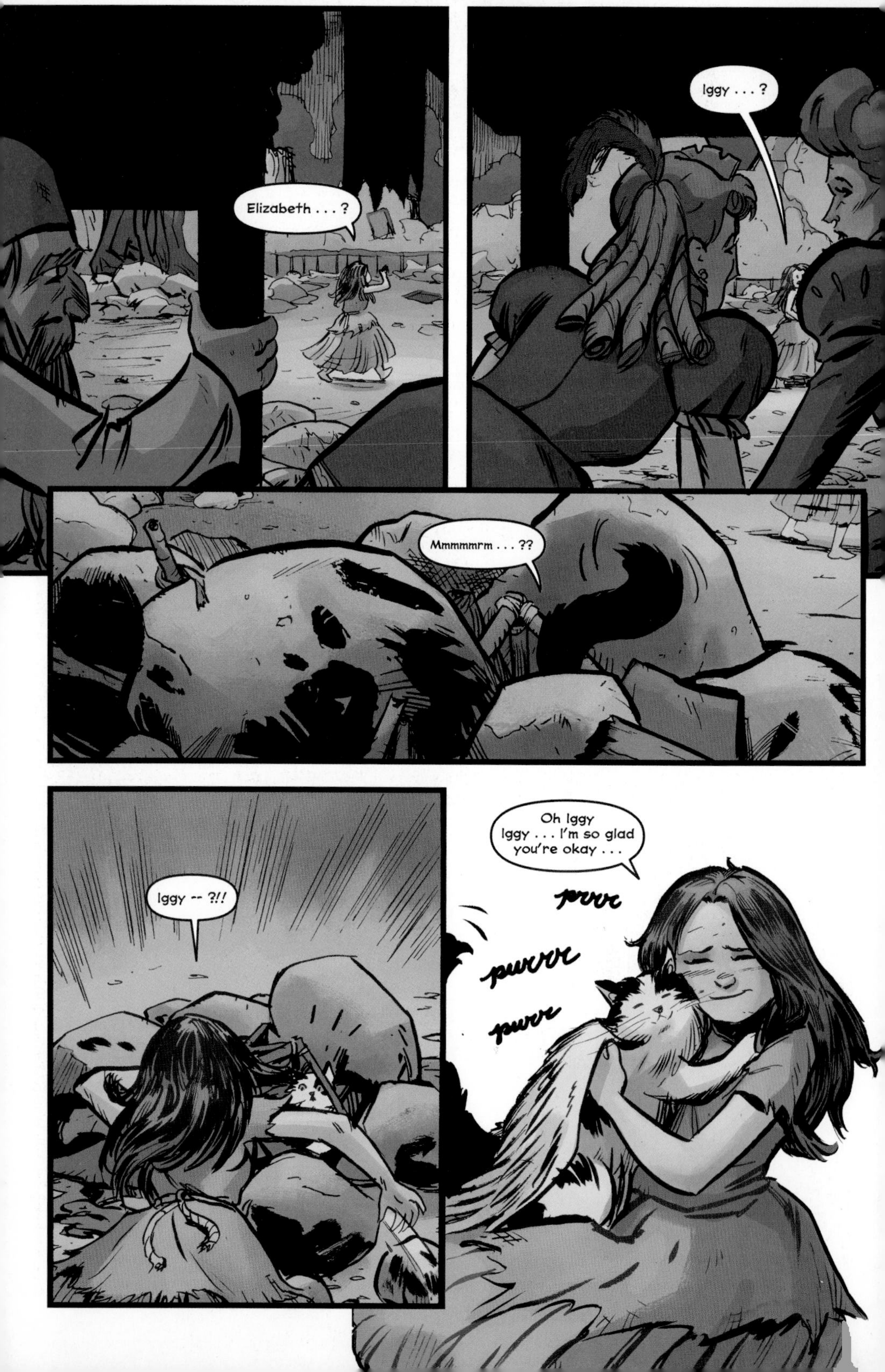
Elizabeth . . . ?
Iggy . . . ?
Mmmmmrm . . . ??
Iggy -- ?!!
Oh Iggy
Iggy . . . I'm so glad
you're okay . . .
prrr
purrr
purr

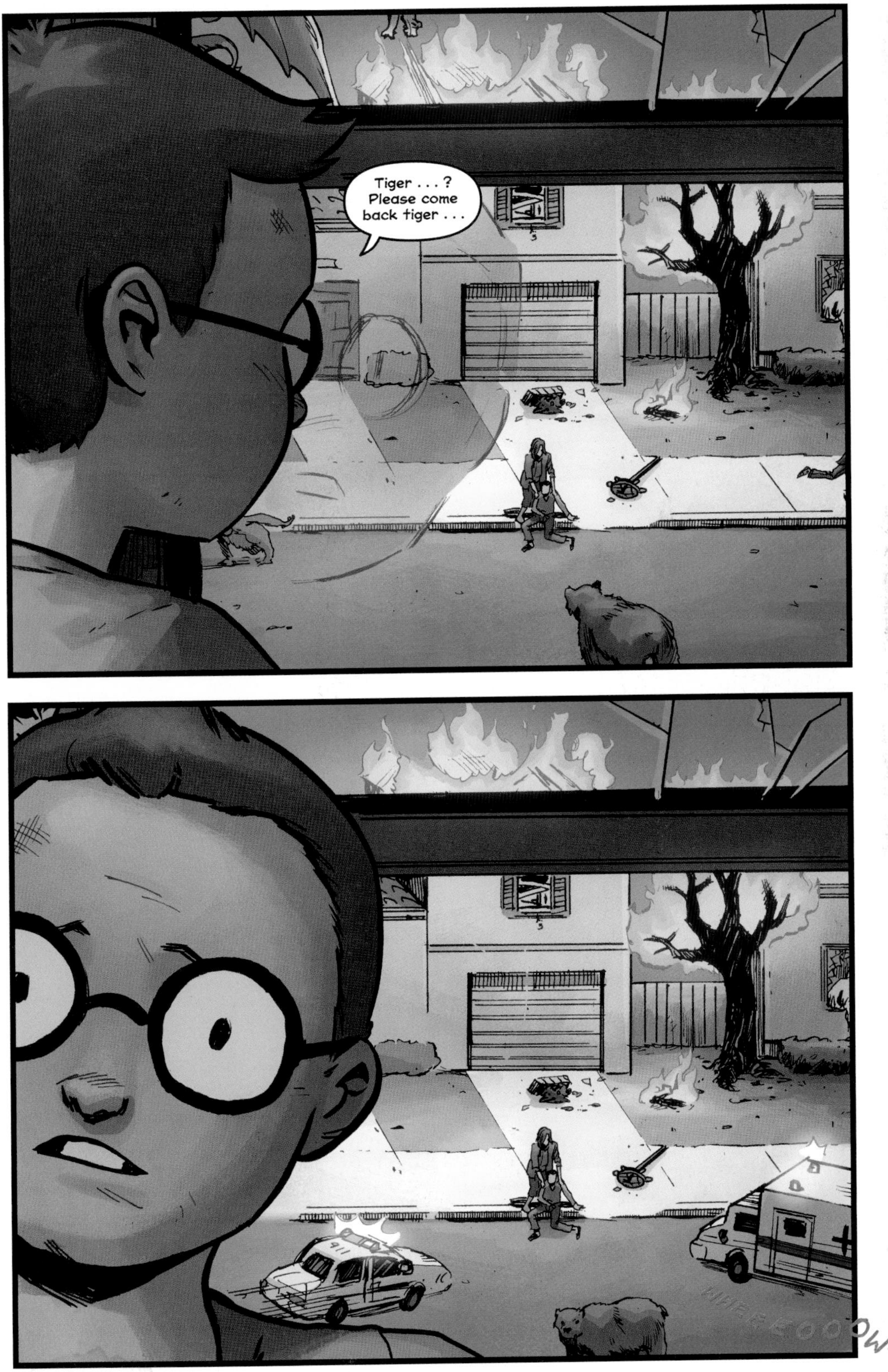
Tiger . . . ? Please come back tiger . . .
WHEEOOOOW

WHEEEOOO WHEEEOOH

Ngggghhhhhhh . . .

Mooooom . . . ?

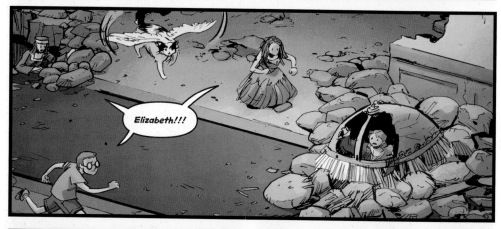

Elizabeth!!!

Omigosh, are you all right . . . ??

Where . . .

Where is it . . . ??

Where, is what, honey??

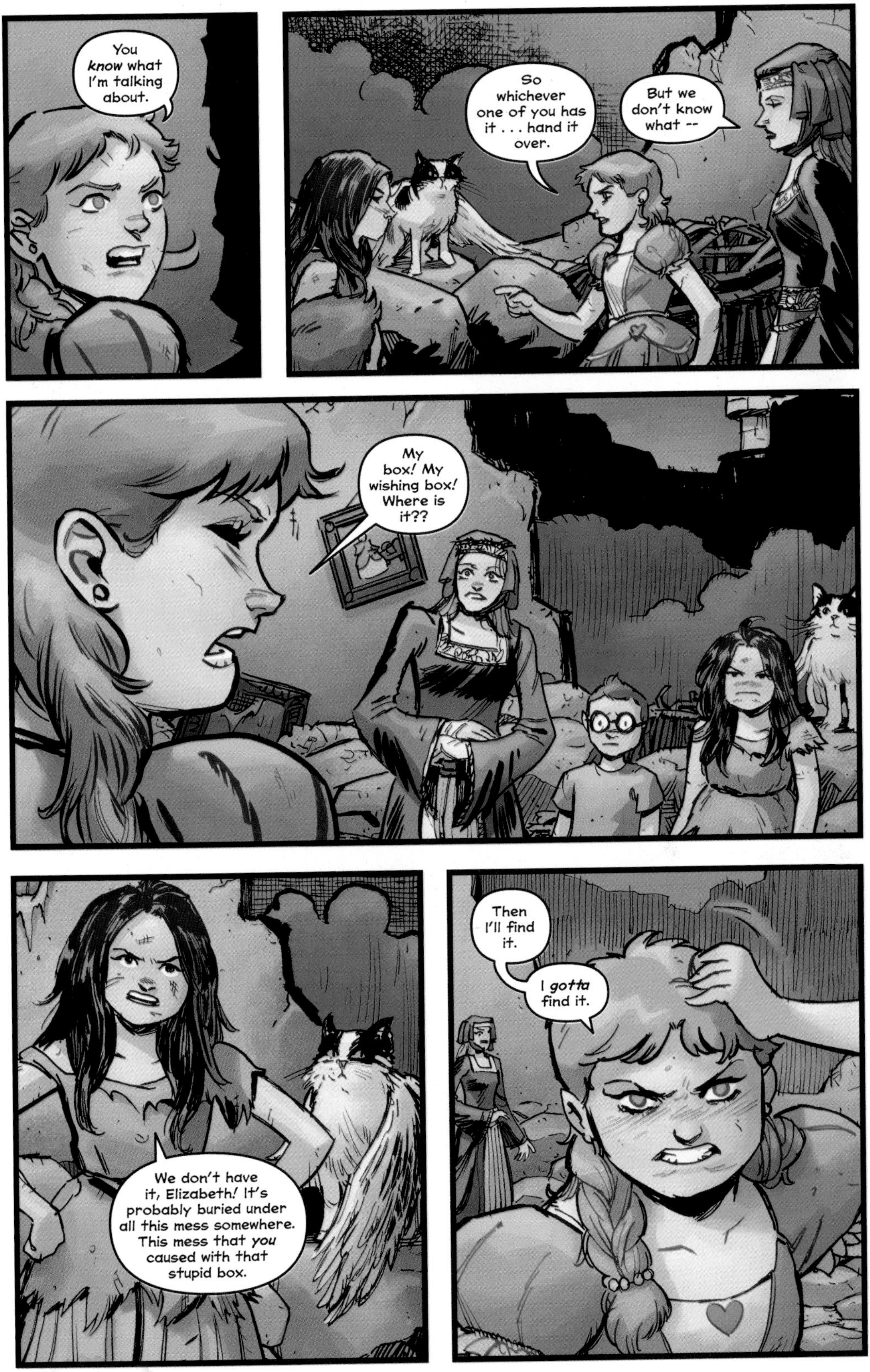
You *know* what I'm talking about.
So whichever one of you has it . . . hand it over.
But we don't know what --
My box! My wishing box! Where is it??
We don't have it, Elizabeth! It's probably buried under all this mess somewhere. This mess that *you* caused with that stupid box.
Then I'll find it.
I *gotta* find it.

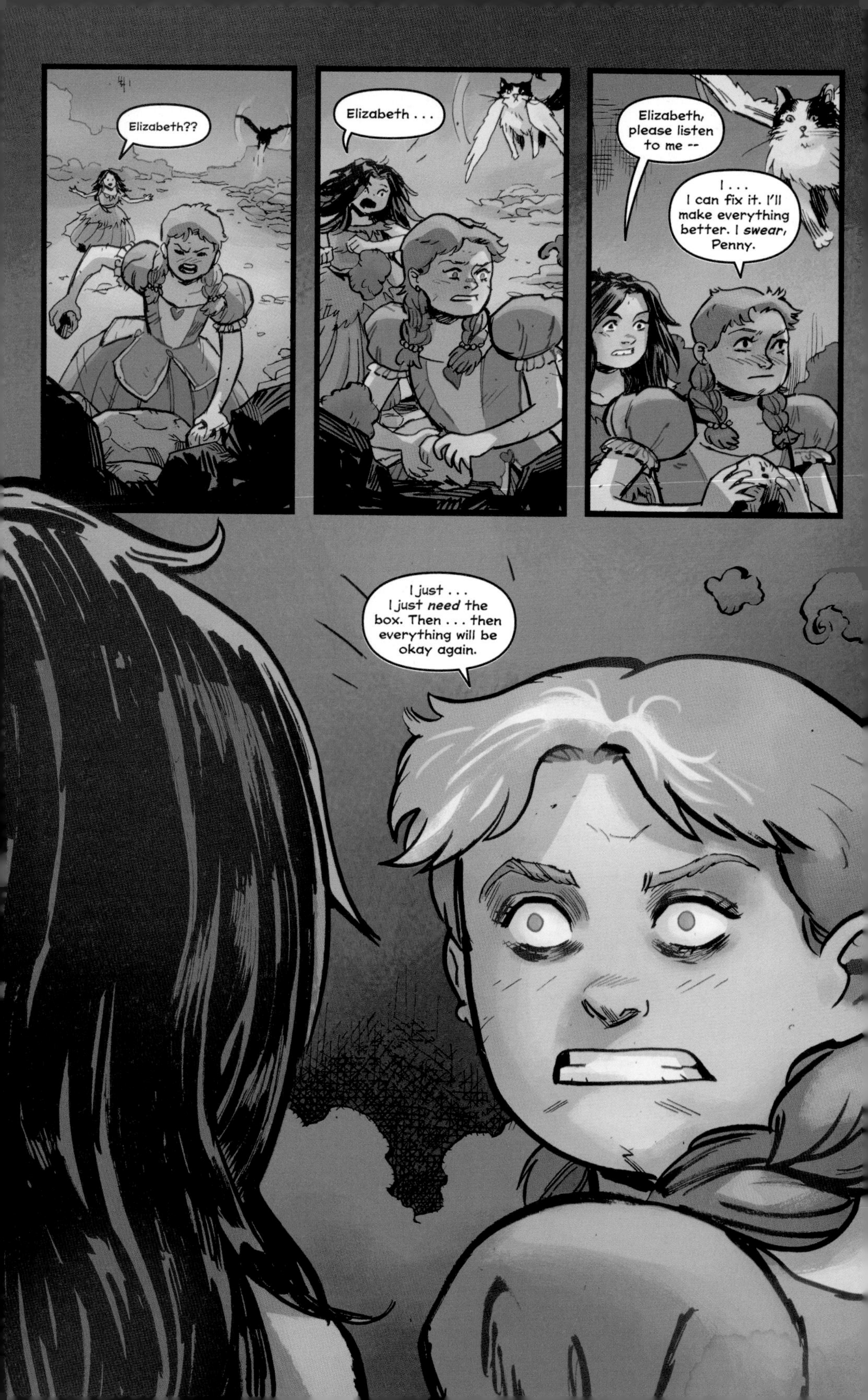
Elizabeth??
Elizabeth . . .
Elizabeth, please listen to me --
I . . . I can fix it. I'll make everything better. I *swear*, Penny.
I just . . . I just *need* the box. Then . . . then everything will be okay again.

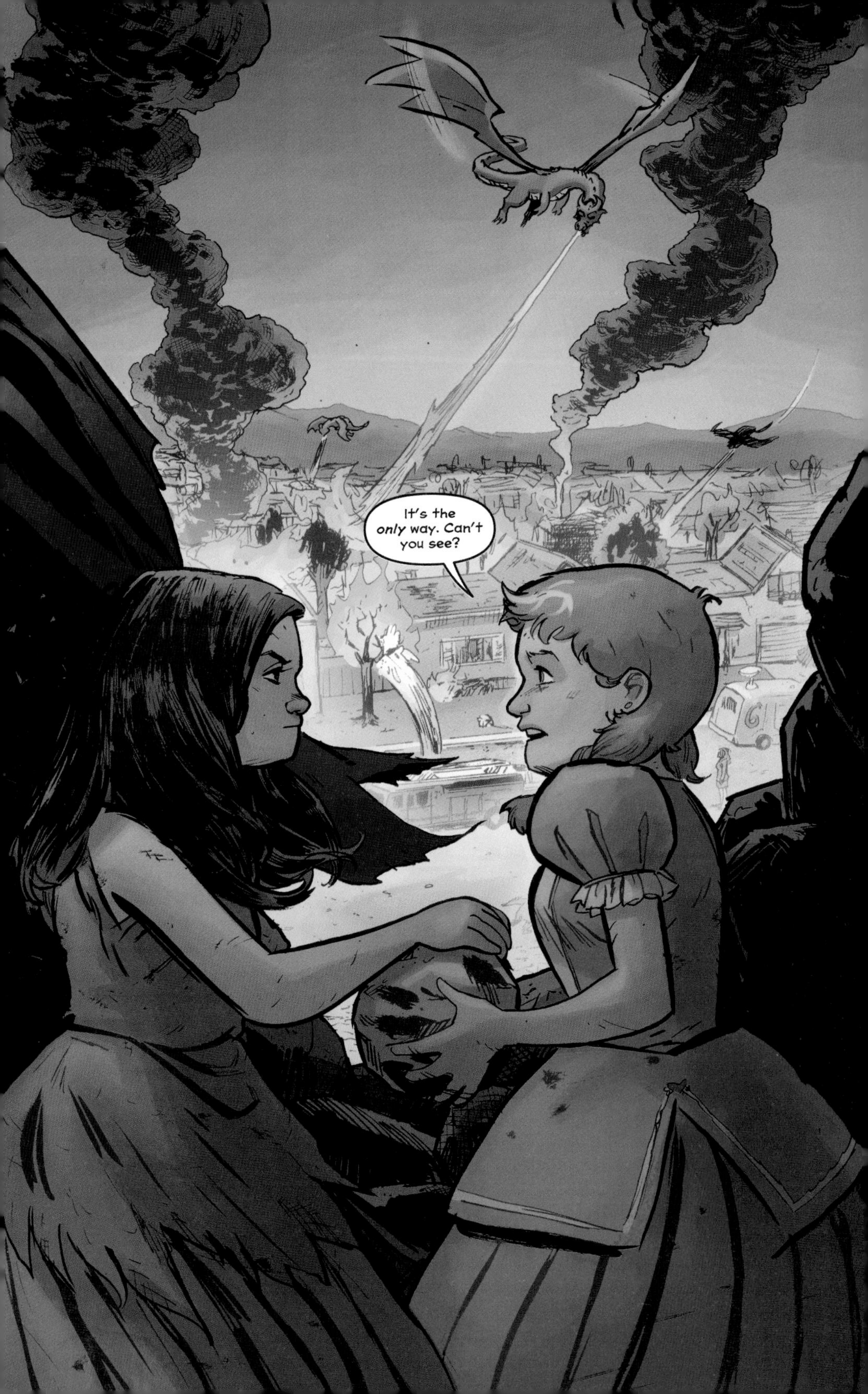
It's the *only* way. Can't you see?

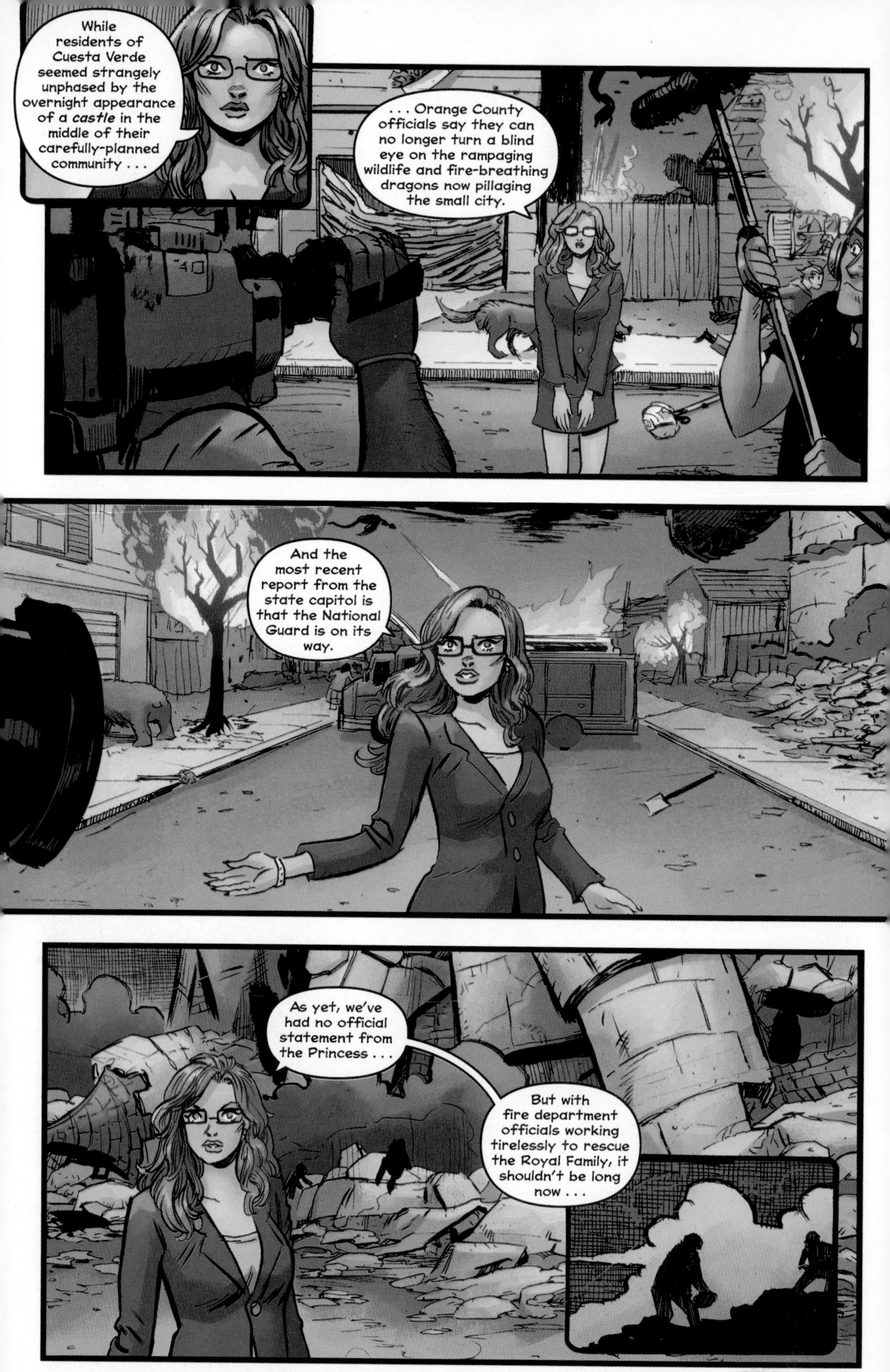

While residents of Cuesta Verde seemed strangely unphased by the overnight appearance of a *castle* in the middle of their carefully-planned community . . .
. . . Orange County officials say they can no longer turn a blind eye on the rampaging wildlife and fire-breathing dragons now pillaging the small city.
And the most recent report from the state capitol is that the National Guard is on its way.
As yet, we've had no official statement from the Princess . . .
But with fire department officials working tirelessly to rescue the Royal Family, it shouldn't be long now . . .

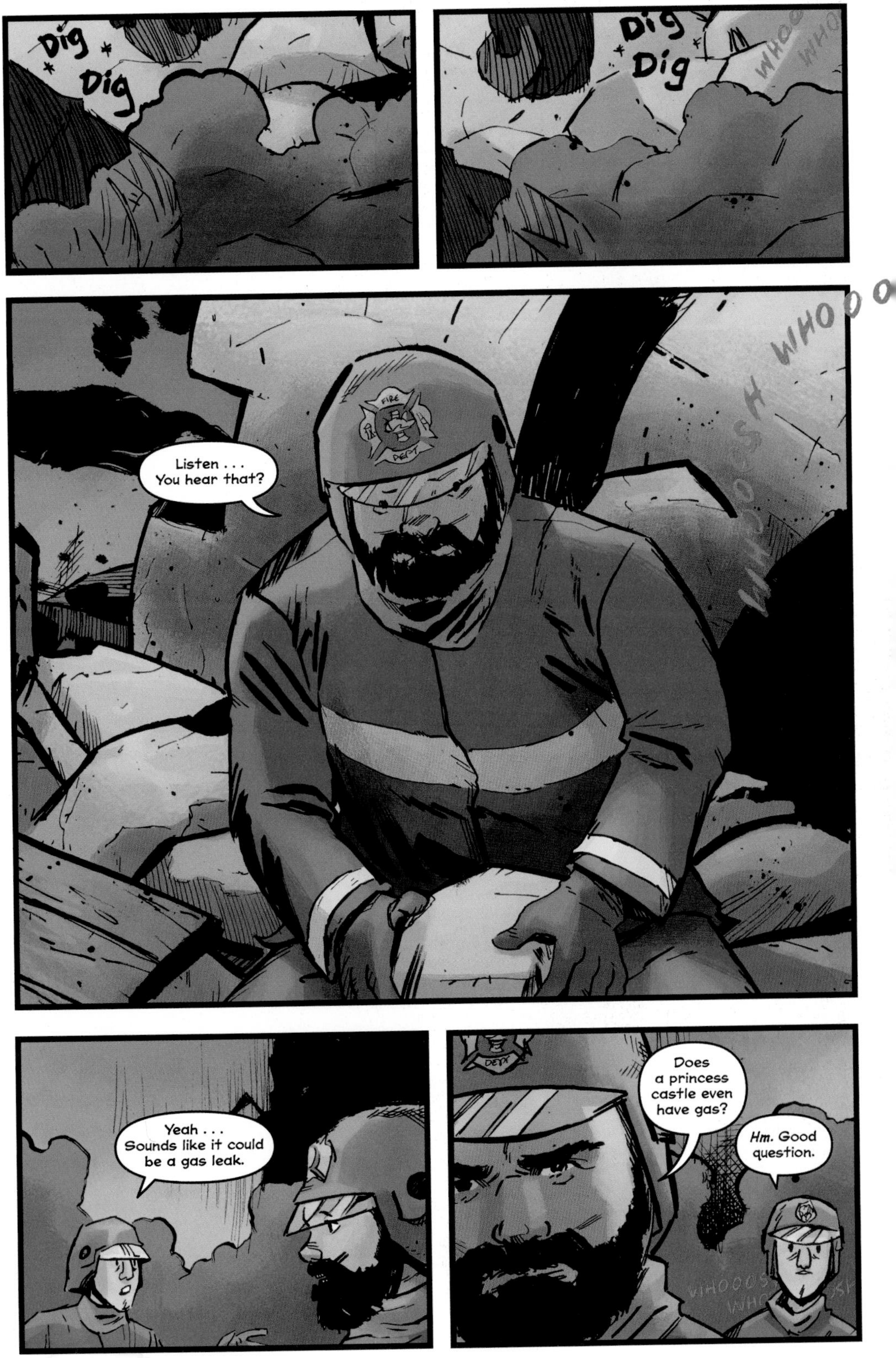
Dig Dig
Dig Dig
Listen . . . You hear that?
WHOOOSH WHOOO
Yeah . . . Sounds like it could be a gas leak.
Does a princess castle even have gas?
Hm. Good question.

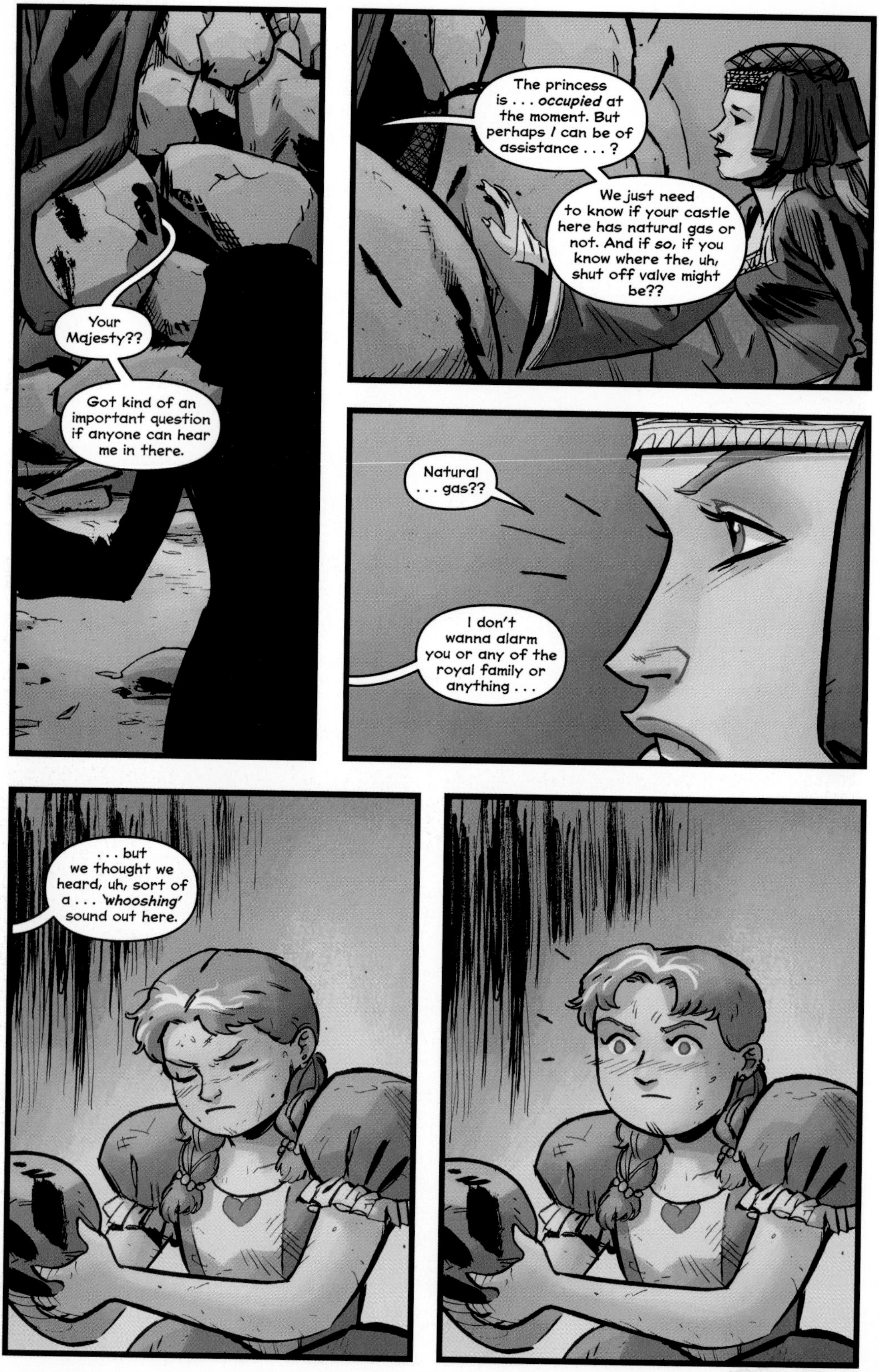
Your Majesty??
Got kind of an important question if anyone can hear me in there.
The princess is . . . *occupied* at the moment. But perhaps I can be of assistance . . . ?
We just need to know if your castle here has natural gas or not. And if *so*, if you know where the, uh, shut off valve might be??
Natural . . . gas??
I don't wanna alarm you or any of the royal family or anything . . .
. . . but we thought we heard, uh, sort of a . . . *'whooshing'* sound out here.

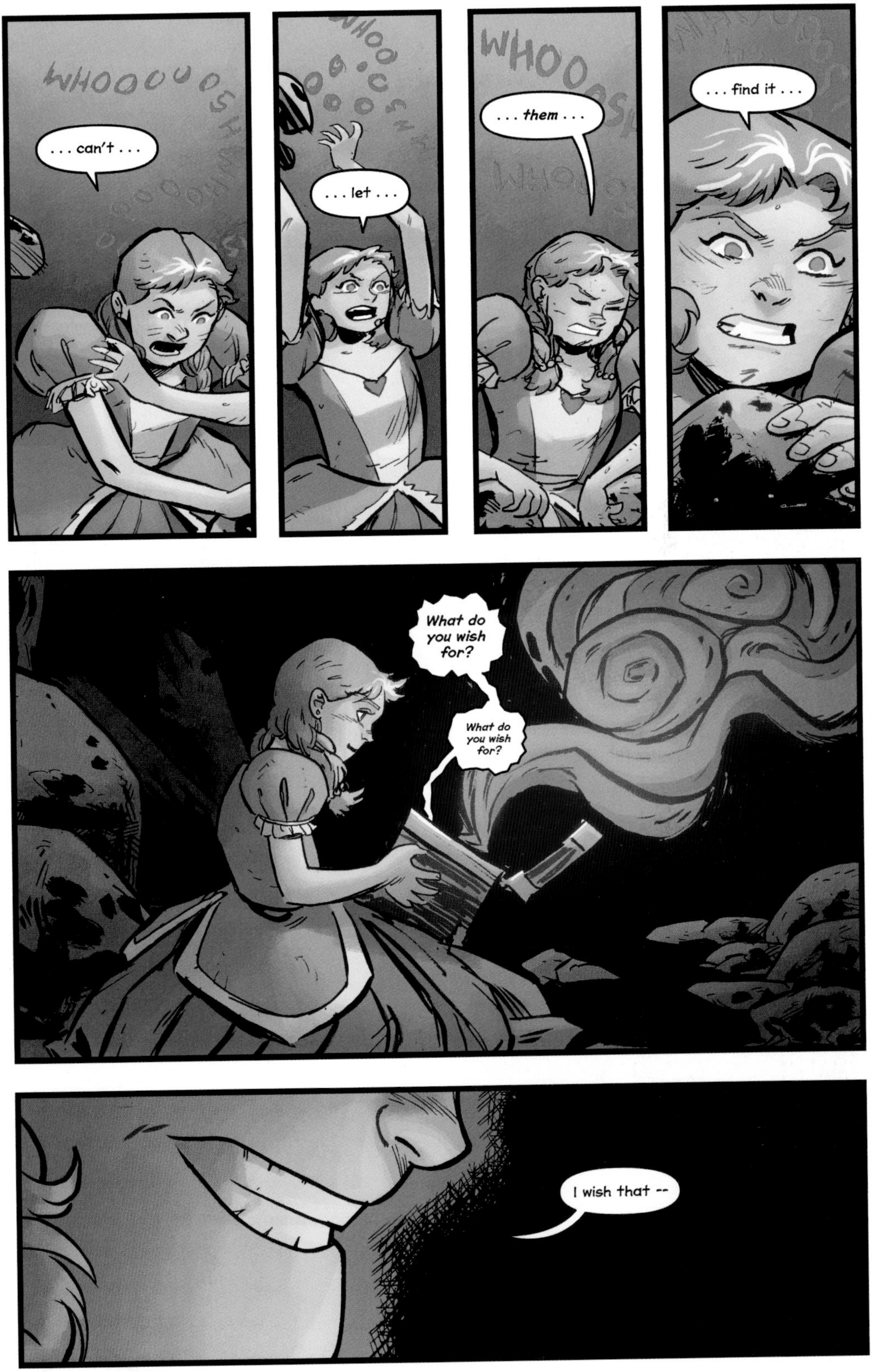
WHOOOUUOSH
. . . can't . . .
WHOOOOSH
. . . let . . .
WHOOOSH
. . . them . . .
WHOOSH
. . . find it . . .
What do you wish for?
What do you wish for?
I wish that --

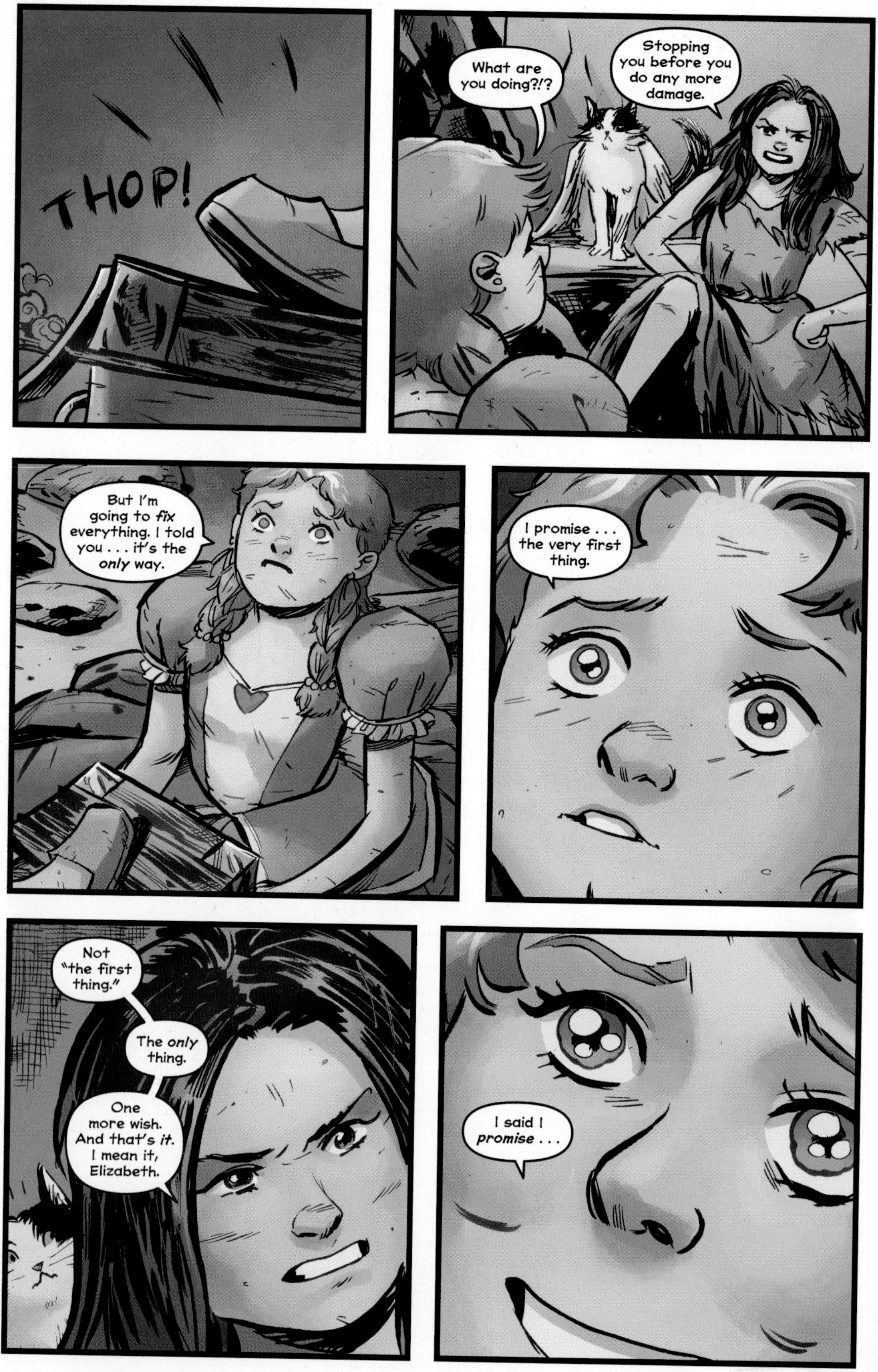
THOP!
What are you doing?!?
Stopping you before you do any more damage.
But I'm going to *fix* everything. I told you . . . it's the *only* way.
I promise . . . the very first thing.
Not "the first thing."
The *only* thing.
One more wish. And that's *it*. I mean it, Elizabeth.
I said I *promise* . . .

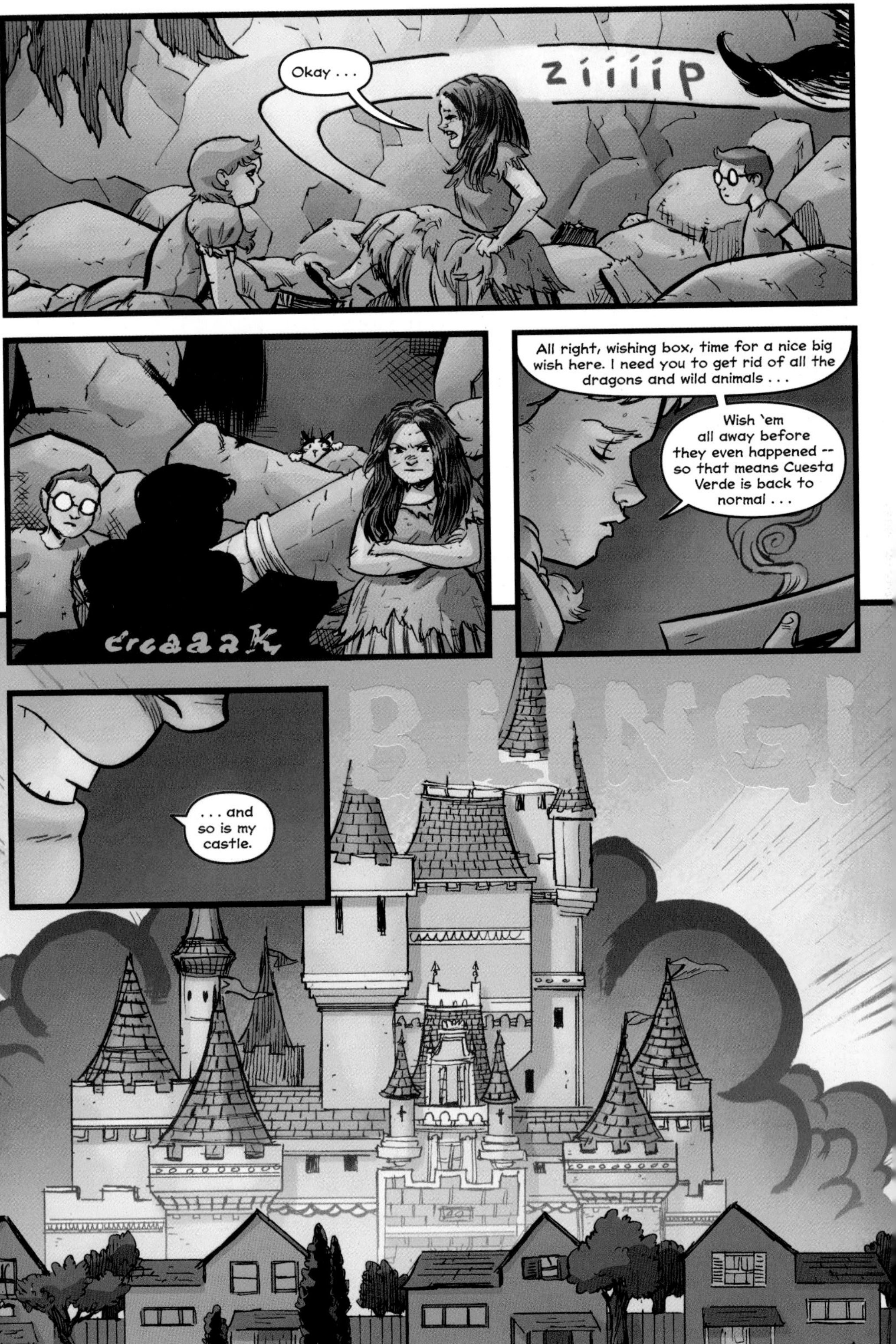
Okay . . .
ziiiip
crcaaaK
All right, wishing box, time for a nice big wish here. I need you to get rid of all the dragons and wild animals . . .
Wish 'em all away before they even happened -- so that means Cuesta Verde is back to normal . . .
. . . and so is my castle.

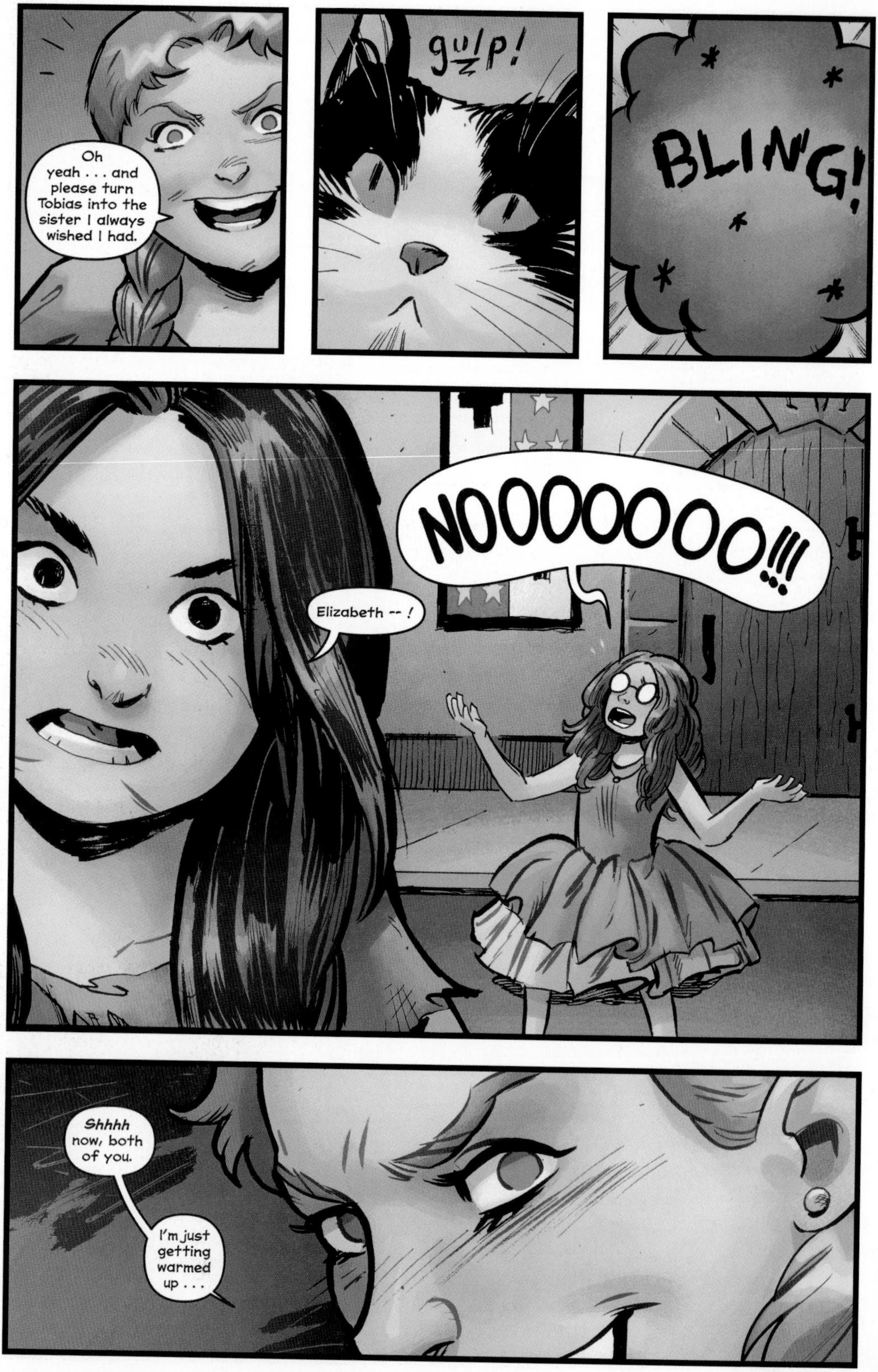
Oh yeah . . . and please turn Tobias into the sister I always wished I had.
gulp!
BLING!
NOOOOOOO!!!
Elizabeth -- !
Shhhh now, both of you.
I'm just getting warmed up . . .

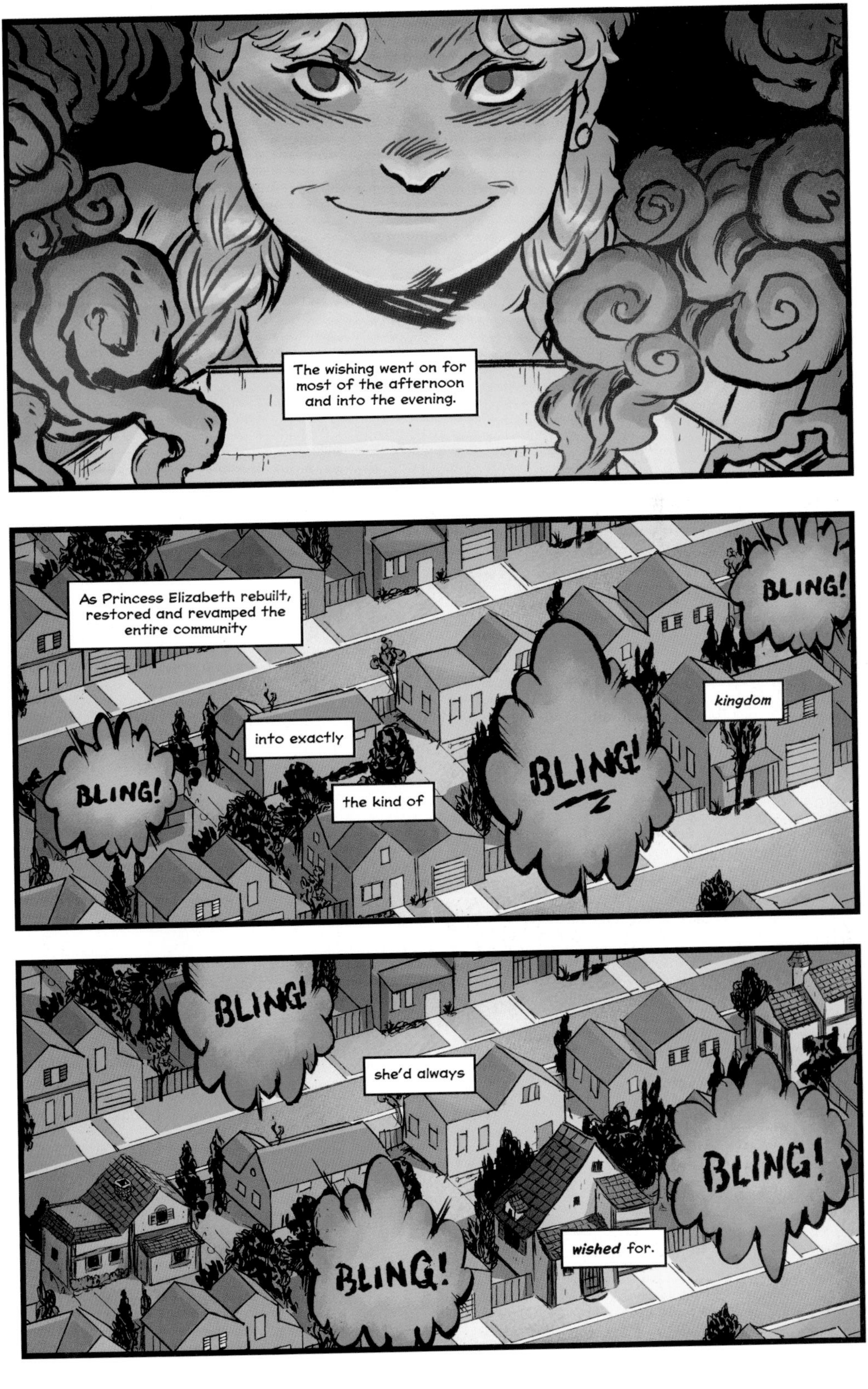
The wishing went on for most of the afternoon and into the evening.
As Princess Elizabeth rebuilt, restored and revamped the entire community
BLING!
into exactly
the kind of
BLING!
BLING!
kingdom
BLING!
she'd always
BLING!
BLING!
wished for.

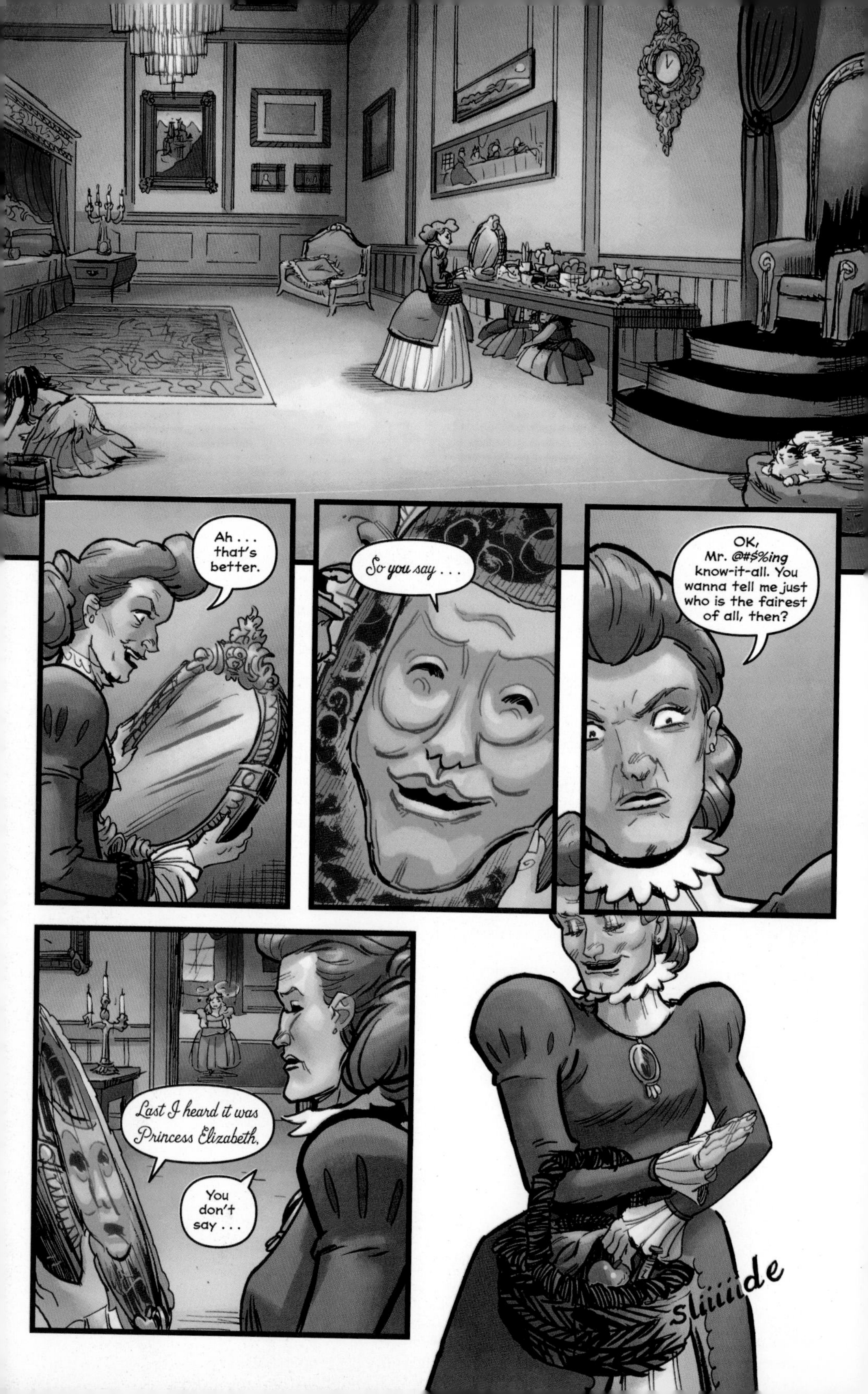

Ah . . . that's better.
So you say . . .
OK, Mr. @#$%ing know-it-all. You wanna tell me just who is the fairest of all, then?
Last I heard it was Princess Elizabeth.
You don't say . . .
Sliiiiide

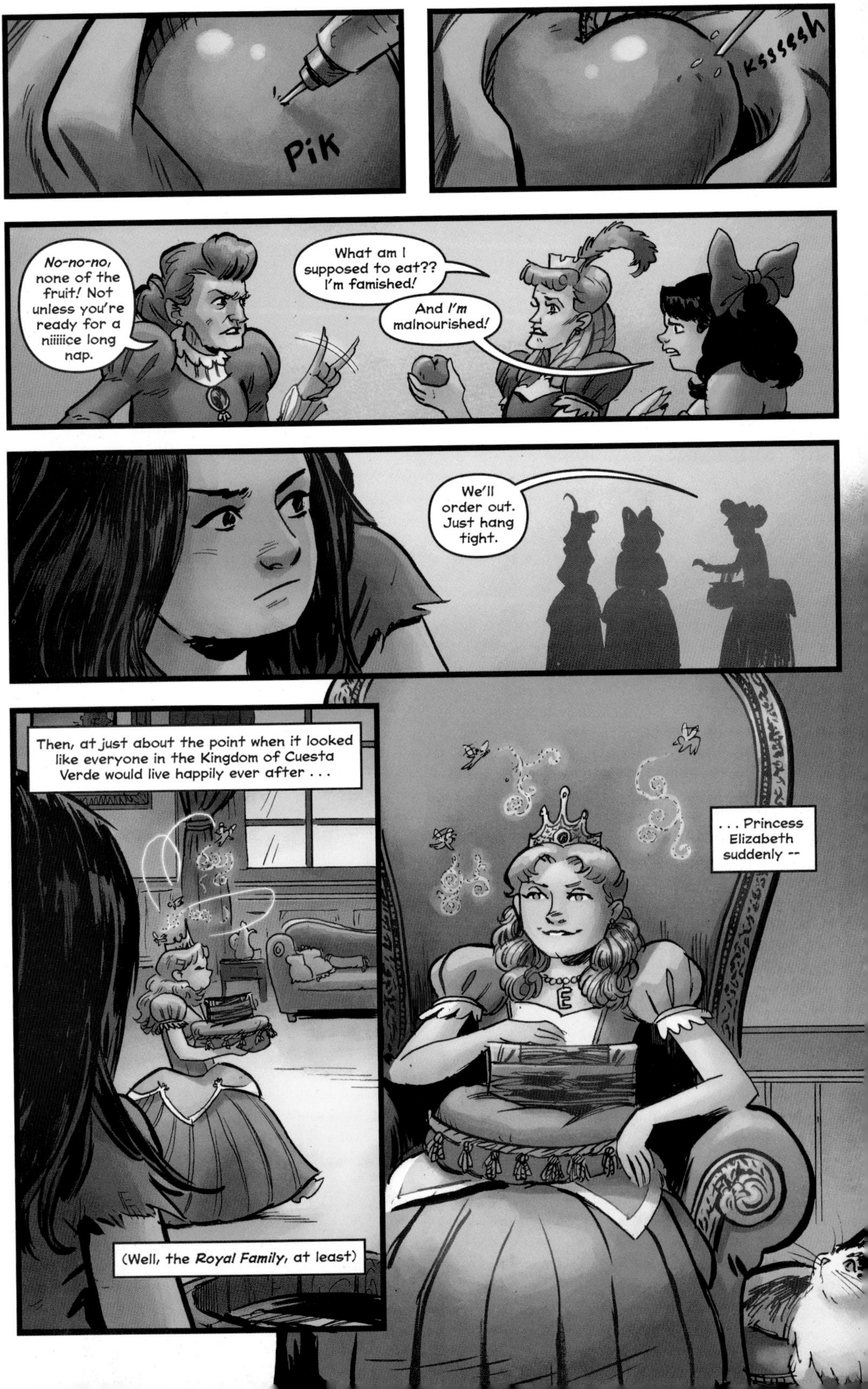
PiK
Ksssssh
No-no-no, none of the fruit! Not unless you're ready for a niiiiice long nap.
What am I supposed to eat?? I'm famished!
And *I'm* malnourished!
We'll order out. Just hang tight.
Then, at just about the point when it looked like everyone in the Kingdom of Cuesta Verde would live happily ever after . . .
(Well, the *Royal Family,* at least)
. . . Princess Elizabeth suddenly --
E

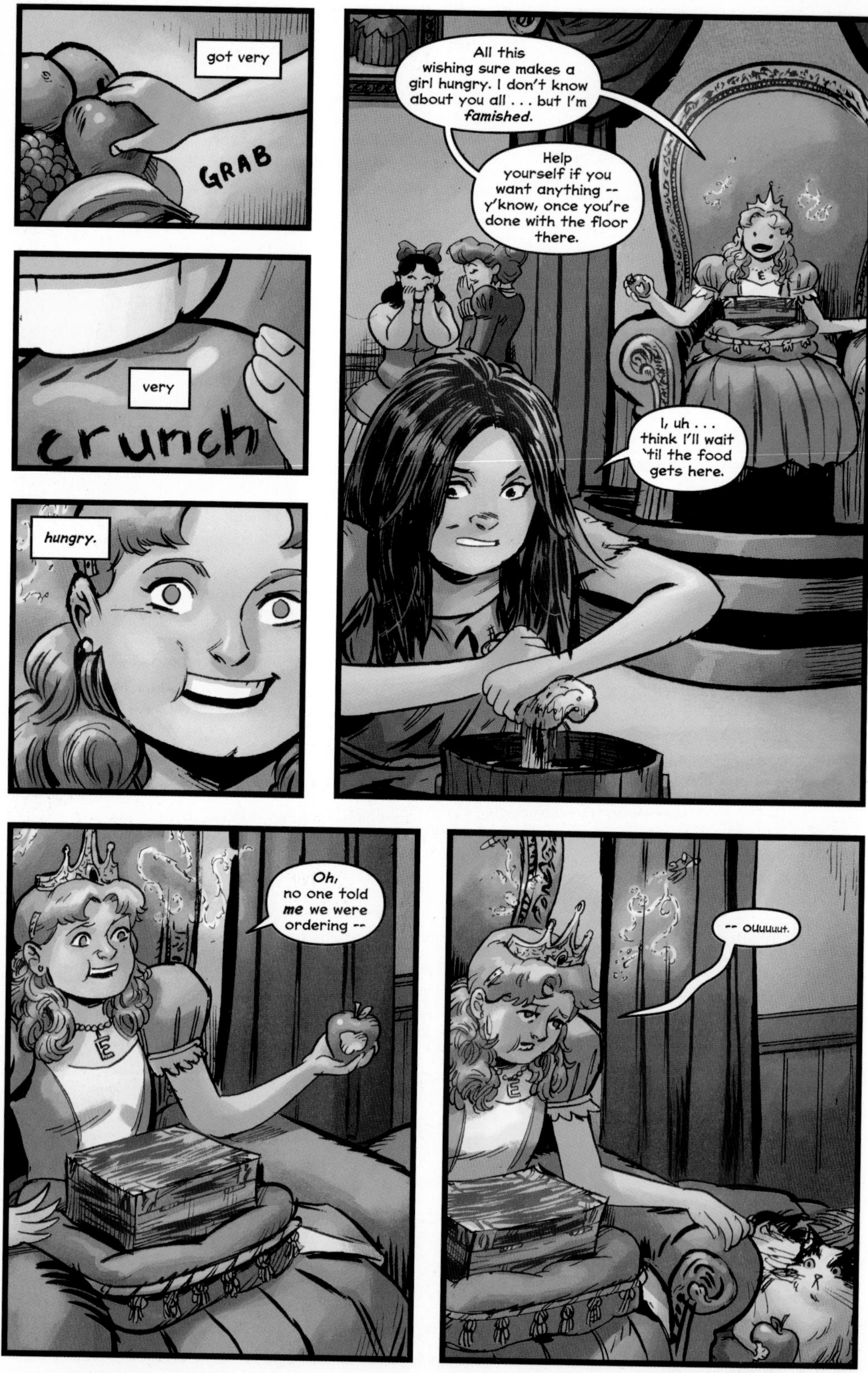
got very
GRAB
very
crunch
hungry.
All this wishing sure makes a girl hungry. I don't know about you all . . . but I'm *famished*.
Help yourself if you want anything -- y'know, once you're done with the floor there.
I, uh . . . think I'll wait 'til the food gets here.
Oh, no one told *me* we were ordering --
-- ouuuuut.

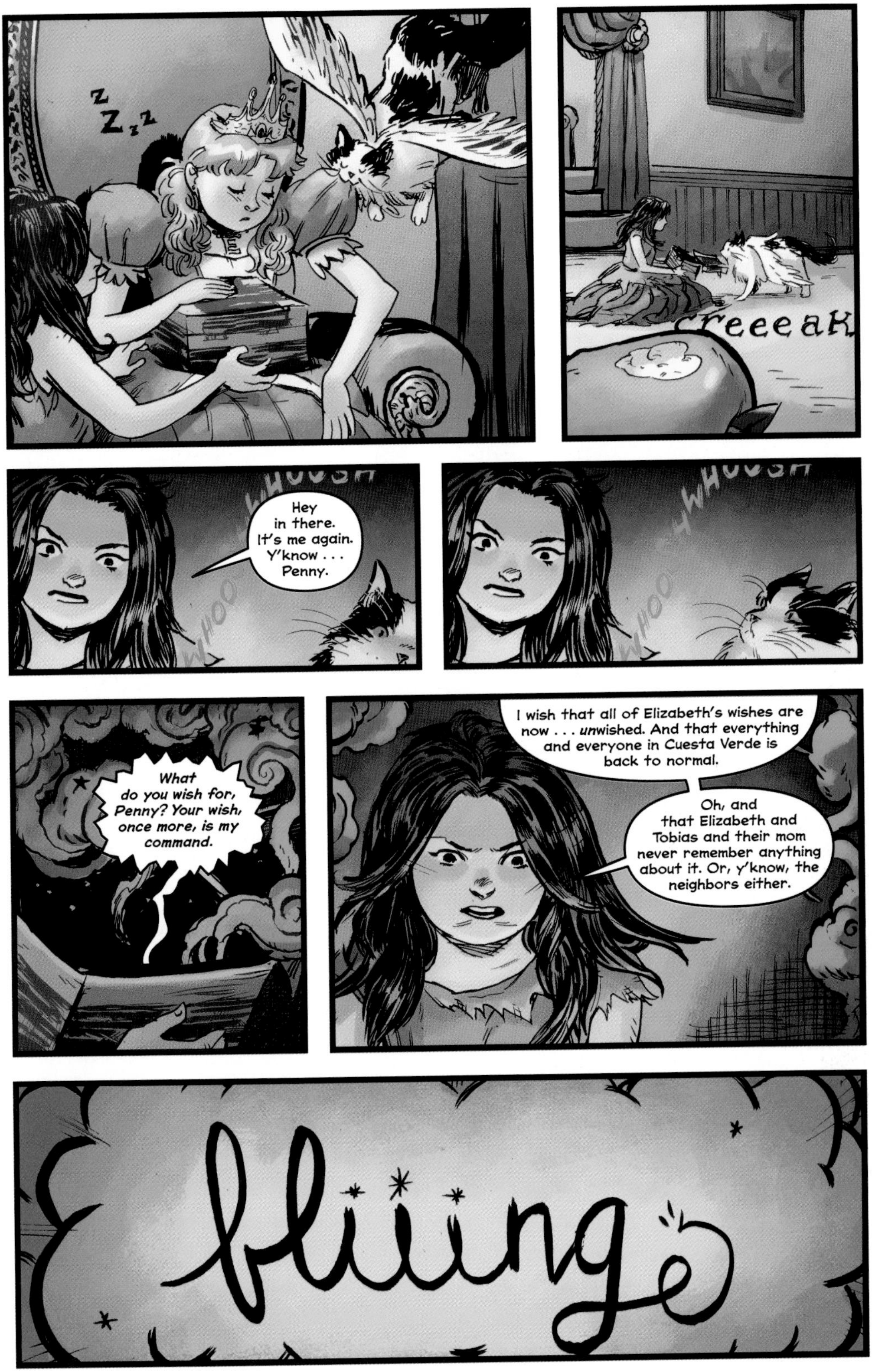
Z Z z z
creeeak
Hey in there. It's me again. Y'know . . . Penny.
WHOOSH
WHOOSH
What do you wish for, Penny? Your wish, once more, is my command.
I wish that all of Elizabeth's wishes are now . . . *un*wished. And that everything and everyone in Cuesta Verde is back to normal.
Oh, and that Elizabeth and Tobias and their mom never remember anything about it. Or, y'know, the neighbors either.
bliiing

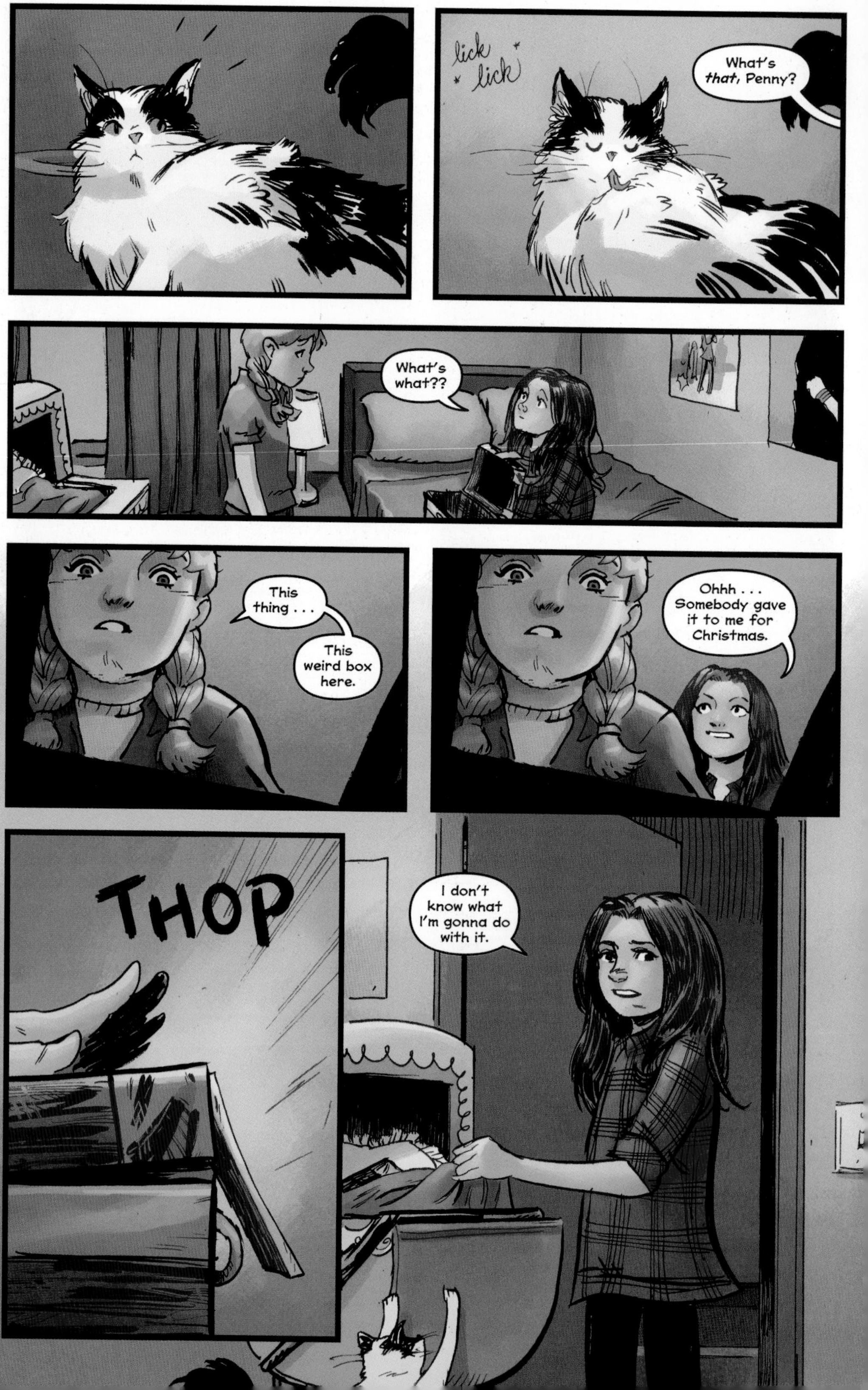
lick lick
What's that, Penny?
What's what??
This thing . . .
This weird box here.
Ohhh . . . Somebody gave it to me for Christmas.
THOP
I don't know what I'm gonna do with it.

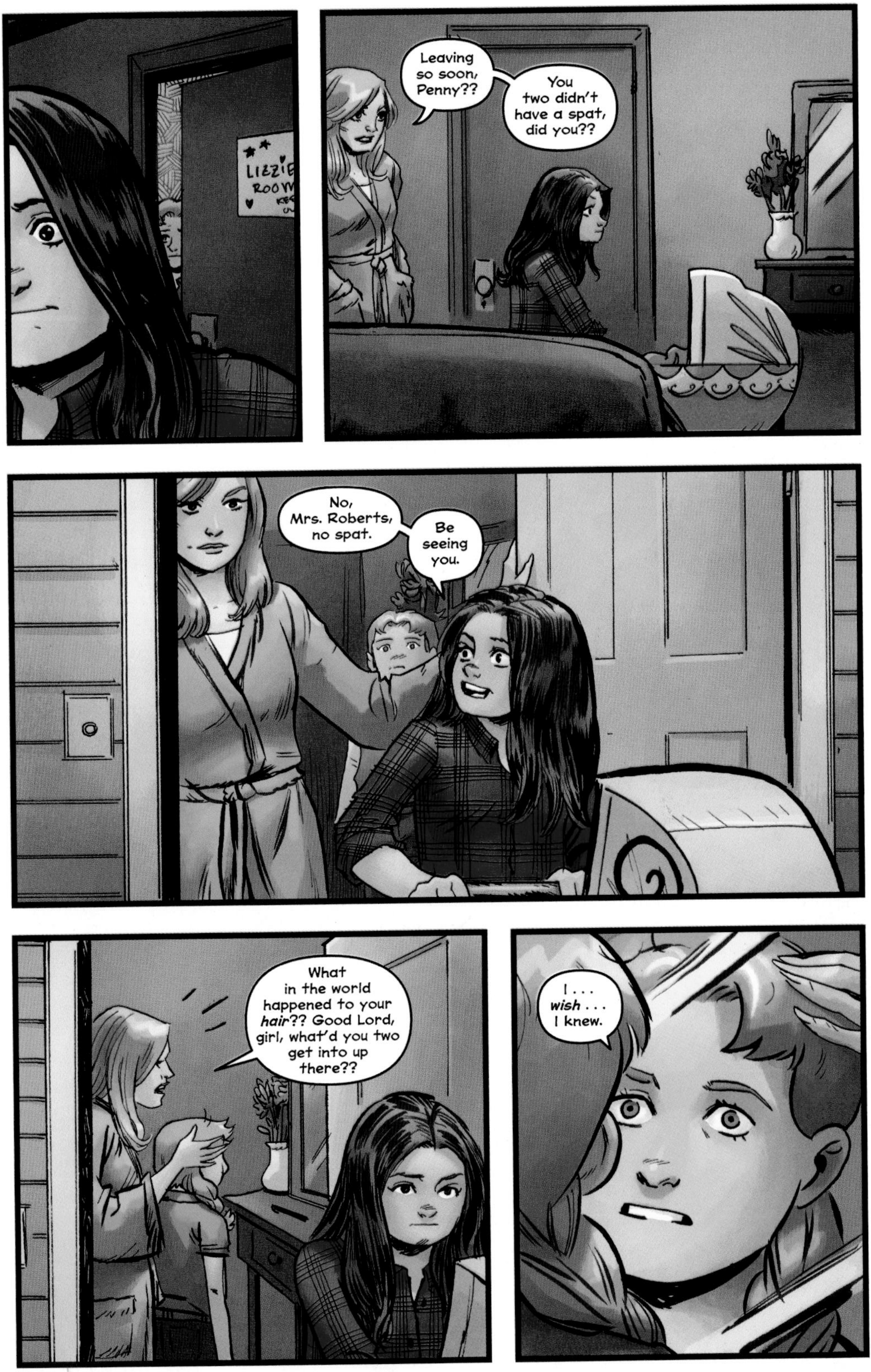
LIZZIE ROOM
Leaving so soon, Penny??
You two didn't have a spat, did you??
No, Mrs. Roberts, no spat.
Be seeing you.
What in the world happened to your *hair*?? Good Lord, girl, what'd you two get into up there??
I . . . *wish* . . . I knew.

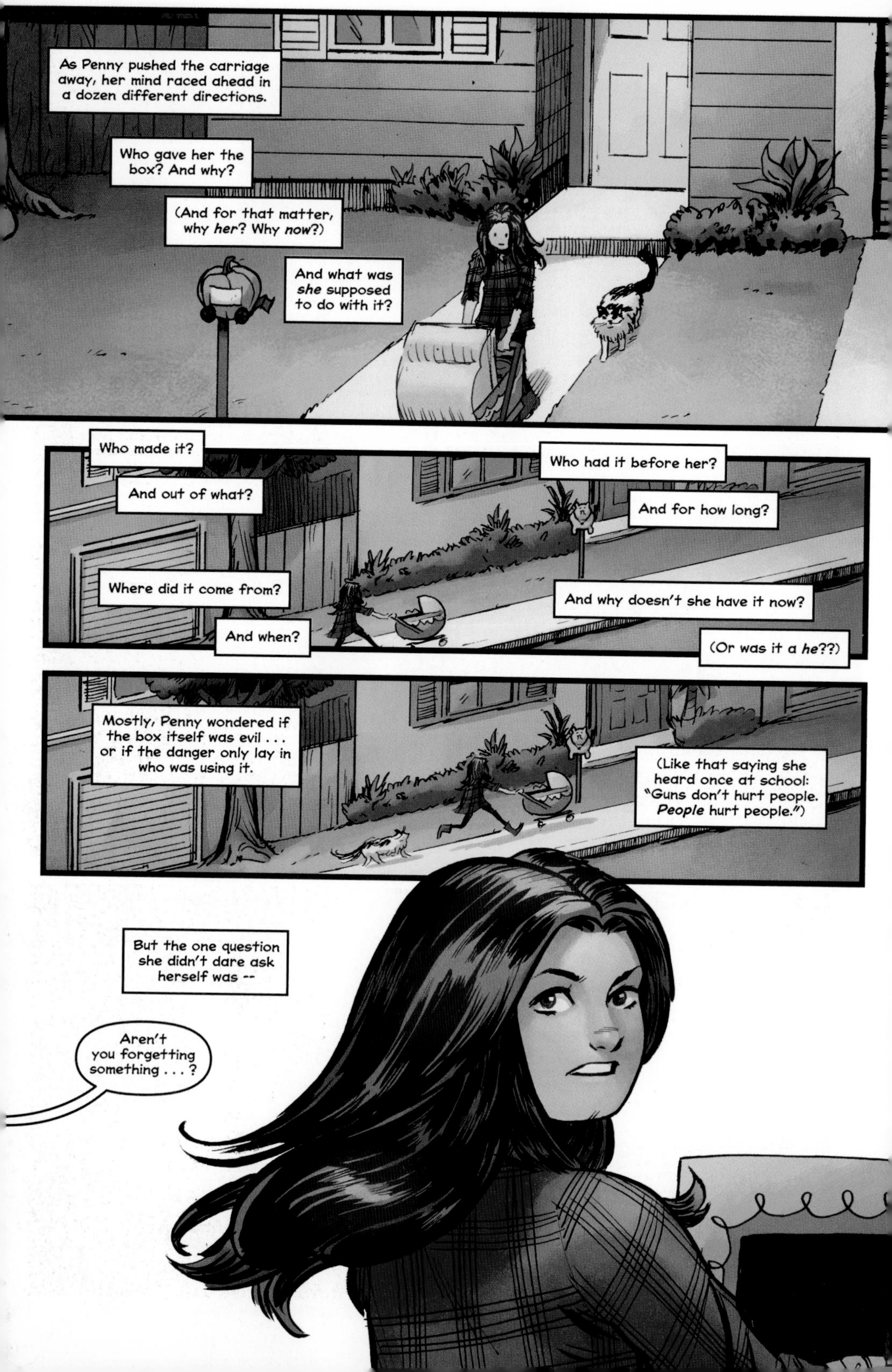
As Penny pushed the carriage away, her mind raced ahead in a dozen different directions.
Who gave her the box? And why?
(And for that matter, why *her*? Why *now*?)
And what was *she* supposed to do with it?
Who made it?
And out of what?
Where did it come from?
And when?
Who had it before her?
And for how long?
And why doesn't she have it now?
(Or was it a *he*??)
Mostly, Penny wondered if the box itself was evil . . . or if the danger only lay in who was using it.
(Like that saying she heard once at school: "Guns don't hurt people. *People* hurt people.")
But the one question she didn't dare ask herself was --
Aren't you forgetting something . . . ?

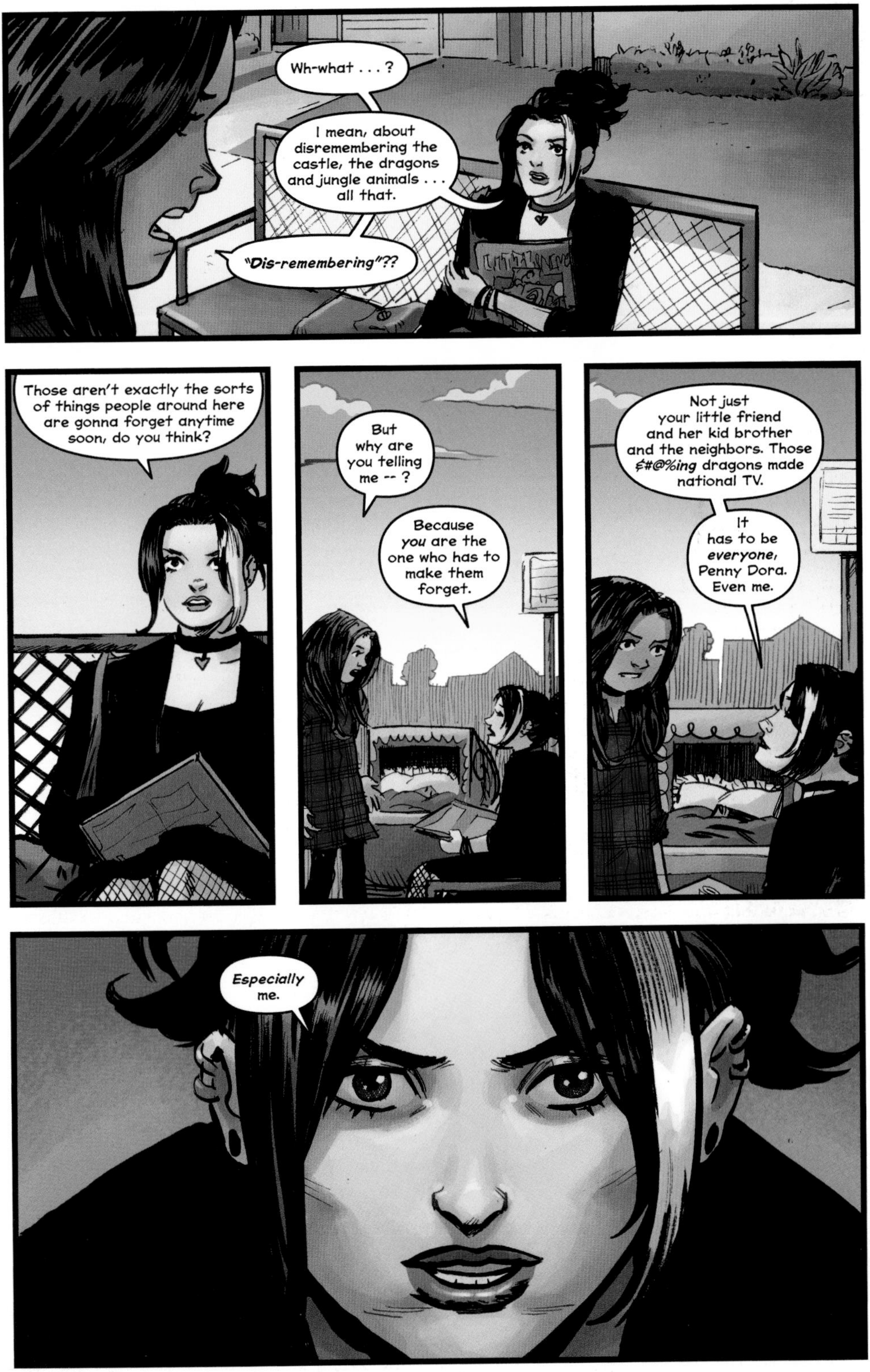
Wh-what . . . ?
I mean, about disremembering the castle, the dragons and jungle animals . . . all that.
"Dis-remembering"??
Those aren't exactly the sorts of things people around here are gonna forget anytime soon, do you think?
But why are you telling me -- ?
Because you are the one who has to make them forget.
Not just your little friend and her kid brother and the neighbors. Those ¢#@%ing dragons made national TV.
It has to be everyone, Penny Dora. Even me.
Especially me.

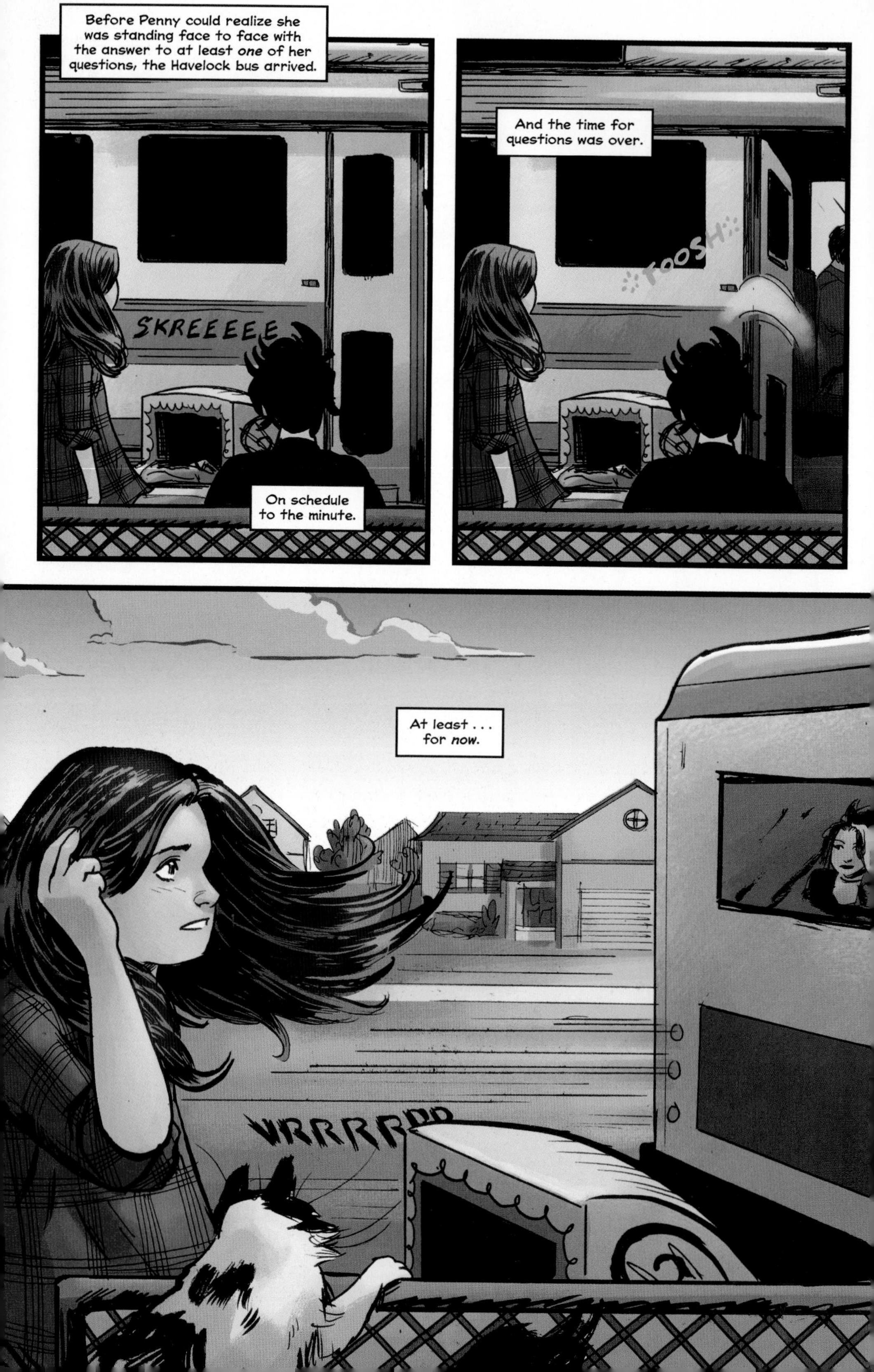
Before Penny could realize she was standing face to face with the answer to at least *one* of her questions, the Havelock bus arrived.
SKREEEEEE
On schedule to the minute.
And the time for questions was over.
FOOSH
At least . . . for *now*.
VRRRRPP

PENNY DORA
AND THE WISHING BOX

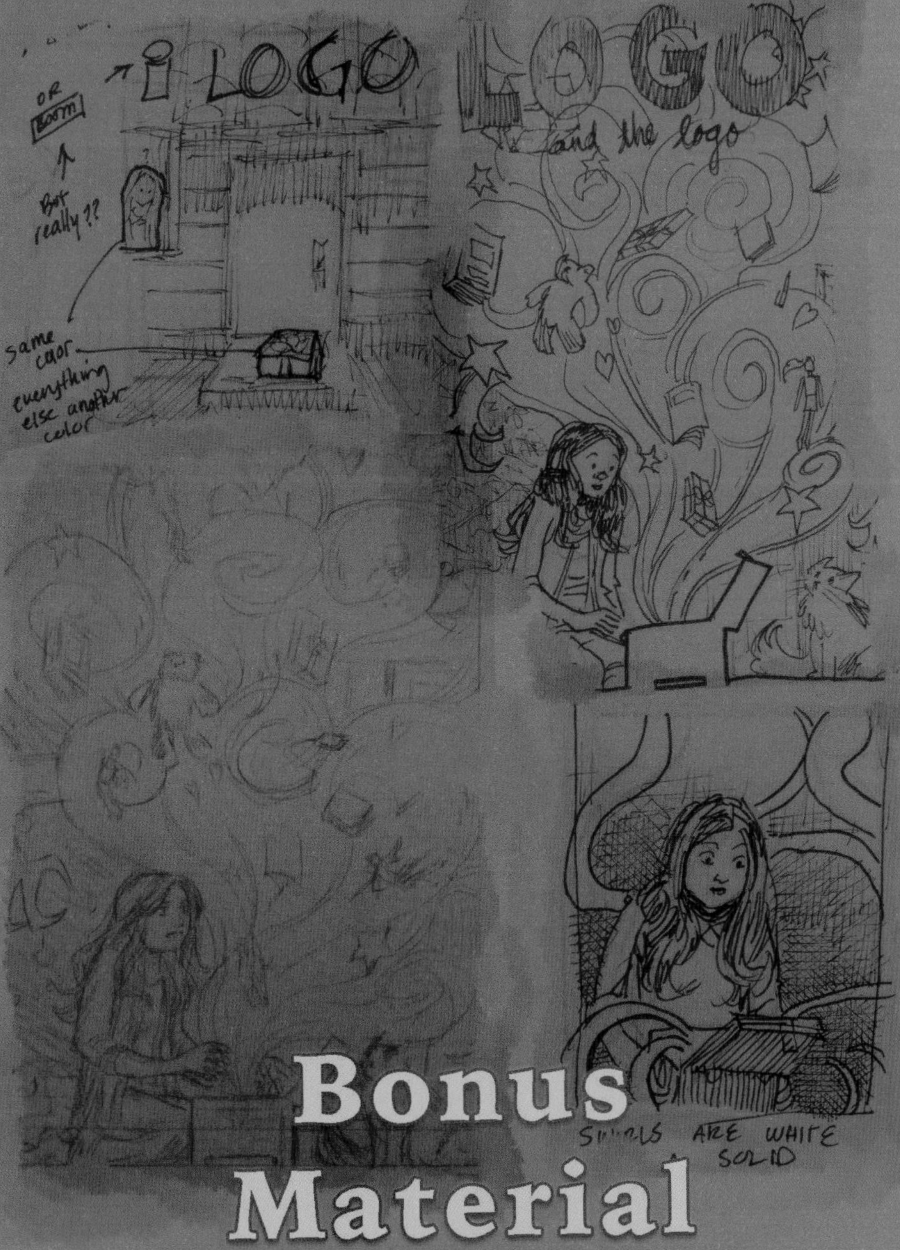

Bonus Material

The book you have in your hands here would never have existed if not for the crackling imagination of my daughter, Nico. Literally. The world of Penny Dora & The Wishing Box was actually created almost six years ago by Nico, who, at the time was just 8 years old.

Her original story, titled "The Magic Box," ran just a half page or so long, and appeared in her school newspaper, The Franklin Times, when she was in 3rd grade. And the first chapter of our book here is for the most part, an adaptation of that! At age 9, Nico wrote a second installment of the story which provides the sort of set up for our second chapter.

Although she never got around to writing another installment of "The Magic Box" (as she originally titled the story), Nico and I talked about all the things that could happen to a little girl who was given a such a thing over the course of many, many mornings on our drive to school and even more nighttimes over many, many meals. Over the years I jotted our plots and plans on napkins and the backs of flyers, whatever was handy. And eventually I logged all these ideas into my laptop in the hopes that Nico and I would return to the story someday...and now we have.

Glad you all can be here too...

xx Michael

P.S. Oh yeah. One final note here. As you will see, in Nico's original story, her hero's name was Katy. Changing her name to Penny Dora was my idea, but something I did only after I got Nico's go-ahead.

THE MAGIC BOX
by Nico Ludwig-Stock (age 8)

Part One.

Once upon a time, there was a girl named Katy. One afternoon on a Tuesday she heard a knock at the door. She opened the door up and on the front stoop sat a medium-small gift. She looked up and down the street but there wasn't a soul in sight. She took the gift and went inside.

The next day it was Christmas. Her mother was passing out the gifts.

"Hey. Who's this one for? It doesn't have a tag!" Katy yelled

"Oh. That is probably for me," her mother replied.

Her mother opened the gift.

"Oh. It's just an old box."

Katy came over and peered inside. It was empty and looked very old indeed. The red paint seemed to be chipping away near the top of the box.

"Can you put the box in the recycle bin for me, honey?" Katy's mother asked.

"Okay," Katy replied.

But instead of throwing it away, she snuck it upstairs to her bedroom. She heard her mother coming up the stairs so she quickly hid the box under her bed. A second later, the door opened.

"Honey. There's still more presents down here."

It wasn't 'til nearly two o'clock that night that Katy remembered the box under her bed. For that was when the weird whooshing sound began.

At first she didn't know where it was coming from. Then she looked under her bed. The box was turning into a different color every second. And now, the box didn't look so old. It looked like it had been made just a minute ago. The paint was also very shiny.

She took the box and opened it.

The box was starting to whisper: "What do you wish for...? What do you wish for...? What do you wish for...?" It was repeating itself over and over and over again. "Katy. What do you wish for? What do you wish for?" it insisted.

Katy got so scared she dropped the box. The whispering stopped and so did the whooshing. It had fallen into the shadows so she couldn't really see if the colors were still changing.

Katy tip-toed across the room and dug around in the back of her closet until she found her favorite red and white striped "Cats Are Cute" Umbrella. Then she slowly tip-toed back to the box. She poked once at the box with her umbrella – very softly.

Nothing happened.

So she pushed the box with the umbrella out of the shadows and into the bright patch of moonlight on the floor in front of her window. Now she could see that the box was no longer changing colors. It was once again a very dull red and the paint was beginning to peel. She used her umbrella to push the box into her closet and she locked it. She pushed her bed in front of her close, got into bed and pulled the blankets over her head.

Part Two.

Katy didn't think about the box when she woke up the next morning. She didn't think about it all day. In fact, when it was time to get ready for bed that night she wondered why her bed was shoved in front of her closet.

"Katy, your friend is here She's ready for the sleepover!" her mother called from downstairs.

"Hold on!" Katy called back as she came running down the stairs.

"Hi Elizabeth!" Katy said.

"Hi Katy!" Elizabeth said.

"I thought you were coming way earlier," Katy sighed sadly.

"I know but we lost the keys to the car when we were getting groceries and we've been looking for them the whole time and we still don't have them and..."

Katy broke in, "You could of called!"

"...Well, Mom also locked her phone in the car too! And we had to walk all the way to your house."

"My, you've had a rough day!" Katy's mom laughed. "Well, if you'll excuse me, I still have to wash some dishes."

The two friends went up to Katy's room.

"Can you help me get my pajamas?" Katy asked.

Her friend looked at her weirdly.

"Just help me pull the bed away from the closet," Katy said again. She started humming as she walked over to get the key to her closet.

"Do you always have your closet locked?" Elizabeth asked her friend.

Katy shook her head, still humming. When Katy finally got her closet opened, Elizabeth noticed the old red box sitting in her closet.

"What's that?" Elizabeth asked Katy.

"What's what?" Katy asked Elizabeth.

"That old looking red thing."

"Oh, that. That's just an old box that I got for Christmas. It's supposed to be a wish for box or something." Katy thought for a moment, wondering if she should mention the box talking to her. She decided to keep it to herself. Maybe some other time she could tell her. Then, out of the corner of her eye, she saw Elizabeth open the box.

Suddenly Katy yelled out, "Stop!"

Elizabeth dropped the box with the lid open. Katy heard her mother coming running up the stairs and Katy quickly closed the box and shoved it under the bed. Two seconds later, the door opened.

"What just happened?" Katy's mother asked when she got in the room.

"Oh, nothing. We were just, um...sort of playing a game." Katy's cheeks turned red.

"Well, okay, but it's time to go to bed now. No more playing, okay?"

"Okay," Katy said.

"Um..." Elizabeth started to say, but Katy covered her mouth.

"Well, good night," Katy's mother said.

"Good night," Katy and Elizabeth said at the same time.

"You know what? I wish I could find the keys to the car and then my mother would buy us ice cream," Elizabeth whispered to Katy.

The two girls giggled together for several minutes after that, thinking of all the different kinds of ice cream they might choose.

The last thing Katy remembered before drifting off to sleep was Elizabeth whispering over and over again, "What do you wish for? What do you wish for...?"

Except it wasn't Elizabeth's voice at all.

MULTIVERSITY INTERVIEW
with Michael Stock conducted by David Harper

David Harper: This is your first comics project in any capacity, but I'm curious, what's your personal history with comics?

Michael Stock: I learned how to read with comics! My mom was a grade school teacher and convinced that books with words AND pictures were the best way to learn. And comics were cheap when I was a kid. So it was easier to buy a stack at a time with your weekly allowance.

One of the small towns near the farm where I grew up in Nebraska had a pharmacy that sold comics. So a lot of my Saturday mornings were spent sitting on the dirty tile floor there reading all the books I wasn't going to buy before walking out with the books I did feel were worth my allowance -- typically, *X-Men, New Mutants, Daredevil...* They also had one of those old school spinners full of dusty old paperbacks and that was where I made the Saturday score of all time (at least I thought so at age 8): a handful of those Pocket Paperbacks reprinting the Marvel Silver Age stuff: *FF, Spidey, Hulk, Avengers, Dr. Strange...* God only knows how long they were sitting there before I walked out with them.

Anyway, I've been reading comics since then. I'm a lifer. And now I'm the father of a 2nd generation comics fan: my daughter Nico. She's 13 now and has been reading comics since she was 6 or 7. She's also a fan of all the great Marvel Silver Age stuff I loved as a kid (not to mention EVERYTHING Archie). This has definitely been one of my favorite parts of fatherhood, getting to share with her all of my childhood favorites; and now, in turn, her sharing with me all of her contemporary comics faves -- like *Tiny Titans, Courtney Crumrin,* Coraline and, most recently, that great new *Ms. Marvel* book.

(Turn the page for more on the creation of Penny Dora, and how the team came together on this project!)

DH: What made you want to try your hand with your own story in "Penny Dora"?

MS: I taught undergrad courses on comic books at CalArts for several years before getting laid off a year-and-a-half back due to budget cuts. I decided this was some kind of sign that I'd done enough talking about comics and it was time for me to start writing some.

PENNY DORA is actually the 3rd book I've written. And my first all-ages book. (The first couple comics I wrote aren't out yet. One, a crime/noir book, and the other a pre-apocalyptic horror book, are both being illustrated right now).

The first issue of PENNY DORA is basically an adaptation of a story that my daughter wrote when she was 8 (!) about a little girl who discovers a mysterious old box on her front step the day before Christmas...a box with the power to grant wishes. Nico read the story on my KXLU radio show one Thursday afternoon. And since then I've gotten a number of calls about it from listeners wondering 'whatever happened to that little girl and her weird Wishing Box?'

One of those calls came last winter, shortly after Nico had given me *Coraline* and *Courtney Crumrin* to read. I started thinking about what a great set up her short story would be for a comic series -- a sort of modern fairytale based on the idea of Pandora's Box being entrusted to child.

DH: In your own words, what's "Penny Dora and the Wishing Box" all about?

MS: PENNY DORA is basically an updated re-telling of the myth of Pandora's Box. Except this time around, the box has been entrusted to a girl of 10. One of the first things we are going to see her learn is that being the keeper of the Wishing Box is less about getting all the things she ever dreamed of and more about keeping it out of the wrong hands. And, what we will eventually find out in the 2nd arc of the book (where we meet Kira, the teenage Goth Girl who gave her the Wishing Box) is that Penny will only have the box until she turns 15, then it's her turn to find the next suitable protector of the box.

DH: What in your mind makes it stand out among other books both at Image and in comics in general?

MS: Well, most obviously, PENNY DORA is one of just a tiny handful of all-ages books at Image -- along with *Howtoons* (which started last month) and *Oddly Normal* (which debuts this month). So it does really stand out at Image right now.

But last winter at the Image Expo, Eric Stephenson mentioned how he'd love to do more all-ages books at Image, so hopefully this is the beginning of a bigger trend -- and one that both Marvel and DC pick up on as well.

As far as it standing out in comics in general?? Well, my daughter said I should tell you it DEFINITELY does (she suggested the ALL CAPS there). Nico is quick to point out that there just aren't enough comics out there for her and her friends -- comics with teenage girl heroes written for teenagers. "Most of the 'kids books' are for LITTLE kids," she points out. So, while *Tiny Titans* was great 3 years ago, and she still enjoys it now, it's comics like *Ms. Marvel* or *The Runaways* OR the great YA graphic novels out there by Raina Telgemeier, Jen Wang and Hope Larson that she and her friends read and trade and re-read again and again.

DH: Sina Grace is a favorite of ours over at Multiversity, and I have to say, I was stunned by just how perfect his art was for an all-ages comic like "Penny Dora". When you were thinking of artists for this project, what stood out about Sina's work, and what do you think makes him such a great fit for a storybook style comic like this?

MS: When I first read *Burn The Orphanage*, I was really struck by this sort of childish sprit that marks all the characterizations that Sina drew. It sort of reminded me of Matt Wagner's earliest work on *Mage* with the unbounded spirit and impish energy of some of the characters. Of course B.T.O is also very violent and ripe with mature subject matter...so I remember when I first brought the idea up of him drawing PENNY DORA, I was like, "I know this sounds really crazy, but would you ever be into drawing a kids' book??" Of course what I didn't know at the time was that he already HAD drawn a kids book for Amber Benson (not to mention a slew of covers for Boom books like Adventure Time, Regular Show, Bee & Puppycat and so on!).

And YES. Sina's art IS amazing!! It's really THE perfect fit for the book!

DH: It sounds like Nico should get a cover credit for this book! Did you ever bump any ideas off her as you were developing it, or was it more of you taking the idea and running with it?

MS: Well, I've definitely run with it in terms of writing the actual story (after basically adapting her short story as the 1st issue). But as far as building the world of PENNY DORA, this has definitely been a father/daughter project from the very beginning!

My typical writing day starts right after I drop Nico off at school at 8:25 in the morning and wraps when she gets out of school, which, these days, tends to be around 5:30 (now that she's doing all these middle-school afterschool programs: writing, art, dance, drum lessons, etc). So, a lot of times on the drive home I'll tell her the next part of the story I was working while she was in school that day. She usually responds with some 'what if's' or 'whattabout's'. Like, 'What if this happened...?' or, 'Whattabout having Penny Dora wish for...?' A lot of times, she will come up with some funny little bit or line, so then I'll try to add that in. I recently started work on the 2nd arc of the book, which focuses on the origins of the Wishing Box, so lately a lot of our drivetime/ dinnertime conversation have centered on the previous keepers of the box, and the rest of Pandora's Daughters...

And actually Nico will be getting the 'based on a story written by Nico Ludwig-Stock (age 8)" credit in each and every book! AND there are plans for her to do an alternate cover at some point (as she is a very promising artist as well).

DH: One of my favorite parts of the book is how it feels like our world, but very much a fairytale, storybook version of our world with some of the details that make it up. For example, I love the mailboxes, particularly the one that is just a case full of cookies. Elements like that give the book a really charming, otherworldly feel in a good way. When it comes to elements like that, what was the importance of including them?

MS: I'm glad you'd already tuned into the otherworldly feel of the world of Penny Dora on the 2nd page! Those mailboxes are our first hint that this is not exactly the sunny southern California you may know (or at least have heard of). This is a world where a Wishing Box has been passed on from one generation of young girls to the next for a long, long time. So there's bound to be some of these little hints that the world has been rewished, reimagined and remade in these little ways throughout the book.

Sina will be happy to hear how much you liked that part! I know he really put a lotta thought into that page (and the really amazing 1st page). Those were the last two pages he finished on the 1st issue!

DH: Also, besides Coraline and Courtney Crumrin, what would you say are the biggest influences on this book?

In many ways, this book, which is based on a story my daughter wrote when she was 8, has become a story about her entering adolescence. (Sina picked up on this as soon as he read the script, and decided to model Penny on Nico, from looks to clothes.) As such, the influences on the book really reflect the comics we've read together over the years. Like *Little Nemo In Slumberland*, for example, which we spent almost 2 years reading; every night a few strips right before bed when she was 5 or so and just learning to read, with me reading the male characters, and her the female characters & narration. Some of the warmth & lightheartedness is inspired directly by the great John Stanley books of the 1950s: *Little Lulu, Tubby, Nancy & Sluggo*. The reprints of that stuff was timed just perfectly with Nico's early childhood, so we both read literally all those stories we could get our hands on. (When I started teaching the History Of Comics course at CalArts, I let Nico select the *Little Lulu* stories which I assigned as a counterpoint to the EC books when we covered the 1950s.) Also, there's a number of times in the script so far where I make references to *Little Lulu* for Sina to check out.

Two of the other big influences on PENNY DORA are *The Sandman* and of course *Lord Of The Rings*. The effect of the box is not unlike the effect of the Ring in the Tolkien books (which I read over and over and over from teendom to twentysomething).

And I'm sure a steady stream of *Buffy the Vampire Slayer* and *X-Files* episodes doesn't hurt either!

(Nico is seeing *X-Files* for the 1st time, and I'm seeing *Buffy* for the 1st time!)

DH: I'm not going to say the book is scary, but there's definitely a certain level of creepiness to the box and Penny's initial interactions to it. Tonally speaking, how do you balance that creepy intrigue with a light-hearted feel for audiences of a certain age?

MS: There definitely is a level of creepiness that runs throughout the book. The sort of storybook narration definitely contributes to that. But also serves to give the reader a safe distance from the creepiness at times, too. So a lot of that delicate balancing is done via that.

But the humor is there all along too, from the wry stuff to outright slapstick by the time the 4th issue hits and the Southern California suburban town of Cuesta Verde has been transformed into the kingdom of Princess Elizabeth (aka formerly Penny's best friend who she loaned the box to overnite in issue #3). Eep, shoulda said SPOILER ALERT there first, I guess...sorry!

Anyway, I think it's this balance that makes PENNY DORA truly for ALL AGES. It's like a starter book for horror fans. Like what you should read before *The Sandman*, *Swamp Thing* and *Sweet Tooth*.

I'm seeing this interest awaken before my eyes with Nico. Film/TV-wise it started with the classic Universal monster movies, then segued into *Outer Limits* and *Twilight*

Zone, and is now moving into **X-Files** and *Buffy*. With comics, it's been *Coraline*, *Courtney Crumrin*, *Amulet*, and most recently that amazing Archie/zombie book, *Afterlife With Archie*.

That concludes the epic and fantastic interview with David Harper over at Multiversity!

Thanks again to David & co. for the opportunity, and thank YOU all for taking a read!

(For your viewing pleasure, one of Sina's earliest designs for the look of our hero, Penny Dora herself!)

* The interview was conducted by David Harper for Multiversity Comics and originally published September 23, 2014 on multiversitycomics.com. Reprinted with permission from David Harper.

The Wish For Box

characters:

Penny Dora	
Elizabeth	Penny's friend
Stevie (Steve)	Elizabeth's little brothe
Kira Welkin	Goth girl
Penny's mom (Mrs. Dora)	parent
Penny's dad (Mr. Dora)	parent

future Penny
Elizabeth
white streaks
Penny
Kira
nose piercing?
white streaks

CHECK OUT NICO'S ORIGINAL SKETCHES FOR PENNY DORA AND HER EVER-GROWING CAST OF ALLIES (OR ENEMIES!?).

WHAT DO YOU THINK- DID SINA DO A GOOD JOB BRINGING NICO'S CHARACTERS TO THE COMIC BOOK PAGE?

ACKNOWLEDGEMENTS

This book would never existed without a number of people, starting of course with my incredibly talented collaborators: Sina Grace, Tamra Bonvillain and Hope Larson, and especially every one of you readers holding this book in your hands right now. (You after all, complete the circuit, and keep the current sparking.)

Secondly, I want to thank all the stores who cared enough about the book to carry the single issues (called 'floppies' by some), and now the stores and libraries who are carrying this special little book here collecting all five of those 'floppies.' And of course a big blushing thanks to Eric Stephenson and the entire family at Image Comics, without whom this book would never have existed. (It was a very literal wish come true having my first book here published by my absolute favorite comics company on Earth, so maybe I should've started with that part, huh?)

Finally, of course, I have to thank the two characters seen here at the bottom of the page--my daughter Nico and our cat Iggy. Not characters of course, but real life people you can see...uh...well, one real life little person and one giant cat if you want get particular. The spark of this story and the world that spun out of it was created by Nico when she was just 8 years old, and inspired in no small part by our giant lovable cat Iggy (who really does love ham so much that we have to spell the word around him to keep him from getting overly excited at dinnertime).

These two are my all my worlds, real and imaginative alike...and I dedicate this book and all that might follow to them.

Thanks to you all...
xxMichael
(June 2015)